HOUSE MADE OF SOUND

Freeman Jayce

Miller's Arch Publishing

ISBN 979-8-218-17437-8

ISBN 979-8-218-16219-1 (ebook)

Cover artwork by: Jennifer Kubicki

Cover concept by: Jason Michael Freeman

Printed in the United States of America

For Shelly

When my train finally rolls in, meet me at the café.

I'll be the one drinking the Earl Grey.

TRACKLIST

HOLLOW MACHINE

-Track One-

Jensen Bennett opened his wallet and counted the bills inside with rising frustration.

Two Grants, a Hamilton, and four Lincolns.

The wallet had housed more presidents when he'd rolled into Springfield that afternoon, but an overpriced drive-through hamburger and his car's fuel tank had conspired to quickly and quietly remove them from office. Now he was left with only a hundred and thirty dollars, not nearly enough to sate the scalper's thirst for highway robbery.

Nothing about the man in question set him apart from the thousands of other ticket scalpers Jensen had seen congregating outside concert venues across the globe, singing the same tune and wearing the same disheveled cloth-ing like members of some interconnected global cult.

"Two tickets, three hundred," the scalper said again, this time with a hint of impatience. There was no finesse in his salesmanship, no pride in the act of transaction, no adoration for the sale. Only raw, unbridled lust.

Jensen tried to connect the dots, to come up with some plausible scenario that would explain why he was negotiating with an amateur outside the gate instead of hanging backstage with the band, helping them numb the pre-show jitters with shots of Jameson. But he couldn't. There once was a time when *his*

1

name was the only ticket he needed, but it had inexplicably lost its value at some point between this morning and now.

This last thought caused him to glare once again at the ticket collector, who paused long enough in her duties guarding the turnstiles at Gate Ten to return his glower with one of her own. It was brief but definitely judgmental, almost biblically so. His name had meant absolutely nothing to *her*; of that he was certain.

"It's a sold-out show," the scalper continued. "You ain't gonna get a better deal."

Jensen's smile was practiced and deliberate. "I don't need two," he said calmly. "Just the one. Hundred bucks."

The man looked insulted. "Hundred? No way. They're going for double that online."

Jensen didn't need to use his parlor trick to know this last bit was a blatant lie; the band used a verified fan program that all but eliminated ticket gouging. But his special talent, his *Bela Lugosi Stare*, as Aimee used to jokingly call it, could still come in handy if he asked the right questions. The answers would come in the corners of the scalper's eyes, the wrinkles on his forehead, the flare of his nostrils.

"Forget what they're selling for," Jensen said slowly. "How much did *you* pay for them?"

"Two seventy-five," he said. "For the pair. I'm barely making a profit."

Jensen leaned in closer, his eyes focused and unblinking. "You sure about that? I'm thinking maybe it's closer to two-fifty."

The man laughed. "Look, buddy, you can take 'em or leave 'em. Three hundred's a steal."

"Two-twenty?" Jensen asked.

And there it was: The man's left eye twitched. It was brief but undeniable. He'd paid one hundred and ten dollars for each ticket.

Good, Jensen thought. *Almost there.*

"Not a bad score, actually," he said. "Biggest band in the world, first show of the tour. In their home state, too. It's just a shame you couldn't unload them earlier when this place was swarming with tailgaters. You could've easily made three. Maybe even three-twenty."

To accentuate the point, Jensen gestured to the gathering darkness around them. The deluge of fans that had been steadily flowing through the parking lot and into Springfield Stadium had indeed thinned to only a few scattered bodies, and none looked in need of a ticket.

"Slim pickings now, though," Jensen continued. "You and I both know that in about ten minutes, those tickets aren't going to be worth the paper they're printed on. But I can take at least the one off your hands for ..."

Jensen thought for a moment as he again sifted through the bills in his wallet. He didn't want to be completely busted, but he also didn't think offering the man only one-hundred was fair; he deserved to walk away with *something* for his troubles.

Jensen sighed. This was going to hurt. "One-thirty. You'll take a ninety-dollar hit, but at least you won't lose your shirt."

The scalper groaned and swept his eyes across the parking lot, no doubt counting the approaching shadows and realizing, as Jensen had, that the math just wasn't in his favor. Six Mississippis later – Jensen actually counted each second of silence – the man looked back and nodded in defeat.

"Okay. One-thirty it is."

Jensen offered the man a friendly smile and relinquished the last of his presidents. In return he received a blue-shaded ticket with the words "Quiet Catastrophe" written across it in large, hostile letters.

"Thanks," Jensen said, and meant it.

"Yeah," the scalper responded with naked contempt. Then he was gone, just another indiscernible shadow in the gathering gloom.

Okay, Jensen thought. *I'm broke, but at least I'm in.*

Then, holding the ticket in the air like a white flag, he approached Gate

Ten and the coiled insanity he could hear assaulting his ears from somewhere beyond it.

***

It was opening night of Quiet Catastrophe's twenty-eight-city tour of North America, and Jensen had expected Springfield Stadium to be packed to the rafters.

What he hadn't expected was the fervor of the crowd, which despite the fact the band had yet to take the stage was undulating across the 15,000-seat stadium floor like a swarm of irritated army ants. Not a single person seemed to be sitting; it was a massive orgy of bobbing heads, flailing limbs and anticipatory shouts. A cloud of pot smoke hung inflexibly in the air despite a steady northeasterly wind, and already the floors were wet with recently spilled beer.

He'd never really seen it all before from this perspective, as a fan would. It was oddly unsettling, like watching a beloved family pet turn rabid.

Entering the stadium through the front gates had also been strange. As recently as a year ago, he would've simply entered through the stadium's rear gangway with the band and road crew, but those days were apparently as gone and irretrievable as the dying melanin now graying intermittent strands of his brown hair. In fact, aside from signing off on a few projects as the band's legal proxy a few months ago, he hadn't even *thought* about Quiet Catastrophe in a long time. Perhaps too long, it seemed.

Bartering with the scalper had given Jensen a fleeting high, a temporary respite. But now the void, familiar and unwelcome, had come home. His thoughts returned to the empty wallet, and to the ousted presidents that once held office there, as he pushed his way through the bedlam and began descending a long, sharply inclined set of stairs that led to stage left and, beyond that, backstage.

It was nearly eight o'clock, and the distant horizon was ablaze with the last remnants of daylight. He'd hoped to be in and out before the band took the stage, on Interstate 55 by nine, and back in Chicago by midnight, if he buried his Hyundai's speedometer the entire way. But that scenario was growing more unlikely by the minute, and he was now down to only his credit cards, all but one of which was maxed out.

This last thought made him sink deeper, but he took a few measured breaths and was able to pull himself back out again, at least enough to function. This trip was too important, and he'd come too far, to stumble.

Guarding the backstage entrance was perhaps the largest man Jensen had ever seen. Two eyes – one a stern navy blue, the other a tired yellow reminiscent of old newspaper – quickly swept in unison across Jensen's face like tenacious searchlights. The giant they belonged to was stuffed uncomfortably into a black T-shirt that showed every peak and valley of his muscled chest, and the word "Security" emblazoned across its front in blocky white lettering appeared a mere pectoral twitch away from ripping apart into syllables. Jensen thought he knew everyone in the band's entourage, but he didn't know this man.

Costumes on, curtains up.

"Evening," Jensen said with a smile. "Band still in the green room?"

The giant scanned his face one final time before replying, his two-toned eyes seeming to note and categorize each line on Jensen's face with cold precision.

"No one past this point," he said robotically, and then jabbed a gigantic finger toward a nearby sign that essentially said the same thing. "Not without a pass."

First a ticket, now a pass, Jensen thought. *What's next, a retinal scanner at the green room door?*

Jensen leaned in close as if confiding a secret to an old friend. Two-Eyes, who reeked of cologne and sweat, didn't lean in to meet him.

"Look, maybe you don't recognize me. I don't need a pass. Never have.

I'm Jensen Bennett."

He waited for a second, sure his name would ring whatever crude, patina-ensconced bell hung inside the ogre's enormous skull. When it didn't, Jensen had no choice but to move into the hard sale.

"Hedley Grange ever tell you his sole source of income used to be playing for spare change in a CTA terminal? Guess who got him out of there," Jensen paused long enough to point at the empty stage, "and up there?"

Jensen was sure Two-Eyes would stand there forever like some cologne-drenched effigy, a timeless and unmoving tribute to the dangers of steroid abuse, when a grin lined with paper-white teeth unexpectedly spilled across his face. The sudden change was terrifying.

"I *know* who you are, Bennett, and I'm only going to say this one more time. No one past this point. Not without a pass."

Two-Eyes and the ticket collector were apparently in agreement: No free entry for Jensen Bennett. Only now, the person denying him access was about two feet taller than the waif manning Gate Ten and wasn't safely caged inside a ticket booth. If the giant snapped – and Jensen could see that definite possibility reflected in the predacious intensity of his two-toned eyes – it would be David and Goliath without the happy ending.

Jensen's fingers found his right temple, where he instinctively began to rub a small pink mark that, despite the passage of thirty years, still vaguely resembled the saluki on his stepfather's class ring. Somewhere inside him a furnace quietly kicked to life and began radiating a soft, unpleasant heat.

He took a deep breath and attempted to fortify his faltering smile.

"I don't think you understand," he said slowly. "Jensen *Phillip* Bennett. Wicked Records. On the Quiet Catastrophe hierarchy, I'm somewhere between a George and a Ringo."

Two-Eyes took a step toward him, and in an instant, Jensen's heart was beating an ancient, tribal rhythm in his ears.

"*Really*, Bennett? 'Cause the Nadmit I got this morning says otherwise.

It has your name, and that asshole face of yours, at number one."

It took Jensen a moment to process this last bit of information. Nadmit – short for "no admittance," usually reserved for tabloid reporters or groupies known to be card-carrying members of Club STD. But Jensen couldn't be on the list, especially not in the top slot, not unless he'd driven through a rip in the space-time continuum somewhere between Chicago and Springfield.

"That's impossible," he said. "Check again."

This time, Two-Eyes did more than just take another step toward him; he grabbed the lapel of Jensen's bomber jacket with one meaty hand, and then balled the other into a fist the size of a softball.

"I *told* you I was only going to tell you once more, Bennett."

The panic that had been idling quietly inside him suddenly exploded like a matchhead being struck. He wanted to run, to slip from the giant's grasp and scurry back into the relative safety of the crowd, but his legs had other ideas and stiffened instead, rooting him to the ground as firmly as the steel pillars that supported the roof of the stadium. All he could do was close his eyes and brace himself for the blow.

But it didn't come. Instead, Jensen heard a familiar, high-pitch voice suddenly shout from somewhere behind Two-Eyes: "What's this all about, then? Looking for a lawsuit? *Down*, boy!"

Without turning his head to see from whom the voice emanated, Two-Eyes immediately lowered his fist and backed away, his searchlight eyes never straying from Jensen's face.

You're lucky, those eyes said. *Damn lucky*.

From the backstage shadows emerged an overweight man who was dressed to the nines and sweating as if it were one-hundred and twenty degrees instead of a brisk sixty. Beneath his receding hairline and hooked nose was a smile that looked less like an expression of joy and more like the grimace of one being subjected to a surprise rectal exam. The gaudy rings on each of his fingers winked in the stage lights as he waddled forward.

7

Jensen breathed a sigh of relief and nodded at the newcomer. "Nigel, will you tell Moby Dick over there to let me backstage? Says I'm on the Nadmit."

Nigel Cuthpit, who for nearly five years had captained Quiet Catastrophe's voyage into celebrity waters, returned Jensen's nod with a wink. It, too, looked forced and painful.

"Funny thing, that list, isn't it?" he said. "I've never managed a band so intent on keeping the troglodytes away."

He extended a hand, and Jensen shook it tentatively. Nigel's palms were wet with sweat, and it took considerable effort for Jensen to resist the urge to wipe his hand on his jeans after the handshake had run its course.

"Been well, I hope? Still addicted to the old ..." Nigel finished the statement by plugging his right nostril with his thumb and snorting like he was clearing his throat.

"No, not anymore."

"Good, that stuff is rubbish. And what of Aimee? I hope she's well?"

"We're separated."

"So *that's* what they're calling divorce nowadays?"

He knew. The sadistic son of a bitch knew and had asked anyway.

"Divorce happens *after* the papers are signed, not before," Jensen said. "Will you let me backstage now, or do you need to know what I had for lunch, too? Cheesy cheddar steakburger. It's knocking at the door as we speak, so I'd appreciate it if we could move this along."

Nigel nodded. "Well, first let me preface what I'm about to say with a compliment, Jensen. You're an incredibly gifted A&R man. Too good, really, if you ask me, for those jackals at Wicked Records. But with that being said, some people within this organization ... well, *all* of them, actually ... have decided they no longer wish to be associated with you. It's rather simple, really. Even if I *could* let you backstage, which I simply can't, as I'm not fond of unemployment lines, no one would talk to you."

Jensen could offer Nigel nothing at first except for stunned silence. The thin sheet of fraudulent cheeriness and flippant humor that sometimes sheltered him abruptly disintegrated. Not Hedley Grange. Nigel, yes. Nigel had *never* liked him, not even a little. Maybe even Zach and Teddy, although that was unlikely. But not Grange, never Grange. They were like brothers. There had to be something Nigel wasn't telling him.

"You're lying," Jensen said. "They'd never do that to me."

"Quite the contrary. They would, and they have. I was just with them. We stood in the wings watching your conversation with Johnny here. And they reiterated to me in no uncertain terms how little they desire your company. They said it less elegantly, but the sentiment is the same."

Jensen loathed the jovial way in which Nigel delivered this devastating news perhaps even more so than the news itself. All he could offer was a variant of what he already said: "I don't believe you."

Nigel turned to Two-Eyes and muttered something, and in response the giant retrieved a clipboard and held it out face-first so Jensen could read it. It was the Nadmit, and sure enough, Jensen Bennett and his face were at the top of the list.

"Believe me now, Bennett?" Nigel said. "Even *you* can't deny the Nadmit. It knows all, sees all."

Jensen's jaw clenched so tightly he felt a particle of dental filling fall from a back molar and catch in his throat. Nigel, Two-Eyes and the flurry of activity backstage blurred into a kaleidoscope of shapes, but he forced them back into focus. There was nothing he could do about his heart, however, which had abandoned its steady canter and was now running at full gallop. He suddenly felt very sick to his stomach, like he sometimes did the morning after a bender, but there was nothing he could do about that, either.

"Let me get this straight, just so we're on the same page," Jensen said, his voice calm and measured despite the fireworks going off inside his body. "I build this band from the ground up, piece by piece, on my own dime. Put my *own* career on the line, take *all* the risks myself. Then everyone becomes

9

millionaires, everyone except me, and suddenly I'm Public Enemy Number One? Tell me how any of that makes sense to you."

Nigel listened to this tirade with a placating smile, which persisted throughout his response. "Same *page*? No. We're not even reading the same bloody book, mate."

Nigel got close, his voice barely a whisper. There was no friendliness in it, duplicitous or otherwise. "We know why you're here. And I'll make this as plain as can be: *You won't get it.*"

"Yes, we *will*," Jensen whispered back. "You're under contract."

Instead of responding, Nigel snapped his fingers, three times in rapid succession. Like a trained dog, Two-Eyes came and cracked his knuckles.

"Johnny," Nigel said, his voice once again loud and jovial, "if this man isn't gone by the time I finish this sentence, you have my full authority to see he leaves the premises in a prompt and dignified manner."

Jensen was gone by the word "authority."

***

Coward. Why was he such a coward?

It was a question without an answer. He was still shaking with adrenaline and fear as he walked back up the stairs toward the sprawling green pasture that was the general-admittance lawn section. He fumbled for his phone, almost dropped it, then caught it at just the right angle to see his colorless reflection in its dead screen.

Long nose, big ears, blocky chin that could really use some facial hair to hide its prominence. Brown hair a wavy, unkept mess atop his head, prehistoric eyebrows guarding a set of almond-shaped eyes that couldn't agree on how far they should be from his oversized forehead. And the kicker, a saluki-shaped mark on his right temple that would stay there until the day he died. He wanted to punch the dumb face that looked back at him until the phone's screen was nothing but cracks and returned a truer image of the man behind it.

Instead, he unlocked it with a swipe of his finger and scrolled down his list of contacts until he found Robbie Tabernacle's name. He wasn't sure how he was going to explain all of this; he wasn't even sure he understood it himself. Whatever the specifics, the band had shunned him, which made the job he'd come here to do all but impossible. Tabernacle would not be happy to hear that.

Before he could make the call, the stadium lights, which until that point had been delicately illuminating the interior of Springfield Stadium in a ghostly blonde light, suddenly winked out. The thousands of fans packing the arena abruptly discarded their impatient, disjointed murmuring and rose simultaneously in a rafter-shaking shriek that threatened to pull every screw and nail from the building's substructure.

As Jensen reached a wide landing separating the stadium's pavilion and lawn sections, he looked down on the stage. About two dozen lights lined along its front had jumped to life and were now showering the darkness in assorted colors. Two flash pots at either end erupted simultaneously, sending sparks and smoke high into the air. An enormous monitor behind the drum riser flashed on, and the crowd noise soared as the words "Quiet Catastrophe" faded onto screen and began to pulsate like an overworked heart.

I *made this possible*, Jensen thought. *I made* all *this possible – the band, the albums, the fans, the concerts – and now I'm just another face in the crowd.*

Was that really true? He still couldn't believe it. He hadn't talked to the band in months, not since leaving the last tour abruptly in Oklahoma City to surprise his wife and, as it turned out, the guy she'd been sleeping with while he was away. Were they angry he'd been so distant? Surely they could understand the personal strain he'd been under of late.

The simple answer to that was *no*, they apparently couldn't. The Nadmit, and Nigel, had proven it.

11

He wasn't wanted there anymore.

The thought made him sad and incredibly angry. He'd let Grange see the *real* him behind the reflection, the cracked and colorless one. It was something very few people ever saw. He'd called the man friend, had treated him like a brother, only to be tossed away like a jury summons. Jensen should have seen it coming.

He became aware of a sound cutting through the clamor and looked again at the stage. Three shadows were slowly emerging from the backstage gloom as the sound – now unmistakably that of guitar peppered with light distortion and slathered in reverb – grew slightly louder. He wanted to leave – this wasn't his country anymore, if it ever was – but he instead leaned against the railing that ran along the lawn section and watched the spectacle unfolding beneath him.

A figure methodically plucking a chipped 1967 Rickenbacker bass guitar reached stage right, where a single shaft of unspoiled light shown down and half-illuminated the features of Ted Choom. He played as if he were the only one in the stadium, lost within the authoritative sound his instrument created as he peered west toward the dying sunlight.

The second shadow lumbered up a short flight of steps connecting the concert floor to a raised platform and all but disappeared behind an enormous, teal-colored drum kit set atop it. The ever-undulating stage lights spilled across drummer Zachary Orrin's face as he began lightly tapping his drumsticks on the cymbals and pounding his foot on the bass drum pedal.

The third and final figure, the one who'd been playing for spare change in a CTA terminal just five years ago but was now a multimillionaire, slowly approached center stage as he began to pluck a more frenzied version of the initial guitar melody. Awaiting him like an unanswered question was a lone microphone, whose stainless-steel frame caught the passing stage lights and reflected them eerily back into the face of Hedley Grange. The crowd noise swelled at the sight.

Despite his riches, Grange looked almost exactly as he had the day Jensen discovered him. His long blonde hair, greasy and unkempt, spilled over his shoulders and onto a Black Sabbath T-shirt that had more than a few rips in it. His blue jeans were likewise torn and looked as if they hadn't seen the inside of a washing machine in ages. Grange's lower lip quivered every time his fingers changed position on the fretboard of his jet-black Les Paul guitar.

Until this point, the song had been building slowly, but as Grange hit a pedal on the floor with his right foot and let out a throaty snarl, the tune exploded like TNT. The band fell into a lurching groove that seemed to saunter in slow motion on the back of an infectiously hooky and distorted guitar riff. Jensen had never heard it before.

He'd always been uncomfortable with the cult-like adoration fans bestowed upon Grange, and even told him that one day while the two were sitting on the front steps of Cannon Studios, sharing a smoke and watching the sun come up over the Chicago skyline. Grange had taken a long, slow drag off the cigarette and continued to stare east at the rising sun as it sent spikes of light spreading like fingers through the skyscrapers. After a few moments of this quiet contemplation, Grange had passed the cigarette back to Jensen, looked him in the eye, and said simply, "It's not really *me* they worship, Benny. It's the music. And I'm okay with that."

But Grange's humility had apparently run its course. He'd let his appointment as the second coming, the savior of music, the saint of rock and roll, destroy what was left of his sense of friendship and loyalty to the one person who had made it all possible. It made Jensen sad to even think these things, but the facts were undeniable.

The divorce papers. The debt collectors. The sudden excommunication from his Quiet Catastrophe family, from his best friend Hedley Grange. And now, the prospect of driving back to Wicked Records only to clean out his desk. It was all too much to bear, and Jensen gave himself over to the emptiness that had been threatening to envelop him since time immemorial.

As he looked for a quiet spot to make a call he very much didn't want to make, Jensen couldn't shake the feeling that his life was spinning out of control, and the only direction left was down.

***

Roughly two-hundred miles to the northeast, Robbie Tabernacle was slowly drifting into what was sure to be an uneven and troubled night of sleep when the telephone beside his bed began ringing. If it were any other day, he would have let it continue ringing until whoever it was realized no one was answering and hung up.

But this hadn't been any other day; it had been the single most gut-wrenching, anxiety-filled twenty-four hours he had ever experienced in his six years as CEO of Wicked Records.

It had begun much like it was now ending, with the shrill, old-timey ring of the rotary-style phone at his bedside rudely stirring him from sleep. On the other end was Scott Miller, one of his West Coast scouts, who had heard a doozy of a rumor: Quiet Catastrophe, Wicked Records' number-one cash cow, had recently rented time at a Los Angeles recording studio. Nine days and seventeen tracks later, a new album was born into the world – an album that, if it really *did* exist, would be the band's third.

Normally, news of a forthcoming Quiet Catastrophe album would be cause for celebration within the Wicked Records ranks, up to and including Robbie himself. The band's first album alone had bought the Tabernacles an eight-bedroom, three-bathroom summer house on the banks of Turtle Lake in Wisconsin, and the second had added a fleet of classic muscle cars to his posh four-level home in the suburbs.

But if the album existed – and at that early point in the morning, Tabernacle had been skeptical that it did – its creation wasn't sanctioned by the label, and no one at Wicked Records knew of its existence. That was a problem, because per the contract they signed nearly five years ago, Quiet Catastrophe still owed him one more album. If the band tracked its third record in secret, Tabernacle wanted to know why.

As the phone rang a second time in the present, Tabernacle remembered the mad rush to his downtown Chicago office, the frantic phone calls to friends in the industry, most of whom owed him a favor or two and spoke under the condition of complete anonymity, and finally the startling confirmation that indeed the album *had* been recorded three weeks prior at Dancing Days Studio in Los Angeles, California.

After learning this, Tabernacle had wasted no time in sending an emissary to the band's show in Springfield, someone with whom the group felt comfortable, someone who could find out why the album hadn't been handed over to the label. Someone whose job it had been to stay on top of things like that, someone who had failed horribly in that regard.

As the phone's bell pealed a third time, seemingly more urgent than the previous two rings despite the impossibility of it, his eyes drifted to the large manila envelope still sitting on his desk by the window. That envelope and the contents within it were the cherry on top of this little garbage heap of a day, and Tabernacle wasn't exactly sure how he was going to deal with it. Not yet, at least.

He picked up the phone before it could ring a fourth time and was unsurprised to hear Jensen Bennett's voice on the other end.

"Talk," Robbie said.

"I'm still in Springfield. Sorry for shouting, but the band is louder than usual tonight."

Tabernacle sat up and grabbed a cigarette from the nearly empty pack on his nightstand. He smoked when he was anxious, and he had never been more so than he was now. "And?"

"And nothing, sir. This little south-bound soiree was all for naught. The band wouldn't see me. I can't even get close enough to wave to them."

"Wouldn't *see* you? The fuck does *that* mean?" Tabernacle lit the cigarette with an increasingly shaky hand and ran a hand across his bald head.

"It means they won't talk to me. It means I've apparently lost any sway I once had with them. I'm not sure what I did exactly, but that's it, snout to tail."

Tabernacle took a long drag of the cigarette while Jensen was talking and slowly let the smoke drift from his mouth as he responded. "I told you to come back with answers, Bennett, or not come back at all. Did you forget that part of our conversation this morning?"

"I didn't, sir. I tried. But short of turning myself into a fly and buzzing backstage, there's not much more I can do here. We'll have to file for breach of contract. I can help with the paperwork when I'm back in town."

Tabernacle crushed his cigarette, only a quarter smoked, and gripped the phone tightly. "Bennett, you're not going *anywhere*."

His eyes again drifted to the large manila envelope sitting on his desk, and for a moment he was tempted to reopen it. But just the thought of doing so conjured up the image of what was inside: An album cover, large enough to accommodate a vinyl LP, with the words *House Made of Sound* written in cheerful letters at its top.

Despite the fact he'd only looked at it once, more than five hours ago, the cover art was imprinted in his mind – every line, every color. The front featured Quiet Catastrophe – Choom, Orrin and that asshole Grange – each giving the camera a middle finger and smiling like jackasses. Behind them, clear as an Oklahoma sunset, was the Wicked Records logo covered in a messy brown substance that could only be human excrement.

The track listing on the back showed sixteen songs, but there was no record inside the sleeve. Instead, Tabernacle found dozens of long strips of paper whose edges bore the jagged scars of a document shredder. Tabernacle didn't need to piece them back together to realize it was the band's contract.

"Sir? Are you still there?"

16

Tabernacle forced the image from his mind and turned to face the window. The city of Chicago was ablaze in a reddish-orange glow beneath him as cars and streetlights and flashing storefront signs fused together to cut deep lines into the darkened earth. Lake Michigan loomed like a starless void in the distance.

"Here's the bottom line, Bennett. The band is in possession of property that belongs to Wicked Records. I want it back. I'm not gonna waste the time and manpower on a lawsuit if there's a simpler solution. You're there, and you're going to *stay* there until you've made all of this very clear to your friends. Do you understand?"

Bennett didn't respond at first, and Tabernacle heard only muffled music in the background. It was barely discernible over the shriek of the crowd.

When he finally spoke again, Bennett sounded different. The placating salesman was gone.

"No, I *don't* understand. I *built* this fucking ship, and yet everyone treats me like the asshole shoveling coal in the engine room. No more. I'm done. I'm getting off. Geffen's been knocking at my door for years. Maybe it's time I finally answered."

Robbie was stunned into silence at first. Bennett had never spoken to him like that before. He had a smart mouth on him, yes, but he'd always been a good, loyal lapdog. Now it seemed he wanted to break free of his leash and find another owner, but Robbie couldn't let that happen.

The guy was talented, of that there was no doubt. He'd single-handedly pulled Wicked Records' nuts out of the fire when he'd discovered Quiet Catastrophe. But it was more than that. They were at war now; the fake album cover and the shredded contract were just the first shots in what could be a very long and bloody battle. But Bennett could end it tonight before it spiraled out of control. Was, in fact, the *only* one who could end it.

But he'd only get this one chance. Jensen had to be fully invested, and there was only one language he understood.

Robbie Tabernacle grabbed another cigarette, lit it with a shaky hand, and then offered Jensen Bennett the deal of a lifetime.

***

"Bennett, I'm going to sweeten the pot, sweeten it so goddamn much you'll get diabetes just looking at it," Tabernacle's voice said in Jensen's ear. "Ready for this? Two percent of album sales or five million, whichever is higher."

Jensen was nearly at Gate Ten – he could see the ticket collector behind the small, glass-covered booth at its side and was about to give her an unobstructed view of his middle finger – but stopped dead when he heard the offer.

"Come again?"

"Bennett, they taught you basic math at Columbia, didn't they? Get me the album – not some second-generation copy but the original master – and you'll get a big ass pile of money. Hell, I'll even promote you to head of A&R, something we probably should've done a long time ago. I'll have legal draft something tonight."

Jensen was speechless. He worked the numbers in his head, and then worked them again just to make sure they were right. Five million dollars, probably closer to seven or eight if the album performed as well on Spotify and iTunes as *Please Rise* had. The numbers were so unbelievably large he was momentarily bowled over by them.

"You said it – this is *your* ship, and I completely agree," Tabernacle continued. "Whether you run it ashore or sail off into the sunset is entirely up to you, now."

Jensen swallowed hard. His throat was suddenly very dry. The realization that this was really happening – under a formal contract, no less – was like having a syringe filled with pure joy injected into his veins.

No more bills. No more worrying. He could vacation wherever he wanted, drive whatever car he wanted, have an adventure whenever he felt like it. Aimee might even reconsider those divorce papers.

But even more exciting than all of that was the prospect of finally opening the nightclub he bought last year, the one below his apartment at Division and Hoyne whose half-finished facade and hollow guts taunted him every day, the one that up until a few moments ago had been threatening to inter him under a pile of past-due notices. With a good business plan, he could turn that five into ten, or twenty, or even thirty. Maybe more if luck was on his side.

"Hedley keeps anything important close to him," Jensen said in a voice that seemed to be coming from far away. "The master should be right here, in the green room backstage. He wouldn't trust something so important to anyone else but himself."

Jensen couldn't see him, but Tabernacle's voice sounded like he was smiling. "Good. That's the kind of talk I want to hear, Bennett."

And with that, Tabernacle hung up. No goodbye, no good luck; just a dead line.

Jensen's head was swimming. Everything that had happened to him so far that day, coupled with the bad soap opera he'd been living for the past several months, all bombarded him simultaneously like the incoherent noise of ten televisions sets all tuned to different channels.

Yet one singular thought cut through the din: *Five million dollars*. The words seemed enchanted, like they'd float away into the ether on a cloud of fairy dust if one dared speak them aloud. So Jensen didn't; he only thought them, over and over and over again as he walked back into the sonic orgy that swelled inside Springfield Stadium.

His sorrow had melted like snow under the relentless gaze of an early spring sun. The void was shallower, too, its teeth blunted. For the first time in a long time, he legitimately felt excited for what might lie ahead.

Yet this newfound elation was seasoned with just enough anxiety to make it all slightly bitter. Five million dollars, maybe more, but only if he found *House Made of Sound*, the band's enigmatic third album. And that wasn't going to be an easy task.

The money and the master, Jensen thought. *You can't have the first one without the second, and right now I have neither.*

But he would. He'd get them both.

Or die trying.

[silence]

In the chaos, a fleeting thought: *She's not here.*

It was a realization born of instinct and dumb awareness. There was no understanding of where *here* was, or who *she* was. Even the words themselves made no sense. But the thought came regardless, floating in the bedlam like a grain of sand caught in a raging current.

Again, this time more panicked: *She's not here.*

These thoughts were brief yet terrifying, pregnant with despair and a sense of cosmic misdirection. *This is all wrong, all wrong.*

But even in the confusion, in that unexpected gale of words neither understood nor misinterpreted, there was a frantic desire to hold onto the thought before it, like every grain of sand, finally succumbed to the surge and disappeared forever into the surf.

Don't let it go. Please, please don't let that horrible thought go.

Then a light, pervasive and driven by a baleful intensity, pushed through the darkness. It sent all thoughts scurrying into the deep, soft, quiet earth beneath consciousness. A final struggle to hold on, and then everything was gone.

In the light, *she* ceased to be, and *here* consumed the world.

VOICES AND VISIONS

D aphne Dartmouth had three problems, two of which were now arguing over which Quiet Catastrophe album was superior – *Shining Morning Face*, the band's first, or their sophomore outing, *Please Rise*.

She knew Tom Kloski and Brad Hendrick were only doing it to impress her, to woo her with their vast knowledge of Quiet Catastrophe trivia, and in a way, she thought it was cute. But neither one had even the slightest chance of ever seeing her naked, and both knew it, although that didn't stop them from constantly fighting over her affection.

The time was coming, and coming soon, when one or (God help her) both would make an intrepid declaration, and she'd have to dust off Unrequited Love's Greatest Hits: I just got out of a bad relationship; I'm really enjoying being single right now; I don't have time for a boyfriend; and so on. It was going to be an uncomfortable situation when it inevitably happened. She liked them, but the truth was that neither was her type. Especially poor Tom, who was trying so hard to be Hedley Grange it bordered on mockery.

But the problem of the dueling lovers paled in comparison to her third problem, which began right around the time the band hit the stage and had been steadily growing ever since.

Someone was coming through. A woman, Daphne thought, short and skinny, with strawberry blonde hair and a pair of beautiful brown eyes. The image was too murky to see much else, but the woman was definitely trying to connect. Daphne wasn't about to let her. She was there to relax and have a good time, not answer collect calls from the great beyond. She just had to fortify her defenses, which at the moment amounted to sheer willpower and a few hits of the White Widow she'd snuck inside. The pot in particular was especially effective in dulling whatever sense it was that allowed her to communicate with the other side, and she made sure to take an extra-long drag before passing the joint back to Brad.

But as she coughed into her hand and tried to ride the wave of euphoria that instantly swept over her, the spirit woman's voice only grew stronger, her image more defined. She was young, probably in her mid-twenties, and cute as a bug's ear. Daphne tried to push the girl away, but she was strong and pushed back. She had a message – didn't they all? – and she wasn't going to leave until Daphne delivered it.

There's gotta be at least ten thousand people here, Daphne thought, directing it at the spirit. *You really expect me to know who you wanna talk to?*

The voice said something in response to this, but it still wasn't clear enough for Daphne to understand. Hopefully, Pretty Ghost Girl would fade away again once she realized her message was getting lost in translation.

Brad and Tom knew of Daphne's "gift," as did most of her friends and family, and they all shrugged it off with a laugh. Daphne let them, because the last thing she wanted was a reputation for being some weirdo who talked to thin air and read fortunes. She'd endured enough ridicule in high school to last a lifetime, had deflected more than her fair share of stupid nicknames like *Daffy* Dartmouth and *Goosebumps* like they were innocent jokes that didn't hurt like hell. She was tired of it, tired of the sarcasm and tired of trying to convince everyone she was telling the truth. All she wanted now was to fit in, and if that meant quieting the disembodied voices and shapes that constantly bombarded her, then so be it.

But as the young woman grew sharper in Daphne's mind, she realized this wasn't a spirit she was going to be able to simply brush off. This woman was tenacious, she was tough, she wanted to say something very badly, and she was going to say it, whether Daphne liked it or not.

Finally, the image became clear enough to make out all the details, even if some were still a little hazy around the edges. Pretty Ghost Girl was only a few steps away, pointing to a man hugging himself for warmth near the front wall of the lawn section. Daphne's breath caught in her chest as she noticed a fine, barely visible black mist emanating from his body. It was an image she knew only she could see, and it meant the man was close to death. Cancer? Car accident? Daphne didn't know, but whatever it was, the man wasn't going to be with the living for much longer.

Words were coming through. The young woman kept repeating them over and over again, each time with increasing urgency and with each word jabbing a finger at the man huddled for warmth.

"Him. Him. I want *him*."

✳✳✳

It was a quarter to ten, and Jensen still hadn't figured out how he was going to get backstage.

In about two hours the band would be on a plane headed for the next show in Boise, aglow in post-concert euphoria and about thirty-thousand feet above the verdant plains of western Illinois. Being that it was opening night, Jensen was holding out hope the band would perform two encores instead of the usual one, which would buy him at least another fifteen minutes before the group left for Lincoln Airport. But in either case, time was growing short, and if he didn't devise a plan soon it would be too late to make good on Tabernacle's deal.

He couldn't let that happen.

His first course of action had been to obtain a backstage pass, which he successfully did by trading his leather bomber jacket with a man who was too drunk to realize it was worth about ten dollars, if that. It had been a gift from his mother, the very last she'd given him before succumbing to cancer more than ten years ago. At the time, weak from chemotherapy and doped up on a cocktail of pain meds, she'd claimed the jacket belonged to his biological sperm donor.

Jensen had struggled at first with the thought of parting with it, despite the fact he'd never laid eyes on the man it supposedly belonged to, if only because it was the only piece of his real father he'd ever had. In any other instance he might have felt a little guilty about the lopsided nature of the transaction, but as it was, he knew he was somehow losing much more than the man was.

Now he stood in the lawn section, not sure how to proceed and hugging himself tightly as a cruel northeasterly wind assaulted his exposed skin. He had a valid pass, and that was a good start, but a pass would do him no good unless he could somehow change his appearance.

It was while he was scanning the crowd for potential disguises that he saw the woman. She looked to be in her early 20s, perhaps late teens, her short blonde hair exposing a long neck that ran into an equally lanky but feminine frame. Her wide, navy-blue eyes gazed unblinkingly in Jensen's direction, possibly even right at Jensen himself, although it was hard to tell with the constant foot traffic and pot smoke moving between them.

The woman was pretty and, if she *was* staring at him, a little creepy, but she wasn't the focus of his attention. It was the two men arguing next to her, and the backstage passes each had clipped to their Quiet Catastrophe T-shirts. One of the men in particular – the one on the far left of the trio – was wearing a floppy hat much too big for his head, as well as a pair of oversized sunglasses, despite the fact the sun had retreated nearly an hour ago.

The ensemble would be his best chance of getting backstage; the only

25

problem was that he had nothing left to barter with – except, of course, for his wristwatch, but it was a Harry Winston knockoff and not worth the cut-rate metals from which it was made.

He'd have to at least try. The trio seemed harmless enough. They were unquestionably "Grangers" – the collective name fans of Hedley Grange had given themselves – dressed in unwashed jeans and dirty T-shirts that were no doubt ripped intentionally in honor of their namesake. The one in the middle even looked a bit like Grange.

Costumes on, curtains up, Jensen thought, then walked toward the group as casually as his now-freezing limbs would allow. The woman stopped looking at him the second he began moving in their direction and reaffixed her gaze to a discarded beer cup lying on the grass.

"Ain't no comparison," Grange-Clone was telling Floppy Hat. "The second album's got no *filler,* man. Good to the last drop. Plus, it just *sounds* better than the first."

Jensen took a spot next to Floppy Hat and leaned nonchalantly against the railing. His body made like it was going to shiver, but he fought against it. It was hard to believe that just an hour ago he'd felt so hot that "spontaneous human combustion" had seemed less like an X-Files plotline and more like a very real concern.

"Actually," Jensen said with a trained smile, "the first album had a better mix. *Please Rise* had a better *master,* yes, but overall it was more slipshod than the first because it was laid down at various studios across the country during the first tour. The sound's a bit cleaner on the vinyl reissue, but the difference is still night and day."

Floppy Hat smiled and regarded him kindly through his dark sunglasses, but Grange-Clone frowned, clearly bothered at the sudden intrusion.

"Best keep your nose on your face," Grange-Clone said to him. "You're wearin' a fucking *tie,* for Christ's sake. The hell would *you* know?"

Jensen nodded, took out his wallet and retrieved from it a business card, which he then handed to Grange-Clone. "A&R rep for Wicked Records," he said. "I was there when both albums were recorded, so I think I know a thing or two about them."

Floppy Hat leaned in toward Grange-Clone to get a look at the card. "Whoa, man, that's awesome!" he said, and then directed his visibly impressed expression to Jensen. "Like, you was *there*, man! In the freaking studio! What was it like?"

Grange-Clone, who seemed less impressed than Floppy Hat but had at least stopped looking at Jensen like he was an impostor, handed the card back. "Pretty cool," he said, "but the second album's still better."

Jensen nodded again and took the card back. "Sure, everyone has their favorite. Me, I like the one they just finished, *House Made of Sound*. A lot of maturity on that disc, if you ask me."

The men's faces lit up at the mention of a new Quiet Catastrophe album. They smiled at each other excitedly, the rift between them temporarily healed, and Jensen relaxed a bit. The woman, however, didn't speak or smile. Instead, she cast a quick glance in Jensen's direction and, when he returned her gaze, she looked back down at her feet. Either she was extremely shy or too stoned to interact socially with anyone, which wasn't good – Jensen needed all three on his side for this to work.

"New album, no kidding?" Grange-Clone said. He apparently had forgotten all about Jensen's tie. "You gotta tell us about it. I swear on my grandaddy's grave I won't say nothing."

Jensen smiled. He'd wanted something to barter with, and now he had it. "I'll do you one better. You guys sound like you're from Arkansas, or maybe southern Missouri?"

Grange-Clone nodded. "Missouri. New Hamelin area."

"It's not on the tour schedule," Jensen continued, "but the band has a show in Jackson in about two weeks. It's a benefit for Hedley's charity, Grange for Change, and rumor has it the place'll be packed with celebrities. Rumor also has it the band's going to play a few tracks from the new album. How would you guys like to be there?"

The friends looked at each other with unbelieving expressions, laughed, and then turned back to Jensen as if they were conjoined twins who shared the same brain stem. "Does a bear shit in the woods?" Grange-Clone said. "Hell *yeah* we wanna be there!"

"Great. I'll get you guys on the guest list the second I get back to Chicago." Jensen leaned in close and lowered his voice for effect. "Before that, though, I was wondering if you guys could help me out with a small problem. I need to get backstage, but there's this reporter hanging by the entrance. I'd rather not speak to him right now. He's been bugging the hell out of me. Wants deets on the next album, but contractually I just can't talk about it. Unfortunately, telling that to a reporter is like trying to snuff a fire with gasoline. I'd like to slip by without him realizing it."

The men nodded as he spoke, but the girl continued to stare at the ground. It now looked as if she were mumbling something under her breath, something that to Jensen looked like, "Leave me alone." She was undoubtedly an odd bird.

"I need something to distract him," Jensen continued. "I'd like to go in with you guys, but also ..." He pointed at Floppy Hat and smiled. "Any chance you'd be willing to part with that hat? And maybe those shades, too?"

Floppy Hat put a protective hand on top of his head, as if Jensen intended to steal the cap right from his head. "My hat?"

He didn't look sold on the idea, but Grange-Clone smiled and nodded. "Yeah, I get it, man. Just sneak right past the dickbag. That's great." He then elbowed Floppy Hat playfully. "Come on, man. Give the guy your hat. You paid, like, five bucks for it." Floppy Hat didn't answer, but he cautiously took his hand off his head.

Jensen looked at the girl and saw she now was having a whispered conversation with someone to her left, despite the fact no one was there. It gave

Jensen the chills.

"She okay?" Jensen asked and nodded toward the girl.

Grange-Clone shot a quick glance at her. "Don't pay her no mind. She's one of them *sidekick mediums*." Then, to the woman, he said, "Come on, Daphne. Cool it. You're freakin' everyone out."

The woman named Daphne suddenly snapped her head toward Jensen and looked at him with haunting eyes. He jumped a little at the unexpected change in her demeanor.

"You're very close to the spirit world, do you know that?" Daphne whispered. Then, a bit louder and slightly agitated, she said, "I got a woman here – I don't think you're related, but I can't tell. She's tellin' me to tell you, 'Wait for me. Wait, please wait.' It's all she keeps sayin'. Wait for me. I told her to stop, to go away, but she won't."

Jensen suddenly felt very uncomfortable. His mouth worked to say something in response, but nothing came out. Spirit world? What in the hell was this lady's deal?

"Wait for you, I *told* him that already," Daphne said impatiently to the air at her left. "Now please, leave me alone. I already told him."

Grange-Clone smiled nervously. "Don't mind Daff, man. She may seem crazier'n a soup sandwich, but she's usually a real picnic." Then, smiling broadly, he removed the hat from his friend's head and handed it to Jensen. Floppy Hat didn't protest. "Here you go, bud. First album, second album, who cares? We're all fans here."

Daphne shook her head and moved her left hand in a shooing motion. "Well, how was I supposed to know? There's gotta be ten thousand people here! Now *shoo!*"

Jensen took the hat, still on edge at the woman's phantom conversation, and put it on. It was a bit too small, but it hid the top half of his face well.

Unprompted, Floppy Hat took off his sunglasses and placed them on Jensen's face. "Here you go," he said. "Just don't be forgettin' them tickets." Now that his face was clear Jensen could see he was young, perhaps not even old enough to drive. "Name's Brad. This jerkoff's Tom. You already met Daff."

Jensen looked at her again. She seemed to have stopped talking to the phantom, the one that had said to wait. Wait where? Daphne looked relieved, but she also seemed a bit embarrassed. She smiled for the first time since Jensen approached them.

"I'm sorry 'bout all that," she said. "They always come to me at the worst times. She's gone now."

Jensen adjusted the sunglasses to sit more comfortably on his nose and managed a weak smile. "No worries," he said. "Happens to all of us. Just the other day, Jim Morrison came to me while I was on the shitter."

Everyone laughed – even Daphne – and Jensen began to feel slightly better. Even still ... it had been eerie. *You're very close to the spirit world*, Daphne had said. What did she mean by that?

It left him with an uneasy feeling he didn't much like.

✳✳✳

Jensen hadn't lied; not really. Quiet Catastrophe *did* have a charity event booked in Jackson, and he was fairly confident that even with his newfound excommunication from the band he could still get his hands on three tickets. The part about them playing new tracks, though? A complete guess. But why on earth would they record a new album and not play songs from it?

His conscience was clear as the Grangers, now a foursome, walked down the pavilion steps and toward the backstage entrance where Nigel and Two-Eyes had not an hour before turned him away. The panic that had been mostly quiet for the past hour suddenly revved its engine again that they were in motion. If his disguise wasn't convincing enough, if Two-Eyes discovered it was him, instead of the master recording of *House Made of Sound*, Jensen would probably get a few cracked ribs and a broken nose. Or worse. The thought made him sick again.

"Remember, guys," Jensen said quietly, "I'm just one of you. Nothing special here."

Brad and Tom nodded, but Daphne again looked troubled. If she went all Shirley MacLaine a second time as they were trying to get backstage, it was show over. Jensen just hoped she could keep her cool long enough for him to make it to the green room.

"Passes," Johnny Two-Eyes shouted over the clamor as they approached. The stadium was near-dark, and he'd popped on a mini flashlight that in his meaty hand looked almost comical.

All four of them grabbed the backstage passes that were clipped to their shirts and angled them so Two-Eyes could see what they said. The giant first shined a shaft of light on the badges, studying each one with increasingly narrowing eyes as if they were some strange mystery, and then swept the penlight slowly across each of their faces. When he got to Jensen, he stopped.

"Hat and glasses off."

Jensen froze. He again became very aware of his heartbeat, which began thudding in his ears like an inner metronome. What to do? Make a run for the green room? Peel off another joke? He couldn't walk away this time. It wasn't just his job on the line; it was his entire future.

"I said hat and glasses off," Two-Eyes said, this time more forcefully. "I'm not going to ask again."

As Jensen moved his hand slowly to the hat, he saw Daphne shoot him a concerned expression. Then, an idea seemed to cross her face and she shouted angrily to the empty air to her left, "Go away, will you!"

Startled, Two-Eyes moved the flashlight from Jensen's face to where Daphne stood. "You alright?" he asked.

Daphne smiled, wide and beautiful, and put a tender hand on Two-Eyes' shoulder. "There someone on your staff named Hank?" she asked. "This woman, she won't leave me be. Wants to talk to a Hank. Does that ring a bell?"

Two-Eyes cocked his head to the side and shined the light directly in Daphne's eyes. "This woman – do you see her ... right now?"

Daphne nodded. "To my left. She's a young thing, very beautiful, but very persistent. I'm pretty sure her name is Gwen."

"Uh-huh," Two-Eyes said and continued to study her eyes for signs of drug use, or insanity. Perhaps both. "Well, I can tell ya there's no Hank here. And even if there was, we don't let crazy people just wander around back-stage."

Daphne looked at Two-Eyes through hurtful eyes. "Listen," she said, "just 'cause you don't understand somethin' don't mean it's crazy. Radio waves have been around since the dawn of time, but we didn't realize it 'till we in-vented machines that could tune into them. It just so happens I'm a machine, too, one that can talk to people on the other side. Just because you can't, don't make fun of *me* for it."

Two-Eyes smiled and lowered his flashlight as a sudden realization dawned on his face. "Oh, you're one of them ..." he snapped his fingers repeatedly as if it would bring the word he was thinking of out of the air. "Mediums, that's it. You talk to dead people and shit."

The corner of Daphne's mouth rose in a half-smile. "Yep, psychic me-dium. They don't come to me as much as they did when I was little, but it still happens now and then."

Two-Eyes nodded, and his grin widened. "Yeah, yeah, I get it. Grange *loves* that shit. Come on through."

And with that, he stepped aside to let them pass.

Jensen was in.

***

Before he made a beeline to the green room, Jensen pulled Daphne aside. The backstage area was teeming with activity as roadies and technicians and groupies swarmed in a hectic dance of concert-night commotion, so he took her to a more secluded hallway a bit removed from it.

"Look, Daphne, thank you. If it wasn't for that act you put on, I'd –"

"It wasn't an act," Daphne said a bit defensively. "Sure, I dialed it up a bit for you, but there really *is* a woman here. Thought she wanted to talk to *you*, but seems she's here for a Hank. Whoever that is."

"Do you really expect me to believe you can talk to dead people? I saw that movie. Bruce Willis was better in *Die Hard*."

Daphne didn't look hurt or angry, just tired – perhaps tired of having this very same conversation. "I gave up tryin' to convert people a long time ago," she said. "All it got me was a silly nickname and a lot of alone time. But I *will* say this, Jensen – there *is* a life after this one, and from the little peek I get at it sometimes, it's great."

"I *want* to believe that. Hell, who wouldn't? Sounds awesome. I also want to believe in a Ramones reunion, but wanting something doesn't make it real."

He expected Daphne to get properly angry this time, but she only smiled and touched his arm gently. "Everyone has beliefs, and I respect yours. But true or not, there's somethin' I gotta tell you."

Jensen saw it in her eyes – whatever she wanted to tell him, it wasn't good.

"When I get close to people, I can see their auras – lights that surround their bodies," she continued. "Yours is tellin' me you're not well. That you're dying. Do you ... have *cancer*, maybe?"

"Not that I know of, but it sure as hell wouldn't surprise me if I did."

Daphne took his hands in hers and looked deep into his eyes. "I don't need my gift to see you had it tough. It's in the lines of your face, in the way you look at me, in the way you talk. Life hasn't been fair to you. You just wanna be happy, but you can't. But don't give up, Jensen. Happiness is out there, for *both* of us. We just gotta know where to look."

Jensen shivered. Either he wasn't as good of an actor as he thought, or

Daphne really *was* psychic. Either way, there was something soothing in her touch, something that made him want to drop the act and be completely honest with her.

"I think I've found it," he said, "but it's not going to be easy to get."

Daphne's smiled widened, and she moved her hand to his cheek. Her skin was warm, comforting. "It's the new album, isn't it?"

Despite being in the heat of the backstage, Jensen suddenly felt very cold. What *was* this? Was this woman really in tune with something beyond? Or was she just a very talented charlatan? "Yeah, it's the new album. *God*, you're good. How do you do it?"

Daphne didn't answer, only put both hands up to her shoulders in a "Who knows?" motion. In the warm spill of backstage lights, she looked both innocent and exceptionally beautiful.

"I don't have much time," he said." It's probably best if you go back with your friends and pretend you never saw me."

Daphne rose up on her toes so that they were eye-to-eye, wrapped her arms around Jensen's neck and then planted a light kiss on his lips. "That's for good luck," she whispered. "Promise me you'll be careful."

Jensen only smiled – no use making a promise he wasn't sure he could keep – and then hurried down the narrow hallway which led to the green room.

The next time Daphne Dartmouth saw him, Jensen Bennett was dead.

***

The hallways were empty and relatively quiet, save for the muffled sound of the music and the hypnotic drone of the crowd both underneath and on top of it.

As the muted notes of what Jensen was pretty sure was the song "Time and Again" echoed through the vacant passageway, he let his mind wander;

34

the song brought back memories, both good and bad.

The track closed out the band's second album and was about the cyclical nature of drug abuse – the intense high, the crushing comedown, the vow never to do it again, and the inevitable return to the intense high. Grange had penned the lyrics one night while in the throes of a week-long, self-imposed, cold-turkey withdrawal attempt from heroin. Jensen had been amazed at Grange's focus and creativity given the agony he was in.

As Jensen approached a door with a piece of duct tape and the words "Quiet Catastrophe" scrawled across it in hasty cursive, the unmistakable sound of Hedley Grange's pristine voice cut through the clatter:

Not this time
I've used and abused
But I think I'll refuse ... this time
Once, I'd taste
But the sorrow and pain
And the thoughts that remained
Laid waste
To me

The lyrics had been more than just a convenient rhyme for Grange; he'd overdosed and nearly died on a hotel bathroom floor in Columbus, Ohio shortly before his self-detox experiment. Jensen had been the one who'd found him, head against the toilet with his eyes closed and a small line of drool running down his chin. If he hadn't already known Grange was a first-class junkie, Jensen probably would've assumed he was sleeping, as everyone else apparently had. Grange's pulse had been weak and his breathing shallow, so Jensen, pretty high himself on a combination of cocaine and ecstasy but sober enough to realize the seriousness of the situation, had called 911. It had been a close call, but he'd stuck by Grange and administered CPR for twelve exhausting minutes until the EMTs arrived to load him into the back of the ambulance.

Grange's second attempt at getting clean, this time using the services of a legit rehab facility, had finally been successful. In tribute, every time the band would play "Time and Again" live, he'd begin by giving a short speech about his near-death experience and how his best friend, Jensen Bennett, had saved his life. Jensen had heard no such speech this time.

He tried the green room door and wasn't surprised to find it locked. Even if the album wasn't in there, Jensen was sure there were other things – practice amps, guitars, personal effects – that the band wanted to make sure were under constant lock and key.

He fumbled a credit card out of his wallet and, checking to make sure the hallway was clear, slid it into the vertical crack between the door and the doorjamb. It slipped under the door's bolt, and Jensen began moving it back and forth. He heard metal against metal as the lock's mechanism resisted the sudden intrusion, and then a loud snap as both the door swung open and his credit card broke.

Jensen pounded an angry fist on his leg as he looked at the two halves of broken plastic at his feet, the remains of what had once been his Capital One card. It was the only one of his credit cards that had even a sliver of money left on it. Why hadn't he used one of his other cards, the ones that were maxed out?

Five million dollars, maybe more.

The thought calmed him some, even as the contents of his stomach began roiling in anticipation of what lie within the green room. He picked up the remnants of his credit card and then slipped inside and shut the door. The song faded out completely now that he was in the room; all he could hear was the indistinct thumping of a bass drum pedal and the muted roar of the crowd.

It was a standard green room. A massive flat-screen TV hung on the far wall and stared at him with its vacant, slightly reflective face. Next to it was a table covered in food, most of which was still uneaten; and next to that, a tall box that he recognized immediately as Hedley's traveling wardrobe trunk, the one Jensen knew had a secret compartment in the back that Grange once used to smuggle heroin and other assorted contraband through customs.

A refrigerator sitting in the corner suddenly kicked on and hummed a monotonous one-note song, and Jensen's eyes were drawn to it. Propped against its door was a painting in progress. Most of the canvass was white, but here and there splotches of color had been smeared over a faint pencil outline that covered the entire board.

Jensen's eyes narrowed as he walked to the painting and studied the ghostly gray lines chaotically etched onto its surface. They looked as if the artist had been trying to hurriedly birth an idea into existence before it escaped the tentative cage of his imagination.

The lines suggested a wall of smooth stone, unbroken and shimmering with a kind of inner light. In the center of this was a triangular hole, and through it Jensen could see a dense forest beneath a sky filled with hundreds of tiny squiggles. Some of these had already been painted, and it seemed no two were exactly the same color. On the lower right-hand side Hedley Grange had already signed his name, as if the painting wasn't a work in progress but minutes away from an art gallery showing.

The painting stirred a memory, a recent one. A few weeks back, a UPS man had delivered to him an oversized package that was flat and wrapped in beige paper. In the upper left was printed a name and address – Hedley Grange, 1204 Seger Road, Royal Orleans, California 95101.

He'd thanked the delivery man and then retreated into his living room, where he tore into the package and discovered a landscape painting, beautiful in its scope and execution. In it, a two-story building slept beneath a cloudless summer sky, rocked gently to dreamland in the arms of an overgrowth of trees and grass. Glints of sunlight winked from the building's windows, which sat in neat rows along the base of the structure's foundation.

Jensen recognized it immediately as the nightclub he and Aimee had been in the process of renovating before their separation, the place above which he still called home despite the bad memories it stirred. In addition to adding façade and landscaping enhancements that didn't exist in reality, Grange had drawn a short, squat sign near the walkway leading to the front door. *Les Deux Figures*, it said. He didn't need to speak French to know the phrase meant "The Two Figures," apparently a reference to himself and Aimee. It wasn't a name they'd considered, nor had Grange ever mentioned it to them.

Jensen knew of Grange's second life as an amateur painter, a hobby he'd suddenly picked up after finally getting clean, but he'd never seen one of his completed works before. *Les Deux Figures* was quite good, but Jensen couldn't bring himself to hang it. Somehow, looking at the club as it existed in Grange's imagination – vibrant, complete, a bit mysterious – filled him with more sadness than living in the actual dilapidated building did. The painting was a representation of a dream, not anything that actually existed. He'd stuffed it into his utility closet and forgotten about it until this very moment.

As Jensen turned his eyes away from Grange's latest painting, he saw a large green sack sitting on a lounger near the TV. It was Hedley's duffle bag, one that he'd carried ever since the day Jensen had discovered him in the Red Line terminal. It contained everything Grange cherished most – handwritten lyrics, a harmonica, a signed copy of Led Zeppelin's *Houses of the Holy*, and, Jensen hoped, the master recording of Quiet Catastrophe's unreleased third album.

Jensen walked quickly over to the bag, just barely containing the urge to run to it, and with shaking hands unzipped the top. There was the harmonica, and Jensen remembered many nights on the road when Hedley would take it out and play for the crew on the tour bus, back before the band had graduated to flying the friendly skies in a renovated 747. He'd blow an open G, stomp his foot a few times to get a rhythm going, and then belt into an old blues number, alternating between playing the harp and singing in a spot-on Junior Wells impersonation. Grange cherished the harmonica; it was his late uncle's.

There was the aforementioned copy of Zeppelin's fifth album, as well as reams of spiral notebooks filled with lyrics. There was also a bottle of Precose for Grange's diabetes, an MP3 player with white ear buds protruding from it, a faded and well-worn AC/DC T-shirt, an expensive-looking mandolin, a few brushes with dried paint coating their ends, a dog-eared copy of Kurt Vonnegut's *The Sirens of Titan*, a few mini bottles of Jim Beam apparently stolen from some long-forgotten hotel room ... and nothing else.

"Dammit!" Jensen shouted to the empty room and again searched the bag, this time actually taking items out and throwing them onto the floor. He went through each notebook, flipping through page after page of lyrics and notes and artwork, and even a whole five-subject notebook with nothing but numbers scrawled cover-to-cover like the ramblings of a lunatic, throwing each to the ground in frustration as he again came up empty.

Nothing, Jensen thought. *Not a damn thing, not even a clue as to where to start looking*.

He slumped onto the lounger in defeat. Had he really expected to find the album here? No, not if he was being honest with himself, but he'd hoped for at least a signpost; something to point him in the right direction.

He could leave now and wait for the label to flex its legal muscle, but that process would take months, perhaps years depending on any countersuit the band might file. He needed the album *now*, because he knew he'd never again get this close. The band simply wouldn't allow it.

As he was thinking, Jensen's eyes dropped to the ground and the contents strewn about it. A picture had fallen from one of Grange's notebooks during his flurry to find the master, and Jensen leaned over to pick it up.

It was a mock *Rolling Stone* cover the band had created for Jensen during the band's second world tour. In the photo, Grange, Choom, Orrin and

Jensen were locked arm-in-arm in front of the band's tour jet, the expression on their faces a kind of delirious excitement that out of context might seem slightly mad. The fake magazine's one and only headline, written in bubbly, '70s-style lettering, read:

"Quiet Catastrophe celebrates Benny's birthday in style!"

And below that, the band had written a simple message where the subtitle should be:

You'll always be our fourth member.
Happy birthday, Benny!
– Quiet Catastrophe

Jensen remembered that day well, which itself was a bit of an oddity. Most of the memories he had of his time with the band were hazy, like looking through a dirty windshield, and he blamed the cocaine. But he remembered his birthday party clearly, especially the gift they'd presented to him that night: the gold record they'd received for *Shining Morning Face*.

Jensen had protested the gift at first, but the band, Grange especially, had been adamant he'd take it. It was his, they'd said, as much as it was theirs, even if it didn't have his name engraved on it. He'd eventually accepted it, and it now hung in his office at Wicked Records.

"Liars," he said quietly to the fake cover as he dabbed his right eye with the back of his left hand. He felt stupid. Stupid for ever believing these guys were his friends.

None of it mattered, not anymore. He only cared about one thing now, and that was getting the money and rebooting his life. Everything else was just background noise. *House Made of Sound* was out there somewhere, just as Daphne had said, and he was going to get it and be happy. But where?

All it would take was a few choice questions and a keen eye to get the location from the band. They wouldn't be as easy to crack as the scalper had been, especially if he had to take them on all at the same time, but they'd eventually spill their secrets. No matter how hard they tried, their faces, their movements, the things they didn't say would betray them.

But for that to work he'd need to be in a place where they couldn't leave; a place where they would be forced to listen to him, a place with no outside opinion to sully his intent. And then suddenly it hit him: The answer was right there, splashed flagrantly across the cover of the mock *Rolling Stone* cover.

When Quiet Catastrophe's plane took off that night, Jensen intended to be on it.

[silence]

Go for the throat. Save the mamby pamby bullshit for church.

His stepfather speaks through puffs of smoke. He's talking business, the only language he knows.

If someone's outselling you, you're doing it wrong.

Richard is close and reeks of beer. When he looks at the boy, which isn't often, there's something unsettling in his eyes, like a thirsty animal trapped in a dry well.

It's hot and humid, the kind of afternoon only a cold swimming pool or air conditioner cranked to ten can rectify. The boy has spent the last few hours at the end of the street trying to sell lemonade, a watery mess with yellow powder floating on the surface. A group of kids is running another lemonade stand a block over, and business there is booming. The boy didn't sell a single cup.

Now, in the suffocating heat of the living room, his stepfather talks on the couch. He's drinking a Coors Lite while *Full House* goes ignored in the background. The room's only fan blows the smoke from his cigarette back into his face as he regards the boy with bloodshot eyes. Richard rarely speaks to him, and when he does it's usually in the form of an irritated command. But not today.

The boy listens with rapt attention, basking in the sudden attention raining down on him. When he's done speaking, Richard reaches into his back pocket and retrieves twenty dollars.

Startup capital. Do what I told you and go back to your stand tomorrow. Don't come home until you double it.

The next day, the boy stumbles back into the oppressive daylight and doesn't just double the twenty dollars – he nearly *triples* it. This time he has better product, lower prices and a motivated staff – namely, a ten-dollar bushel of fresh lemons from the farmers market, a quarter per cup instead of fifty cents, and two employees, older kids he's paid five dollars each to scare the other boys away from their stand.

It's a red-letter day in the boy's life. The gaping hole inside him is filled. It would return; it always did. But for a few days, the fifty-eight dollars that bulged from the front pocket of his jeans had delivered him from desolation.

He'd gone for the throat and had found his salvation.

DOWN TO EARTH

-Track Three-

There was no question about it – Stuart Kidro's job was on the line. They were running slightly behind schedule, but that wasn't the problem. Neither was the flight plan – the skies were clear all the way to Boise, and he'd actually been able to grab a few winks in the six hours before being called to taxi the band's bird onto the runway. He was well-rested and right where he belonged, traveling at five-hundred and thirty knots and maintaining a steady cruising altitude of thirty-one thousand feet.

The problem was Nigel Cuthpit, the arrogant prick who had made Stuart's life a living hell ever since he'd taken the stick from the band's previous pilot. Maybe it was because his predecessor had been caught doing cocaine in-flight, or maybe Cuthpit was just a natural-born asshole, but the limey prick had been so far up Stuart's ass since day one he'd often considered quitting.

Now he wouldn't even have the opportunity. After the brawl he'd had with Cuthpit before takeoff, he'd be lucky to get two wheels on the ground in Boise before that English bastard cut him loose.

Stuart had told Cuthpit, cordially at first, that he was concerned with how the road crew had stacked the band's equipment into the cargo hold. The stages, lights, amplifiers and other assorted concert necessities weighed several tons combined and had to be loaded to strict FAA regs. One crate out of place and it would throw off the entire plane's center of gravity.

Cuthpit had asked Stuart to show him, and he'd guided Nigel to the side of the plane and pointed with his flashlight beam into the darkness of the cargo hold door.

"Looks like it always does," Cuthpit had said impatiently. The band had done an impromptu second encore and thrown the entire night's schedule into the shitter, and Stuart could tell Nigel was at his wit's end.

"Look, Mr. Cuthpit, I know the roadies are running on empty tonight, but they can't just stuff things in here willy-nilly. There's a plan." Stuart had held up a piece of paper and waved it as proof. "Everything has to be put in exactly the right spot."

Cuthpit had ordered Stuart to show him exactly what was out of place, and he'd obliged, walking through the gloom of the cargo hold as quickly as possible, stopping only once when he thought he heard something moving near a wardrobe case tethered to the rear wall. When they'd reached the errant crate in question – an oversized wooden box that was about a foot too aft – Stuart pointed to it and calmly explained the problem.

"Fuck's sake, mate, stop wasting my time," Nigel had interrupted. "It's only a few bleeding inches. I've had longer bowel movements."

Stuart had once again waved the piece of paper in front of Cuthpit's face to accentuate his response. "This isn't some doodle I sketched in my spare time; it's an FAA-approved loading blueprint. I can't in good conscience take off until this crate is repositioned."

Cuthpit had let a long, tired sigh escape from his chest. "Just what exactly are you proposing? That my men unload everything, and then reload it? Are you mad? Do you think my crew has time for a fucking game of late-night *Tetris*? We're due at the Idaho Center for set-up and soundcheck at nine o'clock, and we're pushing it as is."

"Sir, sorry to be blunt, but that's not my concern. I'm going to have to delay takeoff until we can –"

"Oh, fuck off, you stupid git! I'll have Lubbell fly this thing into Boise if you won't, and you can take the trolley back to the fucking unemployment line."

Stuart was momentarily stunned. Was Cuthpit saying fly or be fired? And if so, what then? He could go back to United, or maybe even return to the Air Force Academy, where the commandant – an old buddy of his – said a flight instructor job was waiting if he wanted it. But the money here was insane. He'd never made so much of it in his life.

Stuart didn't think the load would cause a problem, not a measly foot, but he made it a habit of never taking off if something was troubling him, and for some reason, all sorts of alarms were going off tonight inside his head.

Perhaps it wasn't the load that was bothering him as much as the airplane itself. Ever since he'd gotten the job four months ago, he'd simply been uncomfortable flying it. Part of the reason stemmed from the fact she just didn't handle as well as the bird he'd flown at United, but it was also because it was a Combi from the late '80s and had more than 60,000 airframe hours under its belt. There were other problems, too – the captain's chair was uncomfortable, the instrument panel was antiquated, the airframe showed early signs of corrosion ... she was simply past her prime and should've been sent to the bone yard years ago. But it had been a cheap buy, and Cuthpit was nothing if not frugal.

He'd decided to stick to his guns and told Cuthpit he wasn't moving an inch until the cargo was repositioned, and that's when the *real* fireworks had started. Cuthpit had called Stuart a pussy, and Stuart had shot back by calling Cuthpit a limey fuck, which didn't sit well with the Englishman and only caused the argument to kick into second gear. The only thing that kept them from coming to blows was the band's road manager, who grabbed Cuthpit under his arms in a half-nelson and dragged him away from striking distance.

In the end, the road manager had calmed Cuthpit down enough to let Stuart keep his job, at least until Boise, on the condition that they get going and fly a few knots faster than usual to make up for the lost time. Despite his concerns, Stuart had relented – this one flight alone would net him enough money to remodel the library into a nursery and buy all the maternity wear his wife Darlene would need, assuming they could get pregnant.

And now the band – including Cuthpit – was in the cabin, doing whatever it is rock stars did between shows. And when they landed, Stuart was sure to be out of a job anyway and wouldn't be going to California with the band.

When Lubbell got out of the can, he was going to go back and apologize. He wasn't sorry, not in the slightest, but if he wanted to keep his job, he'd have to pucker up and kiss some British ass.

The thought made Stuart shiver.

✳✳✳

Ted Choom had been clean and sober for almost two years. But now, watching Nigel snort lines of coke off the glass tabletop where a row of economy-class seats had once sat, a familiar hunger rose inside him.

Just a bump, Ted thought. *One pull from the straw, one quick snort, and I'd be good for the next two years.*

Ted shook his head and forced his eyes back to the pages of the book he was reading – a collection of song lyrics titled *The Passions of Great Fortune* by Roy Harper. It was interesting to read how other musicians crafted lyrics, and the stories behind them, and hats off to Roy Harper for momentarily taking his mind off the mound of drugs not three feet away from him. Yet he wasn't sure how long it would work.

Just sit down next to him, take a quick pull. No one is going to judge you. Hell, they might even join you.

Ted continued to read. Even through his headphones, which were delivering the warm, laid-back sounds of Booker T. and the MGs into his ears, he could hear Nigel's loud, vulgar snorts. He grabbed his phone and turned the volume up. His ears had already taken a two-hour beating during the show – the amps, the crowd, the stage monitors, Orrin's heavy snare hand, the flash pots – it was a wonder he wasn't already deaf. But the only way he was going to ignore Nigel was if he blocked him out entirely, and if his ears didn't like it, well, tough shit for his ears.

Ted thought about his friend on the road crew, Fred Lehmans, and how he'd helped Ted finally get the monkey off his back. He wished his buddy was on the plane with him right now, and not on the commercial jet the roadies took, so Fred could lend him a bit of willpower. He didn't think he was going to crack, in fact *hadn't* cracked once the entire time he'd been sober, despite Nigel and Zachary still partying day and night like it was 1999, but he wished Fred was here regardless. He wasn't just a great bass tech, he was a friend. Ted owed his sobriety, and his sanity, to him.

From the corner of his eye, he saw Stuart Kidro, the band's new pilot, emerge from the cockpit. He looked troubled, and Ted's first thought was that something was wrong with the plane. His fear waned, however, when Kidro smiled and walked up to Nigel with a hand extended. Ted took out his earphones so he could hear the exchange.

"Look, Mr. Cuthpit, things got a little crazy on the ground. Just wanted to say I'm sorry, and that I was out of line."

Nigel looked up mid-snort, the rolled-up hundred-dollar bill clutched in one chubby hand, a fine white residue caking the inside of his left nostril, and frowned. "For fuck's sake, couldn't this have waited? Don't you have an airplane to fly?"

Ted saw Kidro put down his extended hand after he realized Nigel wasn't going to take it. "Lubbell's in there. Besides, the autopilot's engaged. Even *you* could fly this thing right now."

The second the words left Kidro's lips, Ted could see in his face he regretted saying them. Nigel gently set his makeshift inhaler on the pile of cocaine and stood up. He was a good four inches shorter than Kidro, yet stood to the pilot as if he were nine feet taller.

"And just what in the hell is *that* supposed to mean, you stupid git? Think I'm a simpleton? Can't find his own ass without a fucking map?"   Kidro looked as if he was about to snap – Ted could read it in the lines in his face, how they bent and tensed as if trying to keep some caged animal beneath his skin from escaping.

"That's not what I meant," Kidro said unevenly. "I only came back here to apologize, and I've done that, so I'll be going back now."

Just as Kidro turned to leave, the cabin began to shake violently as though suddenly overcome with a grand-mal seizure. Hedley, who was painting quietly in a carpeted area near the wet bar, cursed loudly as his hand lurched abruptly to the right, causing a long, crimson streak of paint to split the unspoiled canvas like a sinister grin. Orrin stirred in his sleep on the lounger but didn't wake, even as nearly an entire set of glassware fell from the bar and crashed to the floor.

The coffee table containing Nigel's trove of white gold also shifted in the tumult, and much of it – Ted guessed perhaps an eight ball, probably a bit more – fell to the carpet and was lost in the weaving. Nigel stared at it for a moment, perhaps giving the irretrievable cocaine a tear-soaked eulogy in his head, before stirring from this brief trance and angrily pointing a plump finger at Kidro.

"What's this, then?" Nigel said rapidly as one word. He usually was quite articulate in his speech, but when enraged, he would revert to the primitive tongue of his childhood. When he did, it was almost always impossible to understand him.

"Just a little turbulence," Kidro said, the rage still simmering beneath his features. "Relax and sit down."

Nigel stared at him with wide, unbelieving eyes. "You smarmy shit! Just who in the hell do you think you are? *Nobody* talks to me like that!"

Ted saw the anger finally spread on Kidro's face as the pilot stepped forward and poked Nigel hard in the chest with his finger.

"Well it's about goddamned time someone started. I should've listened to my conscience back there and kept us grounded. But I didn't because I was scared of being fired. Shame on me for being such a chickenshit, and shame on you for being an arrogant blowhard who puts timetables over the safety of his supposed friends."

Nigel brushed Kidro's arm away with a quick swipe of his left hand and grabbed the lapel of the pilot's jacket with the other. The combination of the cocaine racing through his system and Nigel's naturally short temper were a bad mix, and Ted didn't like where this was going. He put his book down on the table in front of him and stood up. But before he could say anything, a calm, collected voice softly interjected behind him.

"Nigel, let go of his jacket and sit down."

Nigel and Kidro both looked at Hedley, who was still painting and working quickly with a brush dipped in paint thinner to remove the red mark the turbulence had caused. His eyes never moved from the canvass as he spoke again. "I already lost one friend today," he said. "Please don't make me lose another."

Nigel reluctantly let go of Kidro's jacket and sat down, but he was still clearly worked up over his little boogie with Stu the pilot.

The cabin shuddered once again, this time much more violently, and a strange dropping sensation in the pit of Ted's stomach told him the plane was rising higher. He looked worriedly at Kidro, who managed a feeble smile and motioned toward the cockpit with a quick jerk of his head.

"Lubbell's just climbing to avoid the turbulence," he said to Ted. "Nothing to worry about."

But there was a look in Kidro's eyes that made him uneasy. Ted and his bass guitar had together logged thousands of hours on this jet in the two years since the band had bought it from the aircraft broker, and never had he sensed such an abrupt change in altitude. The plane was climbing at much greater speeds than it ever had in the past.

Kidro seemed to read the look on Ted's face and nodded. "I think I'd better get back up there," he said. "Lubbell may need a hand."

Kidro gave Nigel one final, dismissive look and then disappeared behind the curtain separating the cabin and the hallway leading to the cockpit. That left the four of them – Hedley still painting, Orrin still sleeping and Nigel still fuming – with only the steady hum of the engines thrumming in their ears.

Ted was even more uncomfortable in the newborn silence than he'd been during the escalating argument, so he walked over to Hedley, picked up an overturned bar stool and then sat next to him. Hedley had almost finished removing the crimson streak from the painting.

"Are we ever going to talk about what happened tonight?" Ted asked. "Or are we just going to sweep it under the rug? Because I think Benny deserves better than that. He fucked up, I'm with you on that, but we owe it to him to at least explain."

"There's nothing to explain," Hedley said as he continued to paint. His voice still had the quiet, reflective tone of someone at peace with himself and his surroundings. It was the voice he'd spoken in ever since getting clean a few years back, and although Ted always wanted to ask him about it – how *he* was able to kick the habit so fast and so easily, when the same experience had been nothing but agony for himself – he never did.

"I disagree," Ted responded. "I think we have *a lot* to explain. I don't think he even realizes what's going on."

Now Hedley *did* stop painting and looked over to Ted with patient yet tired eyes. "That's exactly the problem. He *should* realize it. You and I see it. Hell, even Zach sees it, and the only things he usually notices are tits and drugs. That should tell you where Benny's mind is at. He'd have to fundamentally change as a person to understand what's going on, but he won't. Not because he can't but because he won't let himself."

"But Hed, Benny –"

51

"Benny did this to himself. Ted, you gotta remember, this isn't easy for me, either. Jensen was my best friend. I'd be dead if not for him, several times over, in fact. But that doesn't change what he did, or who he is inside. Don't beat yourself up about it. We can't do anything for him. Only *he* can. You have to trust me on this."

Ted went to respond, but he stopped with his mouth half-open as he became aware of something – or, more precisely, the *absence* of something. He strained an ear to the stillness and was able to make out the sound of Orrin snoring and Nigel snorting, but other than that and the constant *whoosh* of the wind lashing the sides of the airplane, the cabin was silent.

Ted suddenly realized with dawning horror what sound was missing and stood up with a jolt.

The engines had stopped.

***

Jensen had been deprived of his sense of sight for so long he was starting to wonder if he'd actually gone blind.

But his nose was working just fine. Although it had been years since it was used to smuggle heroin through airport security, the hidden compartment in Hedley's wardrobe case still reeked of the cayenne pepper Grange once used to keep the drug-sniffing dogs at bay. The smell was pungent and pervasive, amplified by his inability to escape it.

It was a tight fit. He'd crept into the case after putting everything back into Grange's bag but just moments before John Borrowdale, the band's road manager, had opened the door to the green room. In the rush to hide, he hadn't thought about how he'd eventually get out of the secret compartment, let alone the locked wardrobe case, but he was thinking of it now. In fact, it was *all* he was thinking about. Even the thought of the five million dollars and the glorious future it promised had taken second banana to fears of being

52

forever entombed inside a space no bigger than a casket.

And that's exactly what this thing will be if I can't find a way out, Jensen thought, and then tried for what seemed like the thousandth time to break down the fake wall in front of him by jerking his knee up and forward. Again, nothing happened – he was pinned so severely that he couldn't get the range of movement needed to deliver a powerful enough blow, and something, perhaps a piece of musical equipment, had been stuffed inside the case and was keeping the door from swinging open.

He'd lost his concept of time inside what was essentially an antiquated sensory deprivation tank. He could smell, yes, but only cayenne and old mahogany. He could hear, but only the muffled drone of the plane's engines thrumming in his ears. He even tasted something in the air, a dusty, unpleasant musk like cheap perfume.

How long had it been? Four or five hours, maybe six, but it was impossible to know for sure since his phone was still tucked neatly into the front pocket of his jeans where he couldn't reach it. In any case, he knew he was running out of time before the plane landed in Boise.

The interior of the wardrobe case suddenly began to shudder violently from side to side as a labored groan interrupted the monotonous hum of the engines. Jensen's head smacked the side wall with a sickening thump, and as pain exploded on the left side of his skull, he finally saw something in front of him: hundreds of little stars that winked like fireflies in the summer darkness.

Just a little turbulence, he thought, and then shook his head to shoo away the stars. They lingered.

He'd been banking on the roadies putting the wardrobe case in the cabin – Hedley sometimes kept personal items in there that he liked to have near him on long flights between shows – but they'd instead loaded it into the jetliner's cargo hold. He knew this because shortly before takeoff, he'd heard someone arguing – the new pilot, Jensen thought – with a voice that was unmistakably that of Nigel Cuthpit. The Englishman's shrill voice had almost sent Jensen into a fresh rage, but he'd been able to stay calm and quiet.

The thought of Cuthpit, coupled with the stiff pain now slowly spreading throughout his immobilized body, caused Jensen's numb legs to once again rise to action. He delivered a series of vehement knee blows to the partition wall, hoping for at least a crack in its flimsy façade, but again received nothing for his efforts but several fruitless thuds. His legs were simply too weak and too pinned to do much damage.

Then, a thought: *Five million, maybe more, unless I die of oxygen deprivation before anyone realizes I'm trapped in here. Money is of no use to a dead man, and that's exactly what I'll be if I can't get the Christ out of this box.*

He tried to calm down, to relax the heart that was now racing on all eight cylinders inside his chest, but found he couldn't. He was trapped.

This is what Daphne must have meant, Jensen thought. *This is the death she spoke of. A slow, quiet, painful death.*

Then, a second wave of turbulence seized the claustrophobic darkness, this one much more intense than the first. Jensen braced himself as best he could but still hit the back of his head on the wall behind him as the plane began to rise sharply.

Again, stars spread before him, followed seconds later by a disquieting crash as something broke loose in the cargo hold outside. The sound of metal grinding against metal filled the silence, a nauseating squeal not unlike long nails scraping slowly across a chalkboard, only amplified tenfold, and then another crash as whatever it was fell over. As it continued to slide, making that horrifying shriek as it did, Jensen realized the sound was getting closer to him.

Seconds later, he was free.

***

If Stuart Kidro had been worried before, he was downright *terrified* now.

The stall warning was blaring in his ears, and if he hadn't been frantically trying to get the engines started again he would've beat the alarm with his bare fists until it fell silent. If he couldn't get the engines going, there was no way they'd make it to the nearest landing strip in Jackson Hole. He'd have to find a relatively flat plot of land – a hard sell given the fact they were somewhere over Bridger-Teton National Forest – and set the bird down.

This is nobody's fault but mine, he thought to himself as he again picked up the radio and tried to hail air traffic control. *You shouldn't have taken off. You stupid, stupid bastard.*

Lubbell had risen to thirty-three thousand feet to clear the turbulence, but something had obviously shifted in the cargo hold and thrown the plane's balance off-kilter. This caused the plane to rise more sharply than Lubbell had intended, and the wings lost lift. Now the engines were stalled.

Goddammit. Shit and fuck and goddammit.

He tried to calm down, tried to remember his crash simulation training, but was finding it difficult, especially with the stall warning blaring endlessly in his ear.

According to the nav system, ground speed was one-hundred and twelve knots and dropping quickly. Stuart increased the aircraft's nose-up pitch, and the stall warning stopped briefly, but the engines were still silent and they were still dropping from the sky at an alarming five-thousand feet per minute. That number would only increase the longer they went without engines.

Stuart thought of his wife, of the home they'd just bought in St. Louis, of the library that would someday be a nursery for their unborn child, of his mother and how he hadn't had the time lately to call her; he thought of everything and prayed to a god he didn't believe in that he'd live to see all of it again.

But this was bad. This was very bad.

Ted was trying to call his girlfriend.

No bars now, not even a single sliver. He was about to die and couldn't even tell the woman he loved goodbye, to thank her for changing his life, for making him a better man.

He thought about the great successes he'd had – the millions of dollars in his bank account, the throngs of fans who worshipped the ground he walked on, the satisfaction of creating something that people not only respected but cherished – and it all paled in comparison to Emily. She was the one thing that had made the whole ride fun, and now he couldn't even tell her.

Ted looked around the cabin. Orrin was still miraculously sleeping, and Ted had briefly debated waking him. Why? So he could watch as they all crashed and burned? What would be the point? So he let him sleep, and if everything went down the way Ted guessed it would, Orrin would never know what hit him.

Nigel was cowering in the corner, not buckled up and staring out the window wordlessly. The cabin had grown dark, and the slow, pulsing red of the emergency lights fell eerily across his contorted face. He was wringing his hands and shaking his head repeatedly. Ted also considered telling him to buckle up, but in the end, that would be like using a Band-Aid to stop the spurting artery of a severed limb.

Useless. All useless.

Hedley, however, was a picture of calm. Even in the darkness he continued to paint, and a small smile had even formed on the corners of his lips. He looked as if he wasn't in a steel machine plummeting toward earth but in a quiet, contemplative garden. His brush strokes were even, and the hand that dipped into the paint palette was steady and unshaken. He wouldn't come even close to finishing the painting now, of course, but he continued nonetheless, immersed in a deep peace that Ted found amazing.

The sight of Hedley's tranquility actually helped ease Ted's own panic. They were going down, yes. They had a minute, maybe two, before everything – the concerts, the groupies, the drugs, the money – was over forever. But in those few minutes, Ted was going to take a page from Hedley's book.

It's been a blast, Ted thought, and was surprised when a smile found his lips, too.

***

Ninety feet away, Jensen Bennett was in agony.

The oversized crate that had smashed into the wardrobe case had successfully freed him, but at a cost – a jagged piece of wood was now jutting through his left thigh. His nose was bloodied, too, and his right arm felt like it was broken in at least two places, but those pains paled in comparison to the agony now spreading in his leg. He chanced a look down and almost fainted at the tributary of blood streaming down the left side of his blue jeans.

He crawled slowly from the wreckage of shattered wood, every inch a struggle, every movement, no matter how minor, sending fresh bolts of pain throughout his body.

The cargo hold was dark, lit only by a red glow that throbbed like a slowly pulsating strobe light. In the gloom he saw the crate that hit him, tipped on its side with the lid agape. A plethora of trusses, metal legs and broken lights littering the ground told him it had contained the concert stage, or at least part of it, which easily weighed half a ton. He barely winced when his palm fell on a pile of broken glass, and he crept around the crate and into the narrow aisle created by the stacked cargo.

The door that led to the cabin seemed ten miles away. In the crimson gloom it looked like an ominous mouth, one that laughed mockingly from a great and insurmountable chasm.

I'm gonna crawl to it, Jensen thought. *One inch at a time.*

But could he reach it? And if he did, what then? It was sealed, locked tight and impenetrable to someone without the appropriate key card.

He tried to yell out – perhaps someone would hear him – but the only thing he managed was a trifling moan. He crawled toward the door, slowly, using only his left arm to propel him forward (the right was now blaring with agony, and Jensen knew it was definitely broken), meandering past the spilled contents of the crate as he went.

He realized the plane was no longer rising – it was falling, and falling fast. There were no windows in the cargo hold, but he nevertheless could feel the downward movement as surely as he'd felt the sudden upswing moments earlier.

It happened about a minute later as he reached the middle of the aisle. One second, the space behind him was there, and the next it was a gaping black hole rimmed with fragments of twisted metal that poked out like broken teeth. As he grabbed onto a crate with his good arm, leveraging himself against the powerful air current which sought to suck him out, he saw the tail section – and all the crates that had lined its back wall, including the remnants of the wardrobe case in which he'd recently been entombed – tumble into the darkness and then explode in a magnificent ball of flame.

In the light from the blast, he saw the landscape ablaze in a hot orange glow, and by its power he noticed a string of low-lying mountains to the immediate south. The plane, or what was left of it, was flying extremely close to their snowy peaks.

The force trying to drag him through the newly created hole was powerful, and Jensen struggled to hold on, but his good arm wasn't strong enough to counter the dominating pull of the current, and his hand began to slip. Through the hole he saw the ground coming up fast – they were perhaps only a few hundred feet now above the treetops – and Jensen realized that within moments the plane would hit the forest floor.

Before Jensen's hand slipped and he plummeted out of the airplane, the last twenty-four hours flashed by in an instant – the call from Tabernacle, the last-minute drive south to Springfield, the scalper, the ticket collector, the giant, Nigel's revelation, the five-million-dollar offer – and finally Daphne, who had warned him that his life was in danger.

I guess she's the real deal, Jensen thought dumbly, then his hand slipped.

***

Noah DeNova was having a particularly good dream – something to do with a prize, and a podium, and a crowd – when an ear-splitting explosion shook the rafters of the cabin and immediately roused him from sleep.

At first he thought he was in the staff room, where he sometimes napped during his afternoon break between classes. But in the darkness he smelled fresh pine and recently burned firewood, and instantly remembered he was camping with his wife, far away from the bustle of Des Moines University.

He'd heard plenty of explosions back when he was in the Marines, and the one that had just moved through the quiet Wyoming wilderness had been enormous, even bigger than the one that had, in one horrible instant, taken most of his right leg and almost half of his unit in Vietnam. For that, Noah had been awarded the Purple Heart, but he'd always felt undeserving of the honor, since all he really did was not die.

He sat up in bed and saw a faint orange glow streaming in through the cabin window. Yes, an explosion, maybe a fallen satellite or meteor, but more than likely an airplane. His wife of nearly fifty years rolled over in bed and put a warm hand on his back.

"Baby, what is it?" she said sleepily. "I heard something."

"Nella, I need my bag. Do you remember if we packed it?"

Noah's wife, detecting the seriousness in his voice, forced herself fully awake and sat up next to him. "Your bag? You mean your medical bag? Yeah, it's by the fireplace. What's going on?"

"Not sure. Plane crash, I think," Noah said, and then got out of bed and rushed over to his jeans, which were hanging by the fireplace and still felt damp from the rainstorm they'd been caught in during their hike yesterday afternoon. "Call nine-one-one. I'm going to see if there's anything I can do to help."

Nella's eyes widened, and Noah saw the orange blaze reflected in them. "Baby, what're you gonna do? You're a cardiologist, not Superman. Besides, we're in the middle of nowhere."

Noah yanked on his jeans as quickly as his fake leg would allow and then went for his jacket and bag. "That's exactly why I have to go. If it *is* a plane crash, and I think it is, then help won't be coming for some time. If there're survivors, I'm going to tend to them as best I can."

Noah kissed his wife on the forehead and then set out into the crisp Wyoming morning. But as soon as he saw the fireball ablaze on the horizon, he began to wonder if there would be anyone left to save.

[silence]

A lone streetlamp empties unwashed light into the basement through two narrow rectangles, trifling squares which in the daytime look like ordinary windows but in the midnight gloom become the predatory eyes of a malevolent animal.

Somewhere in the vast semi-darkness a clock ticks methodically, its lonely echo the only sound in the stillness, and the boy pulls the covers over his head as he realizes it can only be the sick heartbeat of the creature glowering above him. He's scared and hugs his Cabbage Patch Kid tighter for comfort. It's going to be a long night, one of terrors both imagined and real.

Somehow, sleep overtakes him, but it is thin and troubled. In his nightmares the Wall Monster above his bed stirs, its pale eyes turning upward into malicious half-moons, its rhythmic heartbeat quickening as it extends its gluttonous, mechanical hands into the darkness below, not hurrying, enjoying the helpless fear of the eight-year-old boy sleeping at its feet. Then the hands descend upon him, one covering his mouth so he can't scream, the other scratching a long, thin, razor-sharp finger down the front of his pajamas until his clothes are in tatters.

The boy screams as the finger begins poking him, prodding him, testing the malleability of his young flesh here and there to see if it's ripe enough for harvest. The monster easily stifles the scream, but it can't stop his tears, so he lets them flow like a broken spigot as the hands begin to operate: slicing the skin open, plunging its cold, robotic hands inside and removing organs, lifting them to its wicked eyes in examination, putting them back in all the wrong places, sewing everything shut again, then repeating the cycle all over.

After an eternity of this illogical surgery, he slowly swims up from sleep to find his bedsheets soaked. Blood for sure; probably urine, too.

Until that night he thought the Wall Monster only existed in his dreams, that it couldn't traverse the barrier that separated it from the waking world, but tonight he sees he was wrong. It absolutely *can* cross between worlds. It could hurt him whether he was sleeping or not.

Things were never the same after that.

THE ANONYMOUS MELODY
-Track Four-

The man whose name had been Benjamin C. Clemmons but who was now known simply as The Warden walked with silent deliberation down an elongated passageway that arched almost imperceptibly to the right like the subtle curvature of the earth. The hallway was windowless and aglow in a soft white light that cast no shadows and bathed every inch of space in affable warmth. The light was so inescapable that The Warden had no trouble reading the contents of his clipboard as he moved from room to room, checking off names as he went.

Through the thousands of transparent doors that lined the hallway he saw all sorts of people – some emotional, others oddly detached, but all in wonder at the place in which they now found themselves. In all the time The Warden had been making the rounds in Translucent Tower, he'd never grown tired of seeing how differently people reacted to their new surroundings.

He moved to Cell 12-B and found it empty, but it wouldn't be for long. Any second now, his new inmate would pop into being, dazed and confused but otherwise all right. He decided now would be as good a time as any to take a quick break and leaned resignedly against the cell's outer wall. He felt fine. *Spectacular*, even. But he had thousands more doors to check and welcomed the chance to rest his mind, if only for a moment.

How long had it been since he'd witnessed an arrival? He couldn't remember. Time here was strange. It could have been yesterday, or it could have been a hundred years ago. The Warden wasn't sure, but he knew it was a sight he liked seeing. In those first few moments of awareness, he was able to vaguely recall, however briefly, what it felt like to be momentarily stunned by the strange and mysterious.

And then it happened – the bed sheets rose as if suddenly injected with air and immediately took the shape of a body, which lay in the fetal position (wasn't it always the fetal position?) and didn't move. The Warden knew it would only be a matter of seconds before the man stirred, and his eyes fell once again to the clipboard so he could greet the man properly when he awoke.

Male, thirty-eight, brown hair, gray eyes. Six-foot-one, about one-hundred and seventy pounds. Name: Jensen Phillip Bennett.

***

The pain was gone.

In its place was an immense and powerful wave of euphoria, peaceful and buoyant, like being under the influence of some wonderful drug.

The hard, rough earth of the mountainside had given way to a malleable padding that kneaded his lanky frame with soft fingers, and a breeze pregnant with the sweet odor of freshly fallen rain tickled his face. And there was a sound, too – a soothing tune that hummed quietly from somewhere in the distance. It seemed to be above him, around him and underneath him all at once. It sounded like a million different notes playing simultaneously, a tuneless yet undeniably beautiful song.

Jensen opened his eyes and could actually *see* the music floating in front of his face in faint ribbons of ever-changing color. He moved his right arm – which no longer howled in agony but felt light and almost transparent – in a sweeping motion across his face, and the colorful energy responded by scattering as if it were a cloud of smoke.

As Jensen sat up, the euphoric feeling swelled. His entire body, down to the individual strands of hair on his head, had become a recently plucked guitar string vibrating a single, prolonged note. He blinked dazedly at the sensation and let it wash over him. There was no need to ruffle through his briefcase of counterfeit smiles; the one that crept onto his face now was as genuine as they came.

Someone should market this feeling, he thought. *Put it in pill form and sell it to the masses. The supplier would become a billionaire, and no one would ever again feel unloved and unwanted. Because that's what this feeling is, when it comes right down to it ... unadulterated love, not for something or someone in particular, but for all things.*

The room was small, circular, and made of an immaculate white stone that didn't seem to have a single crack or mortar mark across its smooth façade. A pervasive light, warm and gentle, bled through the stone like sunlight through closed eyelids. Near him was a small triangular hole in the wall that looked out into a cheerful blue sky ablaze with the same ribbons of energy he'd seen floating in front of his face. These, too, were constantly changing color and seemed to move gracefully in union with the unidentifiable melody that played softly in the distance.

Jensen swung his legs over the side of the cot and stood up slowly. Although the pleasant sensations thrumming throughout his body were still intense, he was quickly becoming used to their rhythms; how they seemed to amplify, abate, and then amplify again with each movement of his virtually weightless limbs. Another cool breeze blew through the open window, and again his nostrils were assaulted with the wet fragrance of a coming rainstorm.

His dreams, when he slept long and deep enough to have them, were usually only disjointed nightmares, filled with monsters who slouched from the shadows to slice into his soft flesh. But sometimes, if he was lucky, he'd dream of being inside a small cave carved into an immense stone mountainside, and of a waterfall raging nearby. He'd look down upon the soft green of distant treetops spreading out hundreds of feet below him in every direction, and the fragile mist rising from them, and he'd realize that, except for the birds, this world was his alone.

Then, just as that thought would arise, a girl whose face he couldn't quite see would come, and after an emotional reunion they would make love on the soft earth with only the roar of the waterfall and the echoed chatter of birds as background music. Everything was filled with a mysterious ambiance, and every inch of this dream world seethed with an indescribable sense of adventure. It would end, as all dreams eventually do, but the feeling would stay with him throughout the entirety of the following day.

The room he was now in wasn't that, but it was close, even down to the crisp, rain-swept breeze and the all-encompassing light that surrounded him. He felt as if nothing in the world could hurt him here. Here he was protected, and here he was loved. By who or what he couldn't tell.

He went to the window and, sticking his head out it, was amazed to see he was in an extremely tall tower, one that sparkled with the same white, translucent power as the interior of his room. The tower wall disappeared into a cloud bank both below and above him, obscuring any indication as to how high in the sky he was. The wall, or what he could see of it, was pockmarked with thousands – perhaps hundreds of thousands – of other triangular-shaped windows. They wrapped around the tower in a spiral and appeared to wink at him as the light cast by the energy ribbons passed over them.

"It's a real killer diller, ain't it?" A voice behind him asked.

Jensen spun around, again amazed at how light and agile he felt, like he had lost all vestiges of solidity, and saw a stocky figure leaning against an entryway that fizzled with a nearly invisible energy. The man's short brown hair was cropped close to a head that was square at the top but became steadily more rotund the lower it went. He was wearing some kind of uniform – white button-up-the-front shirt, black tie, black pants – and had a short line of hair beneath his large nose that wasn't quite a mustache but would perhaps someday become one.

The man peered into the room with dark brown eyes that seemed to radiate a kindhearted understanding. Jensen wondered if the newcomer was the source of the feelings of protection and love and then quickly classified the thought as unlikely.

"The view, I mean," the observer continued. "It's quite a sight."

Jensen walked slowly to the man, who continued to lean on the wall outside of the room. Underneath his armpit was what looked like a brown clipboard with a stack of papers tucked haphazardly underneath its metal clip.

"What *is* this place?" Jensen asked. He was still grinning, but the newcomer had startled him, and he spoke in a cautious tone. "Is this ... is this heaven? Am I dead?"

As he said this, a thought occurred, and he poked at his body with an outstretched finger. He was as solid as he'd ever been, despite feeling light as air. He wasn't some transparent specter, and he certainly hadn't sprouted wings and a halo. Aside from the euphoria and buoyancy, he felt perfectly human.

The man didn't answer at first. Instead, he took out his clipboard and thumbed through a few pages, nodding here and there as he read the information contained therein. After a moment, apparently satisfied he'd gleaned the appropriate facts, he looked up and smiled.

"The answer to your question is yes ... and no. Depends on your definitions of 'dead' and 'heaven.'"

Jensen came even closer to the figure, close enough to see the small hairs rimming his nostrils. "What do you mean?" he asked. "Either someone's dead or they're not. There's no in-between."

The man laughed and put the clipboard back under his armpit. "Well, buddy, that's not entirely accurate, but I guess what I meant to say is, yes, you're dead. At least in terms of that sac of fluid you called a body. Whether or not you stay that way, I don't know yet. And about this being heaven? There are many planes of existence, and this one is just one of those many. Whether or not that constitutes heaven is up to you to decide."

Jensen suddenly remembered the spike of wood that had broken through his thigh and instinctively looked down. His leg was fine, and his jeans weren't stained with even the slightest drop of blood. It was if nothing had happened.

"So ... what you're saying is ... I'm here, in this plane, but my body is somewhere else, in another plane. And it's dead. But that could change. Depending on ..." Jensen ended his thought in the form of a question, one that invited the man to respond.

"Depends on *a lot* of things, buddy," the man said. "How quickly help comes. How bad your injuries are. How tough a guy you are. We'll know soon, although I can't say for sure how long. Time's a bit flaky here. A minute over there could be a week here, or a day, or a second."

Jensen thought of the crash and of how remote the area had seemed, and decided it was unlikely that anyone would get to the wreckage in time. This caused another thought to enter his head.

"The other guys – the ones on the plane with me – are they here, too?"

The man nodded. "Yep, and they're fine. Dead as disco in the material world, but just fine here. That bird you were on went down so fast they didn't feel a thing."

Jensen rubbed his eyes. This all sounded so crazy, but he couldn't deny how right it felt. How *real*. In fact, *everything* here – the room, the sky, the man – all seemed so much more real than anything he'd experienced before. Everything else ... his job, his Hyundai, that money pit on Division and Hoyne ... were now just fuzzy fragments, part of some very long dream.

"Okay," he said at last. "Can I see them?"

The man responded quickly and with an authoritative voice that made him seem even more like a cop than his outfit did. "Not right now. For starters, they ain't here; they're at The Terminal. Two, you can't leave. Not yet, not until we know if you're staying or not."

Despite the good vibes flowing through his body, Jensen felt a twinge of anger course through him. "What do you mean, I can't leave? Are you telling me I'm a prisoner?"

The man shifted uncomfortably and turned his gaze toward some unseen point down the hall. "It's nothing like that, Jensen. You're just being detained, in case you go back. There are things here that people on the other side aren't supposed to know about, just like there's things in the higher realms folks *here* aren't supposed to know about. If you go back, and that's still the big question, but if you do, you can't go telling everyone that life continues after you die. It defeats the purpose of living."

"And that is?"

"Again, can't tell you, not unless you're here for good. And to be honest, I'm not even sure I know myself, although I have my suspicions." The man looked back to Jensen, whatever he was looking at down the hall temporarily forgotten. "Look, until we know anything for sure, just sit tight. Enjoy the view. If it turns out you're staying, you can see your friends. I'll even take you to see them myself. They're probably arriving right about now, too, but at the Terminal, like I said. When *I* know more, *you'll* know more. I promise."

"What about the way I feel? These good vibes? Can you tell me what that's all about?"

At this, the man in the uniform looked slightly troubled, as if he'd bitten into something sour. "Jensen, I don't have to tell you the world you came from can be a pretty rough place. I can see on your chart you've experienced a bit of it yourself. Some of the folks who come through here – too many, really – were suffering when they crossed over. Car accidents, murder, disease – the list is too long, but the main thing is they were suffering. What you're feeling, and what everyone feels here, is to help ease some of that pain. It doesn't always work, of course, and folks who are damaged up here," the man pointed to his head, "well, it takes a bit more than 'good vibes,' as you call them, to fix that. Some even arrive in Dim Country and not here because those scars are so deep. But the positive feelings help a lot of people, and for that, I'm glad they exist."

"What's Dim Country?"

A guilty expression crossed the man's square face. "I shouldn't have said that. If you're staying, you'll learn more about it if you want, but it's not a place you're going to want to go poking your nose around in. Just sit tight. I'll know more in a while."

And with that, the man turned and walked out of sight. Jensen tried to follow him through the seemingly open door but was pushed gently back by an unseen force field. He tried again, this time by putting an outstretched fist through the doorway, and was again denied access. Although there was nothing there, Jensen's hand felt like it was encountering an elastic material that gave a bit when pushed, but only a little. He tried a third time, putting all his weight behind his shoulder and pushing, and this time the recoil was so intense it propelled him backward and onto the floor.

The fall didn't hurt; in fact, *nothing* seemed to hurt in this bright wonderland. Nothing except his pride. He didn't relish being caged like a zoo animal, even if that cage was a nice one.

Jensen had little choice. He waited.

***

The man who looked and sounded like a cop had been right – time was indeed flaky here. Without a clock or even a sun by which to judge the time of day, there was no way of telling just how long he sat there before the man eventually came back.

While he waited, a deluge of thoughts flooded his mind, and the fact he was either dead or delirious was understandably at the forefront. But others came, too, like the sudden realization that Quiet Catastrophe was no more. There would be no more concerts, no more music videos and Grammy awards, no more groupies or all-night hotel parties, no more of *anything*. Hed, Teddy, Zach – they were all dead as disco, the cop had said, and they weren't coming back.

The thought was observed rather than felt, like seeing the effects of a devastating earthquake on the nine o'clock news instead of being trapped under a pile of debris at the disaster site. Still terrible, yes, but a detached kind of terrible. A *safe* terrible. Here in this room, his thoughts could present fangs but couldn't bite, at least not hard enough to draw blood.

A wild desire struck him at this last thought, and he suddenly opened his mouth wide and then bit down hard on the fleshy mass beneath his left thumb. No pain, none at all, so he increased the pressure. *Still* nothing – no blood, no teeth marks, not even mild discomfort. He realized he could use a pair of razor-sharp vice grips, and still it wouldn't hurt. It was this place, which was heaven yet wasn't, the man in the uniform had said. Nothing could harm him here; he was invincible.

This couldn't be real, of course. None of it could, and yet it was. He was as sure of that fact as he was his own name. Dreams were disjointed; dreams were foggy. Dreams weren't this focused, this fully formed, this cogent. No, this was definitely not a dream, nor was it some stress-induced fantasy his brain had invented to cope with the terror he'd felt during the last minute of the jetliner's descent. This was as real as anything had ever been. The thought was exciting and scary at the same time. But if *this* world was the real one, what did that make that *other* world, the one he'd just left?

He tried to follow this line of thought, but before he could unravel the mystery, footfalls outside his cell heralded the return of the man in the uniform, the one who held his future somewhere in the pages of the clipboard he carried.

Jensen rose from his cross-legged position on the ground. The mild pain in his back that always flared when he stood was thankfully quiet, alongside every other earthly ailment he'd once begrudgingly endured – no blurry vision, no cluster headache ... even the small, pink mark that looked vaguely like an angry saluki on his right temple didn't seem as defined, although it was still there.

"Well?" Jensen said the very second the cop appeared in the doorway. "Any word?"

The cop nodded and again retrieved his clipboard from underneath his left armpit. "Yep, and it's good news. Hold on a sec while I find your file ..."

The next few seconds seemed like minutes as he anxiously waited for the man to find whatever good news it was he'd come to deliver. Was he being set free? Jensen hoped so, because he didn't want to go back. The happiness here was pristine and effortless, no pill bottle or shot glass or syringe needed. He certainly didn't want to spend the rest of his days locked in a cage, and the man had said very little about what waited for him outside his cell. But even if it contained only a *fraction* of the inexorable bliss that existed inside this room, it was leagues better than even the best day of his former life.

"Seems you're going to make it," the man said at last. "I don't have many details, aside from someone found you, but you're on my *no admittance* list. That means you're going back."

Jensen's heart dropped, even as the euphoria persisted. He was on yet another Nadmit, except this one wasn't denying him something as mundane as backstage access but a world where pain and suffering were apparently just words. Whoever found him, whoever was responsible for his inevitable return, probably thought they were doing him a favor by coming to his rescue. But they weren't.

"When? Right now?" Jensen asked.

"Don't know. Can't say for sure. Like I said before, time doesn't flow the same here as it does where you're from. My guess is you'll probably be here for a while yet, so I'd get comfortable."

More waiting. Now that he knew it was fleeting, the room and its wonderful sense of peace and contentment had become bittersweet.

"And until then? What am I supposed to do?"

"I dunno ... sleep. Meditate. Flog the bishop." The cop, now apparently disinterested in the conversation, shot an impatient look down the hall and put his clipboard back under his arm. "Look, buddy, it's been the cat's pajamas, but I gotta get going. Sit tight and you'll be back in no time."

The cop was already several paces down the hall when three words pushed their way back into Jensen's thoughts: *Five million dollars*. This time, however, they didn't fill him with magical wonder but a sense of unease that seemed to grow with each of the man's fading footfalls.

He was leaving this place and going back, probably very soon. Back to the waiting divorce papers, back to the unfinished nightclub and the apartment above it, back to the overwhelming loneliness that seemed to live there. Back to a friendless world where he was in massive debt without any hope of rescue, especially now that his most successful business venture was in ruin and he'd be forced to see if Geffen's offer still stood. And all of that on top of whatever the plane crash had done to his body. He was facing at least a broken arm and a badly injured leg, and that wasn't even factoring in the fall from the cargo hold. He wasn't looking forward to going back to any of it.

The money was his only salvation now that he'd been dismissed from heaven.

The problem, of course, was that when he returned, he would do so alone. Hedley Grange, Ted Choom, Zachary Orrin and Nigel Cuthpit were here, in this strange and wonderful place, and they weren't coming back. His last chance at cashing in on Tabernacle's deal was *here*. Once he left, that was it. No lost album, no deal, and no money.

"Hey you!" he called down the corridor as he simultaneously beat a fist on the frame surrounding his cell door. "Pal! Come back for a second!"

The cop sauntered back slowly. The patience seemed to have drained from his features. "Call me The Warden. Everyone else does, and it's a heck of a lot more dignified than 'hey you,' don't you think?"

"Agreed. Look, Warden, those guys I came here with ... the guys who were in the plane with me ... any chance I could have a quick chinwag with them before I click my ruby slippers and return to Kansas?"

Jensen expected The Warden to take out his clipboard again, to scan its pages for information on the availability of Quiet Catastrophe, but this time it remained firmly tucked into his armpit.

"Didn't you listen to anything I said before? This ain't a hotel; it's a detainment facility. You think I'm going to just let you waltz outta here and take a quaint little tour of the afterlife? It don't work that way. Most people who leave here and go back don't remember this place anyway, and those who do get it all wrong. Tunnels and beings of light? Gimmie a break. But I can't take the chance that you'll be one of the ones that does."

The Warden began to walk away again, and Jensen's mind raced.

I can't go back empty-handed, not when I'm so close. There has to be a way around this.

"Wait!" he shouted down the hallway. "Just bring them here, then! It'll only take a second."

This time when The Warden returned, he didn't just look annoyed – he looked positively irate. The eyes that before had looked with quiet compassion now glared with disapproval.

"Buddy, read my lips," The Warden said. "You ain't going anywhere, you ain't talking to nobody. You're just gonna sit there and wait. Why is this so hard for you to understand? No contact with anyone or anything, except me and these walls. Got it?"

The Warden didn't give Jensen a chance to respond this time; moving with a swiftness that betrayed his heavy frame, he huffed down the hallway and out of sight.

Jensen couldn't see much of the passageway except for what was directly in front of his igloo-shaped door, but based on the faint echo of his footfalls, The Warden was already well out of earshot. He pounded an angry fist against the cell wall, briefly contemplated shouting an obscenity in the direction The Warden had gone, then decided his time would be better spent looking for a way out. If he could find just one band member – just *one* – he knew all it would take to get *House Made of Sound* was a few well-chosen questions and an attentive eye. Fans would get one last album, and Jensen would get a new life.

A pretty fair deal for everyone involved, Jensen thought.

He began searching the area around his invisible door for some structural weakness he could exploit, some design flaw or sign of shoddy workmanship, but everything looked well-constructed. There were no cracks, no doorjambs, no locks or doorknobs or anything else he could manipulate. It was an effective but cruel prison, designed to look like a wide-open door and not the impenetrable brick wall it actually was.

Through it he could see another doorway sitting like a small expression of surprise on the hallway wall opposite his own, its opening glimmering with the same barely perceptible white energy that crisscrossed his own door. It was undoubtedly another cell, but the odd angle kept him from seeing if there was anyone inside it.

"Someone in there? If you can hear me, say something." There was no answer, but Jensen heard the shuffling of feet. The cell was definitely occupied. "My name's Jensen Bennett. Fell from an airplane and ended up here." And under his breath, he added, "Wherever the hell *here* is."

He was turning to walk back to his cot when a small voice spoke: "Translucent Tower."

Jensen turned and looked back. There was a gaunt little boy, perhaps eight years old, standing in the doorway of the other cell. He was in pajamas – a yellow cartoon sponge was plastered all over them – and his bald head reflected the white light that seemed to be everywhere yet had no source. Jensen didn't have to ask – this boy had cancer.

"Translucent Tower?"

"Yeah," the boy said softly. "That's the name of this place. Warden said so. He said I was going to get to see my mommy again, too."

Jensen repositioned himself so he could better see the boy, whose bright green eyes shone back at him across the hallway like tiny emeralds. "That's great news, kiddo. I'm sure your mom is going to think so, too."

The boy looked down at his feet, which were bare. "I know. But I'm scared. I like it here. There's no stupid doctors here. It doesn't hurt here."

Jensen had found a kindred spirit, it seemed. Hadn't he been thinking pretty much the same exact thing just moments ago? It was oddly comforting to know he wasn't the only one who was less than thrilled at the prospect of returning to the material world, as The Warden had called it.

"What's your name, kid?"

"Leslie, but Carl calls me Lenny 'cause he says Leslie is a girl's name."

Jensen huffed. "Carl? Is that a bully or something?"

Leslie shook his head. "No, it's my daddy. Well, my *step*-daddy. I want to call him daddy but he won't let me."

Jensen looked solemnly at the boy. "You know, I had a stepdad, too. Taught me all about business. Well, the basics at least. He also taught me what being thrown down a flight of stairs feels like, but other than that, he was a real peach. I wanted to call him dad, too, but he wouldn't have any of it."

The boy thought about this for a moment and then shook his head in the comically overextended way of which only young children are capable. "Carl isn't mean, he just likes to tease me. Your step-daddy seems like a bad person, though."

An image flashed across Jensen's mind, one of him behind the counter of Richard's hobby shop, standing on a stool that barely brought his head over the glass display case by the register. He thought of his lemonade stand, how good earning the money had made him feel, how his mother had seen the immediate change in him and begged Richard to let him work a few hours a week after school at the register, how the only times Richard ever seemed to acknowledge his existence was there, behind that counter, under the guise of turning a profit.

"People aren't good or bad, kid," Jensen said at last. "Everyone's just *gray*."

"What happened to your *real* daddy?"

Jensen relaxed a bit against the cell wall. "Well, legend has it he went back to Missouri, but I don't know for sure because that was before I was born."

Leslie looked surprised. "He just *left* you?"

Jensen nodded. "He did. I was about the size of a jellybean at the time, so I didn't much care. Neither did my mom. We were both better off without him, because legend *also* has it he was a certified *asshat*."

Leslie smiled. "You said a bad word."

"Nah, asshat's a *great* word." Jensen smiled back at the green-eyed boy and nodded. "So is Leslie, come to think of it. You tell your stepdad that. And if he gives you any grief, you tell him Jensen Bennett thinks he's an asshat."

The kid put a hand to his mouth in an unsuccessful attempt to stifle the giggle that escaped it. It was a pleasant sound, high and sweet, maybe even a little mischievous, too, in an innocent sort of way. He suspected the boy's illness didn't present many opportunities for fun and games, and Jensen was glad to have made him laugh.

But it was ultimately a brief one. Moments later, Leslie stopped giggling and, without explanation, buried his face in his hands as if struck by a terrible headache.

"Kid? You okay?"

The boy moaned and began shaking his head, but didn't answer him.

"Leslie? Talk to me, kiddo. What's wrong?"

"It's happening," the boy-half said, half-moaned. "I can feel it."

"Feel what?"

"Heavy. Like when I'm really sleepy. Everything is fuzzy. I hear mommy. Nurse Carrie, too. But it's all really far away. There's a beeping sound. It's *really* scary." Then his green eyes opened and he looked right at Jensen. "I don't wanna go back, mister. Don't make me go back."

Then something strange happened: The kid jerked violently upward, his feet rising a few inches from the ground then dropping back down again as if someone had yanked an invisible fishing line attached to his head. Jensen squinted at the sight, sure it was an optical illusion. But then it happened again, and this time, Leslie screamed in surprise and tried to grab onto the doorframe of his cell. But his hands, now transparent, passed right through it.

"Leslie, it's okay," Jensen said in the calmest voice he could muster. "There's no reason to be scared. You're going back home to your mom, remember? And Carl. I'm sure they're gonna be really happy to see you."

The boy moaned again as a third phantom tug lifted him from his feet and then let go. The boy was so ghostly now that Jensen could see the cell wall behind him.

This is what it looks like, Jensen thought. *This is what a return trip to the living looks like from the front row.*

"Don't be afraid," Jensen said. "Everything is going to be okay."

Leslie gave Jensen one final look – was it understanding or terror? – before melting away into nothingness like a pile of leaves caught in an imposing autumn wind. It happened so rapidly that Jensen had to blink a few times to make sure his eyes weren't betraying him, but there it was:

The cell's entryway was now completely empty.

✳✳✳

Jensen felt suddenly lost, as if he'd accidentally taken a wrong exit on the highway and was now meandering through the backstreets of some unfamiliar subdivision.

The boy was gone, and Jensen was next at bat. He had to get out, go to this *Terminal* place The Warden had mentioned, find the band and get what he needed from them. Time was quickly slipping away.

His mind raced. Could he bribe The Warden? No, probably not. The man seemed pretty committed to his job. It didn't matter anyway, because Jensen had nothing to bribe him with. He'd apparently lost his wristwatch sometime during the plane crash, and after a quick excursion into the back pocket of his jeans, he found his wallet and cellphone were likewise missing. The only things he seemed to still be in possession of were his clothes, and he doubted he could barter his freedom with a pair of Levi's and a cheap tie.

That left only one other option: escape. But how? The cell door was impassable, and the walls were a smooth, unbroken stone that would take years to tunnel out of even with the best tools. There was the window, of course, and if he contorted just the right way, he was pretty sure he could squeeze through it. But what then? There was only a single bed sheet on his cot, not nearly long enough to construct a makeshift rope and climb his way down the infinitely tall sidewall of Translucent Tower and into the freedom that he could only assume lie beyond it.

But the window ... the window was the key. It had to be. It was the cell's only weak point.

Jensen walked quickly to it and then stuck his head out as far as it would go. He only got to his shoulders before the triangular frame halted his progress, but from his new vantage point he was able to get a clearer look at the outside. The clouds were still floating above and below him, perhaps two miles in both directions, and the side wall went straight down – there was no subtle curve as it angled toward what had to be a very large foundation on the ground. The sides were just as slick as the interior wall of his cell, and the nearest window was at least half a football field away.

I can't use a rope, and I can't climb down, Jensen thought. *The only thing I can do is jump.*

And then, a voice rose inside of his head: *Let not your heart be troubled, neither let it be afraid.*

The voice wasn't his own. This one was low and distinctly southern; it seemed to be coming from the same unknowable distance as the nameless melody. But the *sentiment* was – he'd told the boy Leslie as much just moments ago. Was he brave enough to heed his own advice?

He remembered biting his hand, how he'd expected blood to trickle down his forearm, and how there'd been none. How there'd been no pain.

No pain, he thought. *Of course. Because I'm already dead.*

Could someone who was already dead die again?

You can do this, the voice, now his own, said. *Be not afraid.*

"I have to be a hundred miles in the air," Jensen said to the empty room. "No way."

Yet even as he spoke, he was angling his body in such a way that he could move further out the window.

It's the only way, Jensen thought. *Happiness is out there somewhere. Are you brave enough to find it?*

Jensen cursed himself, closed his eyes, and jumped.

[silence]

He almost walks right past the flyer, which is just one of dozens tacked chaotically to the school's bulletin board.

An opening on the lacrosse team. A writing contest signup sheet. An advert for the upcoming science fair. A reward for returning a lost Tamagotchi. They're all splayed out like the ramblings of a schizophrenic mind.

But the flyer that catches his eye, the one with the two golden masks on it, is different. One face frowns and the other smiles, but both are connected in the middle, like two halves of the same soul.

He could learn to smile like that. The flyer says so, or at least implies it. And maybe someday, if he practices really hard, it can become a *for-real* smile, like the ones he sees on the faces of his classmates.

But even if it never does, a smile is a smile, at least when it comes to making friends, and the boy wants them more than anything else. He's tired of being a passing shadow, an inconsequential whisper. An invisible kid living an invisible life. The drama club will fix everything. It has to, because he's not sure what else can.

Costumes on! Curtains up! the flyer reads in bright blue letters. He likes the words and says them out loud. A few students look at him strangely as they pass, but he doesn't care. He's used to it.

"Costumes on," he says again. "Curtains up."

Then he walks away, practicing a rudimentary smile as he repeats the words again and again like a mantra.

By the time he gets on the bus that afternoon, he's mastered it.

BENEATH THE SKY
-Track Five-

He'd come across the man almost instantly, which was fortunate – just a few minutes more, and there would have been nothing Noah DeNova could have done except read last rites.

He unslung the medicine bag from his shoulder and crouched down as an unfriendly wind lashed the shallow valley. He'd been a fool for not bringing a warmer jacket, but he'd underestimated how unforgiving the Wyoming climate was in early fall. To his immediate right was an imposing black mountain side that clambered drunkenly into the sky, and in front of him, to the west, murky coils of smoke poured into the cloudless firmament like gray ink spilling across an otherwise serene landscape painting. Whatever had crashed had been big, all right, and Noah was now positive it had been an airplane.

The man in front of him had either jumped or was sucked out somehow, because he'd landed a good two miles from where Noah guessed the actual wreckage lie. Blood streaked down the entire left side of the man's body and seemed to be emanating from a jagged strip of wood that had pierced the upper left thigh. Noah observed with the detached curiosity of a medical professional that both of his legs appeared to be broken in several places; each protruded at odd angles like an overturned box of jumping jacks.

If he was going to save this man, he had little time left in which to do it. He put a hand to the man's forehead and, as much to comfort the man as himself, recited the words his own mother had said years ago, right before he'd boarded the bus that would take him to his first day at the all-white high school:

"Let not your heart be troubled," Noah said. "Neither let it be afraid."

The verse ceased to have any religious meaning around the time most of his right leg and half his unit had been blown to hell somewhere in the jungles near the Cambodian border, but for some reason it still relaxed him, if only because it reminded him of his mother and her comforting smile.

Then, as it always did before he set to work, his mind uncluttered. The broken body next to him wasn't a person; it was a jigsaw puzzle, a riddle that had an elusive but solvable answer.

It was three minutes later when he began to feel a weak pulse beneath the man's jawbone, and eight minutes after that when the helicopter arrived.

***

Jensen again plummeted, and it was frightening at first. Not as terrifying as his instincts had suggested it would be, but harrowing all the same, mostly because he didn't know what was going to happen when he hit the ground.

During the drop, he'd seen the world below gradually materialize through the clouds like an old Polaroid photograph. He'd expected to see some other-worldly scene filled with alien imagery and foreign-looking structures; what he saw instead very well could have been the American Midwest. Directly below him, near the tower's immense circular base, was a dense forest; its treetops looked like millions of individual fibers that had been meticulously woven into a vast emerald rug. Beyond that lay a hilly plain that flowed with the graceful composure of a ballet dancer. Over the hills and far away was a large city that glistened with the same white light of the tower and rose abruptly from the earth like hundreds of inverted icicles.

The sky held no sun but was ablaze with thousands of multi-hued rivers of light that illuminated the entire world and danced silently to the nameless tune still playing somewhere in the distance. There was water, too; streams ran unhurriedly down mountainsides, cut casually through yawning valleys and then joined rivers that moved in a quiet and perpetual journey to join a massive lake on the horizon.

Then the ground rushed up to meet him, but instead of cracking bones and the blackness of unconsciousness, he was greeted with a nonchalant *thump*, as if he'd simply jumped down the short flight of stairs connecting the nightclub's back porch to the pavement below it. No pain, just as he'd suspected back in his cell – his breath hadn't even been knocked from his lungs. His body *did* crumple when it landed, and he rolled several feet before coming to a stop, but this was more out of instinct than anything else.

He stood up slowly, and after a few arm flexes and leg bends to make sure everything was working properly, he turned and regarded the massive prison structure behind him. He was momentarily reminded of the first time he'd looked up at the Sears Tower from its base. He'd felt a kind of reverse acrophobia then, an odd vertigo that was coupled with a sense of grave insignificance, and he felt it again now. Only *this* particular skyscraper had no perceivable top; it simply disappeared dreamily into the clouds above. Its base was wide and contained no doors or windows, only that smooth, unbroken stone that glowed as if lit from somewhere within.

I just fell from somewhere up there, and there's not a scratch on me, Jensen thought.

He wondered if he was the first person to ever escape and decided he probably was. Who in their right mind would *want* to escape? Translucent Tower was peaceful. It exuded a love and warmth that was alien to the material world, and Jensen realized he missed those feelings already, for they *were* gone. Although he still felt wonderfully light, he no longer had waves of euphoria coursing through him. The high hadn't seemed at all manufactured but was gone just the same, albeit without any noticeable comedown aside from the longing to have it back.

He looked up into the clouds, knowing the feeling was still there some-where, trapped inside the cell he'd left. He suddenly wished he had a million helium balloons so he could float back up into the sky, carefully climb in through the triangular hole in the wall, curl up in bed with the sheet over his head, and ride the good vibes all the way back home. But even if he could, it would only be a fleeting high, lasting only hours at best. The money was dif-ferent. The money would last a lifetime if he invested it right.

He turned and faced a part in the tree line. Through it he saw what looked like a paved road that gleamed with the luminance of recently poured blacktop and wound with smooth precision off into the benevolent darkness of the for-est. He didn't know where exactly to go, but the city he'd seen in the distance was as good a place as any to start. He wasn't sure what the Terminal could be – The Warden hadn't gotten into specifics, and to Jensen it sounded grave, like the palliative care wing of a hospital – but someone in the city might be able to point him in the right direction.

With one final glance over his shoulder at Translucent Tower, Jensen walked into the forest.

***

He didn't see the bus until it was on him, mainly because it barely made a sound as it coasted along the neatly paved roadway behind him. But he'd also become too lost in the sublime scenery to notice much else. The weather was absolutely perfect, warm but pleasant, punctuated by a gentle breeze that smelled of some wonderful new flower. The woods around him were dark and peaceful. He heard birds chirping and the soles of his Vans smacking the pave-ment as he went, but nothing else. It seemed he had this strange new world all to himself.

But then the bus came, dispelling the notion. It was made of a smooth material the color and texture of egg shells, and had no markings save for the letters "Tower/City" stenciled across its side. It whispered to a stop on Jensen's left and a side door rustled open, revealing a handsome olive-skinned man with a light stubble and kind eyes. He leaned forward in the driver's seat and smiled at Jensen through the open door.

"You coming from the tower?" the man asked.

Jensen, caught off guard, could only nod.

"Me too," the man said. "Must've just missed you. I'm heading into the city if you need a lift."

Jensen finally found a smile, this one a bit rueful, and offered it to the man. "No cash. Seems I was mugged by the Grim Reaper. But thanks for the offer."

The man laughed so hard he snorted. "*Hermano*, I wouldn't take your money even if you had it. Climb aboard."

"Thanks," Jensen said, and meant it. He didn't usually take handouts, but this was a special occasion – the bus would get him to the city much faster than his legs ever could. As he climbed the short flight of steps and into the bus, he offered the driver an apologetic shrug. "Really, thank you. I don't usually walk around completely busted like this. I wasn't exactly expecting to end up in Narnia today, know what I mean?"

The man nodded. "*Entiendo*. It's a rough transition for some people. I'm sure The Warden already explained a lot of things, but I'd be happy to fill in the blanks for you. I'm Miguel. Miguel Colón."

Jensen shook the man's hand. "Jensen Bennett. Pleased to meet you."

The doors sighed shut and the bus began moving again. Jensen looked around the interior and saw it was about half-full, mostly with people who gazed out the windows with an awestruck and slightly confused look. One man, who was a hundred years old if he was a day, had his eyes closed and was slowly shaking his head as if to wake himself from the dream he was convinced he was having. Another person, a dark-haired woman of about forty, stared out the hazy, electrified window with a look of pure bliss on her face. Near the back of the bus a little girl, no more than seven years old, played with a small teddy bear and seemed oblivious to what was going on around her.

One rider, a slender young woman with strawberry blonde hair that spilled onto her shoulders like a fiery waterfall, was sitting in the seat directly behind Miguel. She looked indifferent, almost bored, and stared out the window with a kind of uninterested familiarity. Her plain white blouse was open slightly at the top, and its hanging flaps partially obscured some kind of logo stitched into the fabric.

As he passed, the woman turned and looked at him with severe brown eyes, the sight of which caused a kind of pleasant anxiousness to briefly flutter in the center of his chest. Her head cocked to the side and her eyes narrowed as if she recognized him. Jensen didn't return the look – he'd never seen her before in his life – but he nodded politely just the same.

As he took the seat directly across from her, the woman continued to study his face with a calm, friendly intensity. Her eyes exuded warmth, but there was sadness in them, too. One side of her mouth rose in a half-smile, and it accentuated a delicate indent between her nose and lips.

"Have we met before?" she asked. "You look *so* familiar."

Jensen searched her face for some kind of memory but found none. He was sure he'd never seen her before, but still ... looking at her now, something *was* familiar, but fleeting, like déjà vu. She couldn't be a day over twenty-five, yet the faint lines that ran from the edges of her nose outward to the corners of her downturned mouth looked like they'd seen an entire lifetime's worth of either laughter or sadness. Jensen couldn't tell which one.

"Sorry, I don't think so," Jensen responded. "I just got here."

The woman leaned toward Jensen and continued to study him through squinted eyes, as if she was trying to read a menu without her glasses. She then put a fist under her chin and supported the arm beneath it on her knee, and to Jensen she looked a lot like a female version of the famous "Thinker" statue.

"Hmmm," she said at last. "Maybe we met before somewhere, then."

Jensen gave her a cordial smile. "Could be." Then, mostly to disconnect himself from the woman's intense but not exactly unpleasant stare, he turned his eyes to the driver. "Miguel, you mentioned The Warden. You know him?"

Miguel cast a quick glance over his shoulder as he continued to drive the bus, which despite its apparent size and weight navigated the road ahead with smooth precision.

"Very well," he responded. "I've been running the Tower/City route almost as long as I've been here. I pick up folks The Warden says are *gratis* – if they want to come, that is – and bring them to the city. It's quite a sight. You're gonna love it, *amigo*."

No mention of an escape, Jensen thought, and relaxed a bit.

He looked over his shoulder again at the other riders, none of whom seemed to notice or care that a new traveler had entered the bus. All except the young woman, of course, who had abandoned her absent window-gazing and was looking at him with a mild curiosity.

"So all of these people just came from the tower?" Jensen asked. "All of them were sprung?"

Miguel skillfully directed the bus around what looked like a black bear and a baby calf walking side-by-side across the forest road. The bear didn't seem at all interested in making the calf lunch.

"You make it sound like jail," he said. "But yes, they're here for good and free to go wherever they want."

The little girl who had been playing with the stuffed bear looked up at Jensen and smiled. Jensen smiled back.

"There are other places to go than the city?" he asked.

Miguel nodded. "Tons of places. *Infinite*, really. Free will is the only rule here. Everyone can go wherever they want. Most gather in places that are similar to the ones they just left, or the state of mind they were in when they passed over. If there isn't a place that exactly matches, they just create one."

"Create one? You mean build a town?"

"Not with their hands; with their minds." This slightly amused response came not from the driver but from the woman sitting across from him. She continued to look at him with that subtle half-smile of hers, one that Jensen found strangely disarming. Her voice was bubbly and peppered with a mild accent – somewhere north, perhaps Wisconsin. "If enough people want something, it'll just pop into being," she continued. "The places some people create are actually kinda neat. Except, of course, when you start to get out into Dim Country. Then it's not so neat."

There was that word again ... the one The Warden had spoken of.

"I get the impression this Dim Country is some sort of badlands?" Jensen asked.

Miguel half-turned in his seat toward Jensen and nodded. He continued to navigate the bus with expert precision despite not looking at the road.

"Badlands isn't quite the word, but you're close," he said. "All you need to know is that you don't want to go messing around out there, not unless you wanna risk losing your sanity. It's like the lady said; collective thoughts make everything here, and the same goes for the Dims. It was created because people had a need for it. But the folks who populate that area are *malas noticias*, for sure. They aren't people you want to cross paths with. Some braver souls go out as missionaries and try to save them, but sadly many of them never return."

Jensen noticed Miguel's smile had all but died.

"It's hell, then," Jensen said with a seriousness he didn't quite feel. "What you're talking about is basically hell."

"Again, no," the woman answered. "There's no devil poking people with a pitchfork or any of that sort of thing. There *is* a place in the Dims that's much worse than hell – we call it The Subdivisions – but most of Dim Country is just lawlessness and selfishness and people being just about as mean as can be to each other."

"And all of this exists ... what, *here*? We could just drive this bus to these

Dims if we wanted to?"

The woman's half-smile grew into a gorgeous grin that showed not only the entirety of her upper teeth but part of her gum line as well. With a jolt Jensen was suddenly reminded of his wedding day.

Aimee had smiled like that, too. Right after she said she'd love me 'till death do us part and kissed me in front of the entire congregation. Aimee's smile had been hiding a sad truth that day, and I think yours, pretty young lady, is hiding one, too.

"Sure, we could drive there, but you can't think of it in such linear terms," the woman said. "There are many levels here. The material world is one, and we're in the level right next door to that. But there are higher levels, and lower levels, and they all exist in the same space. Just on different planes. It's hard to grasp at first, and it's even harder to explain, but you'll get the hang of it the longer you're here."

"Uh-huh," Jensen said doubtfully. "Planes."

This all sounded like complete nonsense. He was here, and the reality of that fact was undeniable. But planes? Levels? People shaping cities and landscapes just by thinking about them? It was so incredibly stupid that it bordered on insane.

"The Terminal," Jensen said, suddenly remembering. "Is that in Dim Country?"

The Warden hadn't been one for specifics, but he'd said Grange and the guys were there, and Jensen would go wherever it happened to be.

Miguel navigated the bus around a curve, and as he did, Jensen could see the city spires poking up from above the tree line. They were getting close.

God, how fast are we going? Jensen thought. *That city seemed like miles away when I was falling...*

"No, The Terminal's in the city," the woman with the chocolate-colored eyes said. Then, in response to Jensen's unsatisfied look, she continued. "It's one of a few entry points for incoming souls – kinda like the tower – but newcomers who arrive there are here for good. There's no cells, no waiting. The bus stops a few blocks from there, but I'm actually headed in that direction myself, so I can show you the way. If you want."

"That would be great, thanks. The Warden said some of my friends might be there, and I really want to see them."

The woman's smile, which never seemed to completely leave, only fluctuate, returned full force. "We all have friends we'd like to see again," she said, and that beautiful sadness floating on the edges of her smile like a restless ghost seemed to intensify. Then, shaking her head as if she'd forgotten something important, she added, "I'm Guinevere Hatcher, by the way."

He leaned over the aisle with his hand outstretched, just as he'd done over so many business tables during his lifetime. "Jensen Bennett. Nice to meet you."

Guinevere took his hand and shook it. Her grip was firm, her handshake strong. "Interesting name. I like it."

Jensen didn't let go at first, only stared curiously at her and continued the up-and-down shaking motion. There was definitely something alarmingly familiar in her features ... something mysterious and a little dark. She smiled and spoke cheerfully, but it was a mask, as rehearsed and unreal as the counterfeit charm Jensen had learned to wear like a costume. There was a quiet, unspoken pain etched into the faint lines and soft curves of her beautiful face, a secret sorrow she tried to hide.

Their hands finally parted, and Jensen tore his eyes away from Guinevere and looked out into the forest wall. It was hurtling by at incredible speeds despite the fact the bus was still emitting that low, almost hypnotic hum. He'd been asked to digest so much information in such a short span of time that he wasn't sure he understood everything. He wasn't sure he'd understand it even if he had an eternity to contemplate it.

But none of it would matter, not if he found what he had come to find. Then he'd start his new life, and the strangeness of this odd world would fade until it became nothing but a disjointed fragment in his mind.

Except for Guinevere, Jensen thought. *She'll linger for a little longer.*

***

The city was as spectacular as Miguel had promised.

There was no slow transition, no sleepy suburb dotted with quaint homes and meticulously landscaped front yards. In a single instant, the bus had gone from the quiet forest, as pristine and flawless as a priceless emerald, and into the sprawling arms of the shimmering metropolis.

The towering redwoods had conceded to immense, see-through skyscrapers that looked as if they were constructed of pure energy and grew from the blacktop like transparent florae. They lined both sides of the road, their glistening tops scratching a cloudless sky ablaze with the same colorful ribbons of light Jensen had seen from his cell in Translucent Tower. They floated in the air as tropical fish sometimes do in an aquarium, darting and dancing in slow-motion, occasionally changing direction abruptly and swooping so low that they'd almost touch the people who were crossing the long, white bridges that connected the transparent structures like intricate spiderwebs high above the roadway.

Vehicles flew up and down the road, which had matured into a six-lane highway with the works – curbs, streetlights, road signs, crosswalks. The sidewalks on both sides of the street were choked with people swarming in and out of storefronts and backstreets. Some people carried shopping bags and children, others strode alone with newspapers tucked under their arms or held hands with the person walking next to them, and some had stopped in the middle of the walkway to engage in conversation. The crowd simply poured around the latter as if they weren't even there.

Miguel turned and motioned to a building on the left. When he spoke, he raised his voice so that everyone in the bus could hear.

92

"This is the Kingston," he said, "and they have pretty much anything you've got a taste for. You don't really need to eat anymore – it's not like you're going to die of starvation here! But some people just can't resist the tastes they once loved, and that's okay! I'm particularly fond of the Kingston's baked parmesan perch, but they serve anything and everything."

"They got Cajun meatloaf?" a voice shouted from the back.

Miguel nodded. "You bet. The best in town."

"Hot damn!" the voice said, then was quiet again.

They passed several more buildings, and as they went, Miguel explained each one. There was a movie theatre, which had every single film, TV show, commercial and sporting event ever committed to tape. There was an oval-shaped stadium that rose above the ground like one half of a sliced cantaloupe, and from it issued a chorus of cheering voices that would make the crowd in Springfield Stadium blush. There was also a recreation center, a beautifully landscaped city park, a public library, an art gallery, rows of restaurants and shops, and a massive fountain that sprayed bubblegum-colored water high into the air.

Then they passed a giant highway billboard that sat on monstrous steel legs and shouted:

LIVE MUSIC!!!
THE ORIGINAL RAMONES
W/SPECIAL GUEST **CODSWALLOP**!!!
COME AND GET YOUR ROCK ON!!!
ONLY IN **TOWNSHIP REBELLION**!!!

Jensen didn't fully understand the sign's message, but he was more than a little intrigued by the notion that his dream of a Ramones reunion was actually happening. There was something else about the billboard that struck him as being vaguely familiar, but he couldn't put his finger on it.

As he was trying to make the connection, someone plopped down in the seat next to him, and he'd been so deep in thought that the sudden intrusion was startling. It was Guinevere, and instead of speaking this time, she just sat there, one leg crossed over the other, hands resting on her lap, studying his face once again through narrow eyes.

A pleasant smell was coming from her – something like coconut – and her pocketed pink miniskirt had been hiked up just enough for him to see she was wearing a pair of black stockings that ran down the length of her slender legs until they disappeared into a pair of even pinker sneakers. The flap on her white blouse had shifted a bit, and in addition to getting an eyeful of milky white cleavage, Jensen could see what was stitched on her shirt: a blue logo that read "United Way" and depicted a cartoon hand cradling a red stick figure.

"I'm telling you, you look *so* familiar," Guinevere said finally. "You sure you just got here? I'm pretty good with faces, and I've seen yours before."

Jensen shifted uncomfortably in his seat, partly because of the question, partly because of how intensely the beautiful girl sitting only inches away was looking at him. Conversations were just dances, and he always preferred to lead. But Guinevere had turned the tables, and everything was off-kilter.

"I must just have one of those faces," he said dumbly.

Guinevere didn't seem convinced, but she didn't pursue the matter. "Must be," she said. "I've been here awhile, myself. You probably gathered as much from all the talking I was doing. I do that a lot. Talking, I mean. I'm kind of a motormouth sometimes. Did I go too fast for you? I probably did. My dad always said I needed to slow down, enunciate, pick my words before I said them. But that's no fun if you ask me."

Miguel continued his tour in the background, but Jensen had tuned him out. He had no intention of staying here long enough to patronize any of the businesses the driver was discussing, as fascinating as they all sounded. Besides, he had his hands full with Guinevere. For some reason, he was having trouble remembering what he usually did in these situations, despite having a lifetime of practice at it.

Focus. Curtains up.

"I'd be lying if I said I understood everything," he said. "My knowledge of the afterlife kinda begins and ends with *Beetlejuice*. But I appreciate the help all the same."

She smiled and began twirling a strand of long, reddish blonde hair in her fingers, but her eyes never left his face. "You'll get the hang of it all. When I first got here I was a mess. Much more confused and panicky than *you* are."

"Well, I'm nothing if not adaptable." Jensen could feel himself relax a little, and he smiled. "My job requires a lot of traveling, so getting used to local custom, and quickly, is something I've become quite good at."

She giggled, and Jensen thought: *Even that* laugh *is hiding something*.

"This isn't exactly Paris or the Bahamas, Jensen, but I tip my hat to you anyway." And with that, she brought a hand to her brow and dipped an invisible hat. They sat in silence for a bit, and then she said, "Your friends. The ones you're going to see. They must have crossed over recently, too, if The Warden said you could find them at The Terminal. Did you cross together?"

"Not exactly."

An odd look passed across her face, one that momentarily erased the smile from it. "*Not exactly* isn't exactly an answer."

Jensen opened his mouth to respond, to make a joke or change the subject, but as he did the bus began to slow and Miguel shouted in a cheery voice, "North and Vine! End of the line!"

Guinevere looked at him with anxious eyes. The interior lights passed and flashed in them, and again Jensen was unwillingly drawn deep into their bottomless depths.

"That's us," she said. "The Terminal's only a short walk from here." Then, she grabbed his arm – her touch was smooth, gentle – and began to stand up. "We can talk more on the way. Come on!"

95

The bus murmured to a stop and Miguel threw open the doors. The sounds of the city immediately poured into the cabin – people talking, feet shuffling, car subwoofers rattling trunks. Not exactly the kinds of things one would expect to hear in heaven, or wherever the hell this was.

Jensen stood and followed Guinevere to the exit, but stopped before she could lead him off. He turned to the driver and put a hand on his shoulder.

"Thanks again for the ride. Just a bit of friendly advice, though ... never give anything away for free, even to a nice guy like me."

Miguel shook his head. "*Amigo*, I told you back in the forest that I wouldn't take your money even if you had it. That wasn't me being altruistic. It's just that money is irrelevant here."

Jensen extended a hand, which Miguel took. "Money's never irrelevant."

Miguel nodded. "I'll take your word for it, Jensen. Enjoy Paradise City!"

"Thanks," Jensen replied, and then stepped off the bus with Guinevere and into the vast city beyond.

✱✱✱

A few other people disembarked the bus as well, and they wandered aimlessly off in scattered directions with heads craned high in amazement at the impossible architecture around them. Jensen was still a bit in awe, himself; this was by far the cleanest, brightest city he'd ever seen, and he'd seen a lot during his tenure on the road with Quiet Catastrophe.

There was no litter, no cracks in the sidewalks, no revolting smell of urine or rotting garbage. The curbs looked freshly cemented, the streets newly paved. The buildings were likewise immaculate and stood not as solid structures but more like malleable ideas that appeared to change with the direction of the wind. Everything seemed alive and in constant flux, and everything seemed to glimmer with the same radiant energy he'd first encountered lining the doorway of his cell.

Collective thoughts create everything, that's what Miguel and Guinevere had said, and Jensen realized with wonder that the energy he was seeing must be the physical manifestation of that process; a kind of primordial electricity that the like-minded could control and shape if so inclined. His previous assumption that the concept was nonsense melted away now that he was staring at the proof. It was hard to argue with the facts.

"*Thoughts* really created all of this?" he asked Guinevere, who was still holding tightly onto his arm with gentle fingers. Now that they were standing, he was about a foot taller than her, and he saw right over her head as the bus navigated into traffic and then disappeared in the organized chaos of cars and bicycles.

Guinevere nodded. "Told you it was neat, didn't I?" And then, not giving him a chance to respond, she grabbed his left hand in her right and shouted "This way!" before beginning to run through the crowd.

Miraculously, it parted like a river around a rock as they moved down the street. Jensen had to work his legs hard in order to keep up with Guinevere, who was running like a sprinter in the last leg of a marathon. But he didn't get fatigued; he supposed he could probably run for hours, *days* even, and still not be tired.

"This city is incredible!" Jensen shouted over the crowd's clamor, and Guinevere smiled at him over her shoulder. "How many people live here?"

Guinevere shrugged. "Dunno! A few hundred million maybe? I never really thought about it!"

Jensen was amazed at how little effort it took to run, and how full of breath he was despite being a bit out of shape. "The city holds them all?"

"Sure! If it needs to get bigger to hold more people, it just grows!"

They reached a side street about two blocks from where the bus had deposited them, and Guinevere finally began to slow down. She didn't come to a full stop, though; she simply scaled her run down into a very fast walk. The souls of her pink sneakers made flopping noises on the pavement as she went.

She unclasped Jensen's hand now that they were walking and relatively clear of pedestrians, and he was surprised to realize he missed the feel of it.

"It's just a bit further down," she said. "You'll see it the second we turn that corner up there."

And see it he did, although it wasn't the grand sight he'd been expecting. It looked like a small subway entrance that jutted from the pavement on the right side of the street like a hitchhiker's thumb. The only indication that it was the place The Warden had spoken of was a sign hanging over the curved archway that read "The Terminal."

A thin man in a long, white cooking smock was casually leaning against one of the two railings that descended alongside the stairs into the darkness below. He took a puff of his cigarette, crushed it beneath his boot, and then waved. Jensen watched in amazement as the discarded cigarette butt seemed to melt and then disappear completely into the pavement.

"There's Bastien," Guinevere said and waved back. "I can't believe he stood there the whole time. I was sure he'd have left for Ladyland by now."

Jensen had no idea what she was talking about, or who Bastien was, nor did he much care. All he could think about was the sign hanging over The Terminal's entrance and the near certainty that Quiet Catastrophe was somewhere beyond it. He was close now.

When they approached the man, Guinevere gave him two kisses – one on each cheek – and then held his hands in hers. "*Merci pour regarder la porte, Bastien*," she said. "*Est-il venu à travers?*"

The man shook his head and frowned. "*Malheureusement, non*," he said, and then eyed Jensen with mild curiosity. "*Qui est votre ami?*"

Guinevere glanced quickly back at Jensen, who was watching them with growing confusion. "Oh, my apologies," she said. "Jensen, this is Bastien Aurand. He's the sous-chef at The Pot and the Pan down the street. Bastien, this is Jensen Bennett. He's here to see some friends."

"A pleasure," Bastien said and made a small bow, which Jensen returned with a friendly nod. "Any friend of fair Guinevere is a friend of mine, for sure." Then, the cook directed his attention back to Guinevere, whose smile looked both amused and anxious at the same time. "He's not at the tower, *eh*? Otherwise you would not have asked if I saw him, *non*?"

"No, although no one at the tower could give me a straight answer. They were running through the hallways like it was the end of days or something. But he wasn't on the bus, so he probably was never in the tower in the first place. He has to be inside somewhere, I'm sure of it. There's no way he'd come out in The Subdivisions or Righteous Country."

The urge to sprint into The Terminal was intense – he was right here, and Grange and the boys were probably somewhere beyond wherever the subway steps ended – but he held his ground. For whatever reason, Guinevere had helped him. It would be rude to go trouncing off down the stairs without at least thanking her. But he wasn't going to wait for long.

"*Non, non*," Bastien said as he fished another cigarette out from the pack in his breast pocket.

Smoke 'em if you got 'em, Jensen thought. *It's not like you have to worry about cancer here.*

"*Votre copain*, from how you speak of him, would not emerge in those horrible places," Bastien said. "*Aurait-il*?"

"Never in a million years," Guinevere said, and then took a cigarette when Bastien offered her one from his pack. The Frenchmen turned the pack to Jensen and raised his eyebrows, but Jensen politely shook his head.

"Not for me, thanks," he said. "Joe Camel and I broke up a while ago."

Jensen hoped his rising impatience wasn't showing in his voice, but he couldn't help it. It would take Guinevere at least five minutes to finish her cigarette, during which time Grange and Choom and Orrin could slip out of sight. He made the decision to go right then and there, manners be damned, when Guinevere spoke and did it for him.

"You've been such a doll, Bastien," Guinevere said and retrieved a pink

Zippo lighter from the right pocket of her skirt. She opened its metal lid and then struck the flint wheel inside with a quick snap of her fingers, making it appear as if she'd summoned fire from thin air. While she held the flame to the tip of her cigarette and took a few quick drags until it caught, she continued to speak from the side of her mouth. "I can't thank you enough for standing watch for me, and I'd really love to stay and talk more, but –"

"But you must go after your *amant*," Bastien said, and a thin, sad smile found its way onto his lips.

Instead of answering, Guinevere leaned in and gave Bastien another round of kisses on each cheek. Then, after a short pause, she added a quick third right on his lips. Bastien's cheeks immediately turned red.

"*Merci beaucoup, beau*," she whispered, and then again grabbed Jensen's hand and led him down the short flight of stairs and into the darkness below.

Before Jensen lost sight of him, Bastien looked as if he'd literally died and gone to heaven.

✳✳✳

The staircase eventually gave way to a long, spherical passageway whose bend concealed what lay ahead. Another sign, this one reading "Rainbow Line This Way," hung from the arched ceiling and began swinging on its silver hinges as the unmistakable sound of wheels on rails suddenly filled the narrow space and then idled with an almost musical resonance.

They were alone in the hallway, but their footfalls were overpowered by what seemed like a million voices from somewhere ahead. Guinevere slowed her pace somewhat as she took the last few puffs of her cigarette, but after she threw it to the ground and stepped on it, she began half-running again.

This was clearly some kind of subway line, or at least this world's version of one. Where the tracks terminated, Jensen didn't know, but based on what The Warden had said, he knew where they began – the material world, *his* world. The tower had been constructed for people who were stuck between realms. The Terminal, on the other hand, was apparently for those whose time on earth was most definitely over. There was no waiting here, and no going back ... this line ran only one way: into the mysterious realms of the afterlife of which Miguel and Guinevere had spoken.

"I don't know French," Jensen said, raising his voice to be heard over the noise. "I failed it twice in high school, actually. But I'm really good at reading people's faces, and Bastien's was like an open book. He has it bad for you."

Guinevere shot him a quick, *you've-got-to-be-kidding* look over her shoulder.

"Yeah, me and every other girl this side of Evermore. Half the women in this city are hot for him, too, at least according to Bastien. He's a regular heartbreaker. He'll be right at home in Ladyland."

Jensen thought about asking her what Ladyland was, but he supposed the name itself was explanation enough and let it go. "It wouldn't matter anyway, right? Because you're taken. This guy you're looking for ... he's your boyfriend, isn't he?"

Guinevere's smile weakened. "Something like that," she said in a low voice, and said no more.

The curved passageway emptied into a vast, rectangular-shaped chamber that despite its darkness stood in high definition to the eye. A low-hung ceiling interspersed every hundred feet or so by ornate stone pillars followed the slightly curved path of the train tracks to their left. There were seven of them, set several feet down in a wide recession that seemed large enough to accommodate a dozen subway trains. Each was a different color – red, orange, blue, green, yellow, brown and black – and each glowed with a quiet radiance that was reminiscent of neon tubing.

Jensen was immediately reminded of the Red Line terminal he took every day on his commute to work, the very same one in which he'd come across a very talented but dejected Hedley Grange playing for spare change. Yet this terminal was different; like the city above, it showed no signs of wear, and the oppressive smells of moving machinery and unwashed bodies so common in many of the El terminals were absent here.

The throngs of commuters milling about the Terminal also didn't seem like the usual riff raff that frequented Chicago's rapid transit stations; many of them were smiling broadly as they meandered about the open spaces like awestruck tourists in a foreign land. Grange didn't seem to be among them, but the chamber was so large and congested that it was hard to pick out individual faces in the crowd. It was a wonder no one was trampled underfoot.

A sobering thought came to him then: *I could search this place for hours only to find the band was already gone. There are just too many people.*

He returned his gaze to Guinevere. "Thanks again for your help. I'd still be wandering the streets looking for this place if you hadn't led me here." And then, for some reason – perhaps it was the quiet beauty in those haunted eyes looking up at him, or maybe he didn't really want to admit to himself that this was goodbye – he lied. "Let's meet for coffee or something. Tomorrow. After you've found this guy you're looking for."

"I'd like that very much," she said. Her half-smile had thankfully returned, and her infinite brown eyes twinkled in the scattered glow of the Terminal's few overhead lights. She gave his hands one final squeeze and then let go. "I don't know exactly where I'll be tomorrow. Probably not in Paradise City. But if I am, meet me here, in the café." She pointed to a small enclosure a few feet beyond the concierge and smiled as a thought came to her. "I'll be the one drinking the Earl Grey."

"It's a date," Jensen said.

He went to open his mouth again, perhaps to wish her good luck in finding her boyfriend, or maybe to come clean and admit she'd be having tea for one – he wasn't sure – when he saw something that caused his heart, or whatever ethereal version of it beat inside his chest, to flutter.

A man was pacing back and forth in front of a bench near the tracks, and he stood in stark contrast to the people around him, like he was the only color image in a black-and-white photograph. Sweat ran down his balding forehead and collected in the crooks of his armpits, and each of his stubby fingers were adorned with what looked like cheap costume jewelry from afar. The transition from life to death had done nothing to quell the constant look of pain etched across the man's face like a stone inscription.

"I think I see one of my friends," Jensen said as a grin split his face. Then, realizing this was probably the last time he'd see her, Jensen grabbed Guinevere's hand and looked deep into her eyes. There was something about her, something hard to define, that he was going to miss. "Tomorrow, then."

She only nodded. The air of finality now hanging between them made Jensen feel surprisingly sad, but he only returned the gesture and then walked away. After only a few steps, he got the sensation that Guinevere was still looking at him with that mysterious, slightly dark smile playing on her lips, and he turned around to give her a final wave.

But Guinevere was already gone.

✳✳✳

Yet the entryway where they had stood wasn't empty.

An imposing figure had entered The Terminal, one who wore a white shirt and black tie, one who only needed a pair of oversized sunglasses and he'd look exactly like a police officer. An expression of calm fury sat on the man's face as he stood framed in the immense archway, flanked on one side by two uniformed men and on the other by another familiar face – the bus driver, Miguel.

The Warden, now sporting a walkie-talkie radio on his right shoulder, stood with his hands on his oversized hips and slowly scanned the interior of The Terminal from left to right like a security camera. Then Miguel pointed and said something. This elicited a nod from The Warden, who then began to gracefully navigate his tall, stocky frame through the masses.

Jensen couldn't see to whom or what Miguel had pointed, but he didn't have to, because it was all right there, engraved on The Warden's features like the sinister taunt of a leering stone gargoyle.

As another train barreled into the station and came to a squealing halt beside him, Jensen realized The Warden was walking right toward him. And he'd come to put the escaped animal back into its cage.

[silence]

His mommy says they're lost, that they took a bad turn somewhere on Interstate 5, but he's not so sure. He can only count to his age, and he has to use almost every finger on his left hand to do it, but he's old enough to recognize familiar words.

The sign back there had them.

Welcome to Woodburn, it had said. Like when Uncle Eric takes them camping and the flames pop and sizzle, and his eyes water from the smoke, and his clothes get all stinky.

He tries to tell his mommy that they're not lost, that she can stop being scared, but she isn't listening to him. She's talking to a mean-looking woman at the gas station, pointing at a piece of folded paper with a bunch of lines all over it. It's a map, but he doesn't need to see it, because he knows where he is.

She's so distracted that she doesn't even notice when his tiny hand slips out of her own. He begins moving down the street, not meandering like a lost child but walking confidently, with purpose. He sees the building and he knows it's a good place. A place of hope.

When he gets closer, he realizes it's not exactly the same. It has brick walls, and a pointy roof, and big, long windows. It's all grown up, not like he remembers it, but still the same anyway, like an old friend wearing new clothes.

No one seems to notice as he crosses the street and sits down on the curb, the one next to the big tree. The *kissing tree*. It hasn't really changed, but the cement in front of it is cracked now.

In its shade, he remembers the kisses, not like the ones his mommy gives him, but *grownup* kisses. He giggles like he's being tickled as memories flood his mind: the softness of her lips, the warmth of her hand against his cheek, the thud of her heartbeat, the promise to always remember this moment, no matter what happens.

Then his eyes fall upon the letters, faint and worn, carved into the cement long ago, back when it was still wet and sticky: A big "W," followed by an even bigger heart, followed by a small, bubbly "B." He stops giggling at the sight. Suddenly his tummy doesn't feel so good.

She's not here, he thinks, and even though he doesn't know what it means, not really, tears squeeze from his eyes and he begins crying, crying so hard his mother hears the wretched sounds all the way down the street and comes running.

He's still crying when they drive into Seattle that evening.

TURNING JUDAS
-Track Six-

Jensen had slipped into the massive crowd, and doing so had bought him some time.

If he was going to risk talking to Nigel Cuthpit, he'd have to do it quickly. The Terminal was as vast as an airplane hangar and stuffed with enough people to fill several football stadiums, but eventually The Warden would reach his position and drag him kicking and screaming back to Translucent Tower.

Nigel was pacing, head down, one hand half-obscured in the front of his pants pocket, the other rubbing a forehead besieged in flop sweat. His lips moved wordlessly in silent prayer. The other commuters must have sensed that Nigel was a pustulous sore just waiting to erupt, because everyone was giving him a wide berth. The two men more or less had an entire waiting station near the green-colored platform to themselves. Jensen just hoped the crowd behind him was enough to mask his location from The Warden.

"Man, the trains aren't on time no matter *where* you go, huh?" Jensen asked.

Nigel jumped a little, torn from whatever rumination was turning inside his head, and looked at him with a shocked expression that was both parts comical and pathetic.

"Bennett? But what ... where did *you* come from?"

Jensen smirked and threw a thumb in the direction the trains entering The Terminal. "Same place as you, Nigel – a seven-forty-seven past its prime."

Jensen risked a quick glance over his shoulder and was relieved to see The Warden had momentarily stopped to talk to a group of young commuters. Miguel was nearby, biting his fingernail and looking as if he had somewhere else to be.

"But that's ... that's impossible," Nigel stammered. Now that the initial shock was gone from his face, that familiar, ever-present grimace had returned. "You left the stadium. You weren't on the plane. It was just the four of us."

"Wrong," Jensen said. "You're forgetting the pilots up front, and myself in the cargo hold. You should've just let me backstage, Nigel. Now you're responsible for seven deaths, including yourself. Surprised you turned up here and not someplace ... a bit hotter."

Jensen was delighted at the angry expression that fell across Nigel's face, and especially at his stunned inability to respond. So he continued.

"*House Made of Sound*," Jensen said flatly. "We know the band recorded it in secret, at some place called Dancing Days Studio in California. Where's the master, Nigel? Where did you guys hide it? Because it belongs to Wicked Records, and I'm here to take it back."

Nigel's upper lip rose, revealing a set of large teeth, and he stared at Jensen through beady, mistrustful eyes. "The *master*? Christ, you amaze me, Bennett. Here you are, in the hereafter, the answer to life's biggest question staring you right in the face, and all you care about is some bleeding *record*? Perhaps you haven't noticed, mate, but you're bloody dead. *Fuck* the album. Christ!"

Nigel's voice steadily grew louder as he spoke, and Jensen saw a few passing commuters throw curious glances in their direction. If The Warden was nearby, he most certainly would hear the Englishman's high-pitched voice and look over, too, but Jensen didn't dare check.

"Nigel, I'm not dead."

"Really? Where'd you think you are then, mate? Bloody *Sea World*?"

Jensen realized he was only irritating Nigel, and he couldn't very well extract the information he needed if the Englishman still regarded him as an enemy. He flashed a friendly smile and made a concerted effort to speak calmly.

"I survived the crash. Or, at least, I'm going to. I'm not sure I understand everything, but I know this much: I'm going back, and I escaped the place I was being held so I could get the album before I do. Look, be reasonable here. I'm the only person who can bring *House Made of Sound* – the last album, really, since the band is gone – I'm the only one who can bring it to light. And I *want* to. For the fans."

Nigel snorted. "For the *fans*. Right. Old Benny, does everything for the fans, with nary a care for his own self-advancement. You truly are a noble among men, aren't you?"

"No, and I never claimed to be. Sure, there's some money in it for me, but what does that matter? All I want to know is where the album is, and then I'll be out of your life."

Jensen expected to hear more of Nigel's trademark ire, but the Englishman only plopped down on the bench with a dejected groan.

"I don't *know* where it is, mate. Not that I'd tell you if I did. We tracked the whole thing in just nine days. No demos, no overdubs, just the gents, live in-studio. Then Hedley took everything – the master, the raw mixes ... everything. Said something about transferring it, or some other such technical drivel. *He's* the man you want to see, Bennett. Hedley Grange is the only one who knows where it is."

Shit, Jensen thought, and balled his hands into fists. "Okay, then where is he?"

Nigel let out a long, defeated sigh. "I don't know. I don't know where *any* of them are. They fired me, and then left on one of these bloody tubes."

"Fired you?" Jensen said. It was evil of him, but he couldn't help but smile as he parroted the same words Nigel had spoken to him in front of the backstage entrance at Springfield Stadium: "As in, they no longer wished to be associated with you? As in, they reiterated to you in no uncertain terms how little they desire your company?"

Well, there goes my brief attempt at being cordial, Jensen thought.

Nigel's sharp, cold look told Jensen he wasn't amused. "Yes, yes, think you're a clever one, don't you?" Then he looked down to his hands, which were slick and glistening under the terminal lights. "I suppose I deserved that. But fired? It's a bit much. Those bastards let me go the second they realized we weren't dead, without even a thank-you-kindly." His eyes returned to Jensen, and they looked as close to sincere as Nigel was capable. God help him, but Jensen even felt a little pity for the man. "They said I caused the plane crash. Rubbish, all of it."

Nigel then scowled as his eyes fell sharply on something just over Jensen's left shoulder. "Christ, lady, can I fucking *help* you with something?"

Jensen spun around, momentarily forgetting The Warden's approach, and saw Guinevere standing at the edge of the crowd. How much of their conversation had she heard? If she'd been there when Jensen admitted escaping custody, she very well might scream for The Warden right here and now.

"Nice friends you have, Jensen," she said quietly. Then, to Nigel, she said, "You're a vile, angry little man, aren't you?"

She didn't call for The Warden, which was a good thing, because Jensen could see him and his posse only a few yards away. Either she didn't hear the part about his escaping, or she simply didn't care enough to rat him out.

He turned back to Nigel and made no effort to hide the urgency now dominating his voice. "Nigel, which train did they take? Which line?"

Nigel crossed his arms and looked defiantly to the left. "Sod off, mate. I don't care if we're in Springfield, the afterlife, or fucking *Oz*. I'm not telling you a bloody thing."

Jensen looked at the set of seven tracks – all different colors – and walked closer to Nigel, so close that even with his head turned the Englishman could see him from the corner of his eye. Jensen could sense Guinevere looming behind him and was grateful that she'd decided to keep quiet.

"Nigel, did they take the Green Line?" he asked calmly, but with authority.

Nigel remained quiet. He shifted uncomfortably on the bench but made no other movement.

"The Blue Line?"

Again, silence. Not a hair moved on Nigel's head.

"The Black Line?"

Nothing.

"The Yellow Line?"

Nigel still didn't say anything, but a grouping of muscles on the right side of his face twitched slightly. It was brief and barely perceptible, but Jensen saw it just the same.

"It's the Yellow Line, isn't it? That's the train they took."

Again, Nigel was quiet, but his lower lip quivered a bit at the question. Jensen grinned at the sight and turned excitedly toward Guinevere. "The Yellow Line," he said. "That's the way they went. Where does it go?"

He expected her to argue, to give him the same lecture The Warden had about Translucent Tower being the proper place for tourists such as he, but she immediately answered as if she'd been turning the same question over in her head.

"A few places, all on the outskirts of the Dims," she said. "Isolation Range. Ladyland. Let me think. There's also Township Rebellion, and Sleeping Village, the Sick Sea –"

And in an instant, Jensen knew why the billboard he'd seen during the drive into the city had seemed so familiar. *Live music!!!* It had said. *Only in Township Rebellion!!!* And, the thing that had sparked the memory he couldn't quite place – *The Original Ramones w/Special Guest Codswallop!!!*

"Township Rebellion," Jensen said with certainty. "That's where they are."

Guinevere took a few eager steps toward him. "Are you sure?"

111

"Positive. A sign I saw said the band Codswallop was playing there. I couldn't remember why that name was so familiar, but now I do – that's what Hed wanted to call the band before the label made him change it to something more marketable! He was beyond pissed about it."

Jensen tried to grasp the timeline – the band had gotten here, argued with Nigel, and then left for Township Rebellion, where they immediately booked a show. All while Jensen was trapped in Translucent Tower and then riding a bus into town. Was that possible? The Warden had said time was flaky here, but was it really *that* flaky?

No time to second-guess himself now. The Warden was so close Jensen could hear him ask a commuter if she'd seen a tall man with brown hair and gray eyes come through, and the woman's quick response that she hadn't. It was Township Rebellion or bust.

"How long until the Yellow Line comes in?" Jensen asked. They were now speaking in hushed tones and huddled together as if hatching some nefarious plot. The crowd of commuters shuffled around them as if they were as inconsequential as the massive stone pillars that supported The Terminal's vaulted ceiling.

"Not long," she said. "The lines come in pretty regularly. The Yellow shouldn't be too far away. We can catch it before The Warden even knows you were here."

So she *had* heard. More importantly, she'd used the word "we," as if his quest had now become her own. Jensen couldn't figure out why she was helping him, but in that moment he could have kissed her for it.

"I hope you're right," he said. "I don't have a floppy hat and sunglasses to hide my face this time."

She didn't ask him what he meant, but gave his hand a reassuring squeeze. "You'll be okay. Just follow me and keep your head down."

Jensen showed his agreement with a slight nod, and Guinevere once again led him by the hand. They left Nigel to sulk and hurried off down the platform, casually but at a brisk walk, and the cavernous archway that Jensen knew led back to the material world inched ever closer.

Like a mouth, Jensen thought, *one that eats nothing but vomits up people daily.*

"I was sure I wouldn't see you again," Jensen said after they'd cleared the green platform and the despondent Englishman who was its sole occupant. "No luck finding your guy?"

"No," Guinevere said, and didn't elaborate any further. There was a hint of irritation in her response that Jensen didn't much care for, and it caused him to wonder if he was the cause of it.

"Are you mad? That I lied to you? I would've told you the truth, but it's very important I find Hedley Grange. I couldn't risk you turning me in."

Guinevere contemplated this for a few seconds. The hive-like hum of the crowd filled the silence between them in the interim. Then, seeming to come to an internal consensus, she said, "You couldn't have known which way I'd go. In retrospect, I understand. And to be fair, you didn't lie about escaping the tower ... because I never really asked you about it." Another pause, another few seconds of crowd murmur, and then, "Your friend back there... Nigel ... he's the manager of Quiet Catastrophe, isn't he?"

Jensen laughed. "Well, Nigel isn't my friend. I definitely *did* lie about that. But yes, he's their manager. Or *was* their manager, I guess. You're a fan of the band?"

She continued as if he hadn't asked a question. "You're after some master recording. You said it was the record label's property. Is that true?"

Jensen realized that she must have been present almost from the very start of his conversation with Nigel. She'd heard everything. No use in keeping secrets now. If he didn't trust her after all her unsolicited help, he never would.

"Yes, absolutely," he said a bit formally. "The band's contract calls for three albums, but they've only delivered two. This new mystery album would be the third and final of their contract."

They'd reached another platform, this one bathed in yellow – yellow benches, yellow flooring, yellow banisters. Jensen chanced a glance behind him and thankfully couldn't pick The Warden out of the crowd. Here they stopped, and Guinevere turned slowly and looked at him square in the eyes. She still had his hand in hers.

"So you're just some record label lackey, is that it?" she asked. "You said you were looking for some friends. Was that a lie, too? Do you even know the band at all?"

She was still smiling, but that darkness hiding in its shadows was more alive than ever.

"Of course I do, Guinevere." She continued to look at him with that unbelieving smile, one which prompted him to further explain himself. "I'm an A&R rep for the band's label, Wicked Records. I'm kind of a go-between. I protect the label's investments by making sure artists don't stray too far off the beaten path."

She gave him an impatient look. "I know what an A&R rep is."

Jensen sighed. "Okay, but did you know *I* was the one who discovered Hedley Grange, who put the entire band together? Not many people do, apparently. Hell, I even paid for the first demo out of my own pocket and put Grange up in a hotel for a few weeks until I could convince the label to bite."

He paused for a moment. Now that he was on his soapbox – on the defensive, if he was really being honest about it – he felt a need to continue.

"I never asked for anything, ever. The band, the label, the concert promoters, the merch guys, they all got rich. But not me. Do you know how hard it is to get a rock band signed these days? Never mind getting them to the top of the Billboard and selling out 60,000-seat stadiums. They got there on *my* blood and sweat, but somehow I can't even pay the fucking mortgage on my place, while everyone else is drowning in cash.

"And all because I trusted Grange. I actually trusted that son-of-a-bitch, thought he actually gave a damn about me, would eventually make me whole.

Turns out he's just another actor, and I fell for his performance. Not anymore. It's my turn. *My* payday. He owes me a whole hell of a lot more than that album, but it's all I want. And I intend to get it."

Guinevere had listened to this lengthy sermon with patience, the smile on her face not fading in the slightest, her large, round eyes searching his face while he spoke. If he'd upset her, he couldn't tell. "And you think getting it will make everything right again." Not a question, but a statement.

"Well, it'll be a start."

They both turned to look as the sound of another approaching train filled The Terminal. Now that he was closer, Jensen could see a single white track jutting from the darkness of the immense inbound tunnel, and it ran alone for several hundred feet before splitting at a junction point into the seven colored tracks he'd seen before. As the arriving train neared this split, it jerked abruptly left and followed the blue track, immediately turning from white to azure as it did.

Without having to ask Guinevere, Jensen realized that all The Terminal's trains entered the station on this single white line and only became one of the seven colored lines after it reached the junction point. They wouldn't know if an incoming train was the Yellow Line until it picked which track to follow and changed color.

"And what are you going to do if you find him?" Guinevere asked as soon as the train's roar had passed. "Beat the information out of him? This isn't exactly the place one does that sort of thing."

Her eyes darted to the crowd behind Jensen and then swept back to again meet his gaze. She must be tracking The Warden's movements, and he was glad she was. He didn't dare turn around and look himself.

"No, not at all. I'm no brawler. But trust me, when I find him, he'll tell me."

"How can you *possibly* know that?"

Jensen sighed again. "Because he owes me, and he knows it. Besides, I have subtle ways of getting people to give up information they don't want to. I did it with Nigel, and I can do it with Hed. It doesn't always work, and I have to ask just the right questions, but Hedley Grange will be easier to crack than a Chicago sidewalk."

The words between them once again withered, and in the silence that followed, Jensen wondered if he really believed everything he was saying. He'd used his *Bela Lugosi Stare*, as Aimee once called it, on countless suits and CEOs throughout the years to close deals and get promotions. But he'd never actually used the stare on someone who already knew he was capable of doing it, like Grange. Did it only work on the unsuspecting? He wasn't sure.

"You know, you might not make it to Township Rebellion at all," Guinevere said finally, and her eyes again flickered momentarily to a point behind Jensen's right shoulder. "You could leave the afterworld long before the train even gets there."

Jensen glanced dreamily down the tracks and saw that while only a few people were getting on the Blue Line, seemingly hundreds were getting off it. Newcomers, Guinevere had called them, and Jensen realized with dim wonder that he'd been one himself not too long ago. Yet it already felt like it was a hundred years ago.

"I know my time here is short," he said finally. "But I'm going to keep pressing on for as long as I have. No matter what."

As if he'd heard Jensen's statement and had taken it as a personal challenge, The Warden's deep voice boomed from somewhere behind him: "Jensen Bennett!"

He knew before the voice had even finished saying his name that he was had. The Warden had quietly shouldered his way through the crowd and got the drop on him, but that wasn't even the worst part. Guinevere *had* to have seen him coming, and she'd said nothing. He didn't want to believe it, but there was no way she wouldn't have noticed his approach – the guy stood out like a coffee stain on a white dress.

116

The Yellow Line was nowhere in sight, and the crowd was so thick he wouldn't be able to get three steps into it before The Warden grabbed him by the scruff of his neck and dragged him back.

There was no way out. He was trapped.

*** ***

"I'll say one thing about you, Bennett, ya got moxie," The Warden said. His face was stern and his posture authoritative, but there was genuine admiration in his voice. "I've had people escape before, but never like that."

Jensen slowly raised his hands about chest level to show he meant no harm and wasn't going to cause a problem. "What can I say? Lock a guy in a room without an Xbox and he's apt to jump out a window."

The pavement beneath his feet shuddered with a delicate vibration, and he craned an ear to hear if another train was coming. He couldn't tell, not with the Blue Line still idling several yards further down, but he thought he could see a feeble white light dancing somewhere in the darkness of the inbound tunnel.

"Yeah, well, thanks to you I'm putting a few bars on those windows the second I get back," The Warden said.

"Glad I could help," Jensen responded, but he was only half-paying attention to the conversation. There definitely was a sound. It was close and approaching slowly, like the leisurely swell of distant thunder. Guinevere seemed to hear it too, because she'd turned away from The Warden and was now looking anxiously down the track.

The Warden shot a knowing look to the man on his left and pointed toward the outbound end of The Terminal. "Grab the wagon, Greg, and take it back to the tower. Me 'n' Tommy'll bring him up on the Green Line."

Officer Greg's startled expression was almost heart-wrenching, especially the way his tired, oval eyes lowered like a puppy who knows his master is leaving the house for a few hours. "You ain't coming back with me?"

The Warden shook his head. "He probably won't remember anything, but just to be sure, I'm gonna take him over to High Country for a wipe."

Officer Greg only nodded and then slunk dolefully into the crowd.

Jensen looked over his shoulder. The incoming train had finally breached the tunnel, its flagrant white exterior shining in stark contrast to the darkness surrounding it. It was still several hundred yards away from the junction point but closing rapidly. Guinevere had moved a few steps further away from him, either to get closer to the tracks or to distance herself from the situation.

The Warden gave her a friendly nod. "The fellas told me you stopped by the tower earlier, Gwen." He jerked a finger at Jensen and added, "Thanks for helping me put this one back in the pen."

Guinevere looked down at her feet. Her pervasive smile was now absent, replaced with a look Jensen could only describe as remorseful. "I didn't really do anything, Benjamin," she said. "I just want to get out of here."

The Warden smiled broadly. "Well, thanks all the same, anyway. Pop by for a visit when you're back in town. Been awhile."

Jensen cursed himself for trusting her. He should have been able to read the deceit in her face, but those eyes, and that smile ... they distracted him from what she really was.

Behind her, the incoming train finally hit the junction point and, after a brief stutter, jerked left and joined the yellow track. As it shed its white luminance and became a dirty gold, Jensen couldn't help but appreciate the sheer fuckery of it all. The train he was waiting for had finally arrived, but now he was in no position to board it. Maybe if he jumped at just the right time, he'd be taken to a second afterlife where he could try again.

As if reading his thoughts, The Warden grabbed Jensen's forearm and yanked him away from the tracks. "As for *you*," he said, "we're gonna fix you right up, then send you back home where you belong."

Jensen turned and offered The Warden a dull but functional smile.

"That's great news. I think I left the stove on, anyway."

His smile lingered even as he thought of his dwindling bank account and the waiting divorce papers still sitting unsigned on his nightstand. Of being turned away in Springfield, and of the painting Grange had sent him, the one of the nightclub that never was. He thought of the endless nights when his apartment was dead silent and the ghosts of what could've been crowded his thoughts, not filling the void as crowds should but making it emptier, deeper.

Five million dollars. Maybe more.

Jensen stuck out the pinky and thumb on his right hand and brought it to his ear. "Don't suppose I get a phone call first?" he said, still smiling. "Got a buddy in Township Rebellion who owes me a few bucks."

The Warden didn't respond, and the Yellow Line came whistling to a stop next to them. Guinevere was practically on the edge of the platform now, well over the place where in the real world a safety line would be drawn, her eyes still looking at her feet. Jensen again wondered why she'd helped him only to turn traitor at the last moment.

"I'm sorry, Jensen," she said, still not looking at him. She opened her mouth as if she wanted to say something else, then apparently deciding no words would suffice, turned and slipped through the open doors of the yellow subway car without another word.

Several people had wandered dazedly off the train, and one of them – a man wearing only a fuzzy blue bath towel around his waist – looked to Jensen with wonder as he stepped into the place Guinevere had been just moments before.

"Where *am* I?" the man asked. "Is this ... *heaven?*"

Jensen could feel waves of familiar euphoria pouring out of the open train car like sunshine, but it did absolutely nothing to quell the panic brewing inside him.

"*Almost* heaven," Jensen said, and his exhausted smile finally faltered. "But not quite."

"All right, Bennett," The Warden said with patient authority. "Green line'll be here any minute. Let's shake a leg."

Without another word, The Warden led him toward the green platform and to the mysterious, mind-erasing place to which it led.

***

The advantages of having his memories wiped clean were twofold: He'd forget Guinevere Hatcher, whose skill at deception would make Benedict Arnold jealous, and he'd no longer be burdened with the knowledge that Hedley Grange still existed somewhere, just waiting to spill his million-dollar secret to anyone who asked. The fact he'd had happiness in his sights but let it scamper away before pulling the trigger wasn't something he was eager to remember. At least he'd have his ignorance back.

Yet as he and The Warden approached the blue platform and Jensen saw the squat, low-riding rear of the subway car parked there, he wondered if it was really as hopeless as it seemed. The end of the last car was adorned with railings and short ladders that gave easy access to a recessed door carved into it. If the last car on the Yellow Line was similarly constructed, and if he timed everything just right, there still may be a chance.

The Blue Line jerked and then began slowly inching toward the outbound tunnel, and after it had passed, Jensen looked over the lip of the platform and onto the colored tracks below. The drop was about ten or so feet – child's play after his fall from the tower. The Warden tightened his grip on Jensen's arm as if sensing the foul play afoot and moved him away from the edge.

A minute, maybe less, and his last opportunity to collect on Tabernacle's offer would pass him by, literally and figuratively. It was time to implement his plan, murky as it was.

Jensen fell to his knees and let a short, dramatic cry escape his lips. The

Warden's grip didn't lessen, but his head darted and his legs swayed a bit at the sudden change.

"Bennett? What's wrong?"

Jensen tried to remember how the boy Leslie had acted in the moments before he'd disappeared from his cell – tried to remember every groan and facial contortion.

"Heavy," Jensen panted. "So heavy, like I've been up for a week straight." And then, remembering how Leslie's body had jumped as if his head was attached to a fishing line, Jensen jerked toward The Terminal's ceiling. "Pulling! Something is pulling me!"

If The Warden suspected the ruse, he didn't show it. Crouching down to meet Jensen at eye-level, he put a reassuring hand around his neck. "Don't fight it, Jensen. You can, if you want to, but it's best to just let go."

Jensen didn't see so much as *hear* the Yellow Line squeal to a start somewhere behind him.

Timing, he thought. *It's all in the timing*.

"We should get you somewhere," The Warden continued. His voice was still firm, but the sudden change in plans had clearly set him on edge. "I don't want these people to see you disappear. That kind of thing only happens at the tower, and I'd like to keep it that way."

The sound of the Yellow Line was close now, perhaps only a few yards behind him. Jensen again pretended to jerk, this one a bit more dramatic than he'd intended, but it was just enough to break The Warden's grip.

The other officer, Tommy, stood a few feet away, watching everything with a kind of dumbfounded detachment. The Warden, who was clearly more focused but was scrambling like a quarterback in a collapsed pocket, tried to reestablish his grip. Jensen avoided this with another series of fake shudders, and this time he was able to roll entirely clear of the jailor and his guardsman just as the Yellow Line roared past.

Jensen wasted no time; he tucked his arms into his chest and rolled off the side of the platform. In the fraction of a second before he dropped over the edge, he saw The Warden's expression fade from shocked concern to grim understanding as he realized he'd been duped.

Then the image was gone, replaced with a faintly illuminated darkness and the sounds of smooth machinery in action. He landed, rolled with a skill he didn't realize he possessed, and then stood up and immediately began running toward the ghostly blonde light that was the retreating end of the Yellow Line.

"BENNETT!" The Warden screamed from above in a mixture of anger and frustration. But the sound was all but drowned in the cacophony of wheels on polished rails and the almost organic churning of gears and pistons. There in the dim recesses of the track line the sounds were dominating, overpowered only by a singular thought that ran through Jensen's head like a song on endless repeat:

Five million dollars.

✳✳✳

Jensen could see the door.

Like its counterpart on the Blue Line, it was low to the ground and easily accessible via a series of rails and ladders that hugged the subway car's squat frame. His escape was right there, floating in the darkness like a yellow phantom. There was only one problem: The Yellow Line was accelerating far faster than Jensen was running, and within moments it would slip into the outbound tunnel and become completely inaccessible.

Jensen ran faster, but the irregularly shaped tracks made his progress difficult. Above him he was faintly aware of The Warden scrambling over the edge of the platform, one leg at a time, but this was less concerning than the fleeing subway car. Even if the lawman was in better shape than his stout frame suggested, there was no way he'd catch up to Jensen in time. He was simply too far behind.

There was a slight bend in the yellow track ahead, and Jensen hoped he could use this to his advantage. Unless the laws of physics were vastly different here in the afterlife, the train would have to slow down in order to avoid derailing as it navigated the curve. He looked down, and in the scarce light he could see a smooth walkway running congruently alongside the rails. He jumped onto it and then began to pump his legs even harder. Now that he was on solid ground he started to gain on the Yellow Line, which was indeed slowing down as it approached the twist in the track.

Twenty feet away, then fifteen. Close enough to see the people in the last car through the rear window, close enough to see that Guinevere wasn't among them. Even if she was, he doubted she would fling open the rear door and reach out a hand to help him onto the train. After what she'd done, he wasn't sure he would've taken it, anyway.

When he was about ten feet away, he felt something grab the back of his shirt. It was a light tug, not very forceful, but it was enough to make Jensen realize he'd underestimated The Warden's tenacity. He could almost feel the jailor's imposing figure behind him, and now that he was aware of it, he could also hear the heavy, cadenced pat-pat of The Warden's boots on the cement walkway. The next few seconds would determine if Jensen reached the train before The Warden reached Jensen.

"STOP RUNNING!" The Warden shouted.

Instead of complying, Jensen gave his legs one final push, and he leapt forward. His fingers flailed in the air for a brief second before wrapping around steel just as the Yellow Line cleared the bend and once again began accelerating. With one hand he held on, feet and legs dragging and bumping on the crossties below, his arm struggling with every ounce of strength against the train's attempts at bucking him off as it swayed on the tracks.

He looked back and saw a dim shadow rapidly fading into the darkness behind him. It looked like The Warden was still running, but the train was going too fast now for him to keep up.

If he could hold on, Jensen was a free man.

**

There was a moment of panic as his hand began to slip.

Then, mustering his last ounce of reserve, he reached up with his free hand and grabbed the railing on the other side. Now he was facing the rear door of the Yellow Line and hanging off the bars on either side like they were handles on a bicycle. His stomach was pressed uncomfortably against the small platform that jutted from beneath the door, and his legs dangled over the edge and onto the track.

The train picked up speed and his body jerked rapidly as both feet caught and bounced between the crossties. It didn't hurt, but it would be enough to throw him off if he didn't do something. Grunting, he pulled on the bars until his left leg found the small set of low-hanging stairs. After that, hoisting himself onto the platform was as easy as stepping from one stair to another.

Finally he sat, partially elated and partially shocked that his plan had actually worked. In the semi-darkness he heard the hypnotic click of the tracks and felt the cool rush of air as the train sped even faster through the tunnel, which was lit in a ghostly tangerine light that threw alien shadows on the walls.

Somewhere in that darkness, probably now miles behind, The Warden was no doubt pumping aggravated fists into the air and cursing the day Jensen had popped into his little slice of heaven. That was okay, because Jensen planned on never seeing The Warden or his squadron of afterlife goons ever again. From here on out, it was just he and Hedley Grange, and a mysterious little place called Township Rebellion.

Jensen was still sitting on the Yellow Line's rear platform, thinking these thoughts, when the train exited the tunnel and entered the dusky and dangerous edges of Dim Country.

[silence]

No one has called the cops yet, despite the fact the room is packed with teenagers and the sounds of the party are echoing off the hotel walls and into the street below.

In the bathroom, the sound is muffled and a bit echoey. Someone, he thinks it's Ben Freise, the guy who played Officer Klein, begins singing a horribly off-key version of that Coldplay song, "Yellow." Something breaks, probably a lamp, and the entire room erupts in laughter.

He's fifteen and has never done what he's doing now, but he knows she has. Her hand is working with practiced care down the front of his boxers while his own is brushing against a mound of hair between her legs, blindly searching for an opening he's heard about but has never seen. He finally finds a thin gap and slides a finger in, and she sucks in a hard breath in his ear.

Not so fast, Debbie says in her real voice, not the affected New England accent she used to portray Elaine Harper. *You gotta get me going first.*

Confused, he begins twirling his finger inside her in a counterclockwise direction. His finger feels like it's in sandpaper.

She again hisses in his ear. *No, not that way. There's a little button there. Find it and rub it.*

He searches for the button but can't find it. What kind of button? He's never heard of that before. He keeps searching but can't concentrate. Why isn't he getting aroused? She's getting bored. He doesn't know what to do. This isn't how he thought it would go.

Until this point, the last few weeks have been nothing short of magical. The school's production of *Arsenic and Old Lace*, and especially his hilarious performance as Teddy Brewster, the delusional nutcase who thinks he's

President Theodore Roosevelt, has garnered him friends and popularity aplenty. No one suspects the goofy, carefree, outgoing kid isn't really him, that it's just a coat of paint.

But now it's not working. No matter how hard he tries, he can't slip into the suit of that other boy, the one with all the friends, the one who first caught Debbie Halverson's eye during rehearsals with an offhand joke.

I want to come, she whispers in his ear. *Make me come.*

He doesn't know how, and her hand is starting to hurt him. The longer they go without results, the angrier her hand strokes get. He can't believe he's so unprepared. There's so much he didn't know. Out on the tiles he sees her pink panties and low-cut jean shorts crumpled in a pile and wonders why *that* part was so easy and *this* part is so difficult.

Make me come, she whispers again, perhaps trying to get herself excited in the void of sensation. The frustration is no longer on the fringes of her voice but front and center.

He panics and begins aimlessly rubbing between her legs, not sure where to go or what to do. He's never done this before, but Debbie doesn't know that because she's never met the real him.

Before he knows what's happening, Brian Riggs, piss drunk and still annoyed everyone is gushing over the new guy who played Teddy instead of his own, nuanced performance as Mortimer, barges in. He sees the supporting actor with the lead actress, *his* lead actress, sees the boy's flaccid nakedness as a show of weakness, sees the boy's fingers half-buried inside the girl that should've been his, the girl he's wanted since auditions, and decides he's had enough of this troublesome newcomer.

The boy, the *real* boy, is terrified. He can't move. He can't breathe. He's unable to defend himself, to even pull up his pants, and the blows come raining down on him, one after the other. Debbie screams and tries to pull Riggs off him, but she's swatted away like an insect.

With each hit, the *pretend* boy, that inspired, colorful stroke of graffiti, is blasted away into oblivion, leaving only the bare wall beneath and the singular message written upon it:

Coward. Why am I such a coward?

ARGUMENT FOR A STATELESS SOCIETY

-Track Seven-

Noah DeNova was losing.

He'd lost patients before. Not many, and never because of neglect, but it had happened. Usually he knew the names of the people he lost, had spent time with them, had met their families. But not this man; he was a stranger, a faceless, nameless puppet whose strings had been cut. And Noah was losing the battle to bring him back.

A light rain had started. It was cold and not at all refreshing. Noah was on his knees, the odd position causing his fake leg to sit uncomfortably against his thigh, and he gave the man another shot of epinephrine and checked for a pulse. The lower legs of Noah's jeans were thick with mud, and he could feel the cold rain pooling in his left boot and spreading to the top of his sock, but he continued, undaunted and determined.

The wreckage, most definitely an airplane, continued to smoke in the distance, sending an angry gray streak into the darkening sky. No hope for the poor souls over there; Noah was too far away to reach any of them in time. But the man at his feet was an entirely different story. His patient would probably never walk again, might even be paralyzed for the rest of his life. But Noah wasn't concerned with any of that right now. Right now, his one and only mission was to make sure the man at least had a *chance* to do those things again.

Then the sky opened and rain began to pour down in sheets, masking nature and man alike in the same gray veil.

✳✳✳

The land had turned flat and dusty, and the skies had faded to a darker shade, but the anonymous melody and the colors of light that danced to it remained like a fragile tether.

Jensen hadn't tried to enter the railcar; there was simply no point. The small platform gave him plenty of support, and he was really too deep in thought and too in awe of his otherworldly surroundings to try making the move. Besides, he rode the rails to work every day, and the inside of a crowded train was nothing he hadn't experienced a thousand times before.

The scenery was new, however, at least to him, and despite being relatively monotonous after the eclectic hustle and bustle of Paradise City, the cracked plains and towering buttes were still quite a sight to behold, and the best seat to view it all was right where he was.

The Yellow Line had traveled for quite a while inside the tunnel, which continued to narrow until the walls were so close Jensen could have reached out and touched them. When the train finally emerged from this semi-darkness and began to follow a yellow-tinged track above ground, Paradise City was nowhere to be seen.

The train hugged the track as it cut through a misty mountain, hopped between a heavy patch of tall trees, and then rushed across a green field dotted with seemingly every color of flower in existence. Here they traveled for a while, but the field became less and less green as they went until, eventually, it yielded to the flat, dirty hardpan he now saw.

The train had made two stops so far – once at the place Guinevere had called Ladyland, and another at a small, quiet hamlet that a passing sign claimed was Sleeping Village. Despite its name, Ladyland was nothing special, at least not that Jensen could see; it was just a small community of what looked like motels and strip clubs, with a few grottos and parks thrown in for good measure. Sleeping Village was likewise unspectacular, its wooden cabins and great stone churches standing empty like long-abandoned relics, and as black smoke silently drifted from the chimneys of some of these structures and poured into the ever-darkening sky, not a single sound dared make its presence known.

No one boarded the train at either stop, but many people got off, especially at Ladyland, which Jensen deduced was some kind of haven for the hopelessly lustful. He was unsure if Guinevere was still on the train or if she'd already disembarked. He tried his best to not care but for some reason did.

Now the Yellow Line was moving again, tearing through mile after mile of vacant desert. It was probably mundane to the casual observer, but for Jensen it held a quiet majesty reminiscent of the American southwest and evoked memories of a better, more stable time in his life. For reasons he couldn't quite put his finger on, the sand-swept plains made him think of the painting Hedley Grange had made for him, the one in which *Les Deux Figures*, the imagined version of his finished nightclub, slumbered under a summer sky.

And as if he'd summoned it, the connection suddenly materialized through the trail of dust the train was kicking up: A small firepit was dug into the dirt, its pitch-black crater the last proof of the heat it once entertained. The memory to which it was tied began in the desert near Las Vegas, sometime before the start of the previous tour, back when things seemed like they might be starting to level off for him. Much like the present, the cracked hardpan of that memory had ambled off into every direction, anxious to meet an early-evening sky that was just beginning to reveal its stars.

In this massive emptiness, four friends were huddled around a makeshift campfire. At one end, he and Aimee were holding each other for warmth, she with her head on his shoulder, he with his fingers tucked into the back pocket of her jeans. At the other end, Hedley Grange was plucking an acoustic guitar, trying to put flesh on the bones of a new song he'd just written. Beside him, Susan, his latest girlfriend-of-the-week, was clapping to the absent beat in stoned ignorance.

But that wasn't the memory. Not exactly. Right place, wrong time. It was a bit after that, after the Southern Comfort had made a few rounds, after the unmistakable red flush of inebriation had colored their cheeks and loosened their tongues. *That* was when he'd spilled the secret about the old restaurant on Division and Hoyne, and their plans to transform it into Wicker Park's hottest new nightclub. How his business acumen and her media connections would all but ensure success, about how they were doing it *together*.

The Southern Comfort made another round in celebration, and Hedley had hugged him, tightly, and told him how much he loved him, how unbelievably proud he was to call him a friend, how the band would be there to play the grand opening, how they'd make sure the line to get in stretched all the way to Lake Michigan.

A summer night, filled with friends and laughter, long ago on the dusty hardpan of the Nevada desert. Now Hedley and Aimee were his enemies, and the would-be nightclub was a bounced check away from foreclosure. He'd taken a wrong turn somewhere and gotten lost, but when or where it had happened was a mystery. Maybe he'd *always* been lost. Maybe *nowhere* was home.

The ride had smoothed a bit now that the terrain was more or less even, and Jensen was able to sit on the platform with his legs dangling over the edge and his feet just inches from the track unfolding beneath him. The train had to be going at least two-hundred miles an hour, perhaps more given how quickly Sleeping Village had first become a dot on the horizon and then disappeared completely, but because there weren't many landmarks from which to gauge speed, it seemed the cars were tracking very slowly across the desert.

Eventually, the track below his feet began to slow to the point where he could see the individual crossties between the rails, and moments later the Yellow Line was pulling alongside a long, narrow structure made of wood. Its facade was beaten a dull brown, the wide platform connected to it worn with the traffic of a thousand shoes. Weeds, yellow and sickly, jutted between the gaps in the boards. Jensen's assumption that this was the town's rail station was confirmed when a sign reading "Township Rebellion: Yellow Line" coasted past him.

He didn't wait for the train to stop and leapt from the railcar, landing a bit awkwardly on the crossties below before catching his balance. From this new vantage point, the track looked like a great steel stitch in the earth that wandered with meticulous precision into the smoldering horizon. How far was he from the city now? A hundred miles? Two hundred? He never would have made it here on foot. Not in time, at least.

As he circled the station to avoid the deluge of passengers now elbowing their way across the platform, he became aware of several sounds, each battling for dominance over the hypnotic hum of the railcar. There was laughter, and breaking glass, and the guttural snarl of a motorcycle engine. There were dogs barking, wooden wheels turning on hard earth, the neigh of a lone horse and a car revving its engine twice and then falling into a monotonous idle.

Underpinning this was a swarm of disparate voices he knew was human conversation but sounded more like the indistinct ramblings of some unknowable alien language. Above it all, playing on the air like mist on a predawn meadow, was the anonymous melody, except now it was joined by another song that was at once part of it and yet separate at the same time.

These sounds were the only thing at first that convinced Jensen he hadn't somehow fallen into one of those John Ford westerns he'd seen on cable as a kid, the ones where a mysterious hero rides into town and takes care of the bad guys in black hats before heading off into the sunset. Despite the rickety station and barren desert, this wasn't the Old West. This wasn't even the same plane of existence, if Miguel was to be believed, but Jensen nevertheless felt like a displaced time traveler as he walked around the ancient wooden rail station and came face-to-face with the organized chaos that was Township Rebellion.

His senses were immediately overloaded with information, and for a brief second he was reminded of the pandemonium he'd witnessed when walking into Quiet Catastrophe's show in Springfield. The dancing, the drinking, the drugs, the half-naked bodies covered in dirt and sweat and excitement – it was all here, compressed into an area that couldn't be more than a few city blocks.

The main road was paved in some areas and trampled dirt in others, with nary a traffic sign or stop light in sight. On either side of the street were buildings of such varying heights and spaced so erratically that they resembled the decaying mandible of some ancient monster, creating a kind of asymmetrical honeycomb which people swarmed around like bees.

And swarm they did: Jensen couldn't see one person who was standing still. If they weren't dancing, they were drinking. If they weren't drinking, they were smoking. If they weren't smoking, they were playing horseshoes, or spinning their motorcycles in the desert dust, or spraying graffiti on walls, or making love, or throwing rocks through storefront windows. It was pure anarchy.

Jensen pushed his way through the torrent of bodies until he came to what should have been a sidewalk but was only a long, rotting board pushed into the dirt at an uneven angle. The crowd was a bit thinner on the boardwalk but he still had to shoulder his way through partygoers as he went, occasionally ducking to avoid the errant limb or cloud of pot smoke. As he passed an establishment that was strangely both a classic Old West saloon and a '50s diner – the two seemed fused together as if an angry child had smashed together opposite colors of Play-Doh – he saw something that made him stop.

Taped to the store's filthy front window was a flyer with the word

"WANTED" stenciled above a black-and-white picture of a man Jensen had tried for three decades to avoid running into. It wasn't his reflection, and in fact was a version of himself that was several years younger, probably from an old driver's license, but he still didn't like the way it stared at him with the same scrutiny as the man in the bathroom mirror did. Below the picture was his name, a brief physical description, and the line, "Please do your civic duty and report this man to The Warden if you see him."

"Word travels fast," Jensen said under his breath, and then ripped the flyer from the window and studied it closer. It didn't say what he was wanted for, nor did it have any kind of reward listed on it. He didn't think anyone would waste their time turning him in if there wasn't cash involved, but just to be safe he folded the flyer into a tight square and stuck it in his back pocket.

As he did, a deep baritone voice soaked in a velvety Texas drawl said from behind him, "Won't do you much good, hoss. Whole street's lined with 'em."

Jensen turned defensively and saw a tall man, made even taller by the gigantic cowboy hat atop his head, eyeing him with what was either amusement or suspicion. One arm across his stomach propped up the other arm, which stroked his salt-and-pepper goatee with practiced care. There was a black dog, probably a German Sheppard, panting obediently at the man's side, but other than that, he seemed to be alone.

Jensen looked down the street and, sure enough, each store seemed to have at least one of his flyers taped to its front window.

"Well, shit," Jensen said to the flyers, as if they'd simply sprung up of their own accord just to spite him, then turned back to the man with a wry grin. "Look, I'm just passing through. I don't see any reason to tell anyone you saw me."

He wondered if the man was going to seize him right there on the spot or ask for something in return for his silence, and he was again frustrated by the fact he had nothing to barter with, save for the clothes on his back. This damn world and its lack of anything resembling currency was aggravating. How was he supposed to strike deals without anything to offer?

The man must have seen the tense look on Jensen's face, because he stopped petting his goatee and returned the grin. "Relax, hoss," he said. "I ain't gonna turn you in. Fact is, Township Rebellion is just about the safest place for an outlaw to be. All of us had hots on for nowhere and ended up here. Warden wouldn't get two feet in this town before we ran 'em back out again." He laughed and looked around at the mayhem in the streets. "Might even say he'd be in a worse way goin' out than he was comin' in."

Jensen relaxed. "Glad to hear. I wasn't exactly looking forward to finding out if your dog is as mean as he looks."

"Well, he is," the man said and extended a hand. "Walter Taram. Wrangler, rider, and all-'round sumbitch."

Jensen took Walter's hand and shook it. "Jensen Bennett. Uh, not too handy with a horse, but I once played Frank Butler in *Annie Get Your Gun*, if that counts for anything."

Walter patted Jensen on the shoulder with his free hand and nodded down the street. "Town square's that way," he said. "Beyond that's the desert, and beyond *that's* the Dims. Warden won't follow you there, and I don't blame 'em."

"Actually, I was thinking of catching Codswallop before I hit the road," Jensen said, marveling at how there was no pain in his hand despite the fact Walter was clenching it like he was dangling off the top of a skyscraper and Jensen's grip was the only thing keeping him from falling. "Know where they're playing?"

Walter nodded and finally released his grip. "Sure, sure. Playin' right now, in fact. Take the main road to the fountain, then hang a left. Can't miss 'em. They're right in the street."

Jensen heard music echoing off the storefronts but didn't recognize it as a Quiet Catastrophe song. Perhaps the tune was syncing up so perfectly with the anonymous melody that it masked the song's structure, or perhaps he'd made a big mistake and this Codswallop wasn't the band he thought it was.

"Thanks, Walter. Good to meet you." He gave the man and his dog a friendly nod, then turned to walk away. Before he could take a single step, another heavy hand fell on his shoulder and spun him around again.

"Just a bit of friendly advice, hoss, since you're new in town," Walter said through the side of his mouth. "People here ain't too keen on conformity. The jeans are a good touch, but I'd lose the tie if I were you."

Jensen smiled uneasily and loosened his tie. "Thanks. Good to know."

With that, he stuffed the tie in his pocket and walked hurriedly down the street, doing his best to look like he belonged but failing miserably.

∗∗∗

There was a moment of dread when Jensen rounded the corner and, straining his eyes toward a small stage in the center of the adjoining road, he became convinced the man playing guitar on it wasn't Hedley Grange. The man's hair was neatly tucked into a blue- and white-checkered bandana, and a pair of wraparound sunglasses hid the color of his eyes. He was tearing through an upbeat blues number Jensen had never heard before, playing a kind of guitar – a cream-colored Gibson Flying V – that Grange never used.

It's not Hedley, Jensen thought, and grit his teeth as he realized he'd wasted precious time chasing a false lead.

But his fears abated when the man began singing and Jensen immediately recognized the distinctive timbre of Grange's voice. Ted Choom and Zachary Orrin were somehow brought into clearer focus by the sound, too, and when put together in this new context, jamming on a small stage in front of a modest crowd in the middle of the desert, the trio didn't look like a multimillion-dollar global phenomenon with multiple Grammys and platinum records under its belt, but some middling cover band playing a town festival somewhere in the American southwest. They were hitting wrong notes, losing the groove, flubbing lyrics. Jensen hadn't seen them play this honestly, and have this much fun doing it, in a very long time.

Jensen's heart raced as he realized he was only several steps and a few carefully placed words away from the end of his journey, and this time there wasn't a three-hundred-pound gorilla or an acerbic Englishman standing in his way. But it still wouldn't be easy. He not only had to ask just the right questions, but he had to do so in a way that didn't upset the apple cart. He had to keep Grange calm. Emotions would only cloud the minute facial tics and muscle contractions Jensen needed to see in order to determine the truth. There was no room for error. He'd only get this one chance.

As he slowly made his way through the dancing and swaying masses clogging the street from end to end, Jensen made a decision: He'd put his anger aside. It was his best chance at walking away with the location of the third album and the five million its discovery would bring.

He forced his thoughts to turn to the good times they'd had together – the eleventh-hour excursion to Betaab Valley in Kashmir during a three-day gap in the first world tour; the all-night rager at Josh Homme's Santa Barbara beach house when they all took ecstasy and swam in the ocean in their clothes; the time Grange was able to get him a last-minute seat at the Grammys by convincing security that Jensen was Paul Rudd's stunt double. Even the not-so-great times, like the race to the hospital in which he'd held Grange's lifeless hand and desperately pleaded with him to fight, had underpinnings of their close friendship sprinkled throughout. Good times, bad times; it didn't matter. He and Grange had been inseparable for so long that recalling their comradery wasn't as hard as he'd expected, despite his anger.

As he neared the stage, he could see the men on it much more clearly. Choom, Orrin and Grange seemed to be reveling in the low-pressure performance, playing just for the fun of it and not to fulfill some rote contractual obligation. All three locked eyes and, with nothing more than a simple nod, eased simultaneously into a syncopated groove and began viciously bobbing their heads in unison. Watching them now, it was hard to believe that only a short time ago they'd all been riding a steel coffin into the side of a mountain. The buoyant vibe that their music and onstage antics exuded was almost enough to bring an authentic smile to Jensen's face.

He made it to the front row just as Quiet Catastrophe, or more accurately, Codswallop, reached the song's conclusion and began to hot dog the ending – Grange with an ear-shattering high note that emanated from his chest like an air raid siren, Choom with a series of rapid scale runs up and down the neck of his bass guitar, and Orrin with a frenzied drum fill on the toms and cymbals.

Then, the last song Quiet Catastrophe would ever play together was over, and the crowd exploded. Jensen was pushed even farther to the front of the stage as the bodies swelled behind him, whistling and hollering for more as they punched the desert sky with zealous fists.

This was it. There was no crowd control fencing, so he took one more step forward, close enough to see the inputs and dials on the back of the stage monitor, and cupped his hands around his mouth to shout at the man now throwing double peace signs at the crowd and grinning like a maniac.

But before he could utter a single syllable, a delicate yet commanding voice cut through the clamor, causing everyone within earshot to stop and look in its direction. Jensen expected neither the woman he saw nor the word she spoke.

The word was "Hank," and the woman was Guinevere.

✳✳✳

Grange slowly took off his sunglasses and blinked repeatedly at Guinevere as if she was the tail end of a bad dream.

"*Gwen?*"

At the sound of her name, she stepped from the crowd, wearing a smile so broad it exposed her upper gums and wrinkled the corners of her eyes.

"It's really me, Hank," she said. "I can't believe I finally found you."

The ribbons swam in her eyes as she looked up with anticipation, biting her lower lip and nervously wringing her hands. Jensen had seen fans swoon over Hedley Grange before, but never with the absolute devotion he now saw in Guinevere's face. She loved him, loved him deeply, and not because he wrote catchy songs or made millions of dollars.

Then it hit him: Hank, short for Henry. Hedley's *real* first name. Grange despised his birth name and had it legally changed sometime before they'd met, but in all their years gallivanting around the planet together like gods among men, Jensen had never once heard anyone call him Hank. Until now, of course.

"*Jesus*, Gwen," Grange said into the microphone. "You shouldn't have come here."

It wasn't the response Guinevere was expecting, and she swayed on her feet a bit as if Grange's words were an autumn gale. Her smile stayed, though, and Jensen began to wonder if *anything* was powerful enough to completely wipe it from her face.

"I *had* to come," she said. "I *had* to find you, to tell you how sorry I am. And that I still love you. I never stopped. I can't quit you, baby, any more than I could quit having brown eyes. And I wouldn't want to even if I could."

The audience, which just moments ago had been worked to such a frenzy Jensen half-expected them to start overturning cars and setting buildings on fire, was absolutely silent. Grange sighed deeply, pinched the bridge of his nose and closed his eyes, but didn't respond. An awkward silence followed.

Jensen decided that if he was going to say something, now was the perfect time. But he hadn't expected this impromptu episode of *As the World Turns* and didn't know exactly what to say. All he really needed to do was inject himself into the conversation, and then somehow carefully navigate it in his favor. It was now or never.

Costumes on, curtains up, Jensen thought, and attached a friendly smile to his face.

"If this is what passes for an encore these days, I think I want my money back," he said to the silence.

Grange spun around so quickly that his fingers unintentionally swept across the fretboard of his guitar and played a short, nonsensical song. Guinevere turned, too, and the look of surprised anger she shot his way gave Jensen a momentary rush of satisfaction.

Betcha didn't expect to see me, his eyes shot back at her.

Grange squinted as if looking into the sun. "Benny?"

Jensen nodded. "Hed. Or should I say Hank?"

Guinevere marched up to where Jensen stood and put a finger in his face. Her smile had been a dam holding back the darkness, and now that it had broken, rage poured across her features in a single, devastating torrent.

This is what she looks like behind that smile, he thought. *This is the* real *Guinevere.*

"Dammit, Jensen, can't you see we're trying to talk?" Now that she was aggravated, her Wisconsin accent was front and center. "You're not even supposed to *be* here!"

Jensen's deal with himself to behave evaporated as he swatted her finger down and returned it with one of his own. He couldn't help it; there was something about her that derailed his focus.

"Yeah, and thanks to you I almost wasn't," he said. "First you help me, then you sell me out. What the hell game are you playing, anyway?"

"Love isn't a *game*, Jensen. I'm here for something that really matters, not some stupid revenge fantasy."

Jensen snorted. "*Fantasy*? It's called money, honey, and it's the *only* goddamned thing that matters."

"ENOUGH!" Grange shouted into his microphone. The sound shot through the PA system and into the streets below, shaking the storefront windows in their frames and causing a nearby horse to emit a startled neigh. Jensen and Guinevere simultaneously looked to Grange, who loomed above them on stage like an angry parent.

Grange spoke slowly, carefully choosing the words as he went. "I don't know how in the hell you two know each other, or how you got here, but this isn't the time or place for *any* of this. I want both of you to leave. *Now.*"

Guinevere's mouth worked to say something, but the only sound that came out was a series of exasperated moans. Jensen, on the other hand, had plenty to say, plenty of questions he wanted answered, but he unfortunately only had time for *one*. Resting his arms on the stage and leaning in, he looked his former friend square in the eyes. Despite the barely contained anger in his voice, Grange's face was calm and clear.

"I'll leave, Hed, and never darken your doorstep again, if that's what you want. I just need to know one thing before I go. The third album, *House Made of Sound*. Where is it?"

And then, to drive his point home, Jensen reached into his back pocket, his unflinching eyes never straying from Grange's face, and unfolded the flyer with one deft shake of his arm, like a magician yanking a tablecloth off a table without disturbing the flowers set upon it.

"Wanted for escaping Translucent Tower," he continued, holding the flyer out so Grange could see what it said. "I'm going back, Hed, because I'm still alive over there. But *you're* not. Don't let the last album die with you."

Grange calmly unstrapped his guitar and laid it against his amplifier, ignoring the feedback that suddenly blasted through the PA and then fell quickly silent. Then he walked unhurriedly to the lip of the platform and crouched so that he and Jensen were as close to eye level as the stage allowed.

"Tabernacle made you a deal, didn't he?" Grange said calmly. "Some ridiculous amount of money, I bet. Five figures, easy."

Jensen ignored the question and kept studying Grange's face. "Is it in your penthouse in the city?"

Grange grinned. "*Six*? My god, that fucking miser actually offered you six figures, didn't he?"

Again, Jensen ignored him and continued to look for a twitch, a squint, an expression that would tell him what Grange didn't want to. "It's at Dancing Days Studio, the one in California."

Grange smiled. "Benny, do you really think your Jedi mind trick is going to work on me?"

"Friendship doesn't change the physics of the human face, *Hank*."

Grange's smile faltered momentarily at this, but it passed as quickly as a single frame in a movie reel. "Tell you what, Benny," he continued. "Let's play a little game. Answer one question truthfully, and I'll do you the same in return. Sounds fair, right?"

Jensen thought about it for a moment. What did he have to lose? If Grange reneged on the deal, Jensen could still get the location of the master the old-fashioned way.

"Sure. Shoot."

Grange leaned in closer. The crowd was silent except for an eager shuffling of feet as hundreds of people moved in to hear the exchange to come. Grange smiled and nearly whispered his question: "Why do musicians make music?"

Jensen was caught off guard. He'd expected something personal, designed specifically for maximum public embarrassment, not some wishy-washy question without a definitive answer.

"You'll have to be more specific, Hed. We talkin' Milli Vanilli or the Sex Pistols, here? Because they ain't the same."

"Okay, fair enough," Grange said. "Me, then. Why do *I* make music? And remember, I want the truth. Not what you *think* I want to hear, but what you really believe. I'll know if you're lying, and I don't even need a parlor trick to do it."

Jensen remembered the red carpets, the throngs of fans, the platinum records, the Grammys, the endless procession of girlfriends-of-the-week, the piles of money almost as tall as the piles of heroin, the constant parade of yes-men and ass-kissers, and how all of that had meant more to Grange in the end than their friendship. The images swirled together to form a complete composite of his former friend, the late, great Hedley Grange.

"Honestly, there's a few answers I could give," he said. "You started playing guitar in high school, sophomore year if I remember right, so at first it was all about being popular and getting laid. Later on, though, it became about survival. A way to get out of that Red Line terminal, or at least earn enough to get a hot meal and a pint of Skol before you crawled into your cardboard box for the night. But after the first album took off and you couldn't go six feet in any direction without hearing a Quiet Catastrophe song ... from that point forward, it was all about the Benjamins, baby. And that's my honest answer. Now it's my turn. Where's *House Made of Sound*?"

Grange smiled devilishly, and Jensen instantly realized he'd messed up. "It's in the United States of America. And that's the truth."

This caused laughter to ripple through the crowd, the first audible sign since the conversation started that they weren't all alone in the desert.

"That's not what I meant and you know it," Jensen said through clenched teeth. "Where *specifically* did you hide it?"

Choom and Orrin were both looking at their instruments, inspecting some phantom defect, trying their hardest to make it look like they hadn't heard a word any of them had said. Jensen didn't need to use his parlor trick, as Grange had called it, to know they were feeling as guilty as Judas on a Friday afternoon.

Grange, however, didn't look the slightest bit remorseful as he stood up, walked casually to the microphone and then made a long, abrasive noise into it, something that sounded like the drone of a game show buzzer. This elicited even more laughter from the crowd.

"Sorry, Mr. Bennett. That's *two* questions. I may have been a bit more lenient with the rules if you'd come anywhere close to answering *my* question correctly, but you didn't. Actually, all three answers you gave were wrong, but for the same reason."

Jensen banged a fist on the stage. "Dammit, Hed. Stop the bullshit. Where's the album?"

Grange scowled. "Okay, Benny. You want to stop the bullshit? We'll stop the bullshit. Maybe these folks would like to know why I won't tell you, and why you wouldn't understand even if I did. How about it, folks?"

The crowd roared in approval, and the pent-up anger simmering inside the sound made Jensen very uneasy. He glanced over at Guinevere and sensed she felt the atmosphere change, too, because her mouth had become a single white line that seemed sewed in place. She returned his gaze with wide, unblinking eyes rimmed with angry tears.

"Here's the deal, folks," Grange said, taking the microphone from the stand with practiced familiarity and then stepping forward to address the crowd. "Jensen discovered me. Put the band together. Convinced the label to take a chance on us. He was our friend, our confidant, our ally. The one person in an industry of liars and frauds who we knew was the real deal."

Jensen listened to the air in the brief silence that followed and heard nothing. It seemed as if the entire village of Township Rebellion, once proud to go their own separate ways, had finally agreed on something to do together: listen to Hedley Grange read Jensen Bennett the riot act.

"I'm telling you all of this," Grange continued, "because it's the only way for you to understand why, in our infinite wisdom, we decided to make Benny our legal proxy, free to act on behalf of the band while we concentrated on making music. I'm telling you this to stress the point that, despite the fact he couldn't hold a tune with a hundred hands, Jensen Bennett was, in every sense of the word, our fourth member."

Grange paused and swept his eyes across the crowd, seeming to look each audience member dead in the eyes. Then, slowly and with a contemptuous tone that made Jensen even more unsettled, he added:

"But we were wrong. Jensen was *never* our fourth member. How could he be, when he didn't give a *damn* about the music? How could any *real* member of this band sell us out to a fucking *fast-food* chain and still sleep at night?"

At this revelation, the crowd erupted in an opus of shouts and curses, and as if choreographed ahead of time, everyone took a collective step toward the stage. He and Guinevere, brought together by the surging crowd, were now trapped in a small semi-circle of dead earth. He was so close he could again smell the faint aroma of coconut emanating from her, could feel her left arm shaking with emotion and anxiety. Inside the human cage, Jensen's heart again began beating an unsteady rhythm in his ears, a thunderous *booming* that was so pervasive that it caused the rest of the world's sounds to go in and out of focus.

The commercial, he thought through the clamor. *That stupid Pluckers Chicken commercial.* That's *what started all of this? It couldn't be.*

"Jensen says I only make music for the money," Grange's amplified voice continued. "Truth is, *he's* the one who's the sellout. I wrote the song 'Savor Me' about toxic relationships, about how abusers eat away at their victims, bite by bite like a delicious meal, until there's nothing left. I wrote it about my ma, how she treated us growing up. Because of that song, I was finally able to forgive her."

Grange turned and pointed a finger at Jensen.

"But with just one signature, this guy took something profound and emotional, something that was an artistic statement on the complex nature of family and how you can love someone and hate them at the same time, and turned it all into a cartoonish plea to buy a chicken *fucking* sandwich. Does *that* sound like someone who deserves to be a member of this band?"

There was no hesitation: The crowd bellowed a collective "NO!" Grange quickened his step as he began to pace back and forth across the stage, the cadence of his voice rising and falling like a Baptist preacher as he continued to shout and point into the crowd.

145

"Now he asks if he can have our last record. The last full measure of our artistic integrity, our very heart and soul pressed into being through sheer creative will. Can you believe it? The man who sold us out now wants to do the same to our final album. Should I let him?"

This time, the crowd didn't even wait for Grange to finish asking the question before answering in the negative with a single, thunderous boom. Jensen could almost *feel* their judgmental stares boring holes into the back of his head. He wanted to say something, to correct the lies Grange was spewing, but he suddenly found it hard to speak, to even move. The crowd was angry and growing more so by the second. They couldn't hurt him, not here, not in a place where he could fall from the sky and walk away without a single bruise, and he recognized this fact even as his racing heartbeat betrayed the thought.

Guinevere began beating the stage with her fists. "Stop it, stop it, stop it!" she said over the cacophony of voices. "This isn't how it was supposed to go!"

As if he'd been waiting for her to chime in, Grange spun on his heel and walked toward her.

"It's hard to believe, ladies and gentlemen, but it gets worse. Jensen's just an ignorant suit who thinks making music is no different than buying a lottery ticket. He's about as dangerous as a bumper car." He stopped at the edge of the stage and pointed a calloused finger down at Guinevere. "But *this* one? *Very* dangerous. She's what you get when you combine the poetic soul of a Walt Whitman, the musical acumen of a Joni Mitchell ... and the killer instinct of a Charles Manson."

Guinevere could hold back her tears no longer, and they spilled across her cheeks and dripped into the collar of her blouse as she violently shook her head back and forth. "No, Hank! Let me explain!"

Grange did no such thing. Instead, he turned back to the crowd and slowly swept a finger across their ranks. "Ladies and gentlemen, Township Rebellion is a place to celebrate individuality, not a haven for cheats and liars. We may rally against the establishment, but we never turn on our friends."

Grange paused long enough to look at Guinevere again and added, "Or our lovers."

The crowd shouted in unified affirmation again, and Jensen was elbowed and pushed and prodded from behind. He knew it was only a matter of time before the crowd's anger turned physical, and the thought, even here in this strange afterlife, made him want to throw up.

Say something, make a joke, defend yourself, do something, *goddammit!* he thought, but nothing happened. He was rooted to the ground, an immovable stone coward.

"Gwen says she loves me, and Jensen thinks I should give him the album." Grange glared down on them with a hard look that was cold and distant. "They're both wrong. She's in love with herself, and he doesn't deserve to even *hear* the album. The only thing either of them deserves is directions out of town." Then to the crowd he shouted, "So let's show 'em the way!"

Happiness is out there, Daphne had said, *you just have to know where to look.*

But he wasn't going to find it. Not here, not anywhere, because it didn't exist. Not in the material world, and not in this dry and angry place where friends became enemies and secrets remained secrets forever. It wasn't really in his cell in Translucent Tower, either, because even *that* was a fantasy, an extremely potent but ultimately short-lasting concoction brewed to treat only temporary wounds.

His mind finally disconnected from the sights, the sounds, the smells of the dusty town square as fingers clawed at his clothes, hands grabbed for his wrists, arms wrapped around his neck, all working in accord to haul him backward, away from Grange and into the sentient mass of limbs from which they sprung. The panic, the nausea, the internal furnace, the slow, battering-ram heartbeat, they were all happening to someone else, someone who was being carried across the crowd like a surfer on a wave and then slammed to the ground near a hitching post and the panic-stricken horse tethered to it. There was a woman with him, too, short and pretty and scared, and he watched as the two of them were bound with thick rope, around their wrists, around their ankles, before being lifted once again and laid face-down across the horse's back.

Then more rope, more enthusiastic shouts, more hands holding the two figures down as both ends of their bound limbs were tied together underneath the horse, pinning them to the animal, which bucked and neighed at the sudden intrusion but didn't gallop away. The man and the woman were on opposite ends, her pink sneakers kicking for freedom just inches away from his nose as the townsfolk tightened the slack with a violent, painless tug. It all happened in a haze of disturbed dust that rose from the ground like smoke, a lucid dream brought to life.

The bound man turned to him and spat. *Coward. Why are you such a goddamned coward?*

He didn't know.

✳✳✳

An anticipatory silence filled the air as Hedley Grange hopped from the stage and then began walking toward the two unwilling riders strapped to the horse's back. The crowd parted to let him pass with such obedient precision that it seemed almost rehearsed.

In the newfound calm, Jensen came back to himself a bit. He wasn't hurt, at least not physically, but he was bound so tightly to the animal that he could only move his head. The Pluckers Chicken contract, just one of a dozen he'd signed for the band that day, had for some inexplicable reason led to this very moment. A standard license agreement, nothing special, and now he was tied to a horse.

The thought was ridiculous but irrefutable.

He remembered that day well. It had been an overcast Monday, hot despite the steady lakeside breeze. He hadn't been to work in two weeks, hadn't shaved in three, and was only at the office under threat of demotion. He'd gotten coffee, forced himself through some trite small talk with the Promotions assistant, then slunk into his office to attend to the mountain of paperwork that had accumulated in his absence.

Business as usual, or so he'd thought. One measly signature was apparently all it took to be excommunicated from the band, without a single text or phone call or email to discuss it. Jensen Phillip Bennett, top of the Nadmit, all because of a stupid cartoon chicken and some B-side no one except Grange even cared about. It seemed improbable, and more than just a little unfair given everything he'd done for the band over the years, but there it was.

The realization that this was the end, not just of his quest for something resembling happiness but of his friendship with Grange, filled him with such an abiding sadness that he very nearly began crying. But he held the tears at bay by affixing a smile, sad but acceptable, to his face instead. He rarely cried, even when he was alone, and he wasn't about to start now.

When Grange reached him, he crouched down and spoke in a quiet voice that only Jensen could hear. "You can let it out, Benny. It's okay. I feel like crying, too."

Jensen stared at Grange, who from this angle looked like a phantom as the bright ribbons overhead outlined his frame in an ethereal glow. "You think you know me so well, don't you? Crying is the *last* thing I want to do right now."

Grange gave him an amused smile. "Really?"

"You bet. What I'd *like* to do is go back in time. Five years or so, to a certain CTA terminal on the Red Line. Go back and tell myself to ignore the bum playing guitar, to just keep on walking. Because our relationship has been nothing but one-sided ever since."

Grange huffed. "Is that right?"

Jensen nodded as best he could. "Yeah, that's right. I pull you out of the gutter, make you an overnight millionaire, even save your *goddamned life*, and all I ask for in return is just a tiny bite of the enormous meal I cooked for you. A little taste of happiness, the kind that lasts longer than a few hours and doesn't leave you feeling like shit afterward. But you can't even give me *that* much, can you?"

Grange furrowed his brow as if Jensen had asked him the solution to a complex math equation. "*You* cooked the meal? I didn't know you played guitar, Jensen, or sang. It must've been hard work writing all those hit songs without an iota of musical talent. Kudos to you."

Grange's tone was mocking, his words soaked in sarcasm, but his eyes told a different story. There was a discreet sympathy in them, an unspoken desire to understand. There was still hope.

"Nobody ever doubted who the creative force was, least of all me," Jensen said. "But put Mozart on the moon, and it wouldn't matter *how* well he played, because no one would be around to hear it. The music is only part of it."

Grange laughed, and it was at least partially genuine. "I'm no Mozart. Not even close. And flattery doesn't change anything, including your blatant ignorance."

But Jensen didn't believe him, not one bit. Flattery *was* changing something: Grange was slowly coming around. He just needed a little nudge in the right direction.

"I'm just asking for a little happiness of my own, Hed. That's all. You can help me. *Please*." Jensen narrowed his eyes and looked at Grange as directly as was possible given the constraints of his captivity. "Where's the album, Hed? In your safe deposit box?"

Grange immediately frowned, and Jensen realized he'd pushed too hard.

"Nice try, Benny. But I've seen *Dracula* a hundred times over, and you've got nothing on Bela Lugosi. I think it's time for you to get a new schtick, 'cause the old one sucks." The compassion Jensen had detected in Grange's eyes had completely vanished, and in its place was a sinister doppelganger of the man he once called friend. "You know what, buddy? I think I'm gonna help you find one. Since I'm so in debt to you and all. Just remember ... payback's a *bitch*."

Then, without another word, Grange stood up and slapped the horse on its rear end, discarding Jensen and Guinevere into the desert wastes and whatever terrors lie inside them.

[silence]

The ballroom is hot and crowded with bodies. Myriad conversations, the constant clink of glassware, the over-rehearsed jazz band playing onstage all create a mess of sound that is strangely hypnotic.

He sees the woman by the bar. Her cobalt eyes are stunning, even if the rest of her features aren't. She's not unattractive; far from it. It's just that she's indistinguishable. Unremarkable. The sight of her doesn't stir any primitive feelings within him, except perhaps curiosity.

The woman has been smiling in his direction all night, but she isn't the only one. Next to Bethany Bree, whose debut album everyone's there to celebrate, he's the star of the evening. There'd been smiles aplenty, and sweaty handshakes, and hard pats on the back, and longwinded speeches about how brilliant he was. There'd even been talk of a promotion if Bree's album sold well. He didn't believe any of them.

But the woman's smile is different. It beckons him, dares him to reciprocate. She seems to sense he's thinking these thoughts and looks down at the empty barstool beside her as she lets one of her red high-heels hang precariously from the tips of her delicate brown toes.

He knows who she is – those blue eyes have looked at him many times before, from the inky pages of the Chicago Sun-Times. But he's never met Aimee Barton in person. Until tonight, he's had no desire to, as her reviews are rarely complimentary to his acts.

But tonight is different for some reason. He can tell she isn't looking for an exclusive interview with Bethany. Her smile speaks of genuine desire.

His thoughts race. Images of women's faces flash across his mind like pictures in a flipbook: Jane from his remedial science class at Northern Illinois

152

University. Stephanie from his temp job at Wessler Electronics. Carrie from the coffee shop, Susan from his statistics class at Columbia, Jennifer from the bar where he'd spent much of his graduate years trying to drink his persistent emptiness away. Each one of them had said they loved him, and each one was now just a piece of debris on the path behind him.

Aimee's Mona Lisa smile, the slightly upturned eyebrow, the seductive way she sips her Tom Collins, all fill him with a sense of frustrating awareness, of being lost on a forest trail and coming across a familiar landmark. He didn't want to go through it all again: the introductions, the life story, the first kiss and the awkward amore that inevitably followed ... it was all so tiring and never led to anything lasting. He can't do it anymore. He won't.

He adjusts his tie and runs a hand through his sweat-soaked hair. He knows he's already made up his mind even as his eyes turn toward the exit sign.

Cursing himself, he closes his eyes and treads the path once more.

GRAVEYARD WHISTLE
-Track Eight-

After what seemed like hours, the horse finally abandoned its feverish gallop and slowed to a relaxed trot.

Jensen could see the tracks its horseshoes had beaten into the desert sands behind them and wondered how far they'd traveled. Township Rebellion was nowhere in sight. *Nothing* was, in fact. Aside from a few scattered sand dunes and the occasional cactus, they had the barren wastes all to themselves.

Now that hooves weren't thumping in his ear, Jensen became aware of two sounds simultaneously. The first was the anonymous melody, and it was now playing a sound not unlike biting into a lemon – sour, but not entirely unpleasant. The second was of Guinevere quietly sobbing – small, mouse-like noises that were heartbreaking in their innocence. He couldn't see her face, but by the way her feet were slumped against the horse's side, he guessed she'd simply given up trying to wiggle free and had succumbed to her emotions.

"Guinevere," he said as kindly as he could. She continued to cry, but the sound of his voice must have startled the horse, because it stopped in its tracks and let out a long and unbroken fart. Jensen tried to turn his head away from the smell that promptly came his way, but all he could manage was a slight twist of his head that did absolutely nothing.

"Christ, what'd this horse have for lunch?" he asked. "Taco Bell?"

Guinevere giggled briefly and then continued to cry. He liked the sound of her laugh; even shaded with tears it was beautiful, and he decided he wanted to hear it again.

"So, Mr. Bennett," he said in an announcer voice, "you died and came back to life, saw untold wonders in the world beyond. What was it like?" Jensen changed his voice back to his own and continued. "Well, Chuck, there was a whole lot of sand. Sand and farts. Horrible, horrible horse farts that smelled like Satan's ass crack and tasted like a burrito supreme."

She snickered again and finally spoke. "*Stop it*. I'm really, *really* mad at you."

"Well, that makes two of us. If my hands were free, I'd probably strangle myself to death. Luckily for my neck, Houdini himself couldn't get out of these knots."

The horse neighed in agreement and turned its head toward the two strange passengers on its back. It snorted, sniffed and then, apparently disinterested at what it saw, turned back to gaze at the horizon.

Jensen thought for a moment, listening to the lemon song above, marveling at how beautiful it was despite the ominous vibe underpinning it. Then he said, "Why did you help me?"

"What?"

"Why did you help me? Back on the bus, and then again in the Terminal? If you were just going to let me be caught, why even bother at all?"

She sighed and sniffed in a few tears. "I didn't intend for that to happen. I was going to take you with me, but then you went on that tirade and I realized all you would do is put Hank in a bad mood. Which, I might add, is *exactly* what happened."

"Hey, don't blame that on me. He wasn't exactly thrilled to see you in the first place. What happened between you two, anyway?"

"It's a long story."

Jensen laughed. "Well, it's not like we're going anywhere, is it? Not unless your arms are really Ginsu knives in disguise."

Her feet wiggled a bit. "No, but I was able to keep my legs apart a little bit when they were tying us up. I think I can slip out, but not with these shoes on."

Jensen looked at her ankles and didn't see any slack. "Okay. Maybe I can ... maybe I can get your shoelaces with my teeth or something. Can you get them closer?"

"I think so." Guinevere's feet squirmed until they were about an inch closer to his face. He stretched his neck as far as it would go, close enough to see the frayed aglet on her shoelace, and tried to bite it. It was still too far away.

"One of us is going to have to scooch a bit closer," he said. "I'm pretty well tied up. Do you have enough slack?"

This time she didn't answer, only wiggled like a worm trekking sideways across a sidewalk, first moving her upper half, then her lower half, then her upper half again until she'd gained about another inch. "I don't think I can go any farther," she said after her body was still again.

"That should be enough," Jensen said and again tried to bite the aglet. This time the shoelace caught in his teeth almost immediately, and as he yanked his head back, the lace unfurled. "Great, now the other one."

She repositioned her sneakers, and again Jensen was able to bite down on her other shoelace and pull it free.

"Okay, you're on," he said to her.

Guinevere began flexing and relaxing her toes, again and again, loosening the shoelace's grip on her feet. Then she used one foot to catch the lip of the shoe on the other and kicked it to the dirt. After doing the same to the second foot, she was down to her stockings and began working her legs to increase the slack in the rope.

Jensen could only stare at her toes through the thin black fabric as she worked. He could see her toenails were painted pink, and a thought struck him.

"This may be a strange question, but why do I still feel alive? I mean, I'm dead, just like you, but my heart still races. I'm still breathing. I blink, I cough, I burp. If I'm a spirit, why would I still be doing all of those things?"

Guinevere grunted, but it wasn't because of the question; at least, he didn't think so.

"Our bodies are all we know in life," she said. "When we come here, it takes a long time to realize we don't need them anymore. A lot of people here never do; that's really something for the higher planes. Truth is, you don't have to breathe if you don't want to. It's all in your head, and mine, and everyone else's. It's just habit."

Guinevere was able to get one foot out of the ropes, and then another, and she let out a small cheer as her shackles fell limply to the ground. She was then able to inch down until her feet were touching the ground. She stood up and looked at her wrists, still tightly bound, and began biting at the ropes.

"Why is everything solid, then?" Jensen continued. "Aren't spirits supposed to be transparent?"

She stopped and gave him a sardonic look that said, "Can't this wait?" before going back to trying to free her hands.

"What! It's a valid question. If we're ghosts, we should've been able to just, I dunno, *materialize* through the ropes. Hell, we wouldn't have been able to be tied up in the first place."

Guinevere stopped again and actually smiled. "Jensen, this isn't *Ghostbusters*. We're solid because here, in this plane, we're all comprised of the same matter, vibrating at the same frequency. The material world is quite sluggish in comparison. If we were there, we'd appear transparent because we'd be vibrating too fast for people there to see clearly, if they could even see us at all. But here, everything and everyone is on equal footing."

She went back to work again, and Jensen sighed. "Why don't you try untying my hands first? Then I can untie yours. You're gonna bust a filling doing that."

She squinted at him and frowned. "I don't believe I ever said anything about untying *you*."

Jensen's mouth dropped. Was she serious?

"Need I remind you that you wouldn't have gotten out of those ropes in the first place if I hadn't pulled a Pac-Man on your shoelaces?"

"Look, Jensen, I plan on going back to Township Rebellion. I have to talk to Hank, to smooth this out. Why you did what you did is your own business, but right now you're a liability to me. I'm sorry."

Jensen couldn't believe his ears. Was she really going to just leave him there?

"Listen, Grange blew that all out of proportion. Licensing songs for commercial use is standard practice, and it's not like Pluckers Inc. even used the actual song. It was the stripped-down, bare-bones version from the demo we tracked to get Wicked to greenlight a full album. I signed off on hundreds of things just like that as their proxy over the years, but for some bizarre reason, 'Savor Me' got stuck in their craw. Really, I *paid* for the goddamned demo in the first place, so I don't think I did anything wrong. I was just selling my own recording."

Guinevere continued to bite at her ropes as if he'd said nothing. Anger suddenly welled inside him, but he closed his eyes and forced it back down again. Yelling at her wasn't going to change her mind; in fact, he was positive it would only reinforce her decision to leave him there. He'd been in tough business dealings before. Never tied to a horse, but close. He just had to find common ground.

"Okay, listen," he said calmly. "Here's why you should untie me. You apparently knew Hed before I met him but not after, because I never saw you around, ever. Each of us knows a bit about him that the other doesn't; me as his best friend, you as ... well, you as whatever you were. What if we worked together? I want the master, and you want to rekindle your romance. We can help each other get what we both want."

Guinevere stopped biting the rope again and thought for a moment. "We didn't do so well together at Township Rebellion."

"That's because we were at odds. Trust me, I know Hed like the back of my hand. I can help you reach him. And maybe you can help *me* reach him, too. He's still in there somewhere. I saw it in his eyes right before he sent us packing."

Guinevere stared off into the desert, no doubt considering the pros and cons of his proposition, and Jensen was suddenly taken at just how naturally beautiful she was. No makeup, no hair products, no jewelry. Just her and that fiery mane of hair, and she was absolutely gorgeous. She could be frustratingly pigheaded at times, but she was also smart and playful and, despite leaving him at the mercy of The Warden, a pretty decent person, it seemed. The more he thought about it, the more he realized Grange was an idiot for turning her away.

She sighed deeply. "Okay, Jensen. We have a deal. But I'm not going to stop until he hears me out. I'll follow him to Beast Country and back if that's what it takes. Are you ready for that?"

Jensen smiled. "Not sure what Beast Country is, but it sounds like Jurassic Park. Always *wanted* to see a real-life stegosaurus." He nodded as much as the ropes would allow. "Count me in."

"You're actually not that far off," she said and, without another word, crouched down and began untying his hands.

It was only a few minutes later when they saw something kicking up dust on the horizon and realized they weren't alone in the desert, after all.

✳✳✳

Jensen's first instinct was to run, but that was instantly followed by a sobering thought: Run where? Even if he and Guinevere mounted the horse and began to gallop at full speed away from the approaching dust cloud, there was nowhere to hide.

As the disturbance came closer, he saw it was being made by a vehicle, something that looked like a Range Rover with no roof, and it had to be going close to a hundred miles an hour. He looked at the horse and decided Old Farty would be lucky to get to a fraction of that speed. Then he turned to Guinevere, who was sitting on the ground and struggling to yank her sneakers back on her feet.

"Thoughts?"

She glanced at the Rover. "Could be anyone, really. There're all sorts of transients out here on the edges of the Dims."

"Dangerous ones?"

"Some of them, sure." She finished tying her laces and then stood up next to him. The Rover was almost upon them, and Jensen could see two figures inside. If they were going to do something, they had to decide quickly.

"Maybe they'll just drive right past us." But even as he said it, he knew it wasn't going to happen.

The Rover began to slow down, and now that it was closer, Jensen could make out the faces of the two figures. One was Walter Taram, the cowboy with the gigantic hat who'd warned him to remove his tie, and he was driving. The passenger was none other than Ted Choom, bassist extraordinaire and perhaps the only one in Quiet Catastrophe's entire entourage who had done more cocaine than Jensen. Had they come to take them back? Or were they here to finish the job the townsfolk had started?

The Rover pulled to a sudden stop, kicking up even more dust and making the two men nothing more than cloudy shapes as they opened the doors and got out of the vehicle.

"If you guys are looking for Albuquerque, I think it's that way," Jensen said and pointed the way the Rover had come.

The men stepped forward, and Walter's walk was broad and aggressive, as if he'd just as soon punch Jensen than say hello. Choom, however, smiled and put his hands in the air in the universal symbol for surrender.

160

"We come in peace, Benny," Choom said.

"Like *hell* we do," Walter said, and walked up to Jensen until their noses were nearly touching. Jensen's jaw clamped down and his heart skipped in his chest, but he held his ground. "I *warned* you, hoss. I warned you and you didn't listen to me. And because you didn't I had to haul ass all the way out here to the goddamned Dims to get my horse back." Walter gave him a final contemptuous look and then walked past them to the horse, which he began petting. "Easy, Dolly. Papa's here."

Jensen relaxed and turned to Choom. "Teddy."

A set of meticulous teeth crept from the center of Ted's brown beard. "Man, I can't tell you how surprised I was to see you back there," Choom said. "How the hell did you *get* here, anyway?"

Sensing that the bassist wasn't there to cause trouble, Jensen extended a hand, which Ted took.

"Same way as you," Jensen said. "I snuck into Hed's wardrobe case back in the green room. Thought I could talk some sense into you guys on the plane, but all I got was a first-class ticket to Hogwarts."

Choom shook his head in disbelief. "It all happened so fast. One minute we were going down, the next we were riding a train. No pain, nothing. I still can't believe it."

Jensen smiled. "Tell me about it."

"So you're really going back? How do you know?"

"A guy called The Warden told me. You probably didn't meet him, but he's apparently the custodian of folks like me, people who are technically dead but not necessarily for good. I guess I was one of the lucky ones."

Or unlucky, he thought. *But only if I come back empty-handed.*

"Teddy, where's the third album?"

Choom laughed. "Man, Benny, you really *do* have a one-track mind, don't you? I don't know, and that's the truth. Hed took the master after me and Zach laid down our parts. I don't know what he did with it afterwards."

Jensen nodded. So Nigel had told him the truth. Wonders never cease.

"I thought as much," Jensen said. "Well, that means we have to go back to town and talk to him again. Maybe if you came with us, we could –"

"You can't, Benny. He's not there anymore."

Guinevere, who'd been watching this reunion in bored silence, finally stepped forward. "What do you mean, he's not there anymore? Where the hell *is* he?"

Choom looked at her and bit his lower lip. "Gwen, right? I'm not sure." He looked back at Jensen again and continued. "After Hed's little outburst, after he sent you guys off, I told him he should've just told you where the album was. It's not like it's going to do us any good anymore, and despite your motivations, at least you can make sure it gets heard. He didn't agree, and we fought. Zach just sat back there on his drum kit and said nothing, like always. You know how he is. But Hed and I really went at it. I've never seen him so angry, so *full* of himself before. Finally, he told Zach and me to fuck off, said he didn't need us anymore. Said *he* was the band, and we were just glorified session players. Said he was going somewhere he'd be appreciated. Then he just stormed off."

"Shit!" Guinevere shouted and walked a few angry paces away from them.

Jensen was able to temper his disappointment enough to continue. "Which way did he walk? Was it this way?"

"I don't remember. Right after our fight I went to find someone who could take me out here to untie you. We may have grown apart, Benny, but I still think you're a good dude at heart. You didn't deserve that."

Jensen put a hand on Choom's shoulder. As was often the case when he was around friends, the smile he offered was a little less forced. "Thanks, Teddy. That means a lot. More than you know, actually. I just wish Hed agreed with you."

"The mirrors!" Guinevere suddenly cried and walked back to Jensen. "Hank said he was the only one who mattered, said he was going somewhere to be appreciated. I bet he's on his way to the Room Full of Mirrors."

"What the hell is that?" he asked.

"A place you'd be an idiot to go to," Walter said from behind them. "Just give it up, hoss. The guy made it pretty clear he wants nothin' to do with you."

Jensen turned and saw that Walter was now feeding Dolly a carrot and gently petting her muzzle.

"Not true," Jensen replied. "I was reaching him. Before he slapped Dolly and sent us out here, I was getting through to him. I just made the mistake of going for the hard sale. If I can get him one-on-one, he'll crack. I *know* it."

Guinevere grabbed Ted's arm gently and smiled. "Ted, any chance you could drive us to The Dark Train? In that Rover we'd be there in no time."

Ted's brow wrinkled. "Not sure what the hell The Dark Train is. Besides, it's not my ride."

Guinevere snapped her fingers. "Yeah, I guess you wouldn't know. You're just as green as Jensen. It's the Black Line. Leads right into Dim Country."

Walter gave Guinevere a sour look. "You're crazier than pig shit if you're thinkin' of goin' deeper into Black Country, woman. I'm a bit spooked just being *here*, and this ain't even close to bein' the bad part."

Jensen wasn't keen on going to this mirror room, whatever it was, but he would if he had to. But he also didn't want to waste what little time he had left. He gently grabbed Guinevere by the shoulders and looked her in the eye.

"How sure are you that he's there?" he asked her.

"Nothing's for sure. I'd say fifty-fifty. But where else would he go? The Room Full of Mirrors is for the vain, people who think they're much more important than everyone else. Hank's state of mind right now, who knows? He might be drawn there."

Jensen turned back to Choom. "Teddy? Was he *that* far gone?"

Choom nodded. "He's never acted like that before. It was like I was talking to an entirely different person. I could totally see him going to a place like that."

Jensen ran a hand through his hair, which was now covered in speckles of sand and dust, and weighed his options. He could return at any moment, and a wrong path would be fatal to his quest. But what other choice did he have? Guinevere knew much more about this place than he did, and he trusted her opinion, if only because she wanted to find Grange as badly as he did.

He looked to her. "Let's do it." Then, to Walter, he said, "Mind if we borrow your wheels?"

Walter looked to Dolly and began rubbing his goatee once again as if it held the answers to all his thoughts. "Can't take her *and* the truck back at the same time. Might as well let you folks use it. But I'm tellin' you, hoss, it's a waste of time. And incredibly dangerous. Don't blame me when the Dims swallow you up for good."

"I won't." Yet even as he said it, something fluttered in his stomach and he hoped Walter's warning wouldn't come back to haunt him.

***

The Rover was only a two-seater, so Guinevere had to sit on Jensen's lap as Choom drove them deeper into the growing darkness. Her small frame was warm against his body, her hair still tinged with the smell of coconut despite the dirt and sand clinging to it. Whenever they hit a rock or crested a sand dune, Jensen would grab Guinevere's thighs to keep her from spilling out of the vehicle. She didn't seem to mind, and neither did he.

The skies had dimmed to a sickly purple, the ribbons of light therein no longer dancing but stumbling across the horizon as if drunk. The melody in the air had changed, too. Now it was playing only in minor keys, a cheerless sound that was a bit unsettling given the darkening horizon.

Jensen thought the desert would never end, but it eventually did after the Rover crested another hill and he saw the sands slipping quietly into an enormous black sea that gurgled and bubbled like boiling oil. Down by the seaside was a small building, beside which wound a malevolent scar in the earth that Jensen realized was a train track.

"There!" Guinevere cried and pointed. "The Sick Sea. Take us there, Ted."

Choom obliged, and Jensen moved his head to the right so he could see her face. "Sick Sea? I thought we were going to some mirror room."

She continued to point. "We are. The Sick Sea is the last place in the Outer Dims before it turns into Dim Proper. The Dark Train makes one stop, right there, and goes straight to the Room Full of Mirrors. This is the way there."

"Grange would've had to come this way, too?"

She nodded as Choom navigated their last obstacle – a large pile of what looked like discarded pill bottles – and pulled the Rover next to the building. Apart from a few discolored panels and a broken window, it looked like a smaller version of the station he saw in Township Rebellion.

The interior of the building looked completely empty, but sitting outside with his legs dangling over the platform was a sallow-looking man with sunken eyes and tattered clothes playing a beat-up old acoustic guitar and singing quietly. The tune was slow and gloomy, the kind of song that would be right at home in a funeral procession. Jensen wasn't sure, but he thought it was a severely detuned and depressing version of Led Zeppelin's "D'yer Mak'er."

Guinevere opened the door and hopped off his lap, and a sudden chill swept through him in the absence of her body heat. He looked over to Choom and put a hand on his shoulder. "Thanks, Teddy. You didn't have to come out here, but you did, and I thank you for it."

"No prob, Benny. Just do me one favor, please?"

"Anything."

Choom cleared his throat and looked down. Jensen had rarely seen Ted emotional, except when his beloved Colts blew a game, but he was very nearly on the verge of tears now. "When you get back, tell Emily I'm okay. Tell her I love her very much. Tell her my life was so much better because of her."

"Consider it done. And thanks again."

Ted only nodded and continued to look down, so Jensen gave him one last pat on the shoulder and then got out. As Choom pulled the Rover around and began trekking back the way they'd come, Jensen realized it was probably the last time he'd ever see him. It made him sad, but he was also glad he'd been able to mend fences with at least *one* old friend.

"Jensen." Not a question, but a statement. He turned around and saw Guinevere looking at him with stern eyes.

"I'm here."

"I just want you to realize what you're getting into before we do this. The Dims are horrible. They make Township Rebellion look like paradise. I've never been there myself, and for good reason – there's a real danger we could get trapped there, even someone like you who hasn't completely shed the material world. The sorrow and apathy and outright evil that dwell in the Dims are like a plague that can infect your soul and make you a slave to it forever."

"I understand," he said immediately. "I'm ready."

He wasn't, not in the slightest, but if he stood here and thought about it for too long, he just might start to doubt his decision to trust Guinevere's instincts. Five million dollars, and perhaps his eternal sanity, was resting on her hunch. It was crazy, but it was also the only option.

He expected Guinevere to press him further, to encourage him to mull it over for a few minutes before deciding, but instead she sighed with relief and smiled grimly.

"Good," she said. "To be honest, I wasn't really looking forward to going in there all alone." Her big brown eyes scanned his face again. "I'm actually kinda glad you're here."

He returned her smile. "Same here."

Sickly Man continued to play as the tune again seemed to meld with the ever-present melody in the sky. These sounds, combined with the gurgling of the Sick Sea mere feet away, gave Jensen chills. He had to be strong; if Guinevere was right, this was nothing compared to what they were going to face.

"What now?" he asked.

"We wait." She grabbed his hand and led him toward the platform. "This train's a bit different than the ones in The Terminal. It comes and goes as it pleases. Hopefully it'll grace us with its presence sooner rather than later."

"Fantastic," he said. "A temperamental train."

As they approached him, Sickly Man ended one song and began another. The notes that crept from the darkness were slow and somber, the kind of sound despair would make if it were sentient enough to speak. He immediately recognized it as "Fell on Black Days" by Soundgarden. Sickly Man even *sounded* a bit like frontman Chris Cornell as he began singing the first verse.

Guinevere must have recognized it too, because she let go of his hand and walked up to the man. She didn't say anything, just stood there and listened. After a moment of this, she began rocking back and forth, very slowly, as if in a trance. When the man began singing the chorus she mouthed the words along with him. The man continued as if they weren't even there.

"Hey," Jensen said. "You okay?"

She made it as far as the second verse before tears began streaming down her face, and as they fell, they cut long, clear tracks into the desert dust that covered it. Jensen rushed over and put an arm around her shoulder, and to his surprise she turned around and embraced him. The tears came faster and she sobbed against his shoulder.

"Hey, Gwen, it's okay," he said. "Don't worry. We'll find him."

But in that moment, holding her tightly against him, stroking her hair, feeling her delicate frame shake in his arms, realizing how graceful even her cries sounded, he wondered if he really wanted her to find Grange, after all.

✳✳✳

That song. That *stupid* song. It wasn't even a love song. Why did it make her hurt so much?

167

She knew why, of course. It was *their* song. The song she'd been playing that night at the bar. She'd broken a High E before she'd even gotten to the first chorus, and he'd rushed to the stage like Sir Lancelot to restring it for her while she continued singing acapella. It had taken him less than thirty seconds, and all she could do was sing into his gorgeous blue eyes as he worked, dumbstruck at their power.

That was the day they'd met, and this depressing song would always be associated with that intense, glorious delirium that had swept over her that night. It was strange, but it was true.

She took a few deep breaths and was able to stem the tears, at least for now. She liked the way she and Jensen fit together, like interlocking puzzle pieces; he was warm and strong and safe. There was also something nostalgic about him, like looking at an old photograph of better days. It could just be a symptom of prolonged denial, but she suddenly decided that Jensen was going to be the one she finally confided in. She hadn't talked about that last night with Hank to anyone, not even her gang at The Pot and the Pan, but for some reason she felt she could unload on Jensen and he would understand.

Guinevere pulled away and looked up at him, arms still wrapped around his torso. "Remember when you asked what happened between me and Hank? I think I'm ready to tell you, if you still want to know."

"Of course," he said and smiled sadly. He looked different somehow, strangely *more* defined than before despite the perpetual dusk of the Outer Dims. She was noticing things that had evaded her in better light: the wavy brown hair, the strong chin, those gray, almond-shaped eyes ... he really *was* quite handsome, even with that unusual scar on his forehead that kind of looked like a barking dog.

She wondered how he'd gotten it – perhaps one of his off-color jokes had rubbed someone the wrong way – but realized then that her mind was wandering and he was still looking at her with expectant eyes. She nodded apologetically and then took his hand, leading him to the other side of the platform, away from Sickly Man and his damned song. When they'd gone far enough that the music was nothing but indiscernible background noise, they took a seat together beside the churning banks of the Sick Sea.

"Okay." She took another deep breath to steady herself. "I know I said before that it's a long story, but it's really not. That was just me avoiding the question. We were only together for a few months. But what a fantastic few months it was."

She told him about the open mic night, how she'd been playing the Soundgarden song, how she'd broken a string and how he'd changed it for her, how lost she'd become in his eyes, how right away she'd wanted to run her hands through his long, blonde hair and kiss those firm lips of his. She blushed a bit at this last part.

"We fell in love. *Hard*. It didn't take long either; a week later he was calling me his girl and we were inseparable. It was like I'd finally filled an emptiness in my life that I always assumed could never be filled."

Jensen's mouth rose in a grim half-smile at this, and she could tell without even asking that she'd struck a familiar nerve with him.

"We became a duo. Two guitars, two voices, and we'd play open mic nights all around the city. We only sang covers at first, because he wasn't very good at writing songs back then and I was too shy to show him mine, but eventually I got a backbone and we started putting some of my originals in the set. We even recorded a demo, can you believe it? He sold his car just to pay for it."

Now came the hard part. She wasn't sure if she could get through it, but she felt like she at least had to try.

"One day after a show, I was approached by this talent scout from Atlantic Records. He said he loved my voice, loved my songs. He wanted me to sign with his label, but I had to drop my boyfriend and go solo. Of course I told him I wasn't going anywhere without Hank, but ... something changed in me after that. I started to get ... started to get, I dunno, conceited? Like my songs were the only reason people were coming out to see us. It's hard to explain."

169

Jensen nodded. "I used to be a talent scout. I've seen it before."

A single tear fell down her cheek, and she made no attempt to wipe it away. "A few weeks later, Hank came up to me and told me he wrote a song. I asked him to play it for me. *God*, Jensen, it was *horrible*. I feel like a terrible person for saying that, but it really was. I tried to let him down easy, but he got angry and said I didn't appreciate him as an artist, that I was just with him because he was a good lay. None of that was true, but it didn't matter. We had the first, and last, argument we ever had. He said my songs were garbage, too, and I got so angry, I … I told him … told him I didn't need him. That I … that I had label interest and he was only holding me back. I …"

She couldn't hold the tears back any longer and let them come again. Jensen again held her until they subsided.

"It's okay," he whispered. "You don't have to keep going."

"No. I want to, Jensen. The end of this story is how I got here. It's how I died."

✳✳✳

Guinevere's voice grew quieter and her pace quickened, as if Jensen was her confessor and she wanted to get everything out before the hangman led her to the gallows pole.

"So we broke up. Just like *that*, and he was out of my life, all because of some stupid song he wrote. And you wanna know the real kicker to everything? When I called Atlantic to reach the talent scout, to take his offer, they told me they'd never heard of the guy before. Turns out he was just some asshole trying to get me in the sack." She shook her head in frustration. "I was so embarrassed. The guy had a business card and everything, even spoke the lingo. I was so stupid."

She paused for a moment to reflect on this and then continued.

"Anyway, our breakup destroyed him. He started drinking. Then he lost his job, his apartment, his *mind*, actually. A few weeks later a friend told me she saw him playing guitar in an El terminal for spare change, and it just tore me up. I still loved him. I wanted him back. But I was too prideful at first to go to him to apologize, because I just felt so stupid for what I'd done and how I'd acted. But eventually the ache got to be too much to bear, and I cracked. I went to see him. I wish I hadn't."

She paused again to collect her thoughts, the war behind her eyes raging on as she struggled for the final words.

"I tried to apologize, but he just kept drinking, and playing guitar, and thanking anyone who threw change into his guitar case, pretending I wasn't even there. I didn't like it. It hurt to be ignored like that, and I got angry. I said some really mean things to him."

She made like she was going to cry again but caught herself just in time.

"I said I hoped he drank himself to death," she continued. Her voice was small and sad. "Said I was better off without him anyway, that I was going to be a big star someday and he'd be sorry he let me go. He didn't respond to any of it. Maybe he was too drunk to even realize I was there, I don't know. He was a wreck. So was I. When I left the El station, I was crying so hard I could barely see. Driving home I was ... I ran a red light. A car hit the driver's side head on. Killed me instantly, or so I was told, because I don't remember the accident at all. And then I was here."

During the last part of her speech she'd barely taken a breath, but now that she was done she inhaled, long and deep.

Jensen didn't know what to say. Grange had told him about losing his job, and his apartment, and about his drinking problem. But not about Guinevere. It was a secret he'd never shared. But their breakup must have occurred just before Jensen met him, because Grange said he was only in the El station a short time when they recorded the demo. Was it Guinevere, and the news of her death, that had brought out Hed's latent greatness? Jensen didn't know, but he suddenly felt like he owed Guinevere an apology.

"I didn't know any of this," he said. "I'm so sorry I brushed you off in Township Rebellion like that. If I'd known, I –"

"It's okay, Jensen. You *didn't* know. And I could have been more truthful with you back in the Terminal. Maybe if I had, we could've come to an agreement earlier and wouldn't be here right now."

They sat in silence for a bit, his arm around her shoulders, her head resting on his chest, each giving the other comfort as the black sea chewed and spat its sickeningly organic sonata around them. This continued for a few minutes, neither one of them daring to break the quiet between them, until the platform began to beat a baleful rhythm beneath them.

Jensen looked down the track and saw a ghostly purple light cutting through the gloom, a pinprick that punctured the veil of darkness like a distant sun on a starless night. Jensen nodded to it. "I'm guessing that's our ride."

"The Dark Train," Guinevere said, as if the words were haunted. "I've heard stories about it but never saw it."

He looked at her. She'd stopped crying, but her eyes and cheeks were still damp with old tears. "This is it, huh? No going back once we get on."

She only nodded solemnly and stood up. He did the same.

A deafening scream suddenly rose from the darkness, a long and mournful howl that was equal parts human and mechanical, and they both instinctively jumped back into each other's arms. Even after it faded Jensen could still hear the sound inside his head, echoing endlessly from some joyless void.

"Was that ... a horn?"

She slowly nodded her head. "I think so." He could see the fear in her eyes and wondered if she could see it in his. "Jensen, I'm scared."

He held her tighter. "Me too."

Seconds later a long, dark shape was rushing in, hissing and churning and struggling, an ancient machine with rusted gears that spilled faint purple light across their faces and exhaled a foul gust that blew their hair back. As it began to slow, he felt her hand creep into his own and squeeze. He squeezed back.

Then The Dark Train was screaming to a stop, no longer a blur but a defined shape, and Jensen could see the individual rivets that pockmarked its swarthy frame like sores. It rippled as if millions of insects were crawling across its surface.

When the train was finally still, idling with the dissonant and sickly sound of damaged machinery, Jensen was struck with an insane urge to reach out and touch the machine, to see if its darkness would dart up his arm and swallow him, but he only stood there, squeezing Guinevere's hand and working up the courage to continue.

The cabin door squealed open of its own accord, startling them both. The sinister purple light above the opening revealed a set of skewed stairs that ascended into gloom, and they looked to each other one final time.

"Jensen, are you sure?" she whispered.

Five million dollars. Maybe more.

He swallowed hard. "Yes. I'm sure."

Without another word, they stepped onto the train, still holding hands, still hearing The Dark Train's murderous horn ringing in their heads, still praying that their one and only salvation was lying somewhere ahead in the perilous shadows of Dim Country.

[silence]

He fumbles with his keys until he realizes the front door is already unlocked. Not a good idea, even in West Town, but he doesn't let himself get angry. He hasn't seen her in nearly five weeks and doesn't want to let an argument ruin his surprise appearance.

Still, he'll have to mention it at some point. The nightclub is under renovation and there's not much inside except for a ladder and a few scattered paint buckets, but that's not the point. In a few months there will be *plenty* of stuff to steal, and leaving the drawbridge down for pillagers simply isn't good for business.

He's exhausted from the tour, which by now is somewhere in Texas, probably El Paso, continuing to rage on despite his sudden departure. He hadn't wanted to go on tour in the first place; he was needed here to help lay the groundwork for their future. But she'd insisted, and so had Hedley, and together they'd worn down his resolve. Separately he could face them, but together they were unstoppable.

He throws his coat on the floor, by what will one day be the greeter station, and moves through the empty space, already imagining the flurry of activity that will soon inhabit it. He calls her name, and when there is no answer, he stumbles through the darkness until he reaches the stairs leading to the second-floor apartment.

He's only halfway up them when he hears it: The squeak of bed springs. There are other noises, too, but he doesn't want to hear them and keeps walking.

He opens the door, and for some reason, it doesn't creak like it usually does. The room smells of sweat and sex and spent candles. Aside from a pair of knee-high white socks that stand in stark contrast to her russet skin, she's completely naked, hands gripping the brass headboard as her knees seek purchase on the silk sheets. He's behind her, head raised, eyes closed, sweat running down his back as he holds her bare shoulders for leverage and works her, again and again. She whispers that she wants it harder, and he obeys.

An unfamiliar moan, at least to him, rises above the squeal of springs and the thump of the headboard, and her entire body begins to shiver as if touching a live wire. He's never made her do *that*, either, not once, not even close. She'd said it didn't matter, that she loved him anyway, but it apparently *did* matter, mattered a lot. He always knew it did, always knew she knew it did, too, but neither one ever told the other they knew, just continued pretending as if nothing was wrong. This is the result of that shared deceit.

Pulling the man off his wife is the easy part; he's shorter and skinnier and weaker, the only indication of his superiority standing like a white stone pillar from between his legs as he hits the floor hard and scurries backward in fear across the carpet. She screams, and so does he as he raises a fist in the air, wanting to beat the stupid, shocked expression from the man's face even as his heart pumps white hot fire throughout his body.

But he can't do it, and he knew he couldn't do it before he even started, because he's a coward, because this is *his* fault, not the terrified man at his feet, not his wife, who's now covering up her nakedness with the bed sheets as if *he's* the intruder.

Before he storms out, to go someplace he can drink this entire evening away, he turns to his wife and shouts, for once not hiding the disappointment and anger in his voice.

Next time lock the goddamned door.

175

BREAKING GLASS
-Track Nine-

When he was seven, Jensen visited the Illinois Railway Museum in Union, where hundreds of monstrous steel beasts sat silently on rusted rails, extinguished headlights staring mournfully off into a horizon they would never again visit.

There had been one exhibit, an old California Zephyr dome coach, splayed out on the tracks like the discarded finger of a giant stainless-steel robot, and from it seemed to emanate the wail of a passing crossing bell, the relaxed blare of a train horn, the hypnotic click of wheels as they turned across the jointed rail. He'd never ridden a train before, had never even *seen* this make or model, but he couldn't shake the feeling of familiarity as he took a few tentative steps into its dimly lit cabin and inhaled the ancient air inside.

He'd been alone, but also not alone. The ghosts of all the people who had ridden the train throughout the decades were there with him, *invisible* but there, reading their newspapers and smoking their cigars and drinking their Scotch on the rocks and going about their lives as if it was still 1949. They were long dead, yet there they lived and would continue to live until the end of time, if only in his mind.

The Dark Train also had ghosts, only these weren't facsimiles of an overactive imagination but real figures that clogged the aisle, slouched in the seats and clutched the pole grips, hundreds of transparent photo negatives with shimmering obsidian eyes and gaping black holes for mouths that all seemed stuck in a perpetual scream. In the pale purple gloom that consumed the cabin, they looked like secret stains exposed by the invisible glare of a black-light.

But it wasn't the sight of the figures that unnerved Jensen so much as it was the *feeling* inside the cabin: an oppressive, abiding negativity that persisted like stifling summer heat inside a locked car. Hatred, fear, prejudice, vanity and hundreds of other emotions too intertwined with each other to clearly define enveloped him as the cabin door squealed shut and The Dark Train lurched drunkenly forward.

The figures slowly turned their heads in unison to scream in silent horror at The Dark Train's newest passengers.

"They aren't real," Guinevere said as if answering a question Jensen hadn't asked. "Not like you and me, at least."

"What are they?"

"Afterthoughts. Kind of like perfume lingering in a room long after the person wearing it leaves."

There was no room to move, so they stood, huddled together in the entranceway, whispering to each other like conspirators. Real or not, Jensen knew he couldn't spend another second where he was. They'd only just stepped onto the train and already his mind was racing with numerous impulses, none of them good. He wanted to scream, to claw at his face until he ripped the skin clean off, to punch the cabin wall until his hand was nothing but bloodied hamburger, to fold into a tight ball and cry the rest of his life away.

"Afterthoughts of who?" Jensen asked as a new thought pushed its way past the others: *She was just going to leave me out there in the desert, tied up and helpless.* He was suddenly struck with an intense desire to wrap his fingers around Guinevere's throat, to feel her struggle against his strength, to keep squeezing until every last drop of oxygen was siphoned from her lungs and the light faded from her eyes.

"Everyone who's ever ridden the train," she whispered back. Her voice wavered as she struggled with the words. "Their negative emotions ... they leave them behind ... God, Jensen, we have to get off this train. We have to leave *right now*."

Jensen knew she was right, but there was no way off. The doors were shut and The Dark Train was now speeding across whatever wastes lay outside. Through a window, he saw the jagged teeth of some distant black mountain rush past and promptly decided he was going to make Guinevere suffer before he killed her.

"Jensen, all I can think about right now is how much I hate you for what you did to me back in Township Rebellion," she said, her voice a mixture of panic and rage. "It's overwhelming. I ... I think I'm going to gouge your eyes out with my fingernails."

"Yes." Jensen felt the balled tie in his pocket, realized he could use it to bind her hands so she wouldn't struggle as he ripped off that pink skirt, pulled down those black stockings, spread those smooth white legs and made her suffer for betraying him. "Yes," he said again, "I think you'll *try*."

The tie was almost out of his pocket when a sane thought clawed its way to the surface: *Positive repels negative.* He took a deep breath and fought the violent voices arguing in his mind, but it was difficult, like trying to swim against a strong current.

"Guinevere, sing one of your songs." *Rape her. Kill her.* "The happiest, most optimistic one you have." *Make her suffer.*

She closed her eyes tightly, forcing a single tear to squirt out and dribble down her cheek. "I can't. I *hate* you. I want you to die."

He grabbed her forcefully by the shoulders and shook her until she again opened her eyes, which he saw were now burning with pure loathing. The urge to kill her right then and there was almost too powerful to resist.

"Yes, you can. You have to." *Choke her.* "Concentrate on the melody. Hear the guitar in your head. Remember the words and what they mean to you."

Choke the bitch. "Sing it for me, Gwen."

"You shook me," she said through clenched teeth. *"Don't* fucking *shake* me."

"Sing, goddammit!" Then, in a scream that was simultaneously a plea and a threat: "DO YOU WANT TO *DIE* HERE?"

This must have flipped a switch somewhere inside her because, despite the hatred still etched into her face, she began singing. It was quiet at first, a small, shy sound that was more like heavy breathing than song.

Jensen reached out and gently cupped the sides of her haunted face with his hands, brushing off the momentary urge to jam his thumbs deep into her eye sockets, and forced the words from his mouth. "That's great, Gwen. Let me really hear it."

Her scowl faded and her voice grew louder, more resolute: "I see the sky and the sea of green ... and to me it seems ... this heaven is just a dream ..."

He immediately felt the atmosphere change as the Afterthoughts surrounding them took a few steps backward, into areas of the cabin more hospitable to their negative energy. The menacing purple light even began to lighten to a softer mauve as she continued.

"But as I gaze into this blue ... I get lost in you ... and I never want to leave ..." Her beautiful voice began to overpower even the sickly rumble of The Dark Train, and as if terrified by its power, the Afterthoughts moved even further into the gloom of the cabin. The sweet, uplifting sound was slowly wearing away the evil thoughts inside his head, too; he could already feel some semblance of sanity returning. She must have felt it, too, because she began to smile. He smiled back.

"*Louder,* Gwen. Sing like you're at Carnegie Hall and there's no microphone."

"Fear is just a sound ... that sinks into the ground ... love and light remain ... to claim this new domain ..."

Grinning ear to ear, she grabbed Jensen's hands, which were still cupping her face, and sang into his eyes.

"Shifting shadows mourn ... a life that's never worn ... a toast to love and friends ... and to a life that never ends!"

She held the last note, her voice confident and powerful as it filled the entire cabin with a friendly pink light. Even the sour notes spilling from the anonymous melody outside seemed to lighten, if only faintly, as Guinevere's voice joined its wanton song. Jensen looked around the cabin and saw the Afterthoughts had completely fled, taking the hateful emotions with them. They were all alone.

The moment the song faded from her lips she laughed, an unrestrained, joyous giggle that he couldn't help but return. "Gwen, that was absolutely *amazing*."

"I didn't think I could do it, Jensen. I thought I'd never sing that song ever again. But you helped me. I don't know why, but focusing on you helped me concentrate."

He shook his head. "I didn't do anything. It was all you. My god, you're a great singer. If you weren't dead as a doornail I could make you a millionaire. Do you know that?"

The smile on her face quickly died and she squinted at him with suspicious eyes. "Why does everything have to be about money with you?"

Jensen looked at the floor, unsure how to respond. In his entire life, he'd only ever told three people about the emotional black hole that lived inside him. Of those three, only Hedley had seemed to truly understand. Aimee and his mother had only offered him worthless clichés like "Look on the bright side" or "There's always someone worse off than you are," none of which helped because they didn't address the real issue: His emptiness was a part of him, like DNA, and couldn't be scared away with hackneyed proverbs, no matter how well-meaning their intent was.

Would Guinevere understand? Was the pit he suspected lie inside her soul just as deep as *his* was? He wasn't sure if it was the change in atmosphere or the fact he just felt more open and vulnerable when he was around her, so *unfocused* and off his game, but Jensen decided he was going to do something he hadn't done in a very long time: confide in someone.

"There's this ... damn, it's hard to describe," he began. "It's like a void, deep inside me, but it's not related to anything specific. It's just ... *there*. It never goes away, no matter what I do. It's kind of like ... there's a piece of me missing, but no matter where I look, I can't find it. The feeling's been with me for as long as I can remember, even when I was a kid, and because of it I had a hard time making friends and fitting in. I just never seemed to feel like I belonged anywhere. I guess my mind always turns to money because ... well, because when I'm working, I feel like the world makes sense. Like I'm not alone. Like the void is a little less deep. It doesn't last for long, but it's always better than the alternative."

Her smile returned, sad and empathetic. "Do you feel it right now? This emptiness?"

He closed his eyes and listened for the sick machinery that always seemed to be churning beneath his subconscious, but all he heard was the anonymous melody and the cruel grind of The Dark Train's wheels as it sped along the track.

"Yes, but it's quieter. Shallower." He opened his eyes and grinned at her. "It must have been your song."

"Yes, because it was a song of love, Jensen. Love is the most restorative feeling in the world. I'm not saying there's anything wrong with making a good living, but it can't be all there is to life."

He gazed into her beautiful brown eyes, and the song came back to him as if she were still singing it; sweet, innocent, hopeful. It really was a wonderful piece of music, something that would have certainly made her a star had she lived long enough to sing it in front of the right people, but he doubted it alone had quieted his inner gloom. *Nothing* had that power.

"Love is what really matters," she continued. "Someday you'll find it. And when you do, it'll change your life."

"Tried that. Just ask my wife, and that twig she left me for, just how re-storative the power of love is."

"Oh, Jensen," she said simply, and then grabbed him in a hug. "You'll find someone. I promise."

As they stood there in that silent embrace, swaying in time to the music now playing a slightly happier melody in the distance, a sudden and scary thought crept into his mind:

Maybe I already have.

* * *

Guinevere was surprised when she plopped down onto the seat closest to the entryway and immediately sunk comfortably into it. The seats had first appeared to her in the purple gloom as hulking black monstrosities lining the cabin walls like a double row of neglected tombstones, but first impressions apparently weren't everything.

She couldn't help but emit an audible sigh as she rested her legs lengthwise across the supple seat cushion and, leaning her head against the window, closed her eyes. In the newfound darkness, the train's sickening *clunk-clunk-clunk* was the only indication she wasn't stretched out on a first-class luxury sleeper bound for some tropical paradise.

"Comfortable?" Jensen asked from his seat across the aisle.

"Very," she responded. Not even the ride to Township Rebellion on the Yellow Line had been this relaxed. If the type of train didn't matter, then perhaps the company *did*. She smiled at the thought.

"Mind if I ask you a strange question?" Jensen's voice said in the darkness. "While we have some time."

"I love strange questions. Shoot."

She could hear Jensen shifting in his seat, and when his voice came again,

182

it was a bit closer.

"How do you know when it's time to let go?" he asked.

She opened her eyes and stared at him. "Let go of what?"

Jensen looked off somewhere behind her, his eyes distant. "Something you know you can never have. Not really."

"I'm not following. Are you talking about money again?"

Jensen shook his head. "No. Not that. Not really. I mean a normal life, or at least something that even remotely resembles one. A nice house. A good car. Peers who respect me, friends who won't abandon me. Kids. Family game nights, trips to Disneyland, school recitals. A wife who understands me. Dinner dates and anniversaries and sleeping next to someone who loves me, warts and all." Jensen looked directly into her eyes. "Why does everyone else get to have those things and not me? And how many more times do I have to try and fail before I finally just let it all go?"

Guinevere swung her legs over the seat and scooted closer to him. In the velvety darkness he looked even sadder than his voice would suggest.

"Jensen, that's simple," she said. "Don't *ever* let it go."

Despite the sorrow in Jensen's gaze, she felt a warmth, an openness that she suspected not too many people saw.

"It *isn't* simple, Gwen." He looked down and fumbled with his hands. "When I was a kid, I wanted to swing through the city like Spiderman, saving Mary Jane from Doc Ock and righting wrongs in a skin-tight jumpsuit. But eventually I had to give up on that dream because, try as I might, I never ran into any radioactive spiders. What I'm trying to say, is ... sometimes you *have* to give up, because some things are just ... too *improbable*."

She inched even closer still and grabbed his hands in her own. They were now sitting across from one another, legs in the aisle, knees touching like they were about to play Patty Cake.

"But there's a difference between reality and fantasy, though," she said. "Like ... I *really* wanted to be the Little Mermaid when I was five. I even insisted my parents call me Ariel for an entire summer. I wouldn't answer to anything else. Annoyed the shit out of them, I'm sure. But even though I never grew a tail, that movie made me want to sing. One was real, the other wasn't."

Jensen thought about this for a moment. "Yes, but ... there's not much of a difference when it's *all* out of reach."

She could see in his eyes he was working something over in his mind, and she squeezed his hands in encouragement. It seemed to work, because he continued, talking in slow, carefully chosen words.

"I have these ... *papers* sitting on my nightstand back in Chicago. *Divorce* papers. I don't know why I haven't signed them yet."

"Maybe because you still love her?"

"No, that's not it. I'm not sure I *ever* really loved her. But I *did* love the *idea* of her – that there was someone out there who would stand in that hollow I told you about, who was so ... *there* that it just ... disappeared. But even though she was never that person, it's hard to get rid of the idea that she *could've* been, if only things had been different. I should sign the papers. I *want* to sign the papers. But I just can't let go."

They rode in silence for a bit, and Guinevere couldn't help but let her mind wander as the dark, unknowable shapes of Dim Country flew past the window behind Jensen. She didn't know why he'd opened up to her like that; perhaps it was because she'd done the same to him on the platform, or maybe he just felt comfortable with her.

If so, the feeling was mutual. Being around Jensen was like returning to a familiar place, one that was warm and inviting and smelled of homecooked meals. The feeling had been there on the bus to Paradise City, and it was there now, on the ominous train barreling toward the dark, deep recesses of hell. In fact, she'd even felt it back in Township Rebellion, despite her anger at his intrusion.

But whether it arose from their shared sadness or something else, Guinevere didn't know. Whatever it was, she was slowly beginning to dread the day it was gone. When Jensen left for good, would she miss that feeling?

She wasn't entirely sure if she wanted to find out.

***

Sometime later, The Dark Train blew its awful horn again and began to slow. They both could feel the negative energy slowly creeping back into the cabin, like a swimmer testing the temperature of a pool by tentatively dipping a toe into its waters. But so far, the Afterthoughts hadn't returned. The power of Guinevere's song was still strong, the lights around them still glowing a vigorous pink.

They'd spent the remainder of the ride talking quietly and watching the alien terrain dash across the cabin windows. Not that there'd been much to see; aside from the ominous mountains sketched across the ebony horizon, Dim Country seemed a dark and enigmatic wasteland of barren trees that poked through the dead earth like broken bones.

Jensen regaled Guinevere with stories of his and Grange's globe-trotting adventures, which she sat and listened to quietly with wide-eyed amazement, her smile swelling in places and fading in others as she no doubt wondered what could have been had things gone differently and she'd been there with them.

In return, she'd told him about growing up an only child on an old farm in Wisconsin and her eventual move to Chicago to find fame and fortune, about the romance novel she'd tried to write in high school, how she started playing guitar at age six and wrote her first song at age seven, how she'd never taken a single guitar or vocal lesson in her life but just took to both as naturally as walking. She even sang him another song, this one a breathtaking rendition of Robert Johnson's "Travelling Riverside Blues." It was as if they weren't in Dim Country at all, but inside a dimly lit restaurant sharing life stories over a glass of wine. Jensen was actually enjoying himself.

That was, until they stepped off the train and saw what lie beyond it. There was no train station, no platform, only a flat, damp mess of sickly green vines that scored the dark earth like veins, twisting and crawling around the dead trees and errant pools of sickly brown water until they reached and then clambered up an immense black structure about a hundred yards from where they stood. The mansion's white-framed windows seemed to witness their approach through the ancient fog with soulless, glass eyes, its crooked turrets reaching toward the firmament like the raised legs of a predatory spider about to strike.

The anonymous melody sang a single, mournful note from somewhere distant as the ribbons of energy, now less diverse in their colors, danced a slow waltz high above the mansion's grotesque silhouette. It was like the covers of the Halloween records Jensen used to check out of the library as a child, only there was no full moon hanging ominously in the sky; no quarter or half-moon, either, just the dark, endlessly depressing heavens above.

"Someone call Stephen King," Jensen said. "I think the afterlife owes him some royalties."

Guinevere took his hand and began walking toward the building. "You joke, but you're righter than you realize. The afterworld influences earthly creativity all the time. It's very possible this place gave Stephen King, or George Romero, or Rob Zombie the inspiration for their stories without them ever realizing it." Jensen suspected she was as uncomfortable with their new surroundings as he was and was simply talking to hide the apprehension she felt. "It's really quite fascinating, if you look at it objectively."

"Not easy when you're standing in the eye of the storm," he said nervously and began searching the gloom for any signs that Hedley Grange had been there. "Are you sure we're in the right place? I thought this was going to be a single room, not an entire building."

They passed a depression in the wet earth that looked to Jensen like a sneaker footprint. It could have been made by Grange, or it could be a mirage generated by his desire to find him. It was hard to tell, especially in the darkness that surrounded them.

"This is just as new to me as it is to you," she said. "I've only heard tales of the Room Full of Mirrors. Never actually saw it until now. But we're in the right place, believe me. The conceited only think about themselves, and that selfishness doesn't leave much room for other thoughts, including constructing a proper living environment. Because of that, you get something like this – a bleak, colorless place without warmth and life."

They were close enough now to the mansion that Jensen realized there were no sounds coming from within.

"I'm guessing this joint isn't as empty as it seems," he said. She didn't answer, so he looked behind them and saw the long, cylindrical shape he knew was The Dark Train still idling where they had left it. "Doesn't seem our ride's in a hurry to leave."

She looked back and shrugged. "Like I said, it comes and goes as it pleases. I'm sure the Afterthoughts are gathering strength again, preparing to torment whoever rides the train next."

Jensen stopped as a thought crossed his mind, and she instinctively stopped with him. "Do you think we'll find the same thing in here? In the Room Full of Mirrors?"

She shook her head. "No. I'm not saying what's in there isn't going to be nasty. I'm sure it is. It's just that it's a more *focused* nasty. The Dark Train collects *all* negative thoughts. This place has just one."

As they turned to continue their trek toward the front door, Jensen saw something that made his heart leap. He ran to it, and she followed, confused.

"Jensen? What is it?"

He crouched down and jammed his arm into the darkness between the wooden porch steps, searching blindly through dust and cobwebs until his hand brushed against something soft. He pulled it out and examined it closely. It was a piece of cloth, checkered with blue and white stripes, and still held the form of the head it once sat atop.

"It's Hed's bandana," he said excitedly as he held it out to show her. "He was wearing it in Township Rebellion. He's here, Guinevere. You were right."

She smiled and took the bandana from him, working it over in her hands and staring down at it with a reverence that was almost religious. "I'm going to keep it," she said. "Until we find him and I can give it back." Jensen shifted uncomfortably as she brought it to her nose and sniffed. "It even still *smells* like him."

He doesn't deserve you, Jensen thought, but held his tongue. As informal as it was, they'd made an agreement to help each other. Jensen would honor that contract, just as he'd honored countless other contracts before, regardless of how he was beginning to feel about the specifics.

"Yeah, well, he'll be glad we found it, I'm sure," he said finally. "Shall we?"

She nodded, stuffed the bandana down the front of her blouse, and then climbed the front steps, with him following a few steps behind. The door was heavy and wouldn't budge when she went to open it, so he joined her, and it howled in protest as together they were able to wrench it free from the doorframe. The sight that immediately filled the opening caused them both to take a startled step backward.

The corridor was packed with corpses.

He'd been quietly meditating when he heard the scream.

He didn't dare open his eyes, not even a sliver, not unless he wanted to accidentally check into this place permanently. But the scream had almost startled them open against his better judgment, if only because it had broken the dead silence that for hours had seemed unbreakable.

Hedley Grange craned an ear to the sound and listened. He heard faint conversation, and while he couldn't discern any words, he knew the cadence of the voice speaking – it was Guinevere. He should have known she'd come, should have planned for that possibility, but it was too late to turn back now. She'd have to endure everything with Benny. It was unfortunate but necessary.

He would wait until the voices were closer before making himself known. He'd only be able to get a few words out before Benny stumbled into the room. After that, there would be no more words; the effect would be immediate.

Eyes still closed, he let himself drift into a deeper state of relaxation. The details of his intricate plan once again unfurled in his thoughts, and he smiled at the justice of it all. Benny was here, and it was finally time for him to take his medicine.

It had been a long time coming.

***

Guinevere didn't like horror movies.

It wasn't because of the blood and gore, and it certainly wasn't because she found them to be the slightest bit scary. In reality, it was those stupid Hollywood scream queens, who'd always lose their minds whenever the movie's monster would appear onscreen, waving a knife or a chainsaw in the air as they lurched unhurriedly from the shadows. Some of the women fought back, sure, but most just wailed and flailed like lobotomized idiots until they were either saved by the movie's hero or brutally butchered. It was a stereotype, and Guinevere hated it.

But despite this, she'd screamed anyway, an involuntary shriek that was born and then died in the matter of a mere second. She wasn't proud of it.

She felt even more ridiculous when she realized her initial fear was unwarranted: None of the corpses seemed to even notice they were there. They simply stood, swaying as the hypnotized sometimes do, gazing with dead eyes into the full-length mirrors that lined the long corridor on both sides. Each mirror was as different as the decaying body staring into it; some were rimmed with ornate brass frames, while others were plain sheets of glass propped against the wall. But each held a secret wonder that only the body in front of it could see, the reflection of a lie each told themselves and believed as truth.

"It's okay," she said. "I was just startled."

Jensen gave her a nervous smile and then took a hesitant step forward, his eyes carefully scanning the sea of sickly skeletal frames that congregated in the corridor. A few wore tattered clothing, others were entirely naked, but all looked completely absent as they swayed together under the dim corridor lights like trees on a soft breeze.

"I don't think they can see us," he said.

"They can't. They're too enamored with their own reflections."

"What are they looking at? What do they see?"

"Whatever it is they *want* to see. The mirrors feed them a false image they think is real. All I know is that we can't look directly into them ourselves. Unless we want to get hypnotized, too."

"You don't have to worry about *me*. The putrefied look is *so* last week."

Jensen approached the nearest body, and after a quick glance over his shoulder at her, carefully waved a hand in front of its face. The figure, an emaciated thing that looked like it was once a woman but was now just a pile of moldering bones held up with invisible wire, didn't register the movement at all, just continued staring into the abyss, jaw hanging at an unnatural angle, with yellowed molars and something resembling spoiled ground beef showing through a large hole in her cheek.

"Let me guess," he continued. "These souls are so busy looking at themselves that they neglect their bodies. Their *spiritual* bodies. That's why they look like they're rotting." He looked to her and flashed a smile full of teeth. "Am I right?"

It was a gorgeous grin, and she felt a momentary rush of heat to her cheeks. "I think you're finally getting the hang of this."

"Well, I can say this much," he said. "These folks could use a few squirts of Febreze. They make me wish I was still tied to the ass end of a horse."

Guinevere couldn't help it – she giggled. Realizing that it was an odd situation and an even odder place to be laughing, she covered her mouth and tried to stifle it, but this only caused her to laugh harder.

"That's real nice, Guinevere," he said, smiling broadly. "Laugh at the poor stiffs. You must be a *blast* at funerals."

"Stop it," she was able to say between chuckles. "You're horrible."

Suddenly the woman next to Jensen let out a terrifying groan, deep and incredibly loud, the sound pushing its way from her rotten lungs and through her unhinged mouth as a line of crimson fluid gurgled from the hole in her cheek.

Jensen instinctively jumped back, and as he did the room was filled with a chorus of groans, all seeming to hit the same off-key note, the sound rising to the vaulted ceiling and echoing throughout the corridor like the pipes of a broken church organ. None of the figures took their eyes from the mirrors as they moaned, but somehow she knew the sounds were for her and Jensen.

"Oh *god*. What *is* that?" Guinevere said as her laugh died on her lips and she began shaking. She tried to stop by hugging herself tightly, but the noise was frightening and she couldn't help it. Jensen rushed to her and put his arm around her shoulder.

"I think it's just a warning," he said. She continued to shake and didn't move her gaze from the frail creatures, convinced that at any moment they would turn to her, stare at her with those clouded, sightless eyes, and then begin to slowly saunter toward her. Jensen must have seen the look in her eyes because he stepped in front of her, blocking her view. "It's okay. I think they're just telling us to leave them alone."

As if in agreement with this statement, the moans faded as suddenly as they'd begun. The echo continued for a brief second before it died, too.

"See? We're all good," he said when the moans had completely subsided.

191

She was still shaking, and she hated herself for it. She hated being vulner-able. Hated the fact that Jensen had *seen* her vulnerable. Most of all, she hated that she kind of *liked* it when he saw her that way, because she also liked the awkwardly sweet way he tried to comfort her. There was only one person who should be able to do that, and he was somewhere ahead.

"I'm okay," she said curtly and shook off his grip. "Let's just go."

Jensen looked at her a moment longer, his mouth working to say some-thing, maybe to ask if she really *was* all right or if she was just saying that to appease him, but he abandoned whatever the thought was.

"Okay, then," he said. "Let's keep our wits about us. No looking into any mirrors."

They exchanged nods and then began walking, separately and guardedly through the narrow aisle created by the mass of bodies. She was terrified and wanted to reach out and grab his hand for comfort, to hear his stupid jokes and see his disarming smile, to feel his reassuring warmth beside her, but she didn't.

She couldn't.

***

The bodies clogging the narrow hallway seemed oblivious to the two intruders now carefully picking their way forward with careful steps, eyes cemented to the floor so they wouldn't accidentally wander into the panes of reflective glass standing on either side. But Jensen was a seasoned actor, and he recog-nized a performance when he saw one: The mansion's occupants were very much still watching, still waiting, ready to revolt the moment he and Guine-vere disturbed their unquiet rest again.

It was deathly silent, save for the creaking of old floorboards and the une-ven, labored breathing sputtering from the sickly mouths of the otherwise life-less bodies enveloping them. His heart was slow and steady in his chest, but he knew all it would take to get it thrashing like an overworked steam engine was some sign, no matter how slight, that their presence would no longer be tolerated. He missed the feel of Guinevere's small, soft hand in his own, because it made him feel safe.

So far, none of the shoes he'd been examining belonged to Hedley Grange. The Vanities, as he was now calling them for lack of a better term, appeared in various stages of decay, and their attire reflected this: Some sported clean clothes and looked perfectly human, while others wore tattered rags or nothing at all, just bone and sinew showing through waxy white skin. But of all of them, Jensen had yet to spot a single pair of red sneakers, size eleven. Jensen was actually hoping he *wouldn't* find them, because if Grange had already selected a mirror, it would be hard to pull him from whatever delusion his mind had created.

This realization brought a question to mind.

"What happens if someone who isn't vain looks in a mirror?" he whispered to Guinevere. They hadn't spoken in a few minutes, and the sound of his own hushed voice was a bit startling, even to him.

When she responded, her voice seemed far away. He wanted to look back, to make sure she hadn't fallen too far behind, but he resisted the urge and continued to focus on the hardwood floor and the myriad feet occupying it.

"Now's not the time for twenty questions, Jensen," she whispered. "I'm kind of in the middle of something here. Besides, I don't know. I'm not an encyclopedia of the afterworld."

Something was bothering her, something more than just fright. He could hear it in her voice, in her short, frustrated response. He wanted to ask her about it but decided not to, at least, not right now.

"All I'm saying is, this would go a lot faster if I could see where the hell I was going," he whispered. "If we're not vain, then it stands to reason we don't have to pussyfoot around these damn mirrors."

She didn't respond, so Jensen threw caution to the wind and chanced a quick glance behind him. She was closer than her voice let on, only a few paces, attempting to navigate around a gaunt figure that had long ago shed any vestiges of humanity.

"Take my hand," he said and put it out so she could grab it. When she didn't, he repeated himself, more forcefully. "Guinevere, take my hand."

"I don't *need* your hand, Jensen. I'm fine. Just keep walking."

Instead of arguing, he turned around and kept going. His next step caused a particularly loud creak to resonate throughout the chamber, and wincing at the sound, he stopped to listen for any protest the Vanities might file against it. All he heard was the sickly sound of broken bodies breathing, so he continued.

A few steps later, he saw the floor split off into different directions, and unsure where to go, he stopped again. Guinevere bumped into him and cursed.

"Why'd you stop?"

"Tell me something – which direction is your favorite?"

She sighed loudly. "You've got to be kidding me. How many?"

"Looks like three. Straight ahead, one going northeast, and one that looks like it goes straight west."

"Dammit. What do *you* think?"

Jensen peered at the three sections of flooring and tried to see some indication of previous foot traffic, but saw none. "Well, I've always been partial to staying the course. Straight?"

Her response was almost out of her mouth when a muffled voice suddenly came from somewhere to his left.

"Try again, Benny."

"Hed?" Jensen looked down the left corridor. There were no mirrors, no bodies. Just a dark hallway that led into a formless void. "Where are you?"

"Tell me something, Benny. Why do you hate your own reflection?"

Jensen began slowly walking toward the sound, which was still muffled but growing louder as he walked. He could feel Guinevere right behind him, could smell her coconut hair despite the putridity in the air.

"I don't know what you mean," Jensen said.

"Sure you do. You never said anything, but I saw. I *always* saw. You'd avoid mirrors like they were toxic. Why? What do you see that disturbs you?"

Jensen disliked Grange's question even more than he disliked the quiet, brooding tone of voice he used to ask it. "Just stay there, Hed. We're coming to you."

"We just want to talk, Hank," Guinevere added. "That's all we want. Please let us talk to you."

"We *are* talking, Gwen. If I'm not mistaken, I just started a conversation with Benny. It's his turn to talk. Why do you hate yourself, Jensen? Be honest. Is it because you're a loser? Or maybe you hate yourself because you can't please a woman, no matter how hard you try. No pun intended, of course."

Grange was very close. Now that he was free to look wherever he wanted, Jensen could see the faint outline of a door forming in the dimness ahead. Grange must be behind it.

"I don't hate myself," Jensen said. "I don't hate anyone."

Grange laughed, the sound even more chilling in the darkness. "Two lies, right in a row! Come on, Benny. I said be honest. Lying will only make me angry, and I can't very well tell you where *House Made of Sound* is if I'm angry, can I?"

Jensen stopped as he reached the door, a simple mahogany rectangle that was covered in dust and cobwebs. He put his hand on the doorknob but didn't turn it.

"I don't know what you're trying to do, Hed, but it's not working," he said.

"No, I suppose it isn't. Well, I tried to avoid this. Can't say I didn't try." Silence, and then: "You might as well open the door, now."

Jensen looked to Guinevere, and she nodded.

195

"Let's go," she whispered. "Let's end this."

Then he turned the doorknob and was instantly transported to paradise.

✳✳✳

Guinevere only saw a quick image, frozen in her memory like a photograph, before she turned her eyes away. Hank was sitting Indian style in the middle of a large, brightly-lit room, arms resting on his lap like he was meditating. Flanking him on both sides were about a dozen mirrors, each turned in their direction.

It had been a trap, and she'd almost fallen right into it.

Jensen hadn't been as lucky. She turned to him, keeping her back to Hank and the mirrors, and saw that his eyes had gone completely white; there wasn't a speck of gray left in them as he swayed slowly, methodically, to a tune only he could hear.

"I guess I was wrong – he *loves* mirrors!" Hank said.

Guinevere didn't dare to look behind her, so she began shaking Jensen furiously. "Goddammit, Hank, why? We just wanted to talk to you!"

She heard him stand up and walk close behind her, close enough that she could feel his breath on her neck.

"Talk, talk, talk," he said. "It always goes nowhere. I'm a man of action, Gwen. No more talking."

She continued to shake Jensen, but his vacant eyes continued to stare ahead, unseeing.

"Jensen, wake up!" she cried. "You have to wake up!"

"No, he doesn't. Not yet. Not until he sees what he really is."

"*Please*, Hank, you have to help me. Please help me. We can't leave him like this."

Again, another breath on her neck, and despite the panic she felt, chills ran down her spine. He used to do that once, long ago, in that other life. It used to drive her crazy with desire.

"You care about him, don't you?" Hank said softly.

She wanted to turn around and face him, but she couldn't chance looking into one of the mirrors. What if she liked what she saw? What if she looked and wanted to keep on looking, forever?

"I care about a lot of people, Hank, but not like I care about you."

Hands on her shoulders. Heavy. Hard.

"I believe you, Gwen."

A faint smile. "You do?"

"Yes," he whispered. "That's why I'm very sorry I have to do this."

Then he spun her around and she was lost.

***

He's faintly aware of someone shaking him, telling him to wake up, but it's distant and unimportant. The images and sounds assailing his eyes and ears are much more interesting, and he leans over the railing and takes it all in.

Below him, hundreds of sweaty, well-dressed bodies are swinging and bouncing to the steady *thump-thump* of a bass drum that is so loud and so pervasive that he feels as if he's crawled inside the chest of a giant beast and is being rocked by the authority of its powerful heartbeat. Passing beams of turquoise light slice erratic patterns through the violet haze and briefly light the faces of the dancers, some of which he recognizes and some he doesn't.

It's his nightclub, complete and alive and thrumming with energy. He runs a hand through his hair and smiles at it all, dumbstruck.

He did it. He finally did it.

Suddenly the music stops and the house lights come up. In the newfound brightness he also sees tables filled with people drinking, eating, laughing. Waitresses navigate the masses with trays perched precariously on one hand. TVs shine with football games and newscasts and reality shows. All of these faces abruptly turn to look at him.

A woman slips an arm around his waist, a woman he immediately recognizes as his wife, and the room hushes as she holds a microphone to her lips.

"We'll get back to the music in a second," Aimee says, "but I just wanted to thank everyone for coming out tonight. We're so thrilled you decided to spend the evening with us."

At this, he looks to her, sees the respect in her eyes, the absolute *adoration*, and in that moment, a realization dawns on him: He's a millionaire. They *both* are, because they've reconciled, and the profits he's made from *House Made of Sound* are sitting in their joint bank account, accruing interest by the second.

He was right to wait on those divorce papers, it seems. She's finally come around. She's standing in his void, trying her best to filter out the darkness. But it's a weak light, nothing more than the momentary flare of a single match, not nearly powerful enough to beat back the eternal night. But it's better than nothing at all.

"I say *us*, but in reality, I'm just a small part of this," Aimee continues. "Tonight's real hero is the man standing next to me. He's given us so many great things over the years –Bethany Bree and Quiet Catastrophe come to mind – but this latest offering is perhaps his greatest. Ladies and gentleman, the owner of *Les Deux Figures*, my husband, Jensen Bennett!"

The room explodes in a chorus of cheers and claps and hoots. His cheeks flush at the sudden attention, and flush even more as the room begins to chant, "Speech! Speech! Speech!"

Aimee offers him the microphone with a beautiful smile. He takes it, unsure of how to begin, suspicious of why everyone seems to be so enamored with him and what he has to say. He didn't do anything. Not that he can remember. But here it is regardless, a corporeal dream. The sea of faces looks up at him expectantly, inviting him to speak.

Costumes on, curtains up, he thinks, and raises the microphone.

"I don't really have much to say, except to thank you from the bottom of my heart," he says to the crowd with practiced intonation and cadence. "This nightclub would be nothing without you, and I'm eternally grateful for your support. It hasn't been easy, but I'm living proof that good things eventually come to those who put in the hard work to get there."

"Why don't you tell the truth?" someone shouts.

The owner of the voice cuts through the crowd below, and as a spotlight searches for and then lands on the figure, he sees it's Hedley Grange, looking as penniless as the day he'd first appeared playing for spare change in the Red Line terminal.

"You don't deserve *any* of this," Grange continues. "You're a complete fraud. *Hard work*? Please. All you did was steal my album and then sell it to the highest bidder. Didn't even break a sweat, I bet." His old friend then turns to the crowd and offers them a playfully malicious smile. "The only thing this man deserves is to be run out of here on a horse."

Some murmurs of agreement come from the crowd. He's momentarily reset to zero and looks blankly to Aimee for support, only to see she's no longer smiling, the respect now completely drained from her eyes. Her light, meager to begin with, has been completely extinguished.

It takes considerable effort to fashion an apologetic smile from scratch, but once he does, he turns back and shows it to the sea of faces below.

"Sorry about my friend here, everyone," he says, adding what he hopes comes across as an amiable nod at the man in question. "He's just a bit angry about being upstaged by a cartoon chicken."

There's a tall figure with barn-door ears and a slumped posture standing toward the back of the club, watching him in silence. There's something very familiar about the man even though he's nothing but a vague shape in the darkness, and his presence is unsettling.

"I can assure you, I'm no fraud," he continues, and to prove it, he allows his smile to mature into an ear-to-ear grin.

"Yes, you are," another voice says, and this time it's Brian Riggs, the high school leading man who played Mortimer to his Teddy, still sixteen years old despite the passage of time. "You're a professional fake, just like me. The only difference is, I take my costume off when the show's over. But not you, right? For you, it's *never* over, because you're nothing but a fictional character living a completely fictional life. *God*, you must be so tired from *pretending* all the time."

More murmurs, more nods of agreement. The tide is quickly turning. His heartbeat quickens and his vision blurs. The dance floor, once as clearly defined as a high-resolution photograph, now becomes a series of brushstrokes, born from the end of a painter's brush. *Hedley's* brush. *Les Deux Figures* isn't a nightclub anymore, but an artist's interpretation of one. But the shadow in the back of the club remains crystal clear, a cardboard cutout of a man. It radiates a malignant intelligence that is silently judging every word he utters.

He does his best to ignore the figure, to pretend it's not there at all, but the room is now haunted and it's all he can think about. Despite this, his smile never wanes, only adapts to the situation like it has thousands of times before, and he redirects it at Riggs.

"Different situations call for different reactions," he says in the same tone he'd use to explain a cash flow statement to an intern. "It's a dog-eat-dog world, and sometimes you have to dial it up a bit to survive."

"Bollocks!" says Nigel Cuthpit, who pushes his stocky frame through the mob and shakes a finger at him. "You survive because you're a *coward*, mate. You run at the first sign of trouble." He turns to the crowd. "An absolute joke, this one."

"Not to mention delusional," Aimee shouts next to him. "He thinks there's still hope for us, but there isn't. Did you know we've never even had *sex*? He can't get it up. Even the pills don't help." She looks to him and scowls. "*Limp dick*. I had to find a *real* man to make me come."

"Limp dick!" a chorus of female voices responds, and looking down he sees Jane, and Stephanie, and Carrie, and Tanya, and Debbie, and countless other women from his past.

Jane steps forward and shakes her head. "Never let any of us get close to him, either. He doesn't know *how* to love."

Things are starting to break apart inside him; he can feel them tearing at his insides like broken glass, but he anchors himself and executes a rehearsed laugh.

"I love plenty of things," he says. "Like mojitos, for instance. How about a round for everyone? On me. Hell, free drinks for the rest of the night!"

Groans and shouts and boos rise up in response to this, so loud that even his attempts to talk over them through the nightclub's powerful sound system are lost. They aren't interested in free drinks; they aren't even interested in dancing and dining anymore. What started as a few dissenting murmurs in the crowd has quickly become outright mutiny.

A loud voice suddenly cuts through the noise, and everyone falls silent to listen to it.

"You're wasting your time on him," the tall, slightly hunched shadow with barn-door ears says from the back of the club. "He ain't worth the effort. Been like this since he was a kid. No friends. No life. A sad little shit who likes to cause trouble."

He squints at the familiar stranger. The smile is still there but now it's taped on. "I'm sorry," his voice booms over the loudspeakers. "Just w*ho* the hell are you?"

The shadow man snickers. "You mean you don't recognize me? You should. After all, you're the one who killed me."

There's an audible gasp as the figure steps forward and the club lights spill across his face. But there's nothing there; no eyes, no forehead, no nose, just a bloody hole where they all used to be. The only thing still vaguely recognizable is the man's mangled mouth, and it speaks again.

"*You* did this to me," it says.

The myriad faces turn from the mutilated figure back to the man on the balcony, and one in particular stands out among them. It's Guinevere Hatcher, still wearing her pink miniskirt and white blouse and that frustrating half-smile. Unlike everyone else, she hasn't already decided his guilt.

"Is that true, Jensen?" she asks. "Did you *kill* this man?"

The microphone becomes a forgotten prop at his side, and his response is delivered directly to Guinevere without any amplification.

"Of *course* not. Do I look like a killer to you? I don't even *know* this guy." His voice is convincingly defiant, but the sight of the man's ruined face has derailed his thoughts and he's speaking in half-truths. Maybe he hadn't pulled the trigger, but he'd definitely done *something* bad to this man, whoever he was. He just couldn't remember.

His answer doesn't seem to placate Guinevere or anyone else in the crowd, especially the faceless man, who's somehow able to point directly at him despite missing his eyes and most of his brain.

"Liar!" the man garbles. "Look what's in his hand!"

And that's when he realizes the microphone is much heavier than before, and looking down he sees why: he's actually holding onto the steel muzzle of an old shotgun. It's splattered with blood, and so is the front of his jacket.

The clubgoers revolt at this revelation, and the room turns into an angry courthouse after an unwelcome verdict. Some in the crowd are more benign in their fury, satisfied to hurl only insults and boos his way, but others actually begin throwing things at him – mostly bits of food from their plates or the contents of their drinks, but also objects that hurt when they hit him, like the cups and dishes themselves. One woman even decides to spit at him, and it somehow defies gravity and lands on his cheek.

He senses movement to his left and turns to see dozens of sweaty, well-dressed bodies storming the balcony's east staircase. He raises his hands in surrender, dropping the shotgun in the process, but it's too late – he can tell by the murderous look in their eyes that he's to be burned in effigy and will be donating his actual body to the cause. Aimee sees them coming and actually steps out of the way to give them a clear sightline.

"I'd run if I were you," she says to him, the corners of her mouth rising into an unfriendly grin. "While you still can."

Her words are like a starter pistol, and he turns on his heel and sprints through the double doors directly behind him, past the receiving station and into the fluorescent sterility of the kitchen. As he rams his shoulder into the door at the other end and spills out into the adjoining hallway, he hears the mob enter the space he just vacated, and their angry shouts and stomping feet are amplified tenfold by the kitchen's small size.

They're close. *Very* close. He has to find a way out.

But he doesn't know which way to go. Everything looks different. There are walls where there shouldn't be, doors that look unfamiliar, strange windows that look out into the pitch-black nothingness beyond. Everything still looks like a painting, and the details are lost in the brushstrokes.

He picks a door and runs into the room it leads to, only to find it's just an empty storage closet with no outlet. He turns to go back, to find another way out, but before he can take a single step forward, bodies are spilling into the small room and he's pushed back into the corner.

He sees Hedley Grange, and Nigel Cuthpit, and Brian Riggs, and the familiar stranger, the one who's face has been blasted away into bits. But it's Guinevere Hatcher at the head of the pack that scares him the most, because the willingness to understand is completely gone from her eyes.

"Guinevere, I ..."

He tries one last time to find the role, to remember the script he's spent years learning, but he knows there's no smile, no laugh, no words that can drive away Guinevere's baleful gaze, and his facade finally crumbles under its unspoken weight.

"Okay, you're right!" he shouts. "*Everybody's* right!"

These are the magic words, and Guinevere motions for the mob to stop by raising her right arm like a cop conducting traffic. They do as instructed, but there's still hostility seething behind each of their eyes, including hers. It seems the bite-sized morsel he's given them isn't nearly enough to satisfy their hunger, and he has no choice but to elaborate.

"I'm a fraud," he continues. Now that the graffiti has been sandblasted into oblivion and he's nothing but a bare wall, looking at the crowd now is like staring into the sun, and he lets his eyes fall to the tips of his black Oxfords. "And I'm a coward. Impotent, too, physically and emotionally. And worst of all, I'm a murderer. I've never fired a real gun in my life but I still killed that man. I admit it. I admit it all. Everything is my fault." Then, in a quiet, broken voice, he says it again: "My fault."

Guinevere aims an accusatory finger in his direction.

"We *hate* you, Jensen," she says.

"I know," he says without looking up. "I hate me, too."

✳✳✳

He'd seen enough. It was almost time to leave. But first he had some things to do.

Hedley Grange brought his lips close to his former lover's left ear and whispered three very important words into it. Guinevere didn't shiver and giggle at the sudden tickle of his breath like she used to do back when they were both very much still alive and in love; in fact, she didn't acknowledge his presence at all. She was completely gone, her limp body continuing to sway to a tune only she could hear, her once-brown eyes transfixed on whatever fantasy the mirrors behind him were creating for her.

He licked his lips and then said the three words again, more slowly this time, just to make sure her subconscious mind latched onto them like he needed it to. The phrase was originally intended for Jensen, but Gwen would do *much* better. She was much more suggestible, more open to new ideas than

Benny was. It was *better* this way. He was glad she'd tagged along.

They'd suffer together.

He stroked her hair and whispered the words a third time, even slower still, then nodded. That was enough. Third time's the charm. She'd either remember them or she wouldn't. Hopefully her mind was as malleable as he remembered.

He did what he had to do with the extra mirrors, making sure to keep his eyes tightly shut the entire time he was working as not to fall victim to their beautiful lies. Then, confident everything and everyone was where they needed to be, he slowly crept out of the room and made his way back down the first hallway, which was empty, and then the second, which was packed with corpses. He carefully avoided them by studying his red sneakers, size eleven, as they slowly and methodically picked their way across the hardwood until he'd reached the front door of the mansion once again.

He opened it and felt a cool rush of air, heard the somber faraway melody, saw the long, dark shape idling quietly in the distance, waiting for him. It was almost as if it knew where he wanted to go and was eager to get moving. But there was one last thing to do before he left.

Turning to face the corridor and the hundreds of bodies swaying in its darkness, he took a deep breath and then unleashed an ear-piercing high note that burned as it made its way from his lungs. The effect was immediate: Every mirror within earshot completely shattered.

Hedley Grange could still hear the angry howls rising from inside the Room Full of Mirrors as he boarded The Dark Train.

[silence]

The record player doesn't mask the fighting downstairs, even though the volume knob is turned all the way up and he's lying with his ear right next to the speaker.

He found a half-pack of Marlboros on a pile of old 45s and smoked one, got high, smoked another, felt sick, and now a blanket of stale-smelling smog hangs motionless in the oppressive and inert heat of the attic. John Fogerty is singing about a town called Lodi, which he pronounces "Low-die," but the boy has trouble concentrating on the words. The argument is just too loud.

Look at me when I'm talking to you! His mother shouts, so hard her voice cracks mid-sentence.

The floorboards groan as his stepfather hurries into another room. His mother's footsteps follow like soft echoes.

Don't you walk away from me, goddammit!

Silence. He can picture his mother's eyes blazing like angry emeralds.

John Fogerty begins a laid-back guitar solo, and he tries to focus on it. The drums and bass bounce together in the background like old friends skipping through a field.

You bastard, his mother says with quiet loathing.

Hey, what can I do about it? His stepfather's tone is mollifying, but there's also an uneasiness to it. *The boy's just weird, Margaret. He has no friends. He's always moping around like someone killed his puppy. That's just how he is, and you know it.*

Mothers understand their sons, even if the specifics are vague, and his is no exception.

Bullshit, Richard, she says. *This is different. He's different. Why won't he come out of the attic? What is this wall monster he keeps talking about?*

The song fades out. The needle crackles as it searches for a way out of the record's groove, finds it, and then thumps endlessly when it can go no further.

I don't know, some dream he had. What do you want me to say? You leave here for a few days and he got scared. End of story.

More footsteps, and when his mother speaks again he can tell she's closer, probably in the kitchen.

If I find out you hit him again, Richard, I swear to God I'm calling the police.

The boy has experienced only eight years of life so far, but he knows enough about the world to realize what's coming next. A slap, the sound of glassware crashing to the floor, his mother's scream. Then a tense silence.

You threaten me again, bitch, it'll be the last thing you do.

Wood groaning again. A slamming door. His mother crying softly. The endless crackle of the needle, *thump, thump, thump,* until the boy grabs the record and throws it against the wall, where it shatters into pieces.

Everything is in pieces.

EARTHBOUND
-Track Ten-

One moment Guinevere was in a field dotted with red and yellow splotches quivering on a tender breeze, and the next she was crumpled on the floor, staring at a mess of broken glass.

There was no gentle transition; it was as immediate as the flick of a light switch. But feelings lingered, like the tickle of his stubble on her cheek and the gentle strength of his arms. It would have been easy to get lost in the intoxicating memory again if not for the approaching sound of dragging feet and the confused, angry moaning that accompanied it.

He shattered them, Guinevere thought, and the realization made her angry. She wanted to go back. There must be a mirror somewhere around here that could bring her back to that field and the man in it. Nothing else mattered, not even those terrible noises in the hallway.

But as she struggled to her feet and looked around, her senses came back to her and the anger turned inward. It had just been an illusion, a trick of light, and she'd fallen for it. Like a weak-minded idiot. Thankfully, Hank had freed her from the terrible lie, and knowing this tempered the shame she felt at needing rescue from it in the first place.

The mirror frames were still set in a semi-circle facing the door, but now they were faceless voids rimmed with sharp, greedy teeth. Jensen was lying on the ground in front of the door, hugging his knees, staring at the glass-littered floor with vacant eyes and murmuring something in a sad and faraway voice.

The color had returned to his irises, but he still seemed to be in a trance.

"Jensen, we have to go," she said and pulled on his arm. He was heavy and barely moved. Glancing through the open door, she could see shapes beginning to take form in the darkness of the hallway beyond it, slender figures sauntering toward them with singular intent. A screech that sounded feminine tore through the corridor, and to Guinevere it sounded like an emphatic "there!" Whether or not it was just the terror of the situation inflaming her imagination, the corpses knew where they were and were closing in.

We didn't break the mirrors, she almost shouted, but stopped when she realized rational thought would be lost on them. The figures had been torn from their fantasies, and someone had to pay for it. It didn't matter who.

She crouched down and grabbed Jensen's face, turning his head so that he was forced to look at her.

"Jensen, you have to get up. They're coming."

"My fault," he said distantly.

She was briefly taken aback. Whatever he'd seen in the mirror had been powerful. Paralyzing, even.

"No," she said, "but it *will* be if you don't get the hell up."

More moans, more shuffling feet, all closer than before. She looked through the doorway again, and in the dim light she saw them more clearly than before, laboring forward on rigid legs, clouded eyes hungry for retribution, naked jaws crammed with crooked teeth working up and down as groans and occasional shrieks shot from them. She felt like screaming again.

"You have to stand up!" she shouted in his face instead. "Right now!"

"Okay," he croaked. "I'm up."

Jensen made it to his knees but froze again the moment his eyes fell on the approaching shapes in the doorway. He reminded her of a music box ballerina she'd had as a child that would abruptly end its dance the moment the spring inside lost tension – no gradual slowdown, just a full and complete stop. Unfortunately, Jensen didn't have a lever she could wind to get him going again.

"We have to get out!" she yelled and swept her eyes across the room, searching for another exit. But it was bare except for the shattered mirrors and a tall armoire wedged into the corner. There were no windows, and no other doors except for the one they'd come through. Their only hope was the armoire, but it looked heavy.

"Jensen! Help me bar the door!"

But Jensen wouldn't move.

✳✳✳

He briefly debated letting the Vanities into the room. Why not? There was nothing about him that was worth saving. Better he served as worm food than continue pretending that life was anything more than a series of spectacular failures, with him in the lead role. At least he'd have a purpose, grim as it was.

But then he thought of Guinevere and realized he couldn't let her suffer for his mistakes. Without his help she'd be doomed to endure the same gruesome fate. He didn't know what kind of damage the Vanities could cause in a world where the only pains seemed to be emotional ones, but he knew she didn't deserve to find out alongside him.

Jensen leapt to his feet at this last thought and slammed the door shut just seconds before the first row of bodies were about to cross the threshold into the room. He looked for a lock but, finding none, put his entire weight against the door and dug his feet into the ground for leverage.

"I don't think I can hold them for very long," he said, and to accentuate this point, a dozen fists began beating a sickening tempo against the other side of the door. "But I'll last as long as it takes for you to get out of here."

Guinevere had been trying to move the armoire by herself to no avail, but stopped and looked at him with concern. "Jensen, you're coming with me. I'm not leaving you here."

He looked down at his shoes. "There's no point. I'm just dead weight."

She marched back over to him and put a finger under his chin, forcing his head back up. He had no choice but to look directly into her beautiful brown eyes.

"Listen to me," she said softly. "Whatever you saw in that mirror, it was a lie. It's not true."

More Vanities must have reached the door, because now it was actually pushing against him with enough force that he had to start pushing back to keep it from bursting open.

"No, that's just it," he said. "I don't think it was a lie at all. I think it was the truth. I *know* it was the truth."

A strange look passed across her face, one he couldn't quite place.

"Jensen, listen to me." The patient tenderness in her voice surprised him given the fear he saw in her eyes. "I don't know what you saw in there, but I know this: You're a good person. Maybe *you* don't believe that, but *I* do. And I'm not leaving you here." She smiled and put a hand against his cheek. "Besides, you're blocking the only way out. You *have* to come with me. Whether you like it or not."

The Vanities pushed again, and this time Jensen's shoes slid a few inches on the hardwood floor in response. Their moans were getting angrier, more frustrated. It wouldn't be long before they were inside.

"Okay, I'll go," he said finally, and smiled back at her. "But only because I *really* hate this neighborhood."

Guinevere nodded. "Agreed. Just keep that door closed, whatever you do. Let me look around."

She left him again and went straight to the armoire, the only other thing in the room worth examining. As he watched her fling open the doors and begin studying something inside, he thought again of how beautiful she was. Not just physically, either. Her voice was like magic, able to clear away the gloom. She'd done it inside The Dark Train, and then again just now, this time inside of *him*, even as literal death was pounding on the door. He wasn't fixed,

211

not even close. But he felt better because of her. And Jensen could think of nothing more beautiful than that.

"Jensen, come over here."

He looked at her with disbelief. "What? Are you *insane*? There's no lock!"

"Just trust me. Come over here. *Quickly*."

He shook his head. "Why? What's in there?"

She turned around and shot him an angry look. "*Mirrors*, Jensen. Six or seven of them, and they aren't broken. Will you just *trust* me on this?"

The door bulged again behind him, but he dug his shoes into the hardwood and was able to keep it firmly against the frame. "Mirrors?"

She nodded impatiently. "We'll each grab one and walk back-to-back down the hallway until we reach the front door."

He smiled at her. "Guinevere, that's *genius*."

She didn't return the smile, only continued to look at him with growing irritation. "Yes, and I need your help to get them out. Convinced yet? Or do you want to talk about it some more?"

"No, I'm good. Just ... give me a second. These things may *look* like the Crypt Keeper, but they *hit* like a linebacker. I've gotta time it just right if I don't want to end up as zombie chow."

Saying it out loud made him realize he no longer wanted to hand his fate over to the Vanities. He surely deserved *some* kind of punishment for his failures, but being slowly eaten alive was a bit much. Thankfully the fog of that terrible vision was slowly starting to lift.

He took a few deep breaths, positioned himself so he could make it across the room in only a few short steps, and then nodded. "Okay. Here goes."

It happened quickly. In the fleeting moment between one swell against the door and the next, Jensen sprinted toward Guinevere. Without resistance, the door swung open, and a mass of bodies began pouring into the room, stumbling over each other as they grabbed for Jensen but found only empty space. He reached her in just a few steps, and together they swiftly removed the first mirror from the armoire and swung its reflective side outward. The Vanities at the front of the pack stopped immediately as they were again transported into their own personal paradise, but the others behind them, beyond the mirror's line of sight, continued to push forward.

Jensen realized he was once again trapped inside a room without an exit as an angry mob approached, and the déjà vu was profound. But this time, Guinevere was his ally, not his enemy. The thought gave him hope that this situation would have a much happier ending than the last.

She looked to him with anxious eyes, and it was the only cue he needed. Making sure she could hold the first mirror by herself, he reached inside the armoire for another. He gripped the next mirror's thick wooden frame on both sides and then tried to walk it out, but heard a hollow thump as it caught on the bottom lip of the wardrobe. It was too large.

"Hurry," she hissed behind him. "We have to get out of here while there's still a path around them."

Jensen wrestled with the mirror until he had it at an angle and then, seeing it would now fit through the opening, closed his eyes and pulled. It was heavy and awkward, but he was able to free it from the armoire and then set it on the ground, mirror-side out. He opened his eyes and dragged it until his back touched Guinevere's.

"All right," he said. "It's heavy as shit, but I have it."

"Can you carry it? It's not far to the entrance, but it'll seem like it is."

"I'll manage."

"Okay. On three."

As she counted, he lifted the mirror, and when she reached three, they set off, her walking forward, him walking backward, both of them using their mirrors as shields as they slowly made their way toward the waiting Vanities.

"It's working," she said. "They're backing up as we go. Just keep going really slow. You may have to angle yours a bit to get any stragglers trying to come at us from the side."

As they passed through the open door and into the dim hallway, he saw at least a dozen Vanities left in his wake discard their angry moaning and begin swaying their hypnotic dance as they caught a glimpse of their reflection in his mirror. As long as they kept the mirrors held out in front of them, they should be safe. None of the Vanities would be able to get close to them without falling under a spell. Yet knowing this did nothing to quell his anxiety, which had kicked into high gear now that they were inside the swarm: the unpleasant inner heat, the tremors in his hands, a jackhammer where his heart used to be, they were all collaborating to usurp his concentration. He closed his eyes and tried to focus on the sound of his footsteps, but the thrumming of blood in his ears overpowered it.

Don't drop the mirror, he thought. *Just don't drop the mirror and everything will be fine.*

The going was slow and methodic. Together, they carefully turned the corner, Guinevere guiding their way and Jensen following by keeping his back square against hers. They hadn't gotten far when Jensen realized he needed something to take his mind off the terrors lurking behind his closed eyes, so he forced his thoughts to return to the five million dollars and what he would do with it. But this only made him think of Hedley Grange, the last man on earth who could give him those things, and something suddenly dawned on him.

"You know, this whole thing was a trap from the start," he whispered over his shoulder to her. Then, when she didn't immediately respond, he added, "Grange came here *knowing* I'd follow. He never had any intention of staying here. He probably sent Teddy to untie us and tell me some bullshit story about an argument just so I'd come after him. What a bastard. He *wanted* me to suffer."

"If that's true, he got what he wanted," she whispered back. "You were in pretty bad shape when you came to."

As they continued down the hallway, he remembered the anger of the crowd in his fantasy and the sobering admission he'd made to them in the storage closet. It had been hell, just as Grange intended it to be. But even though the ordeal was already taking on the characteristics of a bad, half-remembered dream, the undeniable truth of it still remained: He hated himself. Hated everything he was, everything he wasn't, hated how he ruined everything he touched. It wasn't an admission that sat well with him, in large part because he wasn't sure where to go from here.

"Jensen? You sure you're okay?" Guinevere asked gently.

"Yeah. Just took too many red pills in there. I'll be okay. What about you? What did *you* see?"

Silence for a second, and then she said, "Nothing. I was able to look away in time."

Jensen could smell the slightly sulfuric scent of Dim Country and knew they must be approaching the open front door. The anonymous melody, still playing a single, somber note, was beginning to overpower the shrieks of the Vanities further down the hall who'd once again been deprived of their heavenly illusion. They were almost out of this depressing place.

Suddenly an emaciated, crumbling face darted from the darkness and hissed a foul-smelling scream in his left ear. He jumped at the sound, and before he could do anything about it, the mirror shifted in his grip and then crashed to the floor at his feet. The Vanities in front of him wasted no time in letting him know how they felt about his poor grip, rising once again in a horrible moan that was no longer just annoyed but absolutely enraged. The rotting figures once again began staggering toward him, skeletal fingers seizing the air, searching for something or someone to grab. In the darkness they looked like demons, their pallid eyes shining in the dim light like white fire. Jensen froze again, unable to do anything except watch the coming horror, the blood battering his eardrums like some demonic tribal drum as the world waned around him.

But before the Vanities could reach him, Guinevere was in his path, holding the mirror in front of her like a shield. She looked over her shoulder and shouted, "*Run*, goddammit!"

This broke the spell, and he spun around to see they were only a few yards away from the entrance, the outside gloom welcoming despite its apparent malevolence. A few scattered Vanities were in the way, but Jensen was confident he could maneuver around them. But what about Guinevere?

As if reading his thoughts, she shouted, "I have a mirror! Just run!"

She'd wanted him to trust her, and so he did, sprinting with all his energy toward the open door. He easily spun around two Vanities on either side of the hallway but ran headlong into a third that was blocking the opening. He expected resistance, but the figure was so frail that he instantly knocked it to the ground. It fell with a sickening thump as a line of gray fluid shot across the hardwood and its eyes became two dirty cue balls.

Then he was out.

He immediately spun around, ready to run back in if Guinevere's mirror wasn't as efficient as she'd hoped, but he saw she'd already made it to the door and was now carefully laying it against the doorframe, eyes tightly closed as she blindly angled its smooth face toward the corridor.

Then she was out, too, and without saying a word they both instinctively put their palms against the door and pushed it closed. When they were done, they looked at each other again, drunk with adrenaline and excitement, before turning on their heels and running into the sulfuric night, beating their legs until the swirling fog enveloped the Room Full of Mirrors like an ancient shroud and completely erased it from existence.

✳✳✳

They'd hoped The Dark Train would still be there when they returned, its ravenous sliding doors agape in anticipation of swallowing a new lot of passengers, but instead they saw only the long, deep wound in the earth it used to traverse the barren wastes. Unsure of what to do next, they'd decided to follow it and were now slogging through the veil, counting the crossties as they went and wondering just where in the hell Hedley Grange had gone.

For the past several minutes, a strange shape had been gradually taking form in the mist ahead. Jensen thought it looked like an aqueduct; Guinevere thought it was another train station. But as they approached it, they found they both were wrong: It was a bridge, short and squat, rather pedestrian in its appearance given the fantastical nature of everything else the two had seen so far in the Dims. An angry orange streak that smelled of hot iron and secreted a primeval heat ambled gracefully below it; in the gloom, the warm light it cast on the surrounding rocks was almost ethereal.

"Lava," Jensen said simply, and Guinevere nodded in agreement.

"The Flows," she said. "I've heard of them, although the stories really don't do them justice. They're almost beautiful, in a dangerous sort of way." Then, in response to his questioning look, she added, "The Flows run deep into Dim Country, into the real nasty parts."

"It gets nastier?"

"Much. The Room Full of Mirrors is Disney World compared to the other places out there."

He leaned against the bridge's frame, staring into the malleable fire that seemed to stumble over itself again and again as it sailed silently underneath them, taking long sheets of obsidian and dead branches along for the ride, and again his thoughts turned to Hedley Grange and the five-million-dollar secret locked in his brain.

"Exactly where are we headed? I was okay with coming here when we had a lead, but now we have nothing. This seems like a dangerous place to get lost."

"It is. But what choice do we have?" She sighed, long and deep, the sound not unlike the mournful hiss the wind made as it passed through the arms of the broken trees surrounding them. "*God*, I'd kill to be psychic right about now."

217

The words hadn't even finished pushing their way past her lips when a name floated into his mind: Daphne Dartmouth. He jerked so quickly from the bridge frame that Guinevere took a startled step backward.

"Guinevere, you're a genius!"

She laughed. "I think you use that word too liberally. What did I say?"

"Psychic powers. *We* may not have them, but I know someone who does. I met her at the Quiet Catastrophe concert. I thought she was putting me on at first, but she quickly convinced me otherwise."

Guinevere shook a finger at him as a look of recognition passed across her face. "That's *it*! *That's* where I know you from! I've been trying to figure it out ever since I met you on the bus!"

Jensen shook his head. "I don't understand."

"The concert. I was there. And so were you."

The phantom conversation. The spirit woman who wouldn't leave Daphne alone until she'd promised to deliver her cryptic message. It all made sense, now.

"*You* were the one she was talking to."

Guinevere nodded enthusiastically. "There're a bunch of people on the material plane that say they can talk to people on this side. Most of them are lying. But some aren't, and she's one of them. They're a rare breed. Even rarer is finding one that's actually in the same place as the person you want to talk to."

Jensen cocked his head to the side. "Grange?"

"Yes. I told her to tell Hank to wait for me when he got here, but she screwed up and gave *you* the message instead."

Jensen's mind began to race. Daphne. She was the key. She could contact Grange and find out where he was. But there was only one problem – she wasn't on this plane of existence.

"At the concert," he said. "How did you talk to Daphne?"

"In a booth," Guinevere said, and then suddenly the excitement that had been growing on her face drained completely. "But there's only two of us. Dammit."

"A booth? What's that?"

Guinevere began pacing, and in the ruby-orange burn of the lava flow she looked like a sinister angel.

"Remember how I told you collective thoughts create everything here? Well, the same goes for booths. Four, five, sometimes even six people gather in a circle and concentrate, and one eventually appears in the middle. It's like a portal that lets us go to the material plane. Usually all you can do is watch the living do boring stuff like brush their teeth or sleep, but sometimes you run into people like that pretty blonde woman, and you can actually communicate with them."

Jensen again leaned against the bridge and watched as another stone slat drifted beneath him like a boat on a river. "Okay. Let's do it."

She huffed and stopped pacing long enough to say, "No point. Only two of us? It won't work. You need at least three. And even then it's really hard."

Jensen walked a few paces away from the train tracks to a spot that looked relatively empty and focused his gaze on a single point on the ground. "What are you supposed to concentrate on, exactly?" he asked.

"Wherever you want to go," she said distantly.

"How about a person? Could you focus on a person?"

"Sure," she said, and from the corner of his eye he could see she'd stopped pacing and was staring at him with crossed arms. "What are you doing?"

"Thinking of Daphne. I'm not sure where she is now, but if I think of her maybe the booth will take me there."

Guinevere walked toward him, sneakers smacking defiantly on the stone as she went, until she was close enough that he could again smell coconut.

"You're wasting your time, Jensen. It won't work. We'll have to take The Dark Train back to Near Country. My friends in Paradise City can help."

"I don't have that kind of time," he said and intensified the image of

Daphne he'd conjured in his mind. "Are you going to help me or not?"

She sighed, uncrossed her arms and then took a spot in front of him. "What the hell. Might as well try." Then she held out her arms toward him. "We hold hands. It strengthens our connection."

He took her hands in his own and they stood, the anonymous melody continuing its haunting refrain from above, as each focused on their own personal version of Daphne's face. His mind wandered to Guinevere's soft, warm, small hands and how comfortable they felt entwined in his own, how the pleasant smell of her hair overpowered the sulfuric trail of smoke coiling around their feet, how her cute Wisconsin accent would come forward when she was agitated and then all but disappear when she was calm, how quickly she'd plotted the ingenious plan to escape the Vanities, how beautiful her lone voice had sounded on The Dark Train and how its power alone had been enough to dispel the negative thoughts clamping his mind like a vice. She really was something else; Jensen could safely say he'd never before met anyone even remotely like her.

He shook his head as he realized his focus was drifting and forced his thoughts to return to Daphne.

After what seemed like several minutes of this quiet contemplation, Guinevere suddenly broke the silence between them. "Convinced yet?"

"Don't give up just yet. Look!"

A crack had formed in the stone between their feet, a tiny fracture no bigger than a human hair but one that hadn't been there a second before. If Guinevere saw it, she didn't let on.

"Jensen, my circle had five people in it, including myself, and even then it took us forever to –"

The tiny crack abruptly multiplied as the air was filled with a crisp snapping sound and the ground shook softly underneath them. Together the newborn fissures formed an asterisk, and from its center what looked like the top of a wooden post began to push through.

"Ha! See that, Gwen! Keep thinking!" He didn't pause to look at her and confirm his suspicions, but Guinevere's silence suggested she was just as astonished as he was at their sudden progress.

His eyes narrowed and he gripped her hands even tighter as he tried to further clarify the image of Daphne's face in his mind's eye – the shoulder-length blonde hair, the willowy neck, the pair of saucer-shaped blue eyes, the petite chin – as the wooden pole continued to thrust through the stone, at knee level now, the ground trembling even harder with each inch it gained.

And then the pole rapidly shot out the rest of the way, causing them to unlink hands and both take a defensive step backward. When it finally stopped, it stood about eight feet off the ground and was covered in a fine black dust that Jensen suspected was either pulverized rock or volcanic ash. About three quarters of the way up it sat a square box, inside which lay a simple black handset. Despite the absence of a quarter slot and numeric keypad, it looked just like an old pay phone.

"That was ... amazing," Guinevere said as she walked around to his side of the pole. "Incredibly primitive, but still amazing. Your link to Daphne must be very strong. It's the only thing that makes sense."

Jensen scratched his head and pointed to the receiver. "This is a booth? What am I supposed to do? Call collect?"

Guinevere went on as if she hadn't heard him, studying his face with a mixture of awe and suspicion. "Were you guys ... did you guys ..."

He looked to her with an amused grin. "She kissed me."

Guinevere looked off into The Flows, the lava therein reflecting small bonfires in her eyes. "That explains it. Lovers have a stronger connection."

"No, nothing like that. We just ... we had a moment. That's all."

Guinevere didn't respond, so Jensen went to pick up the handset. When she realized what he was doing, Guinevere batted his hand down.

"No, Jensen, not you. I'll go."

He shook his head. "No, it has to be me. The last time you two spoke, all you did was argue."

"That's because she gave my message to the wrong person. It'll be different this time."

She made like she was going to pick up the receiver, but he stopped her with a gentle hand before she could.

"Guinevere, I don't want to fight with you on this. If my link to Daphne is as strong as you say it is, then I have a much better chance of reaching her. It just makes sense that I be the one to go."

He expected more arguing, but she only threw her hands up in surrender and said curtly, "Fine. I'll just wait here and count the ribbons, I guess."

"Thank you. I'll be in and out before you know it."

He waited for her response, but instead she just looked off into the colorless sky and the streams of energy sluggishly swimming across it.

"In and out," he repeated, and then picked up the receiver and put it to his ear.

Seconds later, he was back home.

✳✳✳

She was having the dream again.

It was hot. *Very* hot. Were dreams supposed to have temperature? She didn't know, but this one did. It always did.

She was where she always was, huddled in the corner of her old room, crying and clutching her teddy bear as the flames shot up the wall and began devouring her curtains. That's not how it had happened, not exactly, but it was close, so close that for a brief moment she thought the dream had actually transported her back in time, back to that awful room swarming with heat and smoke and rabid panic. Her eyes burn, her lungs burn, and soon the rest of her will burn, too.

Then the door bursts open and her father's hefty frame fills it. He rushes to her, throws her over his shoulder, begins to rush out of the room, and as always, she drops her doll and begins beating on his back, damning him, cursing him, hating him for choosing her instead of mommy. It wasn't fair, it was never fair, but she's small and can only shout and kick and struggle as she's taken through the flames and out into the freezing Missouri winter. In the evening chill she's jolted awake.

According to the alarm clock, it was six-oh-nine in the morning, but the hotel room was still dark. Soon it would be time to get up, to have the unavoidable and unpleasant conversation that always seemed to follow one-night stands, and then book a night flight back to New Hamelin. But for now, she let herself enjoy the moment. There was no fire, no heat, no smoke. Not anymore. That part of her past was gone, never to return except in nightmares. But this moment was here, it was now, and she was going to enjoy it for as long as it lasted.

She turned in bed, liking how free it felt to be completely naked, and wrapped an arm around the muscular figure snoring next to her. It had been a while since she'd been with a man, and even longer since she'd been with one who actually knew what he was doing, and inching closer to the warm body beside her she let the memory of last night play again in her mind.

He'd seemed a bit intimidating at first, if only because of those strange two-toned eyes of his, but after a few glasses of wine and a hastily rolled joint from her dwindling stash he'd softened a bit, enough to where she'd felt comfortable letting her guard down. Maybe she'd let it down a bit too much, but in any case, it had been one hell of a fun night. She'd even got to ride on the commercial jet to Idaho with the rest of the road crew. She'd felt like a member of the band, if only briefly.

Daphne had almost drifted again into that tentative purgatory between wakefulness and sleep when she became acutely aware of someone in the room with them. Typically, her "visitors," as she called them, would gradually fade into her mind like an old TV set warming up, but this time it was instantaneous: not there and then suddenly there. She didn't have to look to know it was standing at the foot of the bed; she could sense it even with her eyes closed.

Two visitors in twenty-four hours? It was unheard of. She was tired. She wanted to go back to sleep, enjoy the moment before it was gone, and she didn't have time to deal with anyone or anything right now.

"Whoever you are, go away," she whispered. "I'm closed."

The voice that responded wasn't faint and faraway like usual, but right there with her, so corporeal that for a split second she thought an actual physical intruder had broken into the room.

"Can ghosts throw up, Daphne? 'Cause I think I'm about to."

It couldn't be. "Jensen?"

She sat up and spun around, using the covers to hide her bare chest as she scanned the darkness, marveling at how cold the room had suddenly become. She was unsurprised to find a figure standing a few feet from the bed, the first yellow rays of dawn seeping through it like sunlight behind a thin curtain, but was astonished when she saw that it was indeed Jensen Bennett. Daphne was momentarily speechless; she usually didn't see visitors this clearly. Jensen was hardly transparent at all.

"That really you?"

Jensen took a step forward, and as he did his image clarified even more. His tie was gone, his hair was wild and unkempt, and a fine powder, either sand or ash or both, covered his entire body. He looked exhausted.

"Two-Eyes, Daphne? Really? Bestiality's still a crime last I checked."

She smiled despite the shock at seeing him. "Very funny, Jensen. What happened to you? How come I see you so clearly? And *hear* you, too?"

He shrugged his shoulders. "I dunno. This is *your* wheelhouse, not mine. All I know is I need you to do me a favor, and quickly. I don't have much time."

She sighed. It was always a favor, wasn't it? Talk to this person, deliver this message, find this family heirloom. For once she just wanted someone to come through and tell her next week's lottery numbers. Right now, sleep was her only concern.

"What's the rush? You're still gonna be dead after lunch. Come back then and we'll talk. Swear."

Jensen made like he was going to sit on the edge of the bed and then, apparently realizing he would simply sink through it, continued standing.

"Daphne, I'm not dead. I was in a plane crash, a pretty nasty one, but was sucked out before it hit the ground. I guess someone found me and is going to bring me back, and probably soon, which is why I need your help."

She slid back in the bed until she felt the headboard behind her, fully awake now, and ran a hand through her hair. Johnny objected at the sudden movement with a loud snore but thankfully kept sleeping.

"Shit, Jensen. I'm sorry. You get so used to spirits talkin' to you night and day it's easy to forget they're people, too. I'm awful sorry. Was looking forward to partyin' with you in Jackson." Then something came to her and she added, "Wait, you took a plane back to Chicago?"

Jensen looked at her with apologetic eyes. "No, Daphne. There's no easy way to say this, so I just will. It was the Quiet Catastrophe tour jet. It went down somewhere between Illinois and Idaho, probably Wyoming. The band's dead. I was the only survivor. Or, I *will* be the only survivor, when I eventually get back."

Daphne again didn't know what to say. She knew life continued after death; it was a truth she'd known ever since the fire had taken her home, her mother and her childhood all in one fell swoop. But the news still hit her hard just the same, if only because it meant there'd never again be new Quiet Catastrophe music.

"All of them?"

Jensen nodded soberly. "Everyone, even the manager. That's why I'm here. I've been tracking Hedley Grange in the afterlife. *God*, that sounds crazy,

225

but that's exactly what I've been doing. I need to find him, to ask him where he hid the band's last album, the one I told you about, but I don't know where he went. I lost his trail. I need your help. If I go back before I can find him, the album will be lost forever."

Daphne grabbed the glass of water she'd left on the night stand and took a drink. It was warm but still helped to clear the sandpaper gathering in her throat.

"Help how?"

"I need you to use your ability to contact Grange on the other side and find out where he went."

Daphne began shaking her head before he'd even finished the sentence. "My visitors always come to *me*. I don't go to *them*. I tried contactin' someone once but it didn't work. Just always knew I couldn't do it."

"You have to at least try," he said. "You're my last hope. Will you help me?"

"Course I will," she said and then eyed the crumple of clothes on the floor. "But first I need some britches. Don't normally talk to ghosts in the nude." Jensen nodded and continued to stare at her eagerly, so she smiled and made a shooing motion with her hand. "That means turn around, please."

He shook his head awkwardly and then spun around so his back was facing her. "Yes, right. Sorry."

She gracefully slipped out of bed, Johnny completely oblivious to her sudden absence as he rolled over to the space she once occupied, and as she quickly began to dress she thought about a potential reason why Jensen was so clear to her. Of the hundreds of spirits she'd talked to over the years, she'd only seen two people this defined, this real: Aunt Carol and Grandpa George. The links she made with the dead were much stronger among family members than others.

There really wasn't a way to be sure, not here in a seedy hotel room in Nampa, but she and Jensen almost certainly shared a lot more than just a tendency toward unhappiness.

226

She and Jensen probably shared the same bloodline.

***

When Guinevere turned around, Jensen was gone and the handset was swinging eerily from the post by its cord. It was as if he'd never been there at all, just an imaginary friend she'd invented to help cope with the unbearable stress of her quest. The only proof of his authenticity was the muffled and extremely tinny voices quietly emanating from the receiver's earpiece.

She'd been trying to ignore their conversation, but bits and pieces came to her anyway as she stood, gazing up at the ribbons of languorous energy in the sky, wondering again for the millionth time just what in the world she was supposed to remember. Someone had said something to her, and recently, that she knew was *very* important. But she couldn't remember what it was, or who had said it to her, or why it even mattered. The mystery had been nagging her ever since they'd left the Room Full of Mirrors.

Three words, she thought. *Three very important words, but what in the hell* were *they?*

She didn't know and couldn't remember. It was frustrating, like recognizing an actor's face but not being able to place the name that went with it.

A sudden heat flared in Guinevere's cheeks when she heard Daphne's tinny voice say something about being nude. The feeling came and then quickly vanished, a momentary flicker of jealousy that left her feeling more than a little embarrassed.

Why did the very *existence* of Daphne bother her so much? She didn't know *that*, either. Maybe it had to do with that strange, unknowable *something* that was bubbling just beneath the surface whenever she was around Jensen, that comforting feeling of home. But she didn't know anything for sure except that she wanted to stop thinking about it, about *everything*, including what she'd seen in that damned mirror.

227

Three voices, faraway but close enough that she could make out specific words, suddenly cut through the gloom.

"... somewhere on this bridge."

"Could he have gone back already?"

"Maybe, but I don't think so. Let's spread out."

Guinevere turned toward the sound and saw three distant pinpricks of light darting through the mist at the other end of the bridge. She knew the voices well: one belonged to Deputy Tommy O'Meara, one to Deputy Greg Duplin, and the other to their tenacious boss, The Warden.

And all three were rapidly approaching.

✳✳✳

The heaviness of the material world had been the biggest shock, which was strange given that he'd lived nearly forty years of his life there. Jensen had already become so accustomed to the higher vibrations of the afterlife that the lower frequencies of the earthly plane felt like being encased in mud. The air was thicker, his movements slow and labored. Even his *thoughts* were sluggish. How could anyone stand feeling like this all the time?

Another odd thing was how fuzzy everything looked. He was completely solid, but nearly everything else – the bed, the walls, the hairless primate sawing logs on the bed – they were all partially see-through. All except Daphne, who was clearer. Not exactly solid, but not nearly as fuzzy as everything else.

"Any luck?" he asked the pretty blonde woman sitting cross-legged on the floor, eyes closed, hands resting palm-side-up in her lap. She looked up at him impatiently.

"Every time you ask me that you break my concentration. If you want this to work then you're gonna have to zip it."

"Right, zip it. Sorry. I'm just a bit anxious to return. I left someone back there and she's all alone."

228

Daphne nodded and closed her eyes again. "The girl in the skirt. I can sense her."

Jensen took an excited step forward. "Does that mean you're reaching the other side? She's not here; she's there."

Again, Daphne shook her head. "No. I'm not sensin' her over *there*. I sense her in *you*. You're in love with her."

Jensen shifted uncomfortably. "That's ridiculous, Daphne. I hardly even know her."

She opened her eyes again and looked at him. Despite the irritation in her eyes, he also saw compassion, even deep affection. "Jensen, honey, you're lyin' like a no-legged dog. Now, we can dawdle about it if you want, or I can try and find Hedley Grange, but I can't do both."

He put his hands out in front of him. "Sorry, right. I'll shut up now."

Daphne closed her eyes and again relaxed, her back straight as a stack of quarters, her face slack and expressionless. She didn't chant or moan or do anything except sit there in complete silence, trying to connect with whatever force allowed her to communicate with the dead. Jensen had no choice but to wait patiently.

About a minute later, a small, tinny voice suddenly whispered directly into his left ear.

"Jensen!"

It was undeniably Guinevere's, but it was staticky and garbled, like a radio station about one or two megahertz shy of the correct frequency.

"Jensen, can you hear me? I'm going to hang up the phone and bring you back. The Warden found us."

Concurrent with this, Daphne began whispering something, but he couldn't tell what it was because her voice was so low. Worried he might break whatever connection she was making, he walked a few paces away from her and whispered back.

"*Shit*. Look, I think Daphne's getting somewhere. Just give me a second."

The disembodied voice came again, this time more panicked. "We don't *have* a second! He's literally only a few feet away."

"Okay, just give me a second more," Jensen said, then walked back over to Daphne. Now that he was closer, he could hear she was saying "so dark," repeatedly like a mantra.

"Daphne, is that where Grange is? Some place dark?"

Daphne's voice returned to him, distant and alien. "So dark. Stepping stones. Black water. Voices without bodies. Such self-loathing. Such sorrow. Still as a painting but troubled, so troubled. His foot slides on the slippery rock. He almost falls in but catches himself. It's cold. Dark. So dark."

Jensen turned to his left as if Guinevere was actually in the room with him. "Gwen, did you hear all of that?"

When she responded, her whisper was so quiet he could barely hear her. "I did. Dammit, Jensen, I'm hanging up the phone now! I hear footsteps ..."

"Does it make sense to you? Do you know where he is?"

"I ... yes, I think so. I'm hanging up now!"

Jensen looked to Daphne and smiled. "Gotta go, Daff. Thanks."

Daphne didn't seem to have heard him. She was still in her trance, continuing to talk about black waters and slippery rocks and figures without form. He wished he could give her a proper goodbye, a hug or at least a high-five, but her transparency and unwavering daze made that impossible.

"I'll find you when I get back, I swear," he continued. "Bit of parting advice? Ditch the Neanderthal."

Then Daphne and the entire hotel room disintegrated and he was back in the darkness of the Dims.

***

Guinevere returned the handset to the cradle as quietly as she could, and as soon as it was in place, she felt something take form in the empty space behind

230

her. Turning around, she saw it was Jensen, but something was terribly wrong: She could see right through him.

"Jensen, what ..." she went to touch him, but her hand passed right through his body.

The sound of boots clomping on the narrow footbridge next to the railroad tracks grew even closer as the trio of pale lights scoured the ground ahead for any secrets it might hold.

Jensen looked down at her hand in his chest. "What the ..." Then he looked up somewhere to his left and squinted his eyes. "I hear rain ... is it raining?"

"The trip must've loosened your connection to this plane," she whispered and withdrew her hand from his chest. "Dammit, Jensen, I *knew* I should've gone."

He looked at her with large, terrified eyes. "You mean ... I'm going back? For real?"

She shook her head and mustered a weak smile. "Not if *I* can help it. I'll be damned if you're going to leave me out here alone again."

She looked toward the bridge and saw three figures moving in the mist; two lean and lanky, the other broad-shouldered and stocky. If The Warden and his men didn't see them soon, their flashlight beams definitely would.

She turned back to Jensen and saw he had lost even more solidity; the fiery dance of The Flows shown through him like a film projected on a wall.

"*Concentrate*, Jensen. You can fight the urge to go back if you want to. You just have to concentrate."

"I feel heavy. Like I did over there, only worse."

"Jensen, listen to me. Concentrate on the album, on the money you'll get when you find it. Think about it and only it. It'll help tether you here for as long as you can hold it in your mind."

Jensen closed his eyes tightly, no doubt trying to conjure up images of master recordings and piles of money, but after a few seconds of this, she could see it was having no effect: He was now almost completely gone, only a faint ghost of what he'd been.

A tear fell from her cheek at the sight. "Jensen, don't leave. Please don't leave me."

He stared back at her, seeming to take inventory of every line and shadow, and she could see he was crying, too. In a few moments he would be gone forever.

Guinevere didn't know if she could continue without him.

***

The man whose name had been Benjamin C. Clemmons but who was now known simply as The Warden rushed forward the moment his flashlight beam caught a gaunt shape near the side of the tracks.

Greg and Tommy were close at his heels, a little *too* close as always, but this time he was glad for his deputies' company, however intrusive it was. He didn't like this godforsaken place; it gave him the creeps. When he found Bennett, he was going to wring his neck for making him come out here.

But he would get no such opportunity, at least not right now: The narrow shape was only a simple pole sticking out of the ground. Jensen Bennett was nowhere to be found.

"Well, boss, that settles it, I guess," Tommy said, moving his flashlight up and down the pole, searching for clues. "He's not here, and he's not on the clipboard. He must have gone back."

The Warden shined his flashlight over the edge of the bridge and onto the banks of the lava flow beneath it. There was a patch of disturbed ash covering the ground on the side closest to where they stood, and following the unruly pattern with his flashlight he saw it ran back up the side of the steep hill until it connected with a spot neighboring the pole.

"He's still here, Tommy. And by the looks of it, he's not alone."

The Warden leaned over the railing and strained his eyes once again toward the lava flow, but this time he saw something in the distance that made his blood boil.

"Greg, get the wagon," he said under his breath.

His second deputy sounded surprised at the command. "The wagon?"

The Warden spun around and shined the light directly into Greg's face, which looked like a hound dog who'd been caught peeing on the living room rug. "Yes. The *wagon*. You know, the thing we drove here that has four wheels and goes *vroom-vroom*?"

Greg only gave him a stupid nod and then stumbled off into the darkness, and the Warden turned his attention back to the Flows. Two figures were huddled together on a long plank of black stone, floating on the burning river as casually as if they were taking a scenic riverboat tour down the Mississippi.

One was Guinevere Hatcher, and the other was Jensen Bennett.

[silence]

Mommy and Miss Becky say they aren't mad, but both are making angry faces and standing over him like he's been a bad boy. They want to know about the picture, the one he drew during free time. He used a black crayon, the really big one with the wrapper peeled off. It's his favorite.

He wants to be left alone so he can play with his Legos, but they won't go away. They want to know who it is – who the stick figure is supposed to be. He connects a long blue plastic block to a short yellow plastic block, making a big L, and tells them it's Wayne. Wayne with an "E."

Mommy asks if that's a classmate, another preschooler, and Miss Becky shakes her head. No Waynes here, not in her class, and not in any of the others, either.

They show him the drawing again. He doesn't need to see it to know what it looks like. He drew it. But he looks anyway. Because they ask him to.

The stick figure, Wayne, is connected to a long vertical line that comes from above and wraps around his neck like a tie. A blocky shape, meant to be a folding chair knocked on its side, is next to Wayne's stick legs, which dangle just inches above the long horizontal line representing the floor. Wayne's eyes are big black X's, and his head is resting against his shoulder at a weird angle.

Miss Becky asks why Wayne is hanging from the ceiling, and he tells her it's because Wayne was tired of being sad all the time, so he got a rope and kilt himself. Mommy gasps at this last part and crouches down to him, tears standing in the corners of her pretty green eyes.

She asks how he knows about that kind of thing. Was it the TV? Another classmate? Her boyfriend Rob? She needs to know.

He says no one told him about it – it was just there, inside his head, like when they rode Roaring Rapids at Six Flags or went camping with Uncle Eric or visited mommy's friend in Seattle. He knows about being kilt because it *happened* to him.

He knows because *he's* Wayne.

THE DEEP REGIME
-Track Eleven-

Noah DeNova had been so close to giving up that he'd reopened the mental levee keeping his thoughts uncluttered and let the resulting surge wash over his mind. His foremost concern now was the rain, which thrummed around him like the beating of a million tiny drums and had surely washed away the meager trail he'd used to get up here.

Before, he'd been a noble rescuer, but now he was just a fool in the rain. How was he going to find his way back to the cabin, where Nella was probably wearing the floor thin with worry? Would the forest take yet another life this morning when his fake leg caught on some slippery rock and he tumbled down the sheer mountainside to his death?

At that moment, just as he was about to remove his fingers from the man's jawbone and begin packing his bag for the perilous trip back, he felt a weak pulse jump to life beneath the man's skin. It was slow and irregular, but it was there. Noah couldn't help himself – he laughed and pumped a fist into the sky.

He'd never before in his entire career, from his time as a medic in the Marines to his residency in the ER at Beaufort Memorial, revived a patient after they'd been clinically dead for – he glanced at his watch – more than three minutes. One minute twenty seconds was his record, and even then, he'd had the assistance of nurses. This was a miracle, plain and simple.

With that thought, he realized this was no time to rest on his laurels: The man still wasn't breathing. He wasn't out of the woods, no pun intended, so Noah began administering another round of CPR, methodically alternating between pumping the man's chest and putting an ear to his mouth to listen for signs of life.

But as the seconds turned to minutes and he heard the faint thump of helicopter rotors beating a swift rhythm somewhere in the distance, Noah began to worry that the weak heartbeat had been a fluke and he was going to lose the man all over again.

***

The horizon had promised towering obsidian foothills and blistering orange hellfire, and so far it had delivered.

As the stone slab drifted down the molten stream, carrying its two passengers deeper into the craggy and cockeyed landscape quietly burning in the darkness like the dying embers of a campfire, Jensen couldn't help but marvel at their good fortune. Just a moment longer – a second or two at most – and he and Guinevere would've been caught by The Warden and his deputies. But they'd gotten away just in time. He still wasn't sure how they'd done it.

Even more remarkable was the fact he'd been able to remain in the afterlife. He'd rematerialized, but he'd returned feeling like a ship's anchor. His limbs were heavy, his thoughts gluey. The airiness he'd felt ever since arriving in Translucent Tower eons ago had all but deserted him now, leaving no doubt in his mind that he didn't really belong in the afterlife anymore. He'd gone from tourist to alien invader in the blink of an eye, and there was no going back.

A dim awareness of the material world still lingered despite his return, moving in slow motion just outside the limits of his five senses. He could hear the incessant tapping of rain, smell the organic and primitive stink of wet soil, see the greening leaves sagging under the weight of the water falling upon them. And, unfortunately, he could also taste the metallic tang of blood in his mouth and feel quiet spikes of pain shooting through his limbs. It was all there, observable yet distant like the moon.

The stone slab rocked gently as it elegantly circumvented a small island in the center of The Flows and then rejoined the current on the other side. Jensen again looked to Guinevere, who'd taken off her black stockings and bright pink sneakers and was now reclining on the slab as if casually sunbathing on a sun-drenched beach. Something on the horizon had caught her eye, and her head was turned toward whatever it was.

Jensen debated telling her why he was *really* still there. He'd tried to do what she'd suggested by focusing on the five million dollars, on Hedley Grange, on the missing album, but none of it had been strong enough. It was only when he focused on Guinevere, beautiful, mysterious Guinevere, that the material world started loosening its grip and he began to regain his hold on the afterlife. The sight of her now – those bare feet, those tiny painted toes, those long, naked legs that disappeared into the tantalizing shadows of her miniskirt – caused a familiar, aggravating heat to bloom inside him. Desire, yes, but there was also something else ... a sudden dropping sensation in his chest that was both startling and incredibly exciting, like those few seconds after cresting the first hill of a roller coaster, right as it begins to tip over the edge. He smiled like an idiot when he realized what it was.

I love her.

Then again, just to make sure it felt right:

I love her. I love Guinevere Hatcher.

He nodded in silent agreement with himself. It was love, complete and unconditional. Daphne had been right after all.

He hadn't loved Aimee, and he surely hadn't loved any of the others that had come before her. In truth, he hadn't really known what romantic love even *was* until this very moment, floating down a rolling inferno on his way to God knows where. It had always been a fiction written in some exotic language he couldn't understand.

But he understood it now. He loved her. Because she was beautiful and smart and tenacious, but also because of the almost supernatural power she had to summon the *real* him, the one buried beneath costumes and blinded by stage lights. When they were together there was no performance, no audience, no lines to remember or bows to take. Only Jensen Phillip Bennett, completely naked and off-script.

This thought immediately led to another: He didn't hate himself. Not really. He definitely hated the character he'd played to get by, and the broken, miserable actor beneath it. But he didn't hate the person he was when he was around Guinevere. He actually kind of *liked* him – the lack of focus, the looseness of his lips, even the somewhat frightening sensation of letting go of the wheel and allowing the car to take him where it wanted. All of it pointed to one indisputable fact: It was time to finally march the actor out into the woods at gunpoint and dig him a six-foot forever home in the ground. It would be a hole to rival the one inside his soul, the one that nothing could seem to fill, not even everything he'd ever wanted.

And it was all because of Guinevere. Looking at her now, he wanted to feel her petite frame in his arms, taste the warm saltiness of her lips, smell that wonderfully inscrutable scent of coconut perpetually emanating from her hair. He wanted her, *all* of her – the good, the bad and everything in-between. And he wanted it not just today, but tomorrow and for all the days that followed.

But what should he do about it? He could tell her, of course, right here and now. But what then? He was firmly rooted in the afterlife for as long as he kept her face in his mind's eye, but eventually he'd have to return. And when he did, Guinevere would be walled behind the impenetrable barrier separating life and death. And that would be that.

And even if he could somehow breach that barrier, Guinevere was in love with someone else. Her devotion to Hedley Grange was so all-encompassing, so unwavering, that he'd apparently become her sole reason for existing. Jensen might as well be in love with a photo for all the good telling her would do.

Jensen sighed. His epiphany was bittersweet. On the one hand, it felt good to finally love someone for real, and to realize that redemption was possible, even for someone as undeserving as him. But it also hurt like hell to realize she'd never be his, no matter how badly he wanted her, no matter what he did or said. He supposed there was no choice but to carry on and enjoy her company while he still could.

"You still haven't told me where we're going," he said quietly. "You *do* know, right?"

She responded without turning her head, her eyes still lost in the dangerous beauty of the smoldering horizon.

"Of course. The Sea of Sorrow. I wasn't sure at first, but I am now. Hank *wants* us to follow him there for some reason. I can't imagine it's a good one."

Jensen squinted at her. "That doesn't make sense. If he wanted us to follow him he would've left a few breadcrumbs behind. If it hadn't been for Daphne –"

Her head snapped back to him suddenly, the reflected lava of The Flows alive and burning in her eyes.

"*Daphne* didn't do a *damn* thing. Hank whispered where he was going in my ear before he left us in that mirror room. Probably just in case those creatures didn't finish us off. Your girlfriend just jogged the memory loose, is all."

Jensen shook his head in disbelief. "Wait, I know time is a bit flaky here, but that was just a few hours ago. How did you forget about it?"

She looked away again. "I just *did*, okay? I was a little preoccupied."

Jensen smiled and placed a hand on her bare ankle. He didn't want to argue with her. Their time together was short, and every second with her mattered. It was a sad but true reality.

"Okay, Gwen. I get it. I was a little preoccupied, too. Hard *not* to be with the entire cast of *The Walking Dead* coming after you."

She looked back at him apologetically and smiled back. His heart fluttered at the sight of it.

"Your hand feels good," she said. "It's cool. Like an ice cube. Give me the other one, please." Jensen did as he was asked, and she closed her eyes and emitted a long, satisfied sigh that caused the hairs on his arm to rise despite the heat. "Yes, that's *perfect*. Thank *God* you have corpse hands."

"Pretty big talk coming from a dead chick," he said, and they both laughed. Their mutual gaze lingered for a moment before a look passed across Guinevere's face and her grin collapsed back into that enigmatic half-smile.

"Jensen, I know joking is just how you deal with things, and I get it. But this is serious stuff. You should know what you're getting in to. The Sea of Sorrow is in The Subdivisions, which is without a doubt the very worst place in the entire afterworld."

She opened the flap on her blouse a bit wider and began to fan herself. The sweat was beading on her soft white skin, and Jensen tried not to stare as he nodded.

"Yeah, I remember you mentioning it on the bus. You said it's worse than hell, but you didn't elaborate."

The serrated cliffs standing watch on either side of The Flows seemed to grow taller as they passed beneath them, and Guinevere looked toward their menacing peaks as she answered, her eyes sad and faraway.

"I really *can't* elaborate, for a few reasons. One is because I've never been there, thank God, but it's also because it kinda defies explanation." She paused for a moment to brush a sweaty strand of hair from her eyes, and then continued. "I can tell you what *made* it, though – hate. Murderers, rapists, bigots, sadists ... pretty much any sociopathic, psychopathic, ignorant, self-indulgent attitude you can think of came together like the world's worst gumbo to create The Subdivisions. It's one of the oldest and most populated places on this plane. Many of the souls there are older than civilization itself, and they only get more spiteful and angrier and ... *inhuman* the longer they stay in that damp, cold, dark hellhole, feeding off each other's hate. I said before that love is powerful, and it is. But so is hate, and The Subdivisions has it in spades."

She looked back to him, the seriousness in her voice reflected with equal quantity in her eyes.

"There's something else I need to tell you, something you deserve to know." She stopped to gather herself and then began to speak as quickly as her lips would allow. "Your body's alive in the material world. That's why you can sense it. But your soul, it isn't in your body; it's here, with me, on this rock. The longer the two are separated, the greater the chance that when you return … you'll be brain dead. I'm sorry, Jensen. I should have told you right away on that bridge. I should've told you to not fight it. But I was … scared you were going to leave me out there alone."

Jensen blinked a few times as he took a moment to process everything Guinevere had just said. The urge to return to his body was faint right now, but it was definitely there. He guessed by what she'd said it would only get stronger as time went on. The location of *House Made of Sound* would do him no good if he was hooked to a ventilator and had to be fed through a tube for the rest of his life.

In addition to that bombshell was the very Subdivisions themselves. Was braving a torrent of humanity's worst and most primitive inclinations worth five million dollars? Hell, was it worth *any* amount of money? For some reason, the prospect of getting rich didn't seem as exciting as it had back in Springfield Stadium. Either Guinevere's grim description of The Subdivisions was giving him legitimate pause, or something else had taken priority. He shook the thought away.

"I'd be lying if I said I wasn't scared," he said quietly. "But I think I *have* to do this." He looked deep into Guinevere's bottomless brown eyes. "I don't think I could live the rest of my life knowing I had this chance and …" he squeezed her ankles. "And didn't go for it." He took a deep breath that tasted of sulfur and then said, "I'm with you, Gwen."

242

She grabbed his hands and squeezed back. "Good, because I wasn't exactly relishing the idea of going it alone. It's cold and dark and spooky in there. I'm not too proud to admit I'm a little scared, too."

Jensen hoped Guinevere's description of The Subdivisions was just a myth, nothing but a tall tale constructed by people with a penchant for the macabre. But the closer they got to their destination, the busier the butterflies in his stomach became and the less he wanted to find out. But there was no alternative.

For better or for worse, The Subdivisions was where the road led. And there was no going back.

✳✳✳

Not long after, The Flows gurgled around a sharp bend, the stone slab following it like a leaf caught in a rushing storm drain.

As soon as the course straightened again, Guinevere saw their destination a few yards ahead to their right: the toothy maw of an immense cave entrance. Two misshapen outcroppings slightly above the opening looked like eyes, malicious, beady little things that seemed to follow the path of the stone slab with cruel interest. From The Flows, the cave entrance looked like the mossy skull of some ancient giant that had died screaming.

People back in Near Country called it The Crunge, but she wasn't sure why and never really had any reason to ask. In addition to being a deeply unsettling sight, it was one of only a few of entrances that led directly into the belly of The Subdivisions. Hank was somewhere in there right now, alone and probably scared. But she'd fix that. She'd fix *everything*.

"There's our stop," she said, stuffing the black stockings into her left skirt pocket and then quickly jamming her sneakers back on. No time to tie them; the slab was moving faster than she'd anticipated and they'd miss the bank entirely if they didn't act now. "We're going to have to jump off."

Jensen bobbed his head in agreement. "On three?"

"On three."

Holding hands they rose to their feet, the slab wobbling beneath them as they carefully redistributed their weight to avoid tipping over, and slowly began counting. When three came, they jumped from the stone, two paper dolls cut at the feet but joined at the hands, and flew through the noxious air as if swept up in a sudden gust of wind. For a brief moment they were suspended above the warbling river of liquefied rock, its heat sending blistering thorns up the length of her bare legs, and then solid ground was underneath them again and they tumbled forward together, laughing.

They stopped abruptly when a commanding voice echoed from somewhere above.

"Have you completely flipped your lid, Gwen? What're you doing?"

She twisted her head toward the sound and saw The Warden standing on the rim of the cliff behind them, staring her down from his hundred-foot perch, his face a mask of almost comical disbelief. Greg, his constant and faithful companion, was standing closely beside him as usual, trying to mimic The Warden's stern expression but failing miserably. A third figure, Tommy O'Meara, popped his head into view, and the three of them leaned intrepidly over the ledge together and shined their flashlights directly in her face. She squinted and shielded her eyes with her hands.

"What does it *look* like I'm doing? I'm going into The Subdivisions."

The Warden cast an incredulous stare at Tommy, as if looking for confirmation he'd heard what he thought he just heard, and then turned back. "You don't wanna do that, Gwen. You *know* that. What's gotten into you?"

Guinevere stood up defiantly. "*Love*, Warden. *Love's* gotten into me."

The Warden snorted and spilled the flashlight beam across Jensen's face. "What, for *this* guy? *He* make you do all this?"

Guinevere didn't immediately respond. The memory was still sharp in her mind: the field of lazily dancing flowers, the smell of summer rain on the breeze, the stubble that tickled her cheek, the raw, primal heat boiling over inside her. Despite the excitement it stirred, the memory also angered her, *infuriated* her, because it simply wasn't true. It had been an illusion, a trick of glass and light, a complete and utter lie.

"Jensen didn't make me do *anything*," she said. "*No one* makes me do anything I don't want to do. *You* of all people should know that, Benjamin."

The Warden's face flushed briefly, but whether it was due to the heat of The Flows or her words, she wasn't sure.

"Look, Gwen. Jensen. You have no idea what you guys're getting yourselves into. *Please* don't go in there. I'm not just saying it 'cause I don't wanna follow you in. I'm saying it 'cause it's dangerous. *Beyond* dangerous. We're talking eternal suffering, here."

"That's *our* decision to make," Jensen said. "Not yours. No one's forcing you to follow us."

The Warden got down on his haunches and in doing so let the flashlight dip to the ground. "Buddy, that's where you're wrong. I don't have a choice. I *have* to follow you, bring you back. It's my job. You? You *do* have a choice. A choice to not make a damn fool mistake and go in there."

Jensen looked at Guinevere, and she at him. They didn't need to say anything: The expressions they traded were enough conversation. They turned and, without another word, began walking up the pebble-strewn walkway that led to The Crunge. The Warden continued to shout behind them, but the closer they got to the opening, the harder it became to hear him.

Then the gluttonous mouth of The Crunge swallowed them whole and they were gone.

***

The blood-orange light spilling from The Flows outside was enough to guide their way forward at first. But the further they went down the cave's narrow

245

throat, the gloomier it became until, finally, they were in near-total darkness. Only a tiny pinprick of light in the distance ahead suggested they hadn't dissolved into complete nothingness.

But it wasn't the lack of visibility that disturbed Jensen, nor was it the abiding cold that had slowly invaded his bones the deeper they walked; it was the *noises* prowling the arcane darkness somewhere down the line.

A woman's agonized shriek, as if something was slowly pulling her apart. Wet ripping sounds, unintelligible whispers, the frenzied banging of angry fists against a wooden door. Sporadic guttural barks that were neither human nor animal, but somewhere in-between. The deranged laughter of several men who sounded at once amused and absolutely horrified, as if there had been some side-splitting joke at the end of an executioner's noose. Each took turns violating the quiet like the crash of midnight thunder, only to echo into oblivion once they'd had their say.

Jensen broke the silence himself after hearing an especially heartbreaking sound: a woman screaming for help. "Should we do something?" he whispered.

"There's nothing we *can* do," Guinevere whispered back, her voice close and conspiratorial. "That woman's here because she *wants* to be. Maybe that's always been the case, or maybe she's a missionary from Near Country who got stuck here trying to save someone. Doesn't matter, because she's one of *them* now."

"Then why is she calling for help?"

"I don't know. But she definitely doesn't need to be rescued, that's for sure. No one's here against their will. They're just ... *infected*. Not with a virus or anything, but an ideology. A really *bad* one. And if we aren't careful, the same'll happen to us."

Jensen winced and shut his eyes as a short, startled scream, this time from a man, echoed throughout the chamber and then faded away. "Something tells me that's going to get old *real* quick," he said.

In truth, he was far more terrified than annoyed. The sounds were bad, but the images they conjured in his imagination were worse. People being tortured, people suffering. Unending hopelessness and despair. A loveless, everlasting void bereft of light and warmth and happiness, far deeper and darker than any hole he'd ever existed in before. All of it was waiting for them somewhere down the road, waiting for *him*.

His heart suddenly jumped to life at this last thought and began pummeling the inside of his chest like a mallet against a drumhead. The pinhole of light in the distance wavered slightly as if he was seeing it through a haze, and before he was able to blink the mirage away, he felt a wave of nausea overtake him. He wasn't really going *in* there, was he? Into that cold, dark, perilous abyss? It was insane.

"Jensen? Everything okay?" Guinevere asked.

He looked in the direction of her voice and saw only a vague shape in the dark. "Never been more scared in my life, but other than that, sure, everything's just fuckin' peachy."

He felt her creep next to him, wrap her arm around his waist, squeeze tightly. He hugged her back. She was warm and comforting in the darkness.

"I'm scared, too," she whispered, "but we can do this."

He felt his courage return a bit in her arms. "Right. We'll just ... pretend it's a cheesy haunted house. Staffed by overzealous teenagers."

She squeezed his waist again in confirmation, and together they found the resolve to carry on.

✳✳✳

As they went, still holding each other, the insignificant pinhole of light punched into the blackness ahead grew until it was the size of a quarter, then a dinner plate, then the rim of an 18-wheeler. Now it looked like a full moon in the summer darkness, burning with a soft, pale light that was almost bright enough to see the path before them, but not quite. Joining the disturbing carouselambra of despair and delinquency emanating from it was a dangerous, mechanized sound consisting of several elements: two loud, metallic *clunks*, separated by a brief silence and followed by a prolonged *whirring*. The entire cycle kept repeating and took about a minute from start to finish. It was rhythmic, almost hypnotic, like an enormous robot was slowly walking toward them, dragging its giant steel feet on the ground as it went. Guinevere had no idea what could be making the sound and hoped they didn't stay long enough to find out.

She'd expected to find some answers when they finally reached the portal of light and then passed through it into the next chamber, but was instead met with even more darkness and cold. It seemed the guiding light had been little more than an illusion generated by thousands of tiny holes stamped into the ceiling far above their heads. Through the thin shafts of light they produced, she could make out hundreds of slender, unmoving shadows congregating together like a forest of towering redwoods directly in front of them. She didn't know what they were either, but she was near certain they weren't the source of the terrible robotic sounds. They, along with the intermittent cries of the souls entombed somewhere further on, still seemed somewhat distant.

She twisted her head anxiously up to Jensen, whose features were all but lost in the shadows, and pointed to the shapes ahead.

"What do you think *those* things are?"

"Not sure," he responded. "Trees, maybe?" His voice still had the vestiges of a whisper despite the fact he was nearly shouting to be heard over the mournful wailing of a woman who seemed to be calling for someone named Edgar. "What I wouldn't give for a flashlight right about now."

She thought for a second as the cries died down again, then smiled excitedly. "Actually, I have something almost as good." Reaching into the front pocket of her skirt, she pulled out the pink cigarette lighter concealed there and held it up so he could see it. "Remember this?"

He chuckled and took the Zippo from her hand, examining it for a second before responding. "Thank Christ for bad habits. The Surgeon General can suck it."

She looked around, hoping to spot a branch or plank of wood on the ground, but there was only darkness. "We need to find something to make a torch with. The Zippo's too small by itself. Maybe we can use my stockings as a wick."

"No," Jensen said, "they'll burn up too quickly. Grange's bandana is thicker. It'll last longer."

Anger flared inside her and she looked up at him with wounded eyes. "*Absolutely not*. I'll walk in pitch dark before I burn *that*."

"Gwen, it's just a piece of cloth."

"Not to *me* it isn't." She twisted in his arms until she was free of his grip, then took a few cautious steps backward. She stood there, eyes daring him to take the bandana, hands holding it protectively against her chest like it was an injured baby bird. "It's all I have of him. You burn this and I'll *never* forgive you."

She'd expected an argument, but all he did was contemplate her ultimatum in silence and then offer a resigned sigh.

"Fine. We'll use my tie. Never liked it, anyway. Just come back over to me before you break a leg on something."

She stuffed the bandana back into her bra but stayed put. "I know you're just being flippant. As usual. But my legs actually *do* kinda hurt. I'm not sure why."

The tall, black lump in the darkness that she knew was Jensen crouched down and thumbed the lighter's flint wheel, then used the modest light it provided to scan the ground for torch materials. Another loud *clunk*, then the sound of someone laughing hysterically, filled the silence as he searched.

"It's this *place*," he said when the laughter finally faded. "I don't feel great, either. Didn't before we walked in here, but it's much worse now. The cold definitely doesn't help."

He wasn't wrong. She'd grown up in northern Wisconsin and was used to the cold. *Loved* it, in fact, especially when it snowed and the entire farm was completely silent except for the winter wind howling across the fields and the clink of her mother's wind chimes on the porch. But the chill inside The Subdivisions was a different animal altogether – it was cruel and spiteful and existed only to cause discomfort. She very much wanted to be next to Jensen again, for warmth and also for safety, but she hadn't yet convinced herself that he wouldn't try to wrestle Hank's bandana from her by force the second she drew near.

It's just a piece of cloth, he'd said.

It was true. She was being ridiculous, and she knew it. But things were slipping away very quickly, from both ends, and she desperately needed something to hold on to, some tangible reminder of the broken devotion she was so ardently trying to piece back together.

"Got one!" Jensen said suddenly and held up a long, thin shadow in his left hand. "Some kind of bone. I think it's a ... femur? *Blech.*"

He pulled a long, snakelike shape from his pocket – his tie, she assumed – and then began wrapping it around the bone at one end. It was only after he'd completed this task and had moved on to holding the flame to the tie in an attempt to get it to catch that she finally allowed herself to walk back over to him.

"You need to cover it in a little fuel," she said and crouched down to meet him at eye level. "Open the Zippo and squeeze the cotton ball inside all over the tie. But leave some so we can still light it."

"Got it," he said, and began taking the Zippo apart. "Hope you have the fire marshal on speed dial, 'cause this baby's gonna *burn.*"

She hugged her legs for warmth while he worked. It did little good. She was cold and scared and achy all over, especially in her left leg, which had never bothered her before. She tried to think of Paradise City, of its pervasive beauty, of all her friends and loved ones who lived there, but it was extremely difficult. It all seemed so long ago, so distant and unreachable.

Another scream from somewhere ahead, this one cruel and conclusively hostile, shot through the cavern, and Guinevere instinctively jumped at the sound. She was glad it was too dark for Jensen to see her do it. She couldn't believe how arrogant she'd been, how much of an idiot for thinking she could have ever done this by herself. Even with Jensen by her side, it was hard to summon the courage to continue. She just wanted to find Hank and get out of this terrible place.

Finally, the torch was ready, and Jensen reassembled the Zippo and stood up. She did the same.

"Any last words before I send my tie to the great closet in the sky?"

She couldn't tell if he was grinning or not – it was simply too dark to see his face – but she imagined he was and smiled back. "No, but I can sing *Amazing Grace* if you want."

"Your voice is too good for this Louis Vuitton knockoff," Jensen said. "Let's light this puppy."

The torch caught fire with an unexpected *whoosh* the second Jensen put the flame to it, startling them both. Her eyes protested the sudden blast of light, and she instinctively shielded them with the crook of her arm.

When she uncovered them again and Jensen's face came into gradual focus, she saw him giving her a strange look that made her uncomfortable and more than a little self-aware. Something wasn't right.

"What?"

He didn't say anything, just brought the torch close and used its commanding light to examine her face.

"Jensen, *what*?"

He looked to her with sad, shocked eyes. "Gwen, it's your face ... and your legs ... your whole *body*, actually."

It was then that she looked down and saw her legs had lost their healthy hue and were now bruised and pale, like she'd been lying in some coroner's refrigerator for a week. She gasped at the sight.

"You look …" Jensen swallowed hard and locked eyes with her. "Jesus, Gwen. You look *dead*."

✱✱✱

Of course she was dead. So was he. But this was different.

Guinevere hadn't become some walking nightmare like the Vanities, nor had her innate beauty completely vanished. But she was a shadow of the woman he'd met on the bus to Paradise City, with sunken eyes and mottled skin and a complexion that made her seem almost ghostly. Her hair had thinned and she looked malnourished, like she'd lost a good ten pounds since he'd last had a good look at her. He could do nothing at first but stare at her with quiet grief, as if he'd been called to the morgue to identify her body and was now faced with the unassailable truth of her passing.

"I was afraid of this," she said, examining herself by the torchlight and frowning at what she saw. "*Dammit*. How could I have been so *stupid*."

He studied his own arms and saw nothing strange, not so much as a papercut. "Maybe it's just an illusion or something? I seem to be okay."

"It's no illusion," she said dejectedly. "It's this place."

She turned and looked toward the strange shapes ahead that, in the flame's newfound light, were revealed as a dense, dark jungle of rocky spires protruding from the ground. A thick gray mist was darting and swirling and dancing in the impenetrable darkness between them like vaporous ballerinas.

"I'm not tethered to the material world like you are," Guinevere continued. "There's nothing keeping the lower vibrations down here from stripping away my spiritual body like … a river eroding a rock. And it'll only get worse as time passes."

Jensen pointed toward the way they'd come. "Let's turn around, then. Go back and ... I dunno, wait for Grange to come out the other side. This place *has* to have an exit, right?"

"Yeah, the Wicked Garden, but it's clear on the other side. It'll take ages to backtrack and get there. Besides, The Warden is right behind us. We *can't* go back."

"Okay," he said, "we'll stay the course, then. Through these stalactite thingys."

She turned back to him and smirked. "*Stalagmites*," she corrected. "Stalactites are the ones that hang from the ceiling."

He returned the expression and held out the Zippo to her, which she took. "Right. That's what I meant."

Despite the condition of the rest of her body, Guinevere's eyes were still a deep, beautiful, healthy brown, and Jensen realized *that* must be where her *true* soul existed, where she really was. Not in the pointless physical form, which was as malleable as soft clay, but somewhere behind those bottomless brown eyes. He watched her pale lips shudder quietly in reply to the breezeless chill in the cavern, and it took everything in his power not to warm them with his own. In that moment he hated the cold, hated The Subdivisions, hated whatever dared to make her unhappy.

I love you, he thought, and smiled sadly. The phrase still felt good, felt *right*. But he couldn't say it aloud, as badly as he wanted to. Now wasn't the time for the hard sale. Now was the time to just exist with her, appreciating every precious moment they had left.

"You know, this doesn't have to be a bad thing," she said finally, as if answering a question he hadn't asked.

"What doesn't?"

"The way I look. I mean, I'm absolutely *hideous*, but ... it shows how much I care. Once Hank sees what I put myself through just to be with him again ... what I did to myself just to find him ... he'll see that I've changed, right? That I'm not the self-centered narcissist he thinks I am."

Jensen's heart sank. He wanted to ask her how she could still love Grange after what he'd done to them at Township Rebellion and again in the Room Full of Mirrors, what he was obviously doing to them *right now*, all in the name of spite. But he didn't, partly because he didn't want to betray his true emotions, but mostly because he already knew the answer: Love was complicated and seldom made any rational sense.

"I suppose that's one way of looking at it," he said after another scream ripped through the cavern and then scampered back into the darkness. He tried to summon some false expression to hide the disappointment that was no doubt splayed across his face, but he couldn't, not in any convincing way, not anymore, so he turned away from her and aimed the tie-torch toward the forest of tall, narrow columns standing in their way. Its powerful orange light barely penetrated the outer darkness.

Five million dollars, maybe more, he thought. The phrase, once powerful enough to send him dreaming, only stirred a modicum of excitement now.

"Hedley's somewhere that way," he said and pointed the torch northward. "Let's not keep him waiting."

Guinevere looked at him strangely for a moment, like she was expecting him to say something else, then nodded in agreement when she realized he was done. "Okay. Let's go, then. Lead the way."

Without another word, Jensen stepped into the field of stalagmites and began slowly picking his way forward. The gloom parted as they went, the flare of the burning tie-torch sending sparks like startled fireflies into the air. He could feel Guinevere keeping pace behind him and wondered if she realized just how great she really was, how perfect. Grange apparently didn't.

A realization dawned on him: He wasn't just disappointed; he was angry. *Furious*, really. Not at her; she couldn't help how she felt any more than he could. His anger was for Hedley Grange, the self-appointed saint of rock and roll, his former best friend and confidant. Jensen detested him now, for many reasons, but mostly for the way he'd so casually tossed Guinevere aside as if she were a broken guitar string. Grange was an entitled asshole who didn't deserve anything as wonderful as Guinevere Hatcher.

Maybe no one did.

Now that he was inside it, the columns of rock seemed less like stone pillars and more like immense, leafless trees, much like his first hazy impression of them. He glanced upward at the hundreds of tiny holes punched into the cavern ceiling and imagined they were distant stars winking across the vast expanse of space. It was almost beautiful. In fact, aside from the occasional shriek and that bizarre mechanical noise, which definitely seemed to be some giant, sinister machine endlessly *whirring* and *thumping* on dry pistons somewhere in the unknowable gloom, everything was quite peaceful, like a nighttime walk through a wintery forest just moments before snowfall.

But the illusion quickly folded the instant he caught sight of the tall, thin shape lurking in the shadows just beyond the reach of the torchlight. It was a few pillars ahead of him, peeking out from behind it, just a torso and a featureless black head, an elongated perversion of a human figure whose unnaturally long fingers gripped the stalagmite as if depending on it for support. The shadow seemed to study him for a second, stretching its head further out for a better view, before quickly slinking back into the darkness and disappearing.

Jensen stopped and frantically swept the torch in front of him, looking for it again. But it was gone. It hadn't been a man, and it hadn't been a creature, but some strange in-between that seemed to be made of the very shadows in which it hid.

But it didn't stay hidden for very long.

***

The stone forest, already ominous to begin with, became even eerier by torchlight. Somewhere in the shadows, inside the dark spaces where the light couldn't reach, were eyes.

A lot of them.

They were being watched. *Scrutinized.*

She'd experienced similar feelings as a child, late at night when the old farmhouse was uncomfortably quiet and every creaky floorboard or loose pipe became the cautious footsteps of a midnight intruder. Through the slender crack in her bedroom door, she'd picture a tall figure standing in the darkness of the hallway, silently watching her, waiting for her eyelids to close so it could pour into the room like spilled ink and smother her to death in her sleep.

This was like that, only now it wasn't the imaginings of an overactive ten-year-old mind but a palpable danger that monitored and tracked them from somewhere unseen. Even the path behind them now felt crowded with observers, and she couldn't shake the feeling that any attempt at a retreat would be short-lived.

But as uneasy as the eyes made her, they paled in comparison to the dull ache quickly overtaking her body. She felt like she'd been beaten up and left to die on some dirty bathroom floor. She was freezing despite her proximity to Jensen's makeshift torch, and her limbs felt rigid and unresponsive. Even the simple act of *walking* hurt. And as if that wasn't enough, she'd just been treated to an impromptu makeover courtesy of *Maison de Subdivisions*. There weren't any reflective surfaces nearby that could confirm her worst fears, but based on Jensen's shocked and slightly repulsed reaction to seeing her new face, it wasn't good.

Guinevere had never really put much stock into how beautiful everyone always said she was, had even become tired of hearing it, because what did it even mean? The concept of beauty was entirely too subjective to matter. But now that she'd apparently lost her looks, she was surprised at how much it worried her.

She wasn't pretty anymore. She frowned at the thought. Either vanity was finally besting her or something else was.

The Subdivisions, she thought. *It's just got my head all screwed up, is all. Everything will be okay once we leave.*

Just then, Jensen stopped dead in his tracks and began waving the torch back and forth in front of him in a wide arc, searching for something. Her thoughts immediately returned to the eyes in the darkness.

"You see them, don't you?" she asked.

"There was something watching us from behind that pillar up there," he said. "A shadow. But it's gone now."

"No, it isn't. It's still here. I feel it. I feel *them*. Don't you?"

Jensen twisted around to face her and nodded. "Yeah. Like someone's watching me through binoculars or something. Should we go back?"

"Too late. They're everywhere now. Look!"

He followed her outstretched finger and then jumped when he saw what was at the end of it: about a dozen or so amorphous dark shapes were now peering out from behind their respective pillars, their long fingers wrapped around the stone like wire. They looked less like human beings and more like a young child's interpretation of one – featureless, spaghetti-thin stick figures drawn without the slightest hint of individuality.

Jensen raised the torch at them defensively, as if he could burn them from existence.

"What do you think they want?" he asked without taking his eyes from them.

"Don't know."

It was then that she heard another noise casually join the sporadic screams and endless churning ahead: a frantic scratching that sounded like fingernails seeking purchase on the underside of a coffin lid. Something was trying to break free.

"Let's just keep moving," she said uneasily. "Maybe they'll leave us alone."

Jensen didn't respond, only started walking forward again, this time much slower, carefully picking his way through the stalagmites, the tie-torch held out in front of him like a magic talisman. As they passed, the shadow people closest to them would dart back into the shadows and then reappear seconds later behind new pillars further ahead, making it hard to tell just how many of them there actually were. None of the shadows made a move toward them, only watched with their silent, invisible eyes.

It wasn't long before Guinevere realized something that troubled her deeply: The scratching sounds weren't coming from the darkness around them, but from *inside her head*. Something wasn't trying to get *out*.

It was trying to get *in*.

Jensen could apparently hear the noise, too, because he began shaking his head vigorously as if trying to dislodge a bug that had flown into his ear. "What the hell *is* that?"

"It's *them*," she said. "Whatever those things are. I'm not sure, but I think they're trying to read us. Our thoughts, I mean. To make sure we're worthy of getting in."

"Like doormen at a hotel," Jensen said, and huffed. "Man, I'm *really* getting sick of Nadmits."

She wasn't familiar with that term and told him as much.

"It means *no admittance*," he said. "If they're here to vet us, to see if we're good enough to get through the front door, then we'd better call a cab right now, cause there's no *way* either one of us is seeing the inside of this place. Not unless there's a dead hooker in your past you're not telling me about."

He was right. The Doormen, as he called them, would surely realize they didn't belong there and … what? Kindly escort them out? Somehow, she didn't think that's how they dealt with intruders.

"Hank got in," she said. "He doesn't deserve to be here, either. There must be a way through."

Jensen snorted. "Yeah, he's a saint, alright. I'm surprised they haven't added him to Mount Rushmore yet."

She ignored this last bit and tried to concentrate on something bad she'd done when she was alive, something that would grant her access into The Subdivisions. But all she could remember was stealing a carton of Marlboros from a 7-Eleven when she was in high school. That, and the mean, hurtful things she'd said to Hank on the last night of her life. While she wasn't exactly proud of either one, she didn't think they warranted eternal damnation.

She was running out of time. Already she could feel the Doormen inside her head, dirtying the carpet with their muddied boots, trampling filth throughout the house as they sifted through her personal belongings with grubby fingers, examining every crack and crawlspace for some indication she was as diseased as they were. It was now or never. She had to come up with something, anything, even if it was a lie.

She forced her mind to return to that field of flowers, to the soft summer breeze, to the warm, naked body pressed against her own. She let herself remember the way he'd slid perfectly inside her, the delicious taste of his lips entangled with her own, the syncopated music of their flesh colliding, the desire that burned like a patient fire between her legs until, finally, she couldn't contain it any longer and it tore through her body, its flagrant heat consuming her flesh from head to toe until there was nothing left but ash.

I'm a cheater, she thought. *A traitor. A dirty little whore who betrayed the only man who ever truly loved me.*

She found herself getting angry at the lie she was telling herself, but she had to tell it. It was the only way to pass.

I'm glad *I did it, too, because I don't want you anymore, Hank. I want* him.

She gritted her teeth and forced the rest of the thought to form.

I want Jensen.

***

The shadow people wanted to inspect his life, to shuffle through it like a flipbook. But Jensen wasn't going to let them. If he kept his mind cluttered with equations, he was pretty sure he could confuse them long enough to sneak past the gate on a technicality. That was his plan, at least.

Net income equals revenue minus expenses ... assets equal liabilities plus equity.

He wasn't eager to relive his memories anyway, even the good ones. He loathed them all, had spent years learning how to hide them behind carefully constructed disguises or, if that failed, to suffocate them in cocaine and alcohol. All of them were frayed, and if the shadow men were allowed to tug on even one thread, the whole thing would certainly untangle into a jumbled mess. It's not like there was even anything to find, at least not anything that would be useful to them. He wasn't a saint, not by a long shot, but he knew he didn't belong there. The only chance he had at getting through was to avoid being read altogether.

Total liabilities divided by total equity equals the debt-to-equity ratio ... sales minus the cost of goods equals gross profit.

Resisting them was difficult, especially considering the material world still threatened to whisk him back to Kansas the moment his mind wandered from Guinevere. It was a juggling act worthy of Barnum and Bailey, but so far he was managing. It helped that he could still hear her loose shoelaces beating an unsteady rhythm on her sneakers as she walked somewhere behind him. She hadn't said a word since his crack about Mount Rushmore, and neither had he. He wanted to turn around or at least call out to her, to make sure she was still okay, but he didn't want to break his concentration, or hers.

Cash divided by current liabilities equals cash ratio ... profit margin equals net income divided by revenue times a hundred.

He heard the cryptic machine ahead issue a single, decisive *clank*, and then immediately an anguished inhuman howl tore through the dimly lit cavern with such terrible force that it overpowered everything else, even his own heartbeat. The sounds – the *whirring*, the metallic *bangs*, the scattered cries in the darkness – they all fit together somehow, one flowing from the other like a piece of primordial music. He just wasn't sure how.

The shadowy figures ahead seemed to ignore all of it, except for him. They were still popping in and out of existence as he walked, moving as he moved so that they were always in front of him, always hiding behind their stone sanctuaries, their charcoal-black faces craned toward him as they wordlessly tried again and again to comb his mind for information.

Keep trying, shitheads. Nobody's home. Selling price minus unit cost times markup price divided by unit cost, times a hundred, is the markup percentage.

Jensen quietly celebrated as he began to see the hazy edge of the stalagmite field take form in the distance. Beyond it, dimly lit by the thin shafts of light raining down from above, was a large, squat shape that looked like an overturned saucepan. Jensen couldn't tell what the shape was, but it had to be their destination. Only a minute or two more and they'd be there. He just had to hold out a little longer.

Now that he thought about it, the shape ahead wasn't really a saucepan; more like a water storage tank, similar to the gigantic one with the flaking white paint that used to sit behind his grandma's house in Oakworth. He'd go out there often as a kid, sometimes with a book or his Walkman, but usually holding the script for an upcoming school play. He'd run lines with himself, not really caring about the character he was going to play, but obsessed with the persona he was slowly constructing for himself, bit by bit like a patient Victor Frankenstein. God knows he hated practicing in the bathroom, in front of that stupid mirror that hid absolutely nothing, even when he shut the lights off ...

He realized his thoughts were wandering, that he was reliving memories. He needed something stronger than simple equations.

How about ... ROI. Okay. Dude invests twenty-eight hundred in ... I dunno. ShitCo. They sell toilet seat covers or something. Guy decides to rebalance his portfolio, so he unloads the shares a few weeks later for only three G's. Three grand minus twenty-eight hundred is two hundred bucks, divided by the original cost times a hundred is ... about seven percent return on investment. Should've stuck with ShitCo, dude.

The shadow men were becoming frustrated. There was no change in their demeanor, no difference in the intensity of the scratching inside his head, but his refusal to fold was angering them all the same. He could feel it. Perhaps no one had ever fought them like this before. Maybe he was the first. The thought brought a satisfied smile to his face.

Now ... break-even point. Guy opens a small pizza place, six bucks a slice. Fixed costs are three grand a month, probably because it's a rat-infested shithole, with variables at two bucks. Six minus two is four, three grand divided by four is ... seven-hundred-and-fifty slices to get back to zero.

They were almost there – he could see some kind of arch carved into the would-be water tank beyond the stalagmites. Squinting, he could see it was some kind of doorway, at least nine or ten feet high, with a gaping black hole for an entrance that appeared to lead straight into oblivion. It was far from welcoming, but it was an exit. It would have to do.

But before he could take another step, the archway suddenly lifted from the ground with a mechanical *clang* and then zipped out of frame like a startled animal. The *whirring* returned, and he was now able to match the sound with a source: the wall where the arch had been was now spinning.

When it slowed again a few seconds later, Jensen saw a nearly identical doorway move into view and then hammer down into place where the other had just been. A man's panicked cries immediately burst from the new opening, a series of "no's" that quickly devolved into incoherent blubbering and then a disturbing gurgling sound, as if someone had just slit his throat and he was choking on his own blood.

So the sounds *were* all connected, as he'd guessed. The shape ahead was some sort of giant carousel, but instead of plastic horses with painted faces, it consisted of doors. Large, archaic-looking doors that led to places where men willingly endured unimaginable acts of torture and brutality. His confident grin wilted a bit. He was so focused on getting through the stone forest that he hadn't really considered what he'd do about the dangers that lay beyond it.

"They're leaving," Guinevere said, and looking around at the remaining stalagmites, he saw she was right – the beings had all crept back into the shadows while he'd been examining the carousel. Everything was as it had been; a sweep of the tie-torch revealed nothing but barren pillars and swirling mist. Even the scratching in his head was gone.

They'd made it.

He turned to Guinevere expectantly, holding the flame high so he could get a good look at her. Her condition hadn't changed much, aside from a few gray hairs and a slight geriatric hunch she hadn't had before, like she was carrying some heavy load on her shoulders. She also looked angry, and he supposed he didn't blame her. It wasn't fair. He could only hope his expression didn't betray the surprise her new appearance still elicited in him.

"They didn't read me," he said proudly.

"Good for you." She skirted his gaze by looking at something over his shoulder. "It must be some kind of giant Lazy Susan. I saw it spinning before."

He looked back at the machine. The same door was still there, waiting for someone to enter it. "Yeah, I saw that, too. I bet there's other entrances, and this thing spins around to accommodate them all."

"You'd win that bet," she said absently and pushed past him to examine the door, leaving him alone at the edge of the stone forest.

Now that he was closer, the carousel didn't look like a saucepan *or* a water tank; just a tall, smooth wall made of black steel that curved away from the door on either side until it was obliterated by darkness. There was a large platter between the carousel and the ground that Jensen supposed spun the entire contraption, and in the narrow gap between it and the floor were all sorts of gears dripping with a slimy black ooze that smelled like old motor oil.

"This *could* be the right door," Guinevere said quietly, as if talking to herself. She stuck a pale arm through the opening and moved it around, seemingly satisfied when she pulled it out again and it hadn't disintegrated. "Then again, it might not be. There's no way to tell for sure."

He noticed something on the ground near her feet and pointed the torch at it. There, scratched into the dirt in front of the door, were four words:

The memories it steals.

He couldn't help but smile. "Not exactly. Look down."

She did as she was asked, even turning her head a bit so she could face the text head-on. But even in the darkness he could see the familiar furrow of her brow as she shook her head. "I don't get it."

"It's a lyric from a song," he said. "A Quiet Catastrophe song. The full line is, 'Time only heals the memories it steals.' Hed was always *really* proud of that one. He must've written the first half of the lyric on the door he went through, so when it finally comes around again and locks into place, the lyric will be complete. That'll be our door."

Guinevere nodded. If she was impressed by this revelation, or by his shrewd attention to detail, she didn't show it. "But we'll only have a few seconds. I've been counting the cycles. It's about a minute from end to end, so that means the doors only stay in place for – "

Despite the fact they'd been expecting it, he and Guinevere both jumped back when the locks on either side of the arch busted open and the door shot upward, rattling on its greasy tracks until it hit the top with a deafening *clang*. It hung there for a split second and then the carousel kicked to life, sending the door off into the distance.

"About forty seconds," she continued. "That's not much time."

There was an uncomfortable breeze next to the spinning carousel, and Guinevere hugged herself for warmth against it. She was staring off in the direction of the incoming door as casually as if waiting for a bus. In the dwindling firelight she looked like a complete stranger, an emaciated old woman in need of a hot meal and a place to sleep.

The fact she'd made it out, that they'd *both* made it out, suggested something rather obvious to him: Guinevere had been wrong about the shadow people's intentions. It seemed they didn't have the power or the authority to keep *anyone* out of The Subdivisions, even two weary gatecrashers with very little fight left in them. Perhaps they just enjoyed prying into other people's lives, a holdover from their time on earth and, now that he thought about it, probably the reason they were even *in* a terrible place like this in the first place.

But something was definitely bothering her, and it wasn't just her appearance. The shadow people must have read her, forced her to relive something from her past that had mortified her. Was Guinevere capable of doing or saying *anything* that would make him fall out of love with her? The answer was no, there wasn't. His love was complete and unconditional. But she didn't know that. Maybe it would help if she finally did.

Jensen made a decision: He was going to tell her how he felt. Damn the material world, and damn Hedley Grange. They could both go to hell.

"Gwen," he said, stepping toward her, not sure exactly what he was going to say or how he was going to say it. "I know this isn't exactly –"

The rest of the words were knocked from his lips when something big and powerful rushed up from behind and slapped him hard across the back. It didn't hurt, but it was enough to send him staggering forward, hands fumbling the air for something to break his fall. There was nothing, though, and as he fell flat on his stomach with a startled *whump*, the tie-torch fell from his hand and was instantly snuffed out in the dirt. Everything went dark.

Blind, Jensen's other senses kicked into high gear. He tasted dirt in his mouth, heard Guinevere scream his name hysterically, felt something hard but pliable snake around his ankles and bind them tightly together with an uncomfortable squeeze. Then he was being pulled back, but not before feeling her fingers brush against his as she tried to grab his outstretched hands. But it was too late.

As he was dragged back into the stone forest, a voice, singular yet composed of countless inflections and accents, boomed like the voice of God himself inside his head:

You did not conform. Now you will be cast out.

✳✳✳

The Lazy Susan had made three more turns, revealing and then removing three more doors, and Jensen still hadn't responded to any of her calls.

She couldn't see him, either. Neither the meager shafts of light overhead or the small flame of her Zippo lighter provided any clue as to where the Doormen had taken Jensen. The second he'd stepped from their sphere of influence, the stalagmite nearest to him had jumped to life, no longer rigid but springy like a tentacle. It had attacked him, neutralized him, then yanked him backward and out of sight. She couldn't even follow him, because the remaining stalagmites – which were either possessed by the Doormen or obeyed their commands like trained pets – had instantly folded together to block her way through.

She'd been granted access, and Jensen hadn't. She couldn't go back, and he couldn't go forward. It was that simple.

Guinevere had been angry with him, to the extent that merely looking in his direction had made her want to slap him across the face. She'd even thought of darting through Hank's door the second it came around, of running at full speed into the darkness until he was nothing but a bad memory.

But it was just harmless anger, an inevitable result of what the Doormen had made her say to get past them. None of this was Jensen's fault. He wasn't responsible for the actions of a facsimile, or the lies it had made her experience. How could she be mad at him for something he didn't do and didn't even know about? It was asinine. The only thing he was after was a payday, and when he had it, he'd be gone. She'd been expecting it for some time, now.

But not like this. She'd hoped for some kind of goodbye, a hug or at least a handshake. She'd wanted to thank him for being there for her, for holding her when she cried, for making her feel cared for and safe. She'd wanted him to know just how much he meant to her, how much she'd miss him and that familiar feeling of home he exuded.

But now he was gone, and she was all alone again.

Tears suddenly burst from her eyes, hot tears that burned coming out. What would happen to him? Would they hurt him? Trap him for so long that he'd be a vegetable when he returned to the material world? She wished it had been her. *She* was the one who deserved to be punished, not him.

She called out to him again, her voice collapsing into a hoarse whisper from the sheer effort. But there was no response, only the monotonous drone of the machine spinning somewhere in the darkness behind her. When it clanged again, she turned and began quickly examining the newly arrived door with the Zippo. Scant as its light was, she could still see the phrase Jensen had spoken of written on the bottom of the doorframe in what looked like white chalk: Time only heals.

"The memories it steals," she whispered, and then put her head in her hands and cried harder than she ever had before.

It was the right door. Hank was somewhere behind it. But Jensen was out *there* somewhere, lost in the shadows, lost *forever*, as far as she knew. It couldn't be true. There had to be something she could do.

Without thinking, she grabbed the extinguished torch, which was now just charred bone with what looked like the burnt skin of an animal hanging from its end, and jammed it into the crack between the Lazy Suzan and the ground. She needed to buy herself some time to search for Jensen. She couldn't leave without him. *Wouldn't* leave without him.

But twenty seconds turned to forty, then to a full minute, and still her calls, paltry as they were, remained unanswered. Instead, there was a troubling grinding noise and the pungent smell of something burning. Looking over her shoulder, she saw what was causing both: The Lazy Susan was done with

Hank's door and was trying to move it away, but her makeshift wedge was preventing it. Already a hairline crack had formed in the bone, and she knew it wouldn't last long against the force of the immense machine.

This was her last shot. If she didn't go now, it wasn't just Jensen who would disappear forever. She'd lose Hank, too. Maybe even herself.

"Goodbye, Jensen," Guinevere whispered sadly to the darkness. "Don't *ever* let it go."

Then she walked through the door.

[silence]

He's only been outside for ten minutes and already he's pining for the sweltering attic, that wonderland of stale cigarette smoke and dusty album covers,
the place where he can fall face-first into the grooves of a vinyl record and
never come out again. Del Shannon, the Isley Brothers, Cyndi Lauper; it
doesn't matter. He just wants to escape the foul-smelling exhaust and dirty
brick buildings of this horrible outside place and return to the safety of his
private fortress.

Mom said she needs to clean the attic, but he's not stupid. She's worried
about him, wants him to go outside and play, as if the livid heat pouring from
the blacktop will magically make everything better. He didn't want to leave
but does anyway, only because he loves her and knows she's trying to help. But
she isn't. She can't. *Nothing* can, not even the puppy she secretly snuck into
the attic and is planning to surprise him with when he comes in again.

He doesn't see but rather *feels* her sad eyes looking down at him through
the fractured attic window. His heart breaks for her, so he picks up a yellow
plastic baseball bat laying in the front yard, one that a boy who looked and
sounded exactly like him had left there on an ancient summer day long ago.
He cuts through the humidity, then cuts again the other way, and the bat feels
like a weak, insignificant thing in his hands. So he grabs a rock, tosses it in the
air, swings at it, misses.

On his fourth swing he connects, and the irregular shape darts through
the air and slams into the rear quarter panel of the maroon Cadillac parked on
the curb. The sound it makes is startling, and as it joins the city clamor and
fades from existence, he somehow knows Richard heard it.

He debates running away, catching the first bus he sees, getting out of the city, but he knows in his absence Richard will only take his anger out on mom again, so he stays rooted to the ground, letting the bat fall from his fingers and disappear back into the grass. It is the last time in his life he will ever be a child, and the seconds seem to stretch to minutes and then hours as he watches a squirrel in the next yard over drink from a dripping spigot. He smiles at the innocence of it, at the innocence of *everything*, and then closes his eyes tightly as he hears the front door slam behind him.

Richard drags him backward by his shirt, heaving his small frame into the house and away from the prying eyes of the neighbors, and then throws him wordlessly into the stairwell leading to the basement, back into the waiting maw of the Wall Monster above his bed. He falls down the stairs like a doll, end over end, breaking his right elbow on his way down, until he's only a busted heap at the bottom step. The pain is awful, yet it's only just begun.

He sees his stepfather looming in the doorway above and attempts a meager apology, but all he can do is bawl at the ache scattering up his arm. Then Richard's elongated shadow bounces down the stairway, followed immediately by the man himself, who straddles the boy, grabs his hair and forces their noses together, so close that every vein in his stepfather's bloodshot eyes is a lucid scarlet river flowing on milky white stone.

Your fault, Richard barks, spittle flying from his lips like buckshot from a shotgun barrel as the hot tears standing in his eyes tremble and then fall onto the boy's face. His voice collapses into a whisper as he leans in close to the terrified boy, and his breath reeks of beer and cigarettes and sickness. *I tried to be good, didn't I? I tried but you wouldn't let me.*

Richard begins slamming the boy's head against the cement floor, again and again until the smacks begin to sound wet and small crimson specks splatter onto the collar of Richard's immaculate white shirt. His stepfather stops and looks at these new stains, and after a moment of detached inspection, grows even more enraged and drags the boy further into the darkness, where he punches the small, round, slightly chubby face, knocking out teeth,

270

breaking a nose, swelling an eye socket. From somewhere distant he can hear his mother scream but he can't see her face, because now the world is beginning to wane around him, ebbing and surging in snippets like a slow-motion strobe light.

Before he blacks out entirely, the boy sees a cocked fist and a shiny metal object on its third finger, the words *Southern Illinois University* and a snarling red saluki engraved into the ring's unwieldy face. Then the dog rushes toward him and the world turns black.

WORLD'S GREATEST DAD

-Track Twelve-

It wasn't just Guinevere who was fading away. It was *everything*.

That other world, which seemed oddly alien now, was starting to reassert itself in her absence. He couldn't let it. Not yet.

Jensen concentrated on the darkness, on the taste of dirt in his mouth, on the abiding cold and the rough hands that were taking turns dragging him backward like a plaything, away from *her*.

Her. Guinevere. The woman he loved, his tether to this bizarre place. She was his anchor, his safe haven, and he couldn't let her go. But she was rapidly slipping from his thoughts anyway.

Someone was hunched over him, working on him, grunting at the effort. It was pouring rain. Somewhere far off, the thumping blades of a helicopter fought for dominance over the rolling of distant thunder. His body was in ruins, his legs mangled and useless. The pain was excruciating.

He was there, a crumpled heap lying motionless on that rain-soaked mountainside, but also here, in The Subdivisions, being jerked and pulled through the gloom by something unseen. The two worlds were at war inside his head, and the one that held Guinevere was moments from surrender. It felt as if he was teetering over the edge of a cliff, flailing for a handhold that didn't exist. All he could do was stare dumbly at the instant death etched into the craggy rocks below and pray like hell that the fall wouldn't be as terrifying as it looked.

Guinevere. The way she'd felt in his arms, the intoxicating smell of her hair, the beautiful song that had spilled from her lips on The Dark Train. How she'd unknowingly stripped him bare, had chiseled away the parts of him he despised to reveal the flawed but authentic sculpture beneath. It was all still there. He just had to focus.

Jensen came back a bit, long enough to realize that the situation was hopeless. The darkness of the cavern hid the details, but he didn't need sight to understand what was happening: His application to join The Subdivisions had been rejected, and he was now being escorted to the exit with extreme prejudice. He wasn't sure what was grabbing him, manhandling him, tossing and turning him this way and that, but he suspected it had something to do with the stalagmites and the shadow people he'd seen cowering behind them. Soon he'd be back at the entrance, and Guinevere would be out of reach. Without her, he'd surely return to that empty, useless world for good, with nothing to show for it but the burden of knowing what could have been.

Sadness and despair turned to anger. This wasn't right. It wasn't fair. He was losing despite doing everything right this time. And it was all because of Hedley Grange, the self-appointed savior of music, the saint of rock and roll. Hedley was going to win, *again*, and not just in his quest to torture and humiliate Jensen. Guinevere would find him, would somehow convince him to reconcile. The name Jensen Bennett would become an inside joke to them, a laugh to be had when they needed one.

Hedley didn't love her, didn't deserve her, and yet still he was going to get her in the end.

He could hear Grange laughing now, in fact. Laughing at the fact that Jensen had bought into the lie of their friendship, laughing at stealing the love of his life from under his nose, laughing at the pain and emptiness that Jensen would be forced to endure for the remainder of his life. Laughing at that painting, *Les Deux Figures*, that he'd sent Jensen weeks before their falling out, as if it hadn't been a kind gesture from an old friend but an elaborate taunt, a mockery, an acknowledgement that Jensen would never achieve his dreams, that they could only exist in the fantasy of Grange's much superior imagination.

All he had to do was tell me where the goddamn album was, Jensen thought. *He couldn't even give me that much.*

Jensen's hatred boiled over, and as he continued to be dragged across the dirt, hitting rocks and errant bones as he went, he remembered the scream he'd heard echoing from the carousel as they'd approached it.

It had been *Hedley's* scream, he now decided, and smiled.

Grange had wandered down the wrong path, had been caught by whatever lived down there, had been stripped naked and strapped to an operating table. He'd struggled against his restraints as some demonic lump of bruised flesh emerged from the shadows on warped legs, knife raised, and put cold steel to flesh. Then his throat had been slit, long and slow until his terrified shrieks had been drowned in blood. Guinevere would never find Grange, would never be with him, because he wasn't where she thought he'd be, not anymore. He was in his own personal hell, where he belonged, getting what he truly deserved.

The moment this last thought entered his head, Jensen felt the vice around his waist relax and then slip away. Momentum carried him for a bit longer before he came skidding to an awkward stop. He took a second to get his bearings, taking slow, long breaths until he'd recovered some modicum of calm, then groggily got to his knees and looked around.

He was alone. No voices, no shadows, only the mist catching in the beams of light overhead as it waltzed between the lifeless stone pillars around him.

It seemed he was worthy, after all.

***

Jacob Hatcher once said that his daughter had loved her first word so much –

it had been *apple* – that she'd spent the remainder of her life filling the silence with them. He'd called her Motormouth, or sometimes just Mouth for short, and it was a term he used with both affection and annoyance, depending on the situation.

But Guinevere Hatcher was speechless, now. There was nothing left to say, and no one left to say it to. She was completely alone.

She thought she was accustomed to the feeling. She'd gone from growing up an only child in the rural wastelands of Wisconsin to a self-reliant runaway singing for scraps in the sprawling metropolis that was Chicago, all without ever batting an eye. Even in the afterworld, surrounded by throngs of friends and distant relatives, she'd felt like a sovereign nation of one. Being alone had always just been a part of her uncompromising independence, and for the most part, she'd been okay with it.

But this was different. This was scary. This didn't seem like a minor blip that she'd eventually get over; it seemed permanent. She'd only ever felt this way once before, in those horrible last few weeks of her earthly life, when the breakup with Hank had set her adrift on a sea of regret and self-loathing.

Jensen wasn't Hank, but he'd still taken something from her when he'd left. Something she needed, something she desperately wanted back.

She *should* feel relieved. Jensen had been just a mild curiosity at first, a handsome stranger in need of help, but his single-minded pursuit of that damned album and his anger at Hank had ultimately turned him into an out-right inconvenience. God knows how much farther along she'd be now if she hadn't helped him find the Terminal, or untied him from that horse. Really, if she was being honest with herself, Jensen had been nothing but a distraction from the very start.

So why did she miss him so much?

The lump in her throat threatened to erupt into another fit of tears, but she held them at bay by taking a series of long, measured breaths and focusing on the reason she was there. Hank was somewhere ahead. When she caught up to him, she'd need her wits – and a little bit of luck – to win him back. She'd only have one shot to make everything right again. Her emotions would only get in the way.

Jensen was the past. Hank was the past, too, but also the future. She just had to find him.

Guinevere finished making her new torch and stood up to light it. When it finally caught after a few flicks of her Zippo's flint wheel, she was woefully unimpressed with the dismal light it produced. Jensen had been right about the stockings – the flame was weak, and the torch was already starting to die out. That wasn't good. She'd need all the light she could muster to navigate her way out of this godforsaken hellhole.

She had to get going, and not just because the rapidly vanishing torchlight had now become a timer. The Subdivisions wouldn't simply stop after it had pilfered the last relics of her beauty; it would keep on digging, through muscle and bone if necessary, until it had punctured her very soul. She had to get out before it did. With or without Hank.

Guinevere looked around at the new room she'd entered. The torchlight only revealed some of it, but from what she could tell, it was an immense grotto whose ceiling was shielded in rust-colored spikes that looked eerily similar to the ones that had littered the Doormen's stone forest, the ones that had jumped to life and unceremoniously whisked Jensen out of her life. Water dripped incessantly from each. She eyed them distrustfully as she passed beneath them, but they thankfully didn't move.

Directly in front of her was a lengthy shoreline being thrashed by what looked like liquid obsidian. She couldn't see much, not from here, but it seemed like a fairly large underground river. From it came the repugnant smell of decay, like a moldy basement left to rot. There were small, glistening black stones scattered across its surface – a kind of bridge, it seemed – but wherever they led was lost in the gloom.

It had to be The Sea of Sorrow. The place Hank had whispered into her ear, and the one Daphne had described during her trance. She'd only heard stories of it, but everything seemed to match those bleak accounts.

"Hank?" she called out. "It's me. It's Gwen."

Her voice echoed away, and there was no answer.

"I'm coming. Just wait where you are."

This time there *was* a response, but it wasn't from the darkness ahead, but from somewhere behind.

"I really hope you brought a canoe," a familiar voice said, "because I forgot my snorkel at home."

Guinevere spun around and saw Jensen standing there in the firelight. His clothes were ripped and dirty, and his hair was a tangled mess, but his handsome smile was immaculate. Unbridled joy swept over her at the sight.

"Jensen!"

There was a brief moment of silent acknowledgement between them – she, shocked to see him returned, and he, savoring her surprise like fine wine – before Guinevere rushed to him on raised toes, delirious and unthinking, and began passionately kissing the place where his smile had been.

Jensen held her close as they kissed, and the world fell away in his arms.

***

The kiss was paradise, especially after the lonely, blind trek back to the carousel and the tortuous wait for it to spin around to the correct door again. Until this very moment, Jensen hadn't been sure he'd even ever *see* her again, that perhaps he'd taken too long to get back and she'd already moved on to places unknown.

But Guinevere was still there, beautiful even despite her macabre transformation, and she wasn't just happy to see him; she was *kissing* him. It wasn't a platonic peck on the lips, either, but the long, savory kiss of a lover. He'd been expecting a kind greeting, maybe even a hug, but not this. Her lips were cold but felt wonderful against his own. He didn't want it to end.

But it did, rather abruptly, only moments later. Guinevere sucked in a surprised breath as some realization seemed to dawn on her, and she pushed him violently away with her free arm like he was a mugger trying to steal her purse. Jensen staggered backward, confused at the abrupt change in her demeanor and demoralized at the way she now looked at him, eyes wide with stunned horror, lips working to form words that wouldn't come.

"Gwen, that was –"

"A mistake," she finished, and looked around guiltily as if someone had seen them. "Oh my God, that ... that wasn't me. I was just ..."

"It's okay, Gwen." He went to embrace her, but the moment his hands touched her shoulders, she shook it off and backed away in disgust.

"Get away from me! Haven't you already done enough damage? Just *leave me alone*."

Jensen tried to read her face, to glean something from it that would explain this sudden outburst, and why he was now the villain, but it was so distorted by anger that it was little more than a blank page. Was there some kind of negative energy here, like in The Dark Train? If there was, he didn't feel it.

"Guinevere," he said calmly. "I don't understand. What's wrong?"

"Everything!" she screamed. "I had him, he was mine, and all I had to do was hold on. But I let go, and now he'll never be mine again." Fresh tears fell from her eyes. "Never again."

Jensen tried again to put a reassuring hand on her shoulder, but again she brushed it off by stepping away.

"And you!" she shouted and jabbed a finger in his face. "It should've been Hank I saw in that mirror. Why was it *you*? You ruined *everything*!"

Jensen was momentarily at a loss for words. She'd seen *him* in the Room Full of Mirrors? Based on her guilty expression, it had been a pleasant experience. His heart picked up speed as he realized what this meant – Guinevere had feelings for him, too. *Real* feelings, not just a random kiss born of a dire situation. And it was conflicting with her lingering desire for Grange.

Despite the oppressive sense of gloom that permeated the room, he wanted to shout for joy.

"Gwen, think about it – why do the vain flock there?" he asked, his mind working through the logic almost faster than his voice could follow. "It's because they see a fictionalized version of themselves and get lost in the lie. But people like us, people who are considerably more modest, we apparently see the opposite – facts. Truth. *Brutal* truth, in my case. The reason you saw me in your reflection is because ... *I'm* your truth. You want me." He paused and swallowed hard. "But that's okay, because I want you, too."

The words hit her like morphine; her eyes dreamed, her face wilted, her pursed lips relaxed. Jensen smiled and stepped toward her, but stopped when she came to life again and threw the torch on the ground at his feet.

"You're *wrong*! All you want is that album. Save me the sappy speeches and just *fuck off*, already."

Jensen didn't back down. "Gwen, I'm not here for the money anymore. Hedley Grange can go to hell. When I was disappearing back on that bridge, it wasn't the thought of the five million that brought me back. It was the thought of *you*. Because you're my truth, and I'm yours."

She marched up and shouted so forcefully that warm spittle landed on his cheek.

"*Liar!*"

Then she turned and walked off.

***

He'd only been half-listening at first, humming a quiet mantra as he sat cross-legged in the shadows somewhere near the exit. But his ears perked up at Guinevere's emotional admission, and Benny's measured response.

He slowly eased himself out of the trance, making sure to taper it off at the end to maintain the peace he'd been constructing. It wasn't easy now that the argument had escalated into shouting, mostly from Guinevere, but his inner calm prevailed and he was finally able to open his eyes. It was too dark to see anything aside from a dim flicker of light in the distance, but their voices carried well across the cavern and he was able to hear Benny calmly say he could go to hell. He smiled.

"Already there, buddy," he whispered. "You'll be joining me soon."

It seemed Jensen was hot for Guinevere, and Guinevere was hot for Jensen. *Sizzling* hot, by the sound of things. Subjecting her to the mirror had just been a last-minute adjustment to the plan, nothing more. Jensen had been the true target. But never in his wildest imaginings would he have predicted what she'd see in the reflection: Love, or at the very least, lust. For *Benny*, of all people. It was a wrinkle in the plan that he wouldn't iron out even if he could.

Hedley Grange stood up, still listening as the conversation ended abruptly and silence once again ruled the darkness. He debated calling out to them – a trap was no good without bait – but held his tongue when the faint smacking of shoes on wet stone from somewhere in the darkness told him they were already coming. Which one would be the first to find the stepping stone he'd greased for them? Whoever it was would win an all-expenses-paid trip into The Sea of Sorrow. And thanks to the new wrinkle, the other would surely follow. Two birds, one stone, as the saying went.

He wasn't sure what, if anything, was waiting for Guinevere down there. But he knew what Benny was in for, and it wasn't pleasant. In fact, it was the ghastliest thing Hedley Grange had ever seen in his entire life.

And it had been waiting for Jensen Phillip Bennett for a very long time.

✳✳✳

I want you, too.

The words were barbed on one side and smooth on the other.

As Guinevere made her way across the stone path and away from Jensen, the phrase coursed through her thoughts like some wonderful yet poisonous new drug. His admission meant the mirror image could be real, if she wanted it to be. All she had to do was turn around. Turn around and renounce Hank. It was a pitiful, treacherous, spineless thing to even consider, so she forced it out of her mind and continued walking.

He was following her. Of *course* he was. She didn't need to look around to confirm her suspicions; the soft orange light tickling the darkness behind her was proof enough he'd picked up the torch and trailed her.

Using the remaining fumes in her Zippo, she'd been able to negotiate a good deal of the bridge, which in reality was just a collection of small stones that wandered indiscriminately in the same general direction across the impossibly black river. But the lighter was very nearly out now, and the space around her became less defined the farther away she got from Jensen's torch.

The ground beneath her feet was wet and slippery, the air brutally cold, the darkness beyond her field of vision alive with strange gurgling noises that were made all the more unnerving by the absence of a discernable origin. This was the place Daphne had described, she was sure of it. Hank had been here, was maybe even *still* here. Once he realized she'd walked through hell to get him back, had *gone* through hell to get him back, he'd have no choice but to fall in love with her all over again.

I'm your truth.

"Stop it," she whispered to herself.

She hadn't even *hesitated*. In fact, she'd done the exact *opposite* of hesitate – she'd *sprinted* to him like she was on fire and he was a bucket of ice-cold water. A mirror could lie, even one that cracked open your soul and reached into its depths. But the second thing? That was all her. No mirror, no tricks, just her own thoughts and emotions.

You want me.

"*Please*," she cried. "Please just leave me alone."

The Zippo's flame began sputtering in a series of violent death throes, then went out entirely with a pathetic flash. She sighed and flipped the lid closed for the last time. It was now just a cold, dead thing in her hand, a useless trinket that had outlived its usefulness. So she dropped it to the ground, sentenced it to rot in the bowels of hell for the rest of eternity.

Poor lighter, she thought. *What did you do to deserve such a horrible fate?*

The longer she stared at the Zippo, the easier it became to see. Jensen and his archaic flashlight were getting closer. No time for a funeral. She crouched down, partly to make herself harder to see, but also because it was easier to gauge the distance to the next stone. It was a good six feet away, or exactly one Jacob Hatcher. She'd have to jump for it.

"Easy peasy, right?" She asked the darkness, which only continued to gurgle in response. Now that she was focused on it, the gap was probably closer to seven feet. And wasn't the target stone a bit slimier than all the others?

"Okay, chicken. Stop stalling. Time to jump."

She coiled her muscles and leapt.

***

There was a tiny light shivering in the darkness ahead, and from Jensen's distant perspective, it looked like the directionless dance of a lone lightning bug.

It was Guinevere. How she'd gotten so far ahead of him, and so quickly, he wasn't quite sure. She'd gone from an old woman hobbling on corpse legs to a methed-up roadrunner in the blink of an eye. Perhaps adrenaline and repressed desire were to blame, or maybe he was just being too cautious in selecting his steps. Either way, he knew he had to do better, go faster. He had no idea where she was headed or just how he'd go about finding her again if she slipped away.

Motivation came to him not long after. The dancing light suddenly winked out and, seconds later, he heard something large break the surface of the water. He called out her name, and when there was no reply, he began frantically bounding between the stones, moving Guinevere's crude torch in quick semicircles at his feet, simultaneously searching for the source of the sound and his next foothold.

It didn't take long to find what he was looking for: Guinevere's lighter was lying on one of the stones. Was the water around him rippling, too? It could just be the way the torchlight was hitting it, or it could be his overworked imagination, but he didn't think so.

He called her name again, and for a second time received no response, not even the sound of her sneakers squeaking.

She'd fallen in.

Without hesitation, he dropped the torch and dove in headfirst after her.

***

The closest Jensen had ever been to deep space was his eighth-grade trip to Adler Planetarium, whose high, rounded ceilings had given him a glimpse, however fabricated, of faraway alien worlds teeming with magic and adventure. Jensen's imagination, seemingly always on overdrive in those days, had let him experience that universe. It was a dark, cold, weightless world devoid of anything resembling intelligent life.

The Sea of Sorrow and its frigid depths were identical to this childhood delusion in every regard except one: There was life down there, and lots of it. Despite being virtually blind, Jensen sensed hundreds, perhaps *thousands* of people floating aimlessly in the void like discarded bits of space debris. Countless individuals, all dreaming troubled dreams in the infinite deep, all aware of his presence just as he was aware of theirs. He tried to sense Guinevere in the static but couldn't.

After nearly a minute of battering the icy nothingness with his limbs, Jensen began to panic. She wasn't here. Moreover, he was sensing an entire city's worth of people but had yet to physically run into a single one. If the lake was as wide and as deep as that suggested, it would take a literal eternity to search the entire thing.

She wasn't here. She wasn't *anywhere*.

Her absence was again wearing away the feeble grip he had on the afterlife; he was heavier, more sluggish, less spry in both mind and body. The image of her face was still strong in his mind; he was sure there was nothing that could ever completely erase it from his memory. But without the woman it belonged to, his ability to counteract the material world was growing weaker. If he didn't find her, and soon, they'd *both* be lost.

Jensen decided to swim back to the surface and gather his thoughts, maybe even scan the waters again from the safety of the bridge and draft a better plan of action than simply flailing away at the darkness. A few kicks later, he was nearly there when the water sloshing at his feet suddenly grew very cold and a soft, sad sound filled his ears.

Noooooooooooooooooooo ...

As it continued, the whisper rose in volume, resonating from somewhere below but also from inside his head, too. Unlike the arbitrary scratching of the Doormen, which was more akin to a shotgun blast with lots of collateral damage, the whispering moan was a laser-focused shot directly into his brain. The water at his feet rapidly solidified, causing his kicking legs to slow and then stop completely. Then the weight of the ice block around his ankles grew sentience and began dragging him back down again, deeper and deeper until the modicum of torchlight dancing on the surface of the black river above dimmed and then winked out entirely.

Come baaaaaaaaaccccccccckkkkkkkkk ...

Jensen tried to reverse his descent using only his arms, but quickly realized it was pointless; the weight at his feet was simply too great. But gravity wasn't the only culprit. Something was pulling him deeper into the abyss, something that he knew, something that knew *him*, something that wanted him to stay for a visit and never ever leave again. The deeper he sank, the clearer that *something* became in his mind's eye.

It was his stepfather.

***

A lone streetlamp empties unwashed light into the basement through two narrow rectangles, trifling squares which in the daytime look like ordinary windows but in the midnight gloom become the predatory eyes of a malevolent animal. Somewhere in the vast semi-darkness, a clock ticks methodically, its lonely echo the only sound in the stillness.

As Jensen pulls the covers over his head, he realizes he's not a man, but a child, stuffed into cotton Transformers pajamas that he outgrew long ago. He doesn't like this place, he doesn't like the Wall Monster he knows is looming just inches above his head, but he knows he can't escape, because it's already happened.

Somehow, sleep overtakes him, but it is thin and troubled. In his nightmares the Wall Monster, its pale eyes turning upward into malicious half-moons, its rhythmic heartbeat quickening, extends its gluttonous, unseen hands into the darkness below, not hurrying, enjoying the helpless fear of the eight-year-old boy sleeping at its feet.

Then hands are wrapped around him, one covering his mouth so he can't scream, and the boy realizes he's no longer sleeping. The hand covering his face is calloused and smells strongly of cigarettes. The other one is moving slowly down the length of his right thigh. This is no Wall Monster; this is a man, and the boy can feel something warm and hard beating a rapid pulse against his leg. Hot breath that smells of stale beer brushes the back of his neck.

"Shhhhh," a voice says. "Just lie still."

It's quick and painful. He cries silent tears the entire time. At the end, the figure next to him sucks in a shuddering breath, and immediately Jensen feels something warm and alien gush inside him. Then the shuddering stops, replaced moments later by a soft, anguished, uneven sobbing.

"You did this to me," the voice whispers in his ear. "This is your fault."

The bed squeals and then lifts as the figure stands up, moves across the cement floor with rapid footsteps, clambers upstairs, shuts the door with a startling crack. Jensen's sheets, his pajamas, his pillow; everything is wet. Blood, for sure, and probably something else. The Wall Monster leers overhead, its rhythmic heartbeat continuing its sickening refrain, its dull eyes mocking the boy's tears.

"My fault," Jensen whispers in the voice of a child but the mind of a man, and then stuffs his face into the pillow and cries uncontrollably, yet silently, so no one can hear. He doesn't want to remember, has in fact done everything to expunge the memory from his mind, but there's nothing to be done, no escape, no way out of the nightmare, because it's already happened and there's no going back.

✳✳✳

The unrelenting cold and absolute panic woke him, but only momentarily. His lungs were screaming for air but he wasn't drowning, *couldn't* drown, in fact, but no one had told his body that.

As he thrashed and jerked in the icy water, trying in vain to counteract the pull of the ice gripping his ankles, he looked up and saw nothing at all. No light, no dark; just the emptiness of nonexistence.

But he could still hear faint whispers – hundreds, thousands of them – so close they had to be surrounding him, but there was absolutely nothing in all directions.

One voice was clearer than the rest, like the ghost of radio station music between static. And it called him by name.

Jensen ... follow me ... follow me ... follow me ...

He had no choice but to submit to the command.

***

The boy stops crying when he realizes he's no longer in his pajamas. In fact, he's no longer a boy, but a man, dressed in faded blue jeans and a white button-up-the-front shirt in dire need of a wash.

He sits up in bed, blinks, and looks around the basement. There is no Wall Monster, only a cheap, battery-powered clock hanging above his bed. The deluge of dark shapes stretching across the cement floor aren't ghosts but shadows cast by neglected furniture and packed boxes in the basement. He is alone, and he is safe.

"Follow me," Jensen says. He nods at his own words, gets out of the miniature bed, and walks slowly to the basement stairs. "Follow me," he says again, and looks up at the closed door at the top. He nods again, then cautiously begins ascending the staircase. The boy had fallen down them, had broken his elbow. But he walks up them a man, confidence growing with each step, heart galloping faster in his chest as the door approaches. He reaches it and grabs the handle, hesitates, then turns and swings it wide open.

His stepfather is sitting at the kitchen table, head in his hands, not weeping but simply staring at the scratched surface of the wooden tabletop with the bored familiarity of a man who hasn't seen anything else in decades. He looks at least seventy years old; his hair is paper white, his face lined with deep wrinkles that look like dead tributaries. Despite the lanky frame and barndoor ears, he's not the same man who once towered over him as a child; this man is old, weak, beaten. Without asking, Jensen somehow knows this is his prison; this cluttered, claustrophobic kitchen, an ethereal twin of the one that once existed in reality, has become his entire world. Jensen approaches him.

"I did what you asked," Jensen says. "I followed. Now let me go."

The old man looks up and smiles, but there is no happiness there. "No."

Jensen walks to the chair next to Richard and sits. He's shaking, but his voice is calm. "You raped me."

Richard nods and closes his eyes, and as he does, tears squirm from them. "Yes."

Jensen leans forward, not afraid of the miserable figure sitting before him, not anymore. "Why?"

His stepfather looks down and begins fiddling with his hands.

"Don't know, kid. I'd say it was because my daddy did it to me, too, but that's just an excuse. Truth is, I couldn't help it. I tried to stop myself. I did for so long. So long. But then your mamma went away and I had you all to myself. I couldn't help it."

At this last bit he begins sobbing, speaking through his tears, which flow almost as quickly as his words.

"I hurt you bad, boy. Real bad. Nothing can ever change that. I just wanted you to know how sorry I was. How goddamned sorry about it all I was."

Words float to Jensen's mind, and he speaks them. "My fault."

The old man's face contorts into a mess of wrinkles as he regards him in surprise. "No, never. You did nothing wrong, son. Nothing. Except make me realize what I really was."

"Which is what, exactly?"

A sad smile pushes its way through the tears. "Something I just couldn't live with no more." He looks around the kitchen and frowns. "After they took you to the hospital and your mama said she was leaving me, I knew I couldn't go on. So I ended it," he points to the drawers beneath the kitchen sink, "right there. One squeeze and I was gone."

Silence fills the fabricated room; the usual sounds of cars drifting down the street and birds chirping in the oaks outside the window are absent. This is a dead world, a snapshot of the way the kitchen had looked the day Richard had taken his life. On the counter there was even a piece of half-eaten custard pie, the after-supper treat his stepfather had been enjoying when the sound of the rock hitting the quarter panel of his Cadillac had roused him to action.

"I loved you, you know," Jensen says at last, surprised that a tear of his own is now slowly tracking down his cheek. "Looked up to you. You were my dad."

The old man shakes his head vehemently. "No. I should've been, though. I should've loved you like a father should, but ..." Richard's eyes wander to the scar on Jensen's right temple and linger there momentarily before darting away again. "But I broke you instead. Took out my shame on you, blamed you, but I was the guilty one." His stepfather sighs, looks around the kitchen. "And now I'm here. Where I belong."

Jensen leans forward. His voice is level, powerful. "Richard. Let me go."

Again, the old man shakes his head. "No. I can't. I can't let you go."

Jensen breathes deep. He's no longer shaking; in fact, he's as still as a lake on a windless day. He should be in a rage, but he's not.

"Richard. I forgive you."

The old man doesn't respond this time, but he still shakes his head. He looks like a petulant child refusing bedtime. Jensen grabs his stepfather's hands in his own, and the act surprises Richard, who stares at him with bloodshot, tormented, tear-rimmed eyes.

"Richard, I forgive you," Jensen says again, more sternly. His eyes don't lie, and his stepfather sees this.

The old man's lip quivers and his eyes drop. "I don't deserve it."

"Maybe not. But I forgive you anyway. You can let go, now. Let me go."

✳✳✳

Guinevere wasn't feeling well.

It had started innocently enough as a tickle in her stomach, a nervous flutter that would be right at home at a job interview. But as her body sunk deeper into the obsidian sea, its cold, infinite void negated all of her senses and the tickle became a hundred sharp nails clawing for freedom from deep within her abdomen.

This isn't water, she thought. *It's consciousness. The collective thoughts and emotions of everyone whose hopelessness brought them here. And it's eating me alive.*

The panic set in then, and she began beating her arms and legs in a hopeless attempt to reach the surface. Nothing could survive the crushing isolation and self-loathing that existed down here. It was equal parts remorse and grief, magnified to a paralyzing degree by the staggering number of tormented souls she sensed nearby. If misery did indeed love company, then The Sea of Sorrow was where it gathered. She had to escape before the emotions liquefied her into an oily paste and she became just another futile voice whispering in the darkness for forgiveness.

But she had lost all sense of direction and couldn't be sure which way was up. There was no light to guide her, no shoreline to aim for, only complete and utter darkness. She could feel the icy liquid working her limbs; they were slowing now, and any progress she might have been making was lost as her body began to sink like a stone toward whatever seabed lie below.

She was trapped. No amount of struggling was going to change that fact, so she stopped thrashing and let the grief wash over her. Her lungs begged for air even though they didn't require it, just one of many earthly necessities she hadn't yet learned to shed, so she obliged the impulse and opened her mouth. Thick, freezing slime poured into her throat and down her stomach, bringing with it an abiding despair that spread throughout her like a sudden illness.

Nothing matters anymore, she thought as her body continued to sink. *I ruin everything I touch. Love is a lie. Happiness is a lie, a bedtime story we tell ourselves to mask the reality of existence. It will never stop hurting. Ever.*

She sensed another voice, too, this one much deeper than her own, and it didn't sound like the others. It wasn't whispering but shouting, blaring like a car alarm in the middle of the night. She couldn't tell what it was saying, nor did she care. *This* was her existence, now. She was home.

When the arm wrapped around her waist and began pulling her to the surface, she didn't register the sensation at all.

Guinevere Hatcher was gone.

***

Jensen lifted the frail body in his arms onto the craggy stone outcropping first, making sure she was on solid ground before exiting the water himself and joining her. Then he collapsed and laid on his back for a minute to catch his breath. Above him were an army of stalactites hanging from the cavern's ceiling like stores of ashen rock candy, an upside-down doppelganger of the Doormen's stone forest. His clothes were wet and sticking to his skin, but other than that he felt fine.

In fact, he felt *excellent*. Much like his jog through the streets of Paradise City and the subsequent mad dash down the Yellow Line to catch the subway car, his body didn't ache. His mind was even clearer, lighter, more focused. In truth, if not for the heaviness of the material world, which still remained at the edges of his perception like a viscous fog, he would have thought he was back in the loving and nonjudgmental arms of whatever omniscient force dwelled inside Translucent Tower.

For the first time in what seemed like an eternity, he felt unburdened. *Free*.

He became aware of a sound then, faint but loud enough to overpower the subtle gurgling of The Sea of Sorrow. It rumbled from the darkness somewhere behind him like a raging waterfall, roaring a single, monotonous tone that would have been soothing if not for how angry, how utterly and completely *wrong* it seemed.

"Gwen," he said, the word coming back to him seconds later as a ghostly echo. "Talk to me."

When she didn't answer, Jensen lifted himself up on one elbow and looked down at her. But he didn't see the woman he loved next to him, but a strange skeletal creature wearing her clothes. The pale, emaciated figure was barely recognizable as being human, let alone female; it looked like something an archeologist would find while plundering an ancient tomb. In fact, if not for the blue- and white-checkered bandana tucked between its breasts, Jensen would have thought he'd dragged the wrong person to the surface.

But he hadn't. It was Guinevere, the last of her beauty finally siphoned off by the toxic sea. Her eyes were wide open, looking sightlessly into the space above them, but her irises, once a deep russet, had become jet black and flowed like spilled ink across white parchment. She didn't seem to register his presence at all, even as her chest rose and descended slowly with each labored breath. There was also a fine, gray mist rising from her body like fog from dry ice, and a line of black liquid he could only assume was seawater dribbled from the corner of her mouth.

"Gwen, can you hear me? Gwen?"

Near hysterics now, he quickly got on his knees and put an ear to her lips. The soft push of air against it told him she was definitely still breathing. That was good, even if they were in a place where oxygen wasn't necessarily needed to survive. He next put two fingers against the right side of her neck beneath her jawbone and nodded to himself when a strong, steady pulse met his touch.

What was going on? Why wasn't she responding to him? Her body was there, but *she* wasn't. Whatever intangible thing that made her who she was, that true soul he'd detected in her eyes before, was nowhere to be found, now. He was only looking at a shell. The thing that Guinevere had left behind.

It couldn't be.

Jensen lifted her shoulders and then cradled her head in his arms. The gray mist trembled in the air but continued to pour from her body, coiling around her arms and limbs and chest and face as if feeding on her. Her body was as limp as a ragdoll. He could feel himself on the verge of tears but somehow willed them away.

"Guinevere, talk to me. Say something."

Her emotionless eyes continued to stare unseeingly past him, the dark irises wobbling slightly at the sound of his voice but making no other indication of sentience. Even looking as she did, a mere whisper of the woman he knew, a withered, sexless husk, Jensen still loved her.

Something came over him, and he leaned in and kissed her. It was little more than a peck, but her lips warmed the instant he touched them with his own. He pulled away and said her name again, but there still was no response.

"Gwen." All he could muster was a whisper. He put a hand to the side of her face and began stroking her cheek. "Where did you go? Come back to me."

He wasn't sure at first if it was only the meager light coming from the tunnel immediately behind them playing tricks, but at these words, Guinevere's eyes fluttered. For a brief moment, a bit of brown crept back into them, fighting the black before eventually being overpowered and fading away again.

He leaned in close and cupped her chin. "Gwen," he said, this time more forcefully than before. "I love you. Come back to me."

Again, a bit of brown squirted into her irises, and this time, it lingered a bit longer before again being overwhelmed and scurrying back into the swirling ink.

"You're still in there," he said. "Whatever's happening, *Fight* it, Gwen. With everything you've got."

This time, the brown not only returned, but her chest rose swiftly as she inhaled long and deep. Then it faded, and her eyes once again became the color of night.

He had to get her out of this place. Away from The Sea of Sorrow, yes, but also the entire Subdivisions. He wasn't going to reach her with such a powerful force working against him, not if he had all the time in the world, which he didn't.

Carefully resting her head back on the stone floor, he stood up and then lifted her entire body into his arms. She was light as air but as cold as a bag of ice. He glanced down at her ruined face and smiled. The woman in his arms was his everything; the world could crumble to dust around him and it wouldn't matter in the slightest, so long as she was there. The feeling was so intense he had to look away until it subsided.

"We're getting out of here," he said, eyeing the entrance behind him. The sound of the bizarre, broken waterfall seemed to be spewing forth from somewhere within it.

Then a voice, faraway and echoey, called out from the darkness.

"*Where* are they? Greg, you gotta *enunciate*."

There was a crackle and a tinny, indiscernible muttering, then the voice returned.

"*Jesus wept*. I have to stop 'em before they get there."

Despite the fact he didn't care at all for that voice, and cared even less that it seemed so close, Jensen was relieved The Warden had been able to get past the shadow people unscathed. The jailor may have a raging Captain Ahab complex, but he was a good man, and Jensen felt a bit guilty for putting him through so much grief since escaping from Translucent Tower.

"Tommy, you see him come back your way, knock 'em upside the head for me. Both a'you, head back to the Tower without me if I don't check back in five. Whatever happens, *don't* come in after me. No matter what. That's what they used to call back in the service *an order*."

Why couldn't he just give up? Was he really chasing Jensen out of some misdirected sense of duty, or was there something else? Jensen decided he didn't want to stick around long enough to find out.

"Come on, Gwen," he whispered to the figure in his arms. "Let's blow this place."

With that, Jensen walked into the next cave entrance and the deafening waterfall that lie somewhere inside.

***

Except, the sound wasn't a waterfall; it was people. *Thousands* of them.

Jensen held Guinevere close as he looked at the grisly scene playing out below him. The tunnel had converged with dozens of others and then deposited them on a wide, stony ledge jutting precariously over a shallow pit gouged into the earth. Inside it, throngs of naked bodies, so deformed and filthy it was hard to tell man from monster, were pummeling each other with bare fists or, if they could find them, rudimentary weapons like large bones or jagged boulders. They whooped and hollered and shouted and screamed as they fought, the dirt and blood and spit flying into the air and settling on their bodies like warpaint. The carnage was bathed in an eerie orange light courtesy of hundreds of raging bonfires scattered across the crater floor.

"Holy *Christ*," Jensen said, but his voice was lost in the chaos. The scene below him wavered like a mirage as blood began pounding nails against his temples. He felt hot and faint and faraway.

The more details he noticed, the worse it became. The valley floor appeared to be covered in a thin layer of crimson sludge that smelled like excrement and sloshed around the ankles of the man-creatures as they battled. There were bits and pieces of meat and bone floating in it, too, like the killing floor of a vast slaughterhouse. His stomach shuddered and briefly threatened to expel the ethereal remains of the overpriced hamburger that had been his last earthly meal.

A creature directly beneath them, something that looked like melted flesh poured over a vaguely human skeleton, picked up a sharp rock and, unrestrained rage distorting its already ruined features, brought it down hard on the head of a relatively normal-looking man who'd been crouching naked in the muck nearby, watching the bloodshed. The resulting blow cracked his skull open, and through the new opening Jensen could see bone and brain and blood. The victim jerked for a moment before falling face-first into the sludge and instantly dissolving into it like melting ice. But death here wasn't permanent, and the man began reforming moments later, piece by piece, an arm here, a leg there, using the sickening stew as raw material until he was more or less complete again, save for a slight malformation on his head where the rock had hit it. Thoroughly unfazed by this astonishing resurrection, the newborn man-creature immediately rushed screaming at his attacker, starting the cycle anew.

Scenes like this were being played out across the crater floor, hundreds of mini tragedies that had no end, only brief intermissions. If there was a literal hell, he was looking at it now – a seemingly endless dance of murder and brutality and suffering that none of its participants could seem to escape for very long. Jensen could feel what was fueling it all: noxious, uncompromising *hate* was wearing and tearing at the vast room like an immensely powerful cyclone. It was primitive and ancient, the well from which all other wicked desires sprung. And it was trying to worm its way into his head.

"Guinevere," he said, and looked down at her. He had to get her out. Nothing else mattered, not even the hatred for Hedley Grange that was again blossoming inside of him like a mushroom cloud.

He either had to cross the battlefield or turn back; there were no other options. But even as these two alternatives presented themselves in his mind, he knew both would be near impossible: He couldn't move. His legs felt fixed to the ground, his arms stiff as cement, his heart wild with adrenaline and fear. His encounter with Two-Eyes at Springfield Stadium, the mass of dead flesh lurching toward him in the Room Full of Mirrors, even the angry mob at Township Rebellion hadn't been this bad. Going back meant being captured by The Warden, and going forward meant mutilation and certain death, over and over again, reforming from the sludge until he wasn't human anymore but some hate-filled nightmare who could only reason in terms of bloodlust. He couldn't do it. He just couldn't.

Coward. Why am I such a coward?

"It's not cowardly to walk away from a fight you know you can't win," he said, but he didn't hear his voice, only felt the vibrations in his chest.

As if she felt it too, Guinevere squirmed in his arms, and he looked down at her again. The gray, smoky discharge was still curling around her petite frame, and her irises remained jet black. They even seemed a shade darker, now, if that was even possible.

He realized in a sudden swell of emotion that she really and truly was the only thing he cared about now; *House Made of Sound*, Grange, the five million dollars ... none of it mattered to him like she did. If he didn't move, and move now, he wouldn't be the only one spending the rest of his existence in perpetual darkness. The color had returned to her eyes before, however briefly, and it would do so again. He was sure that if he could get Guinevere out of this horrible place, she'd come back to him.

Okay, he thought. *I go forward, as insane as that sounds. But how?*

Jensen gazed across the pit to the other side and saw a dark spot that he thought could be an exit, but he wasn't sure. The room was too large and too dimly lit to see anything but the shapes of faraway things. There was something else on the other side, too – he squinted and saw a man, sitting cross-legged on the ledge, his head bowed and his upturned hands resting on his legs, a sinister Buddha somehow meditating peacefully while absolute chaos unfolded just yards beneath him.

Jensen had no second thoughts: It was Hedley Grange. He didn't have to see the man's individual features to recognize the smug, pretentious aura of self-importance his former friend always seemed to carry with him, even when he was trying like hell to be modest.

The bastard's just sitting there, Jensen thought. *Waiting. Watching. He wants to watch me suffer. And why? All because of a stupid Pluckers Chicken commercial? How is my eternal torment a fair trade-off for* that?

He grimaced as he felt the hatred surge again. It wanted to take control, was *begging* him to let it. Grange's throat could be slit for real, not just in his imagination. And Jensen realized he could be the one to do it himself. Long and slow, using the most jagged and rusted piece of metal he could find. In a place like this, he could do it over and over again for as long as he liked.

"Stop it," he said. "Just stop."

But he couldn't, so he decided to occupy his mind with thoughts of escape instead. He looked left, then right. He couldn't walk the circumference of the ledge to the other side, because there wasn't one to walk on; it went on for a bit in both directions before gradually collapsing into the crater beneath it like an interstate offramp. His only way out was through the mass of bodies between his current position and where the ledge rose once again to meet the other side. From there, he'd be able to climb up and access the shape that he was pretty sure was an exit.

Guinevere squirmed again in his arms as if she was having a nightmare. Despite the fact her eyes were wide open, she probably was. If he wanted to have any chance of bringing her back, he had to move. There was little time for debate.

Closing his eyes and praying he wasn't making the worst mistake of his short afterlife, Jensen's legs unfroze and he quietly slipped into the muddled anarchy below.

✳✳✳

Before, he'd been only a spectator to the endless bloodshed, watching it unfold in a detached sort of way from the relative safety of higher ground. But now that he'd been pulled onstage and the hell of the situation was spread out before him, he found his legs once again locking, his panic a jagged piece of hot glass being drawn slowly across the length of his body.

The smell was horrible. A piece of bloodied sausage, probably a part of someone's intestines, floated by on the bile. He closed his eyes.

I can't do this. I just can't.

But he *had* to do it, for Guinevere's sake, but also because there was no way to climb back onto the ledge now that he was off it. He brought her closer to his chest and willed his right leg to move forward, then his left, the sludge sloshing around his feet as he went, on and on until he'd reached the edge of the thin ring of inactivity that encircled the pit.

He opened his eyes again and saw about fifty people in his line of sight, punching and stabbing and bludgeoning each other, dodging and thrusting like they were dancing to some sick, choreographed ballet. There didn't seem to be a clear path through them. The noise was even more deafening now that he was in the thick of it. He'd been witness to some large crowds in his tenure with the band, but this was much worse.

The closest thing he could compare it to was RDS Arena in Ireland, where Quiet Catastrophe had stopped during its first world tour. Drug-addled and weak, Grange had collapsed onstage smack dab in the middle of the band's bluesy take on Zeppelin's "Living Loving Maid," ending the show nearly a full hour too early. The audience had reacted to the announcement with unified fury, tearing up seats, throwing beer bottles at the stage, screaming to the rafters about the injustice of it all. It had been chaos, but not nearly as loud or tumultuous as the hell he was now in.

The Afterthoughts on The Dark Train. They'd been defeated by negating their energies with an opposing force, something so strong it washed away all ill effects and rendered he and Guinevere virtually untouchable.

Would it work again?

There were so many people here, so much hate. The love he felt for Guinevere was intense, by far the most powerful thing he'd ever felt in his life. But it couldn't be nearly enough to dissuade the thousands of enraged savages, who maimed and killed and tortured as easily as one scratched an irksome itch. Could it?

Jensen lifted Guinevere slightly and kissed her again. A man screamed at the top of his lungs and shot past him, but Jensen didn't look up, concentrating instead on the cold, dead lips that were entwined with his own. Somewhere from deep inside whatever darkness she was held, Guinevere responded, slowly, dreamlike, reciprocating his kiss, her lips warming, her eyes fluttering, the pallor of her wrinkled skin growing slightly redder.

He pulled away and saw that tinges of brown were floating in her irises, quivering like the last drop of water from a faucet. He smiled at the sight.

"I adore you, Guinevere," he whispered, the sound lost in the grumble of screams surrounding him. "With all my love."

Then Jensen began walking through the crowd.

***

Hedley Grange opened his eyes and instantly spotted them.

It wasn't a sixth sense; not really. It was just that there was so much hate swirling about the room that the presence of such abiding love cut through the noise like a lighthouse through thick fog.

He smiled sadly at the sight of his old friend cradling his ex-girlfriend in his arms as they slowly made their way through the hordes of thrashing bodies, which parted like Jensen and Guinevere were toxic and couldn't be touched. That was, after all, a pretty accurate description of what was happening: Benny and Gwen were so completely in love with each other that they were cancer to the vile, heartless, cruel creatures surrounding them.

"Your time is gonna come, Benny," he said as he got up from his crouched position and began dusting off his blue jeans. "Just you wait."

As he turned and walked out of The Subdivisions, a snatch of an old Doors song came to him and he began singing it as loudly as his lungs would allow:

This is the end ... my only friend ... the end.

[silence]

Jensen.

Her voice startles him from a troubled sleep, and he rolls over in the cot. Last night is murky, a kaleidoscope of images and sounds that make little sense on their own: neat white lines laid out on reflective glass, the sound of something big shattering, someone yelling, the uncomfortable leather seat of either a taxi or a cop car; he can't remember. The headache is crystal clear, however, and as he sits up, he winces at the sharp pain that blooms behind his eyes.

Jensen, she says again, and this time he looks in the direction of the voice. Aimee is standing behind the bars, the frown on her face made all the more profound by the lines under her eyes and the disheveled mop of jet-black hair atop her head. She looks as exhausted as he feels.

He stands, falls, stands again. His head is protesting the sudden movement, but he ignores the pain and joins her.

Tell room service they forgot my mint, he jokes, but there is no humor whatsoever in his voice, nor does he crack a grin.

I posted your bail, she says flatly. *There isn't anything I can do about the mirrors, though. You'll have to talk with the owner about it yourself.* She looks to her feet. *He's pressing charges, if that wasn't obvious by now.*

He shakes his head, and the act seems to bring last night into clearer focus: leaving the apartment to tie one on at Bonzo's Montreux near the El. Getting drunk and scoring a teener from the bartender. Doing lines in the men's bathroom and breaking every last mirror in it with the trash can. Being arrested and falling into an inebriated sleep.

I didn't know what to do after ... what happened. Is he okay? The guy you were with? I threw him pretty hard.

301

She huffs, surprised. *You want to know if the guy I was fucking behind your back is* alright? She shakes her head. *You should be furious at me.*

I am, he says.

No, you're not. I can see it in your eyes. You think this is your fault. And it is. But it's also mine. Jensen ... we don't love each other. We never did.

He grabs his head. The headache is a roar now, a million microscopic jack-hammers working feverishly in his brain.

Don't say that, baby. Come on home with me and we'll figure this all out. We can still do that. It's not too late.

I'm not your baby, Aimee says in a flat, almost irritated tone. *I never was.*

Silence as he mulls this over. He searches for his character, tries to remember his lines, but the headache is making it nearly impossible.

I'll quit, he says abruptly. The smile he offers is half-hearted and weak, a paltry performance worthy of scathing reviews. *It'll be easy. Cold turkey, one and done. I'm not even going back on tour.*

She's heard this all before and frowns.

This isn't about the cocaine.

His wife in nothing but knee-high white socks, the stranger working her from behind with silent accuracy, the sweat, the groans, the headboard bang-ing against the wall like they'd *wanted* it to be heard ... it all comes rushing back, and he lets it, because it makes him angry.

You lied to me. On our wedding day. You lied and said it didn't matter.

She wipes away a tear with her forefinger.

It doesn't. Not in the way you think, at least. I accepted the fact I'd never know you in the bedroom. So I tried to know you outside of it. But four years later and I still haven't met the real you. She fishes a Kleenex from her purse and dabs her eyes with it. *Even when you're here, you're not really here. I just can't do it anymore, Jensen. I'm not like you. I'm not a pretender.*

He grabs the bars, leans in as close as they allow. He knows his breath smells like vomit, that he looks like an exquisite disaster, but there's nothing he can do about either one. He's all out of resources.

So that's just it, then? We can't talk about this?

She shakes her head, and the certainty of it breaks his heart. There's nothing to be said or done. He's lost her, just like all the others.

Aimee looks down the hall and nods at someone, then turns back to him with an air of finality.

I have to go, now. Take care of yourself, Jensen.

Then, without another word, she turns and leaves. As her footfalls echo down the corridor and then disappear altogether, he slumps back into his cot and screams into his pillow.

Moments later, the screams turn to tears.

BRIGHTER SKIES
-Track Thirteen-

Noah DeNova had to shout over the rumble of the helicopter rotors, which were thumping at a steady pace about fifty yards away. "Where are you taking him?"

"Teton Valley over in Driggs," the EMT shouted in return. "It's the closest place."

Noah nodded. "I don't suppose you have room in that chopper for one more?"

The man scanned the horizon and the black smoke that was still pouring into the early morning sky despite the heavy rain that had passed through the area.

"Sorry, no," he said. "We're full up. But there's another one inbound, ETA five minutes. Could have you there within the hour. I'll radio it in." The man looked over at the body being strapped into the airlift gurney and nodded. "Friend of yours?"

Noah chuckled. "You could say we only recently met."

The EMT flashed him a smile full of perfectly white teeth and extended a hand. "Damn good work, doc. Don't know how you did it, but I think he's actually got a chance in hell."

Noah took the man's hand and pumped it three times before letting go. "I'm as equally impressed with you. How you were able to see me down here in all this mess is a damn miracle."

"It must be that kind of day for miracles, doc," the man said and gave him a final nod before walking to join the others.

"Miracles, indeed," Noah said to no one but the trees.

***

Once he'd mounted the ledge at the other end of the crater and was safely removed from the violence below, Jensen laid Guinevere on the ground and gently leaned her back against the wall. She remained unresponsive, and the gray mist still poured from her body like waves of heat from blacktop on a sweltering summer day.

But something, probably their proximity to the exit, had restored her femininity; she no longer looked like some mummified exhibit on display under glass at the Field Museum, but a significantly older, sicklier version of the headstrong, resourceful young woman he'd grown to cherish more than anything else in the world – material, astral or otherwise.

In the dim orange light, he checked her eyes for any new signs of sentience and, finding none, stood up to examine the way he'd come. They'd survived unscathed. The rioters hadn't bothered them at all; had, in fact, acted as if he and Guinevere were the bubonic plague, parting like the Red Sea to let them through. A few had even stopped murdering each other long enough to regard the pair with an unholy blend of revulsion and envy as they passed by.

"All you need is love," Jensen said to the bedlam below, and smiled despite the horrific things he was seeing.

He turned back to Guinevere and again crouched beside her. A strand of hair, darkened by the water still dripping from it, had fallen across her eyes, and he swiped it aside with his finger. Her lips curved slightly into a half-smile at his touch, even as her eyes continued to stare blankly forward. There was a bit of brown in them – not much, but just enough for him to crack a smile of his own.

"Whatcha say, beautiful? Wanna blow this joint and grab a burger or something?"

He put one arm in the crook of her knees and the other behind her neck, intending to lift her again, when he heard someone shrieking and stopped cold. It was markedly different from the other wails emanating from the pit below; it wasn't angry or howling in pain. It was terrified. Jensen turned and immediately located its source.

The Warden had made it about three-quarters of the way through the pit before being stopped and cornered by a group of man-creatures, one of which was armed with a long, jagged blade that looked like a scimitar but wasn't. They were advancing on The Warden slowly, as if the terror in his eyes was a drug they wanted to savor for as long as possible.

The Warden blindly searched his belt with his left hand, brushing past a pair of handcuffs, and retrieved a black Billy club, which he began waving in the air as if he were trying to swat a fly. If not for the horror of it all, Jensen would have found the sight comical: an overweight Achilles making his last stand against the denizens of the deep.

A series of images flashed across his mind then: his stepfather's steel Saluki and the smell of the musty basement; Brian Riggs, still dressed as Mortimer Brewster, straddling him in a hotel bathroom; Johnny Two-Eyes cracking his knuckles, and Hedley's enraged mob tying him to a horse. They joined the countless others in his life who had towered over his courage and made him feel small and insignificant. A lifetime of fear and cowardice and inaction, punctuated by brief moments of clarity when he wondered just how different his life could have been if only he'd stood up to just one of them.

Then the memories faded, just winked out of his mind like an old tube TV being shut off, and kissing Guinevere on the cheek, he left her and ran full speed down the length of the collapsed ledge. On his way he scooped up a large stick of wood, something that looked like a gnarled, knotted tree branch lying near a portion of the cavern wall that had collapsed, and rose it above his head as he sprinted headlong back into the swarm of bodies infesting the crater floor.

***

Benjamin C. Clemmons was *fucked*.

He'd never much cared for colorful expletives, even the tamer ones that were really just misappropriated from regular words, like *ass* and *dick*. His mother had always punished that kind of language with one swift swipe of the slotted spoon she'd kept above the kitchen stove, and he supposed years of that had beaten the urge to swear out of him.

But mother wasn't here, and there was really no other way to put it: He was fucked, utterly and completely.

The creature with the bladed weapon slowly advanced on him, its face featureless save for a pair of small ears and a monstrous mouth that protruded like a dog's snout. It smiled at him, revealing a double row of oversized, blood-stained teeth dripping with saliva and adorned with bits of rotting flesh. The sight was terrifying, but not as much as the sound its jaws made as they began snapping together, *tap-tap-tap* like typewriter keys pounding paper. The other three creatures dropped back a few paces at the sound.

Either the Snout-Man was some sort of gang leader ordering his minions to back off so he could be the one to draw first blood, or the four beasts had simply decided to put their differences aside for the moment to make sure the terrified man in the uniform couldn't escape. It really didn't matter either way, because The Warden was comically overmatched. His Billy club was useless against just one of them, let alone all four.

He still had his walkie, but what good would calling for help do? Tommy was guarding the entrance, and Greg was all the way out by the wagon. Neither would get to him in time.

The Warden jumped back just as Snout-Man swung its massive blade, but he was a bit too late and the tip grazed the front of his button-up-the-front shirt, slicing it open and drawing a thin line of blood in the supple flesh beneath. The Warden looked down at the wound in shock – not so much at the sight of the blood, but at the fact it hurt. Everything he knew about this place told him things weren't supposed to hurt, but this did.

The Billy club slipped from his grasp as he fell to his knees. He tried to put his hands across his chest to stem the bleeding, but it only gushed through his fingers. The smell of blood and fear sent Snout-Man into a wild frenzy, and it began chattering its nightmare teeth again as it resumed its slow, predatory advance toward him.

It was almost on him – so close that The Warden could smell centuries of victims' blood on its breath – when a figure suddenly emerged from the shadows and, without introducing itself, sent a swift and brutal blow raining down on the creature's head. Its skull instantly cracked open and it dropped to its knees in agony. The other three figures who'd been waiting patiently behind it began to whoop and holler in approval of the brutal act.

"Come on," the shadow said. "He won't stay down for long."

A hand reached out to him, and he took it. In the dim firelight he saw the face of Jensen Bennett before him. He was covered from head to toe in blood and dirt but looked otherwise unharmed.

"Stabbed," The Warden said dumbly.

Jensen looked confused. "I don't see anything. You sure about that?"

The Warden looked down and saw Jensen was right – his fingers, which had been wet with blood just seconds ago, were now bone dry. Even the pain was gone, although his shirt *was* ripped. Everything except the attack itself had all just been in his head.

"Mind if we get going, now?" Jensen said, and motioned to the downed creature. "*Jaws* was a great flick, but I'm not one for remakes."

The Warden nodded and had even taken a few steps when Jensen stopped him and pointed to the Billy club lying in the sludge.

"Grab that," he said. "You're going to need it."

***

Jensen had almost reached the second ledge when he heard it: a soft, leisurely thumping. It sounded like a mechanical heartbeat, and it wasn't coming from the Rioter Room but inside his head.

"Why'd you stop? We're almost there!" The Warden cried out from behind him. His shirt and pants were now grimy, and much like Guinevere, the negative influence of The Subdivisions had left him looking more than a little worse for wear, but the wide, excited look on his face told Jensen he'd snapped out of his fugue state and was once again alert and ready.

"I hear something," he said. "Sounds like ... a helicopter?"

The Warden wrapped an arm around his shoulders and forced him to keep walking. Only when they were back on the ledge and next to Guinevere did he turn Jensen around to face him.

"It's the material world. My guess is it's a rescue chopper. You don't have much time now."

Jensen nodded solemnly but didn't respond. He had to get Guinevere out of this place; all other concerns were secondary. He crouched down to pick her up but was stopped by a gentle hand on his shoulder.

"Jensen," The Warden said calmly. "Thank you. You didn't have to save me, but you did."

Jensen grinned. "What can I say. I love a man in uniform."

Then he scooped Guinevere's limp body into his arms and began walking toward the exit he'd seen from across the room, The Warden quick on his heels. The moment he touched her, the thumping of the helicopter blades fell to a dim, almost inconsequential hum. Her body was even warmer now, and it felt good in his arms as he navigated the long, rugged tunnel toward a small light in the distance.

"It's the damndest thing," he said after they'd walked for a bit and the hellish roar of the Rioter Room had faded enough to allow for civil conversation.

The Warden huffed. "What is?"

"I *saved* you."

"Yeah, buddy, I know. How many thanks you want?"

Jensen shook his head. "I'm not fishing for compliments. It's just that, ever since I was a kid, I've either frozen up or turned tail and run. I never fought anyone in my entire life."

The Warden was silent for a moment. When he spoke again, his voice was soft and contemplative, almost fatherly. "Trauma's a terrible thing, Jensen. I know from experience. Mine was my momma, and then the war. Yours was your stepdad. He beat you so bad it just stayed with you. Made you scared of everyone and everything."

Jensen went to ask how he could possibly know that, but then it came to him: the clipboard. The Warden probably knew almost *everything* about him, even things Jensen himself didn't.

"Yeah, I guess that's true. Except, that didn't happen this time. I just ran out there. The fear was gone."

"That's a good thing," The Warden said. "Maybe it means you don't have to be afraid anymore."

✳✳✳

When they were close enough to the exit that it nearly illuminated the entire tunnel, Jensen decided to make his move.

"So, where *is* your clipboard?" he asked. "Strange seeing you without it."

"In the paddy wagon with Greg. Told him to pull around 'case you squirmed out somehow." He pointed in the general direction of the cave opening and sighed. "He should be waiting for us somewhere out there. Assuming he didn't follow my orders, which is pretty much always." Jensen could tell the adrenaline of their recent fight was already wearing off, but The Warden was starting to look like himself again. "I should probably walkie him, come to think of it."

Jensen took special note of the phrase "waiting for us." Despite everything, The Warden was still hellbent on taking him back to Translucent Tower. Jensen couldn't let that happen. Not because of the money; that had become only a dim thought in the back of his mind. He needed to stay for Guinevere. To make sure she was okay, yes, but also because he was dreading the moment he was torn from her. It didn't matter if they only had minutes or even seconds; he was going to savor every last drop.

As The Warden talked to Greg via the walkie-talkie strapped to his shoulder, Jensen scanned the cavern wall. It didn't take long to spot what he was looking for: a thin segment of rock jutting from the stone. It was hollow in the center but attached to the wall on both ends like a drawer handle.

Jensen stopped when he was relatively near the protrusion and grunted. "Man, I really underestimated how heavy Gwen was." He shifted her in his arms and grunted again to sell the lie. "I think someone's way overdue on renewing their afterlife gym membership."

"Here," The Warden said, reaching out his hands. "Let me carry her for a bit."

Jensen shook his head. "I couldn't ask you to do that. I think I'd have to turn in my Man Card."

The Warden smiled warmly and poked his hands out further. "Please. It's the least I can do, after what you did for me."

Jensen feigned a sigh and, nodding as if conceding a hard-fought battle, handed Guinevere over to the Warden's burly arms. The moment she was secure, Jensen grabbed the handcuffs that were hanging off the Warden's belt and, in one deft motion, wrapped an end around the jailor's left wrist.

"What the ..."

Before The Warden could finish the statement, Jensen had wrapped the other end of the cuffs around the protrusion and then clicked them shut.

"Hey, just what in the hell do you think you're doing?" The Warden's face was a canvass of shock and anger.

Jensen first unclipped the small radio from The Warden's right shoulder and casually tossed it over his shoulder, then took Guinevere back into his arms. The Warden was too busy struggling with his new shackle to resist either action.

"Sorry, Warden. But I can't let you take me back. It's nothing personal."

The Warden began yanking at the handcuffs, but all he managed to do was cause some cavern dust to float down from the wall. The makeshift handle would hold, but probably not for long.

Jensen looked down at Guinevere, who felt soft and warm in his hands despite the chill in the air. Just a few moments more and she'd be out of that vile place.

"Well, Benji, I guess we're gonna groove. It's been real. We'll have to do this again sometime."

The Warden's face went red with rage. "Jensen, uncuff me *right now*!" With one arm he continued to struggle with the cuff, and with the other he reached out to choke Jensen. Neither effort was successful.

Jensen turned and took a few steps toward the exit when a thought struck him and he spun around. Guinevere groaned in his arms; she was definitely shaking off whatever bad mojo had a grip on her. Even the gray mist that had once covered her head to toe had dwindled to what looked like nothing more than a trick of light.

"Seriously, though. Thanks for everything. You've been a royal pain in my ass, but I'm actually gonna kind of miss you." The Warden didn't respond; his full attention was now directed at the handcuffs and the protrusion to which they were connected. "I'll come back here, someday. And when I do, I'll be sure to swing by Translucent Tower. We'll share a laugh. Maybe play some Scrabble."

With that, Jensen carried Guinevere out of The Subdivisions and into the world outside, The Warden cursing his name the entire way.

***

Once they were outside, the anonymous melody returned in full, that single, sour note blaring from somewhere above in the eternally darkened skies. It sounded like a lone horn heralding the arrival of some wrathful deity, and its ominous discord would've been terrifying if Jensen wasn't so elated at making it out in one piece, with the woman he loved in his arms.

The Subdivisions had deposited them in a large garden filled with hundreds of enormous plants – tall, sickly green monstrosities that looked like oversized Venus Fly Traps. The plants *moved*, too, pivoting ever so slightly on their thick stems and seeming to regard the man and the woman in his arms with guarded eyes. They looked malevolent, and Jensen had half-expected a flurry of massive mouths lined with sharp teeth to descend on him as he passed beneath them. Instead, the plants let him pass, but their silent, brooding shapes sent one clear and unified message: Get moving or else.

A few hundred yards from the strange plants, an eerie outline began to take shape on the horizon: A large, four-wheeled contraption that looked like it belonged in an old *Keystone Cops* movie. It was the paddy wagon, but he didn't see any sign of Greg, The Warden's faithfully pathetic sidekick.

As he continued to walk toward it, he glanced at Guinevere and saw that her eyes had very nearly returned to their vibrant shade of brown; only a few squiggles of inky black darkness swam in her irises like confused tadpoles. The gray mist was now completely gone, and while she still looked unwell and underfed, the wrinkles on her face had smoothed out and her skin was a shade redder. Her hair was even fuller now, too, the strawberry blonde waging a successful war against the gray that had infested it.

But she was still comatose, and Jensen began to worry that she might *never*

313

come around, no matter how far away from The Subdivisions they got. This thought made him decide to chance another kiss and, for the third time, he leaned over and brought her lips to his.

The response was immediate: Guinevere not only began kissing him back, but actually wrapped her hands around his head and started running her fingers through his hair. Warmth flooded Jensen's body as his heart quickened. Her lips, warm and soft, tasted faintly of bubblegum. She groaned and slid a tongue in his mouth, and he returned the gesture. The moment was pure magic, the weight of the material world lifting from his shoulders and seeming to float away into the sky like an unwanted thought. Even the slow thump of the helicopter rotors was silent. It was a slight return to the paradise of their first kiss along the banks of The Sea of Sorrow.

All of which made the slap across his face that came moments later even more surprising. He recoiled from the blow, and when he turned to face her again, he saw Guinevere regarding him with wide, shocked eyes that had at some point fully returned to their original color.

"How ... DARE you!" she spat.

Jensen couldn't help it – he laughed. The heavenly feeling lingered despite the shock of the slap. "Hey, you were kissing me, too."

Something passed across her face – realization, perhaps? – but her eyes continued to shoot daggers at him. "Put me down, Jensen. *Now*."

He did, but the moment her feet touched solid ground they began to wobble, and Jensen had to catch her in his arms again.

"Easy," he said.

She pushed him away, propelling both of them backward until they fell on the ground with an unceremonious thump. They sat that way for a minute, looking at each other, he with a bemused grin on his face, she with a scowl on hers.

"And just what in the hell is so goddamned funny?" she asked finally.

"Nothing. Just that I'm so in love with you I could throw up."

Her cheeks flushed at the admission, but the pointed glare didn't falter. "Stop *saying* that."

"No," he said simply. "I love you. And whether you want to admit it or not, you love me, too."

She huffed and looked to her right. There was nothing there to see except fog. "You're delusional. We barely know each other."

"That's bullshit and you know it. I don't think I've ever known anyone as well as I know you. Not Teddy, not Aimee. Not even Grange." He scooted closer to her, half expecting her to recoil. When she didn't, he continued. "Since I've been loving you, everything I thought I cared about before – the album, the money, opening that stupid nightclub – it all just seems so *boring*. We *have* something. You didn't see your eyes. They were black. Like, *oil slick in the middle of the night* black. They only came back – *you* only came back – when I kissed you." He realized he was still grinning and decided he didn't much care. "The eyes don't lie, sister."

She seemed to contemplate this for a moment, watching the mist curl across the ground like sentient smoke. When she responded, however, it wasn't the question he'd expected. "Where are we?"

"Dunno." He pointed to the Venus Fly Traps and nodded. "About two football fields away from those creepy plants."

Guinevere regarded the enormous shadows standing watch in the distance with a quiet wonder. "The Wicked Garden," she said. "It's magnificent. In a glum sort of way."

"What the hell *are* they?"

"They're guardians, kinda like the Doormen, I guess. Their job is to make sure no one leaves The Subdivisions with negative energy attached to them. That stuff is bad for the environment."

"Well, whatever they are, they let us go. And just in time, too." Jensen pointed to the blocky shape on the horizon. "Our cab is waiting."

Her gaze followed his finger. "A car?"

"Yep. The Warden's very own personal chariot. I'll have to deal with Barney Fife, but I don't think he'll be much of a problem."

She looked back to him, some of the anger gone from her face, but not all. "And where do you suggest we go?"

He scooted even closer to her and grabbed her hands. Again, she didn't recoil. "Wherever you want."

She looked him dead in the eyes and said, "I want to go wherever Grange went."

She said Grange, not Hank, Jensen thought, and then immediately dismissed the idea as wishful thinking. The truth was, he couldn't make her see if she didn't *want* to see, and right now she was as blind as Stevie Wonder. He couldn't care less about Hedley Grange or his damned album anymore, but if it meant spending his last remaining moments by her side, then he'd go anywhere she wanted to go.

"Okay, then," he said. "After you."

***

Now that he wasn't holding Guinevere, the trip to the paddy wagon was a short one. Officer Greg, whose lanky frame blended into the vehicle so completely that Jensen almost didn't see him, was leaning against the driver's side door smoking a cigarette, a look of utter dread on his face.

"Got a light?" Jensen asked.

Officer Greg darted his head toward the sound and, seeing the two newcomers – both looking like they'd walked through the very heart of hell and back, especially Guinevere – took a few defensive steps backward.

"Hey, I don't want no trouble." He flicked the cigarette to the ground and put his hands in the air. "Take the car."

Guinevere laughed. "*Jesus*, Greg. Grow a pair, will you?"

Greg squinted as recognition crossed his face. "Gwen? That you?"

"Nope, it's Aileen Wuornos," Jensen said, "here to claim her eighth victim."

Guinevere ignored this last bit and walked forward. "At ease, soldier," she said kindly. "We come in peace."

Officer Greg relaxed, but only for a moment. "Where's The Warden? He ain't responding."

Jensen pointed back the way they'd come. "Benji's still checking out The Subdivisions. Said he's thinking of getting a summer home there. Needs your help picking out some drapes."

Officer Greg peered into the fog, trying to see what Jensen was pointing at and no doubt imagining a whole host of horrors lying in wait somewhere. "I ... don't know. I don't think I can do that."

Jensen walked up to the officer and flashed a smile. It was amazing how good he felt, how absolutely *himself*. There was no need for fakery anymore. "Greg, this is serious shit. The Warden asked specifically for you. Said no one else could help him."

Officer Greg's chest swelled. "He did?"

"You bet," Jensen said. "Just make a beeline straight that way. Warden's in the caves right at the edge by the garden."

Officer Greg swallowed hard and bowed his head. "Okay, then. If the Warden needs me."

Jensen gave him a pat on the back as he passed, and together he and Guinevere watched as Officer Greg first became a billowy figure and then disappeared completely into the fog.

"He's so fucked," Guinevere said.

"Yep," Jensen responded, then tried the handle on the paddy wagon. It opened wide, revealing a cramped interior that belied the size of the vehicle.

"How exactly are we going to find Hank?" Guinevere said as she made her way to the passenger side and swung open the door. "It's not like we have a GPS attached to him or anything."

Jensen pointed at the clipboard lying on the driver's seat and smiled. "Actually, we kinda do."

***

"*Evermore?*" Guinevere shouted, so loudly that Jensen almost lost control of the paddy wagon. He was probably driving a bit too fast in the dense fog, but Guinevere had insisted on it.

"What?"

Guinevere put the clipboard down and shook her head. "Evermore. In High Country. It's where people go to have one last party before walking the Path of Reflection and reincarnating at the Hall of Rekindling."

"Gwen, you're going to have to slow down. I have no idea what in the hell you're talking about."

She took a deep breath and then continued. "Hank is going to Evermore. Actually, he's already *at* Evermore, according to this clipboard. Must've caught the Green Line somewhere. Anyway, he's going to leave the afterworld and go back, in a new body, to live a new life." She paused for a moment before continuing. "I can't believe he'd just *leave* me like that. Without even saying goodbye." Then, after a pregnant pause, she added, "Maybe he's not the guy I fell in love with anymore."

Jensen turned the wheel sharply to the left to avoid a rocky formation that seemed to materialize out of the fog. When he was on the straight and narrow again, he looked to her. She'd just made a startling admission, but he didn't want to press the issue; it held much more power if she came to the realization on her own.

"So ... you can go back?" he asked conversationally.

"Yes," she said absently, and a bit dejectedly. "People live many lives. Me, you, everyone. We live, we die, we spend some time here, then we go back."

"But ... why?"

"I don't know, Jensen. We just do."

They rode in silence for a bit. Could he really have lived multiple lives before? If so, who had he been? And why couldn't he remember it?

"This Evermore," he said finally. "You said it was a party. What do you mean?"

"It's a way for people to shed all their earthly desires – sex, drugs, booze, you name it – so they can be completely clean when they walk the path and see all of their past lives. There they learn what they did wrong, what they did right, and so on. They come out as one person but with all the memories and emotions of their past selves. Then they take all the lessons they learned into the next life, to work on things that still need working on."

Jensen didn't know what to do with this information; it was heavy stuff that would take eons to unpack. So he remained silent, watching the road for obstacles and hoping beyond hope that, when they reached this Evermore place, Hedley Grange was already long gone.

✳✳✳

It didn't take long for the skies to lighten and the melody forever playing in the atmosphere to become sprightlier and less ominous. They'd been driving for only a half hour, but already Jensen could see they were once again on the outskirts of the Dims. It looked similar to his approach to Township Rebellion, only instead of hardpan desert, the craggy outcroppings and dense fog had given way to a flat, barren field that was slowly but surely becoming greener the farther they went.

The drive had cleared his mind a bit. Despite the euphoria of being with the woman he loved, of finally feeling free of all the weights that had shackled him his entire life, he was more than a little ashamed of the grisly fate he'd concocted for Grange in his mind, the one that had freed him from the Doormen, as Guinevere called them. His hatred in the Rioter Room could be dismissed as nothing more than a toxic influence wearing away at his resolve. He *was* human, after all. But that first thought, that had been his alone. And he hadn't just invented it; he'd *relished* in it.

Hedley Grange was now his enemy, but he'd once been his friend. More than a friend, really – he'd been his brother. Jensen hadn't loved too many people in his life, but he'd loved Hedley. The fact he'd wished such unforgivable acts on someone he once considered family, even despite the rift between them, made Jensen reexamine everything. He probably shouldn't have signed off on that commercial. The song wasn't his to give away. He should've reached out to the band, to Nigel at least, to make sure they were all in agreement. But he hadn't, and it had cost him the most precious friendship of his life.

"I never did thank you," Guinevere said suddenly. "For saving me from The Sea of Sorrow, I mean."

Jensen smiled, glad to have been torn from his thoughts, but kept his eyes on the road.

"I'd wade through a thousand Seas of Sorrow for you. Besides, you saved my ass in the Room Full of Mirrors, so that makes us even."

Guinevere sniffed. She'd been crying on and off, silently as not to alert Jensen, but he would've been able to tell regardless; the sadness was in her voice.

"Actually, twice," she said. "I also saved you on The Dark Train."

Jensen shook his head. "Nope, doesn't count. It was my idea for you to sing. That one was more of a team effort."

He felt something warm on his arm, and looking over, he saw Guinevere had put a hand there and was staring at him with tear-rimmed eyes. Despite the sadness in her smile, she looked absolutely gorgeous again, the influence of The Subdivisions completely vanished.

"We really do make quite a team, don't we?" she said.

Jensen took his right hand from the steering wheel and held her hand.

"Like Abbot and Costello. Only much, much sexier."

Guinevere laughed, and then did something he wasn't expecting – she pulled Hedley Grange's bandana from its nest between her breasts and, rolling down the window, flung it out into the lessening darkness.

From that point onward, the rest of the long ride to Evermore was a happy one.

***

Their destination sat on a platter-shaped acre of land that neighbored an imposing waterfall, one which casually oozed liquid blue into a sleepy river dreaming immediately below it. A thick, emerald forest guarded the acre on all sides, and the river muttered contemplatively as it meandered around the perimeter of the platter and then squeezed through the tight embrace of the trees, disappearing into the placid darkness therein. Opposite the waterfall was a large, stone staircase with uneven steps that gradually rose into the forest until it joined the side of a nearby mountain. In the ethereal light it looked like a stairway to heaven, or at the very least, a path to something more mysterious and profound.

The patch of matted grass in the center of it all was teeming with activity. Hundreds of tents were scattered about like a small village; some were just crude sheets held up with sticks that looked like they would break in a mild breeze, while others were more elegant and seemed firmly rooted to the ground.

People were everywhere. One man was sitting in a circle with a dozen other people, chuckling loudly and taking a drag from what was either a hand-rolled cigarette or a joint, the small bonfire between them popping and hissing as the flames hungrily consumed the four sticks that formed its structure. A lady who was completely nude except for a silver necklace that hung from her neck like a gaudy noose stood near the river and hummed while she painted a picture of the waterfall. In the center, a three-piece band was playing a boisterous folk melody – a woman on fiddle, and two men on acoustic guitar and bongos, respectively – while a group of people danced enthusiastically in circles around them. Near the southern rim of the forest wall, a man and woman made silent love on a blue blanket spread beneath them. No matter where he looked, he saw throngs of people, and they all seemed to be having the time of their lives.

"Evermore?" Jensen asked. "Looks more like Woodstock."

Guinevere squeezed his hand but didn't respond. They'd parked the paddy wagon about a mile up the road and had walked the rest of the way along a small dirt path beaten through the forest, she swinging their linked arms between them like a Girl Scout on a nature hike. Something had changed in her since leaving The Subdivisions, which now seemed like nothing more than a blurry nightmare. Whether *he'd* been the cause of this change or something else, Jensen wasn't sure, but he liked it all the same.

As they walked into the circle, Jensen looked up and saw that the skies were gray. Rain was coming, but despite this, he could still distinctly hear the anonymous melody playing a series of contemplative, happy notes somewhere above. He could even see thousands of faint squiggles moving in the sky beyond the storm clouds. The ribbons, it seemed, felt like dancing again.

Everything had a strange familiarity about it – the waterfall, the mountains in the distance, the taste of rain in the air, even the chattering of birds in the surrounding forest ... he felt as if he'd been there before, if only in his dreams.

"I can't believe a place like this exists on the same plane as a dump like The Subdivisions," Jensen said. He stopped and turned to her, their hands still intertwined. "There's an energy here, a ... *force*. It's not like the one in Translucent Tower or The Terminal, it's ... magical. Almost *mythical*. Can you feel it?"

She smiled up at him, both with her lips and her eyes. Despite her dirty, tattered clothes and disheveled hair, she looked absolutely stunning in the meager light falling from above.

"It's like the stories I used to read when I was a kid," she said, "with sorcerers and dragons and princesses."

"And sexy little Hobbits with hairy toes?"

She giggled and scanned the crowd. "I don't see any of those around. A few *Gollums*, maybe."

They stared into each other's eyes for a moment, and the magic seemed to radiate *there*, too.

"Come on," he said at last. "Let's join the party."

As they entered the circle and the celebration churning within, the battle of Evermore's competing sounds assaulted them: raucous laughter, groans of pleasure, idle conversation and at least three separate songs being played by various disparate groups scattered about the camp. Yet none of these elements stepped on the toes of the other; they existed in harmony, some even complementing the other sounds, all swirling into the sky and joining the pleasant, unknowable tune ceaselessly sounding from the heavens.

They stopped near the folk band in the center and watched as men and women, some naked, others not, shimmied around the trio as the beat propelled their feet forward. All of them looked stoned, either on the moment or something slightly more manufactured, their wide grins and wild eyes seeming a bit insane. As the band ended one tune and began another, this one a stripped-down, almost medieval-sounding version of Led Zeppelin's "Bron-Y-Aur Stomp," the dancers didn't miss a step and began circling the musicians in the opposite direction, their collective bare feet slamming into the earth in time with the driving beat.

"All of these people will be born into new bodies before too long," Guinevere said from his side. "It's really kind of beautiful. Life doesn't end." She looked to the dancers and smiled. "And neither does happiness."

"And neither does love," he said, wrapping his arm around the small of her back and gently pulling her close, so close their noses were nearly touching. She looked scared, but it wasn't fear of *him*; it was fear of her own desire. He could see it in the squint of her eyes, the quiver of her lips. She put a soft hand against his cheek and began to stroke it tenderly.

"I'm sorry I slapped you," she said softly. "We were in the Dims, so I bet it even kinda hurt a little."

He reached up and grabbed her hand, and now they were standing like two dancers, waltzing to the music of Evermore.

"I shouldn't have kissed you. Not like that."

They began to sway, and now they actually *were* dancing – slowly, meticulously, enjoying how they felt in each other's arms.

"Oh, yeah?" The smile returned to her face, big and bright and beautiful. "How *should* you have kissed me, then?"

"Like this," Jensen said, leaning in. To his amazement, she leaned in to oblige him, and as their lips met a light rain began to fall upon their shoulders. They didn't seem to mind, and neither did anyone else at Evermore.

"I love you, Guinevere," Jensen whispered into her ear.

The words she whispered back sent chills down his spine.

"Maybe you'd like to show me just how much."

✳✳✳

From his perch halfway up the staggered steps leading to the Path of Reflection, Hedley Grange saw it all: the swaying masses, the lively music, the immense waterfall and the large, pregnant storm clouds, which suddenly opened up and began pummeling the area in a cool, revitalizing rain.

He saw *them*, too: two hazy shapes running for the nearest tent and laughing the whole way, their hands never unlocking even as they were forced to jump over a man lying on the grass. A tear fell from his eye, and it was immediately obliterated by the rain.

Good for you, Benny. Good for you.

He smiled, knowing there was nothing left for him to do. Jensen was happy, truly and utterly happy, just as he'd requested. It had been a hard road, for Jensen and Guinevere and Teddy and Zach, but also for Grange himself, who'd been forced to set aside his own anger and see the bigger picture. But he'd finally done it – he'd finally paid Jensen back for all of his love and friend-ship over the years.

Hedley Grange stood up and began walking up the steps that led to the Path of Reflection and, somewhere beyond, a brand-new existence.

[silence]

He feels sluggish and disconnected, like the first few minutes upon waking after a long afternoon nap. He can only open one eye and, when he talks, the words come out all mangled. But mothers understand their sons, even if the specifics are vague, and this is no exception.

How long until I can go home? the boy asks. *I don't like this place.*

His mother regards him with sad eyes that seem in dire need of a good night's rest.

Just a bit longer, baby. She squeezes his good arm, the one that isn't in a cast. *But when you get out, we're not going home. We're gonna stay with gram and grandpa for a while.*

Through his good eye he sees a tear roll down his mom's cheek, but she doesn't start crying. Her well is bone dry, and one tear is all she can muster.

What about Richard? Is he coming with us?

She averts his gaze and looks out the hospital room window. There's nothing to see there except the side of the building next to it and the somber, colorless sky above. His stepfather is already dead; the police found his body that morning, propped against the kitchen sink with the shotgun still in his hand and missing the majority of his face. But the boy doesn't know that yet, and neither does his mother.

No, honey. Just the two of us. Like it was before.

Despite everything, this makes him sad. He never had a father and he'll miss Richard. But he won't miss the Wall Monster, and he tells his mother this.

There're no monsters at Grandma's house, sweetie. Grandpa checked last night, just for you. Only homecooked meals and a whole lotta love.

The Teenage Mutant Ninja Turtles flash their cartoon smiles at him from the TV above his bed, but he doesn't feel like smiling back. None of this was supposed to happen.

A long silence, and then his mother speaks again.

Honey, who is Beverly? You talked about her in your sleep. Is that a friend of yours at school?

The boy shakes his head, and doing so hurts. There are bandages everywhere: on his head, on his nose, on his eyes. He's a miniature mummy come to life.

No. I don't know who that is. I don't know any Beverly.

But even as he says the words, something in the back of his battered mind knows he's lying; he *does* know a Beverly, knows her well, but he doesn't know how or why or even what she looks like. She's a dream, a phantom who doesn't belong in this world.

Well, whoever she is, you seem fond of her. You kept calling out to her, asking where she was. I thought maybe it was one of your nurses, but it wasn't.

His mother squeezes his arm again, and he gives her a meager smile in response.

Get some sleep, honey. I love you.

But he knows sleep is something that will be difficult, now and for years to come. There may be no Wall Monster at Grandma's house, but there's one inside his head, and he visits it again and again every time he closes his eyes. He may be able to escape Richard's basement, but he can't escape the creature that lives there. It's inside him now.

Forever and always.

NAMELESS DAYS
-Track Fourteen-

J ensen held Guinevere for some time afterward.

He knew time was short; the thumping of the helicopter rotors had returned. Even despite the warm, naked body cradled in his arms, he was finding it harder and harder to concentrate on her, and the heaviness had begun to return to his limbs. He didn't have much time left, but what little he had, he wanted to spend right there, inside the dimly lit tent, the rain song tapping a gentle beat on the vinyl roof, the soft breaths of the love of his life sighing next to him like a beautiful melody.

There had been no performance issues. In fact, despite the fact he'd never had sex before – not *real* sex, not penetration – he'd done everything right. They'd made love not with the frenzied pace their short time warranted, but slowly and with careful, deliberate movements – he on his back, gently clasping her petite breasts, she on top of him, head leaned back, eyes dreamy. They'd even climaxed together, a romantic conceit he thought only happened in fiction. It had been the greatest experience of his life.

He laughed in the darkness, realizing that for the first time in his entire, miserable existence, he was truly happy. The world made sense.

Yet the joy was tempered a bit by something he couldn't quite put his finger on, a lingering emptiness that seemed to endure. How could he still feel it, after all he'd been through and all the demons he'd faced and defeated? What more was there to do? He couldn't think of a single thing he wanted other than what he already had, yet the hollowness persisted deep inside him like an ornery cold.

Jensen became aware of a sound, quiet and restrained, coming from beside him. It took him a moment to realize it was the sound of Guinevere crying.

He turned over on the mattress and began stroking her hair, which was still a bit damp from the recent thunderstorm. "What is it? Did I do something wrong?"

She laughed through her tears. "*God*, no. That was wonderful. *You* were wonderful. I've ... never been with a man who makes me feel the way you do."

Jensen's brow furrowed. "Then why are you crying?"

She inched closer to him. Their naked bodies were so close that he could feel her heartbeat.

"Because ... it wasn't supposed to be you."

Anger rose inside of him. The *thump-thump-thump* of the helicopter grew louder in his ears.

"You still love him." He huffed and rolled over on his back. The tent ceiling was caving in a bit from the rain collecting on its roof, and water was dripping from a hole in the plastic. "After everything he's put you through, after rejecting you time and time again, you still love that bastard."

She got up on one elbow so she could look him square in the eye. The blanket fell away from her, revealing the smooth, silky white curvature of her breasts. He tried to ignore the fire that once again leapt inside him but couldn't.

"I love you *both*," she said. "I ... don't know how, or why, but I do."

Jensen didn't know what to say, so he said nothing.

"I know this isn't what you want to hear," she continued. "It hurts, I get it. It hurts me, too. But it's the truth, and you mean way too much to me for anything but."

He also got up on one elbow, and now they were staring across from each other like two friends chatting at a late-night slumber party. "Who do you love

329

more? Me or him?"

Thump, thump, thump. Even louder now.

Guinevere's face scrunched, causing a little squiggle to form in the flesh between her eyes. "That's not fair."

"I think it's *very* fair. I've been there for you the whole way, and he's just been a giant pain in the ass who's made it very clear to you that he's moved on. To me it seems pretty simple. I love you, and he doesn't."

More silence, interrupted only by the sounds of the rain and the party still carrying on outside despite it. She looked to her hands and began fumbling with them as she spoke.

"Maybe ... I just need closure. To talk to him one last time, just to say goodbye." She grew silent again, seeming to struggle with a troubling thought. Then she sighed deeply and continued. "I know this sounds terrible, but ... when we were making love, I ... I felt like I was with *both* of you. Like you were both inside me, physically and mentally."

"*Jesus*, Gwen," Jensen said threw the covers off his body. "You're absolutely right. That doesn't just *sound* terrible, it *is* terrible."

This elicited another round of sobs from Guinevere, but this time Jensen didn't console her. He was livid. How could she say these things to him?

"Go, then," he said. "Get your clothes and get out of here. I think that stone path across from the waterfall is where you'll find him. I saw him watching us during the dance."

"Jensen ..." She reached out to him, but he pulled away and stood. His clothes were in a heap by the entrance, and he quickly began getting dressed.

"Please, don't do this," she said, the tears flowing now. "I don't want this to end. Not now, not ever. I really *do* love you, so much that it scares the hell out of me. Being with you is like ... it's like coming home. I don't know what to do."

Jensen pointed to the tent flap that led outside. "I know what you can do. Go find your boyfriend and leave me the hell alone."

With that, Jensen stormed out of the tent, leaving Guinevere to cry alone in the darkness.

✳✳✳

Jensen watched from a safe distance as Guinevere slowly ascended the staggered stone steps leading to the Path of Reflection.

The thumping of the rotors in his ears had now been joined by a sensation of movement, of wind in his ears, of treetops and mountains glistening in the aftermath of a pre-dawn rain. His legs felt weighted, his mind packed with cement. It was becoming harder and harder to stay focused on Evermore, and the throngs of naked and half-naked bodies that were still celebrating like Jensen's world hadn't just crumbled to dust around him.

Guinevere turned around, gave him one final, sorrowful look, then disappeared beyond the point he could see her.

He was alone again. It was a familiar feeling but one that for some reason felt alien this time. Just moments ago, he'd had the love of his life in his arms, everything he'd ever wanted and then some, and now she was gone. The only thing waiting for him was a cold, heavy, pointless world of politics and war and meaningless garbage.

Five million dollars, maybe more.

He hadn't thought those words in an eternity, but there they were, regardless. Robbie Tabernacle had promised him a veritable treasure trove for the master recording of *House Made of Sound*. And while five million dollars – hell, five *billion* dollars – could never make him as happy as he'd been with Guinevere, it sure as hell beat the alternative: waiting for a slow and sad death to eventually take him back to this place, where more loneliness awaited.

He nodded to himself and stood up. It wasn't what he wanted, not anymore, but it would have to do. Hedley Grange would spill his secret, even if Jensen had to beat the truth out of him to get it. Guinevere would try to stop

331

him, but he wouldn't let her. Not this time.

"Okay, then," he said to himself. "Let's bring it on home."

Then Jensen Bennett began walking toward the Path of Reflection, his pace quickening with every step, the material world growing to a roar in his ears as he went.

This was the end. Of that, he was absolutely certain.

He was about halfway up the steep climb when he saw it: a single wet footprint, women's size six. It was *her* footprint, made just a few moments before by how defined its shape still was. She was probably only a few paces ahead of him. He could run, catch up to her, tell her he loved her and that it didn't matter if he wasn't the only one she wanted. He could do it and then spend the next few minutes – for he was sure that was all he had left – in her arms.

But instead, he wiped the footprint clean with the tip of his shoe and kept walking. It was just too late.

Even though time was running short, he paused to take a quick look back on Evermore. The party was still raging, especially now that the rain had stopped. From this height, the people looked like figurines, some model maker's idea of a Woodstock or Coachella. He envied them, if only because he'd been one of them just an hour before but was now a lifeless husk who was only going through the motions. He also realized they were probably the last people he'd see in this strange afterlife, aside from Guinevere and Grange, until he returned someday. It had been a strange journey.

"Goodbye," he said and continued up the path.

***

After what seemed like forever, the steps finally ended at a large wrought iron fence that disappeared into the hilly forest in either direction. Above its double gates was a small sign that looked rather pedestrian given the almost gothic nature of the fence itself. It said:

"WARNING: You will be reconstituted
once you pass this gate."

Jensen leaned in and tried to see what lie beyond it, but everything was completely dark.

The anonymous melody, the old friend that had stuck with him from the time he'd entered Translucent Tower to this very moment, was much louder now that he was on the mountain. He still couldn't tell what song it was playing, or if it was even playing an identifiable song at all, but it was beautiful. It reminded him of Guinevere. He was sure everything would remind him of her, from now until the day he actually died for real. It was going to be a long, hard road. The thought made him sad, but he willed the tears away.

Five million dollars, maybe more.

"Fuck you," Jensen said to the voice in his head, and then opened the gate.

The second he was across the threshold, Jensen Bennett ceased to be.

***

Murky. Dark but just a glimmer of light filtering through the surface above. Not cold or hot; no feeling at all, just the dark, mysterious, wonderful deep. Food. Evacuation. Division. Death.

***

Water again, only warmer and brighter. Bigger. Stronger. Swimming against the current. Food. Procreation. Evacuation. Big wave, a useless struggle to resist it. Land. Solid ground. Can't breathe. Death.

***

Underground this time. Warm and safe and dry. Plenty of food to survive the cold above. Procreation. Children. Family. Evacuation. Starving. A perilous trip above ground. Large creature, hungry and desperate. Jaws. Pain. Death.

***

Trees. Beautiful sunset. Swinging, howling, mating. Food and children and quick dunks in the pond to cool off. Old age, gray fur. Full moon, big and beautiful in the night sky. A peaceful death, surrounded by family.

***

Consciousness came back to him slowly. He still wasn't sure who he was, or where *here* was, only that he was alive, and that he *knew* he was alive. Images came like machine-gun fire, one after another, yet he completely understood each one, remembered all of them as if they'd happened to him. Because they had.

The creature in the woods that looked like a man but wasn't, the one who lived only seventeen years before dying of some strange shaking disease. Next came the woman, whose reflection in the lake was stunning but who had a strange ridge above her eyes and a large, flared nose, the one who was tasked with gathering berries and got lost from her tribe, dying of exposure. The man in the desert. The man in the mountains. The woman in the freezing wasteland. One after another they came, each with a full lifetime's worth of memories. A man, a woman, another man, another woman. They were him, and he was they.

The faces changed, but the soul inside didn't. There were people he knew, people he'd always known, life after life after life. Daphne Dartmouth. Nigel Cuthpit. Richard Metliff. Bethany Bree and Aimee Barton and Ted Choom and Zachary Orrin. His mother and grandparents and Uncle Eric. They were all there, but sometimes they would be his sister or mother, other times his father or brother, sometimes only a friend or casual acquaintance. The lone exception to this seemed to be Guinevere, who was always his lover, however briefly their paths crossed in each life. Yet no matter what form they took, everyone was there, as intertwined with his life as his own reflection.

The further he went and the more lives he re-experienced, Jensen slowly came back. Cobbler. Housewife. Soldier. Farmer. Working girl. Healer. Train conductor. They marched past him, each one as real as the life he'd just left, each one helping him understand the virtues he'd mastered and those he still needed to work on, a millennia-long tapestry of what is and what should never be. He not only saw the lives, but the lives *in-between* lives, those brief moments of respite where he could rest and ready himself for the next. It was as if Jensen was in a darkened movie theater, watching all the people he'd once been flash and pass across the screen in seconds yet understanding every single individual story, from the mundane to the extreme.

It was only as he approached what he knew was his most recent past life that he slowed down a bit. Without knowing why, he realized some great truth would be revealed when the story was complete, something that would bring everything into focus.

It started out like nearly all the rest, with an uneventful birth and a more or less stable home life. His name had been Wayne Culver, no middle initial, the youngest of seven children born to Mr. and Mrs. Louis Culver of Salem, Oregon. With so many brothers and sisters, Wayne wasn't sure his middle-class family would ever be able to afford college, so he learned how to play bass guitar and fell in with The Pluto Gang, a three-piece punk band named after the group of hooligans in Kurt Vonnegut's *Breakfast of Champions*. If he couldn't get an education, he'd become a rock star. It made perfect sense to him at the time.

But he went to college after all thanks to a presidential scholarship and traded his pink mohawk for a shot at a bachelor's degree in economics from the University of Oregon. His freshman year he met Beverly Werner, who hid her beauty behind a thick pair of black glasses but was gorgeous all the same, at least to him. She helped him get through English Lit, and he taught her the bassline to "Blitzkrieg Bop." They shared their first kiss in the quad, their first awkward sexual encounter in the back of his baby-blue 1978 Ford LTD Country Squire with wood paneling. It was the best time of his life.

Then came the breast cancer diagnosis that sent Beverly back home to Woodburn for a radical mastectomy that removed the entirety of her left breast. Wayne followed her, forgoing the remainder of his sophomore year to help her through the darkest days. And for a while, things were better. She'd sometimes cry and say she was ugly now, that he would never want to see her naked ever again. He would cradle her and say she could lose all her limbs, gain three hundred pounds and go completely bald, and he'd still want her just the same.

But the cancer returned, this time in her liver, and before each chemotherapy session they'd sit beneath the large oak tree outside the clinic and talk about all the things they were going to do once she beat it; the kids they would have, the house they would buy, the romance novel she would write. They promised each other they'd never give up, no matter what happened. They'd kiss beneath it each time before going in, and they began calling it the Kissing Tree. It was a symbol of hope for a brighter future. They'd even cemented their love quite literally in the freshly poured pavement beneath it, a big "W," followed by an even bigger heart, followed by a small, bubbly "B."

Then, the news they'd been terrified of hearing: the cancer had metastasized to her brain. He'd sneak her favorite candy, Nerds, past the nurses at Salem Hospital, and she'd tell him that she didn't need them because she already had the sweetest nerd of all. The days grew shorter, and Beverly wasted away before his eyes, her body failing but the beauty in her boundless brown eyes never fading, not even on the day she took her final breath.

Wayne said goodbye to his Beverly, the love of his life, his everything, and moved back home. But without her, life was a meaningless drudge devoid of all light and love. He didn't eat or visit friends. He didn't play the bass, or even listen to music. Everything reminded him of her, and nothing mattered. The world became gray and desolate. It was too much, and in a drunken stupor one night he hanged himself from a ceiling fan with one of his dad's work ties. The year was 1983.

Then Wayne was in The Sea of Sorrow for what seemed like forever. Time had no meaning there. He'd spend his days in a single room, the hospital room in which Beverly had died, only the bed was empty and there were no nurses or doctors. She wasn't there, only his grief at her loss and the growing feeling that she was never going to be there because the room was a construct of his own mind.

This realization eventually freed him, and Wayne wasted no time looking for her once he'd emerged through the Wicked Garden and out into the strange world beyond. He had to be with her again. He couldn't live without her.

But she was nowhere, not in the strange shimmering tower, not in the city that looked like icicles, not in the hardpan desert or the vast forests. She could only be in one place – back where he'd met her, back in that world he'd come from. But what if she wasn't?

He was torn. Literally.

A part of him stayed behind in hopes Beverly was still out there some-where, and the other part left to rejoin the living, convinced she was already gone. Indecision triggered mitosis on a spiritual level, and one soul became two.

He didn't know what happened to the part of him that stayed behind –

his life as Jensen Bennett was now playing in his mind's eye, from his birth all the way to the unfortunate fall from Quiet Catastrophe's airplane. His mother, Richard's lemonade stand advice, the Wall Monster, the record player in the attic, the dent in the Cadillac, the move to his grandma's house in Oakworth, Mortimer Brewster beating him senseless, discovering Hedley Grange playing for spare change in the El, even Aimee were all there, and he relived each moment again, experiencing it from an omniscient perspective that allowed him to see and understand the thoughts and emotions of everyone he'd come into contact with, as well as himself.

As the movie reel ran out of film and began spinning into space, Jensen's thoughts returned to his other half but could only guess where it had gone, what it had done, or if it even still existed somewhere.

Yet even as he pondered this, he knew: The second him, the piece of his soul that had stayed behind to wait for Beverly, had eventually returned to the land of the living to begin its own, separate life. It could only be one person, the only person, in fact, that had made just one appearance in all his many lives – the final and most recent one.

The piece of him that was missing was none other than Hedley Grange.

***

The moment Jensen's left foot hit the ground on the other side of the iron fence, the gate banged shut behind him as if propelled by some unseen force.

He was stunned into silence by the experience he'd just had, which neither seemed real or a dream, but a strange combination of both. He'd been all of those people before, and now he was all of them once again. All of their memories where now his, every single triumph and failure, every last love and loss. All of his friends and family and lovers throughout the ages rushed back into his thoughts simultaneously, and it was simply too much for him to bear. He fell to his knees and began sobbing uncontrollably.

338

A shadow fell over him, and at first he didn't look up. The emotions surging through him kept him locked in place, head down, palms on the wet earth, heaving great cries which wracked his body. When he felt them subsiding a bit, he finally looked up at the owner of the shadow and saw Beverly Werner, also known as Guinevere Hatcher, the love of his life, the woman who had been by his side for centuries and would continue for centuries more. She was also crying, but her tears were no longer of pain but happiness. She looked down at him and smiled, eyes wet and puffy. He stood and immediately wrapped her in a tight embrace.

"I finally found you," Jensen said, struggling for the words between sobs. "After all these years, I finally found you again."

Guinevere laughed and nodded, a fresh stream of tears falling down her cheeks, and the two reunited lovers kissed, long and deep, just as they'd done a million times over since the world first began.

***

"I'd say this is getting uncomfortable, but the truth is, I'm kinda turned on right now."

Jensen tore himself from Guinevere's kiss – a difficult task given how great it felt – and looked behind her. They were in a small, circular garden teeming with the colors and fragrances of nearly every variety of flower known to man. Rimming the edge of this floral smorgasbord was a series of simple wooden benches, one of which sat next to a door that shimmered with the same, invisible energy Jensen had first seen guarding the door of his cell at Translucent Tower. Hedley Grange sat on this bench, legs crossed, arms on his lap, smiling at Jensen like a proud parent.

"Hedley," Jensen said, a smile of his own beginning to take shape. "Or should I say Jensen Junior?"

Grange laughed. "*I'm* the world-famous rock star. I think if anyone's a junior, it's you." The words were playful, without a tinge of malice in them, and he followed them with an incredulous look. "I knew I always liked you, Benny, but I never realized it really was just a strange form of vanity."

Jensen and Guinevere walked to the bench, fingers still entwined. When they were near enough to Grange, he stood up suddenly and wrapped them both in a hug. They held the embrace for a moment, each one of them over-joyed to have reconciled with the other two.

Grange was the first one to break the silence. "Hug me any harder, Benny, and we just might squish back together."

Jensen disengaged the hug but still kept his right arm around Guinevere's hips. She turned to Grange with curious eyes. "What are you talking about?"

Jensen cleared his throat. He wasn't sure how to say it, so he just did.

"Hedley and I are the same soul. Or, we *used* to be, until we broke apart looking for *you*."

Guinevere took a step backward and put a hand to her forehead. "I ... saw everything. All my lives. You were both in them. That ... that's impossible."

Jensen went to answer, but Grange beat him to it. "That's because you know both of us in *this* life, as two separate people. Tell me something – were the two of us ever in the same life with you, together?"

She shook her head. "No, now that you mention it. Wayne was Jensen. But Allen, the train conductor, was *you*, Hank."

"That soul you kept seeing was *both* of us," Grange said. "You just saw it one way in one life, and another way in another, because you're connected to us both in *this* one."

Guinevere looked to Jensen, then to Grange, then back to Jensen again. "Is that why I love you *both*?"

Grange nodded. "That's my guess. But it's okay, Gwen. Jensen is the one you belong with." She looked to him, confused, so he continued. "Back when you were Beverly, and *we* were Wayne, Jensen had the courage to reincarnate into an unknown world just on the off chance you'd be there. Me, I was too scared. I played it safe, opting to stick around here instead of going after you. *Jensen* is your true love, because he risked it all for you."

Guinevere looked to Grange with sad eyes. "So what does that mean? For us?"

Grange put his hands on her shoulders and looked deep into her eyes. "It means we will *always* love each other, in this life and the next. But as close friends, not lovers."

Guinevere didn't respond, only nodded slowly in understanding and then gave Grange another hug. Jensen didn't intervene, but watched them with a fondness he hadn't thought himself capable of just hours before.

When they were done, Grange looked to Jensen and smirked. "You had me worried there for a few, Benny. You asked me to help you find happiness, and I did, the only way I knew how – by taking you to places that would make you face those things that were making you unhappy. First the mirror to break you of that act you put on – to reset you, so to speak, open you up to the pain it was hiding – then onto The Subdivisions to face your demons. You almost didn't make it."

Jensen grinned. "But I did." He moved back over to Guinevere, wanting to take her into the flower bed and make love to her over and over again but knowing there wasn't time. He was leaving, and leaving soon.

"Yes. Yes you did. The only question is ... did it work? Are you happy?"

Jensen stared at Guinevere. "Absolutely."

Grange turned to the shimmering doorway and eyed it cautiously. "Then I guess my work is done. I was too afraid to go back before. I'll not make the same mistake again."

"You're really going through?" Guinevere asked. "Back to the material world?"

Grange ran a hand through his long blonde hair, which was surprisingly combed and presentable for once. "Yep. Gonna take a new ride out for a spin. There's nothing left for me here."

A thought occurred to Jensen – his emptiness, the result of having a piece of him missing, was still there. "So we can never become one soul again?"

"I don't know," Grange said after mulling it over for a second. "Maybe. But truth is, I wouldn't do it even if it were possible. I kinda *like* being me. And I think you're going to like being *you* from now on, too. See, I've lived with the same emptiness all my life that *you* have, Benny. But I've come to realize the power it holds. For your life to have any real meaning, I think you need a little pain now and then. It reminds you how good everything else really is by comparison. So the answer to your question is yes. We can never be rejoined. That's my last gift to you – an emptiness that you'll just have to fill with other things. *Great* things."

"I can live with that," Jensen said. "But I'm holding onto the gift receipt just in case."

Hedley smiled. "Fair enough." Then, with an air of finality, he added, "It's time. This isn't goodbye. Not really. The three of us are going to have plenty of adventures together, someday, somewhere."

"I'm looking forward to it," Jensen said. Grange gave them a friendly wave and was almost at the door when Jensen shouted, "Hed, just one last question."

Grange turned slowly back to face them, that smirk still planted on his face. "You want to know where the album is, don't you?"

Jensen nodded. He did, despite everything, if only because it was a mystery that needed solving.

Grange leaned against the door frame and sighed. "I was here once before. During my overdose. Like you, I escaped the tower. Had a little adventure of my own. When I came back – after you revived me – I only remembered glimpses of it. The tower, the strange melody that always seemed to be playing somewhere, the awesome lights in the sky. But that's not all. I found I could see people's auras, their life force. That's how I knew Quiet Catastrophe was coming to an end, why I urged them to record the album in the first place.

One day I looked in the mirror and saw the black mist around me, and then I saw it around Teddy and Zach, too. Even Nigel. I knew whatever was going to take us would take us all, and that I had to make my last months count."

Grange paused for a moment and looked to the sky. "But that melody. It's beautiful, isn't it? Its mood may change, but no matter where you go, the song remains the same. It stayed with me when I came back, especially when I was painting. It reminded me why I make music – not for the money, or the girls, or the drugs, or any of that sort of thing. I make it because it connects me to something greater than myself. It makes me feel alive."

Grange now pointed to the sky, which was swimming with more ribbons than Jensen had ever seen before. "Those colorful lights? That music? It's *life*, Benny. Literally. This place makes music, and those vibrations create the material world you and I both know and love. Reality on earth is just a house made of sound. Without music as its foundation, the material world would simply fall apart."

Jensen nodded. "That's real heavy, Hed. All of it. But it still doesn't answer my question."

Grange laughed and turned back toward the gleaming doorway. "Music is life, Benny, and life is art. Once you realize that, you'll find the album."

And then, with two steps, Hedley Grange disappeared into the door, and Jensen and Guinevere had the world to themselves.

***

There were birds inside the garden, chirping an after-shower song as they sat on branches, grooming their wings or watching with fixed eyes as the flower petals danced to the wind. There were bees, too, buzzing and swooping from flower to flower, forever in pursuit of a food source they no longer needed. The anonymous melody, soft and achingly beautiful, fell from the heavens with the tenderness of a fond memory, the ribbons that produced it swimming languidly in the atmosphere like dust particles caught in sunlight.

It was the perfect moment, but one that was destined to end.

"Babe, I'm gonna leave you soon," Jensen said. "But I don't want to."

"How long?" Guinevere asked. She was crying again, and the words came out jumbled.

"Not long," he responded. "A minute. Maybe less." His own tears were standing just behind his eyes, waiting for the ache inside his chest to welcome them forward. He'd never been so happy, and so utterly sad, at the same time.

Guinevere grasped the sides of his face, bringing it close. He wrapped his arms around her waist and brought her even closer. Their lips were inches apart now, so close they could kiss, but they didn't, only stared into each other's eyes with unspoken desire. They *would* kiss, and it would be magic, but not yet. Neither one could bring themselves to do it because they knew it would be their last for years. Perhaps decades.

"Guinevere," he said, and at the mere mention of her name, the tears began to fall in droves. "You saved me. I was drowning but you saved me." He brought his right hand to her cheek and wiped away the tears holding congress there with a brush of his thumb, but it was no use; more came to take their place. "You're the love of my life, my *real* missing piece. As long as I have you, I'll never be empty again."

Guinevere shook her head. "I don't want you to go. Please don't leave me." She ran her forefinger slowly across his lower lip, wanting so badly to taste him but knowing doing so would smother their last words. "What am I going to do without you?"

Thump-thump-thump. So loud it hurts his eardrums. So loud he has to shout to hear his own voice. His entire body seemed made of concrete. Guinevere's face began to fluctuate, like a video conference with bad Wi-Fi.

"What you're going to do is *sing*. Make music again, great music like you did on The Dark Train." He was speaking hurriedly now, trying to get the words out before the world around him faded. "Sing for anyone that will hear you, sing for the ribbons in the sky, and sing for *me*, because I'll be listening. And one day I'll be back, and I'll step off that train and see you there, in that little café at The Terminal, and you'll look at me, and I'll look at you, and without a word we'll know that we're both completely and utterly whole again."

She blinked, and an unbroken stream of tears fell down her left cheek. "You won't have to look too hard. I'll be the one in the pretty pink skirt, the one drinking the Earl Grey."

Then they kissed, hungrily tasting each other's lips, she in his arms and he in hers, together like interlocking pieces, two souls casting one solidary shadow across the grounds of an immaculate garden that daydreamed under a rainbow-colored sky, somewhere beyond the shade.

When Guinevere Hatcher finally opened her eyes, the garden was silent and she was alone. Jensen Bennett was gone.

[silence]

He's ascending, and as he does, a fleeting thought: *I'm forgetting her.*

The realization came suddenly, violently. He was weightless, formless, an assembly of atoms held together by nothing more than his thoughts, thoughts which he was rapidly losing hold of.

Remember. You have to remember. Strawberry blonde hair, bottomless brown eyes, cute Wisconsin accent. The subtle half-smile that accentuates the delicate indent between her nose and lips. The squiggle of flesh that forms on the bridge of her nose whenever she's confused. The playful giggle, the one that causes butterflies to take flight inside your stomach. Remember.

Higher now. She was fading, melting before his eyes like snow under a hot sun. He's breaking apart, atom by atom, an ozone baby slowly dissolving as it leaves its crib and enters the vacuum of space. Panic sets in.

Remember. Remember. Translucent Tower. The Warden and his clipboard. The Anonymous Melody. The boy Leslie disappearing into thin air. Remember. Running through Paradise City to meet the Frenchman, chasing the Yellow Line into Township Rebellion. The warning from Walter Taram, the mob at the Codswallop concert, Dolly the farting horse and the evil train. Guinevere's song, her wonderful, beautiful song. Remember. Remember, goddammit.

Higher still, thinner still. Molecules drifting apart as the memories fade.

The mirrors. Shattering glass. Strange phone booths, scorching lava flows, the chill of the deep and the scratching of the Doormen. Old Richard, begging for forgiveness, Guinevere's blackened eyes, the perilous walk through the Rioter Room. Remember. Remember. Evermore. Making love, slow and calculated, savoring every second. The stairs, the iron gate, the many lives coiled into one. The last kiss, overwhelmingly cathartic despite its brevity. Guinevere.

346

Remember. Guinevere. Guinevere.

Then a void, starless and infinite, scatters his atoms into space, sending all thoughts scurrying into the deep, soft, quiet earth beneath consciousness.

A final struggle to hold on, and then she's gone.

Everything is gone.

NEVER TO RETURN
-Track Fifteen-

There was absolutely no pain, only a muffled beat that pulsated slowly like the relaxed thud of a kick drum. *Thump. Thump. Thump.* It was calculated, timed, perfect. It was his heartbeat.

The void had color now, a marriage of reds and oranges, but it was only a suggestion, a ray of sunlight filtering through closed eyelids. He floated in the nothingness, consciousness without shape, gesture without motion, drifting toward a horizon with no end.

He began counting the thumps: one, two, three, on and on until he'd reached the millions, never once stopping to wonder why he was doing it. There were no clocks here, no setting sun and waxing moon by which to judge the time. There was only the magnificent void; dark, deep, and endless.

He stayed there for a very long time.

***

He hears voices talking. The first, a deep baritone, says something indiscernible, the seriousness dripping from every syllable. The man grows quiet, and then the second voice, high and feminine, offers a short reply that begins life as words but dies as a series of heaving sobs.

She cried like that, he thinks, but whoever *she* is, he doesn't know.

He opens his eyes and sees a bright square hovering above him in the darkness. There's an image on it, a man and a woman. The man is holding a microphone, and the woman is crying into it. There's something written below them, something about a plane crash and a survivor in critical condition, and this sparks a distant memory. But before he can fully recall what it is, the invisible lead weights hanging from his eyelids plunge him into darkness again, and he rejoins the void.

***

There's a quiet, steady beep that seems to be keeping time with his heartbeat, and a strange sucking noise that pumps sterile-tasting air into his lungs. The voices are gone, but he can hear others – muffled, as if they're coming from behind a closed door.

He forces his eyelids open, and florescent lights perched somewhere above his field of vision immediately send railroad spikes into his eyes. The pain subsides and a hospital room comes into focus, clean and blindingly white. He can only move his eyes, and with them he scans the area in front of him.

There's little to see save for an inactive TV set hanging from the ceiling at the foot of his bed, and its giant, cyclops eye sends the reflection of a broken body back in his direction. His badly bruised eyes are the only part of his face he can see through the mess of bandages taped to his face. A tube connects him to a noisy machine nearby; he can feel something large and uncomfortable running down the length of his throat. All of his limbs are encased in thick casts and his neck and head are pinned in a giant black contraption that looks like a metal spider.

Seeing this miserable image makes him realize he can't feel anything below his waist, but the thought doesn't worry him for some reason. He's happy. The drugs coursing through his veins are partially responsible, but there's more. There's a boundless joy standing just outside the edge of his perception, a friendly face without form. He tries to coerce the shape into presenting itself in his mind, but it resists and steps even further into the shadows.

The muffled voices suddenly become clearer, and he decides to focus on them.

"... broken vertebrae. The hemorrhaging in his brain has stopped, thank God, but his brainstem reflexes don't look good."

"No response to supraorbital pressure?"

"Not yet, but it's still early."

"What do you make of the EEG? The spike was rather curious. Seems he regained consciousness, if only briefly."

A long, unbroken sigh. "Doctor DeNova, is it?"

"I prefer Professor, if it's all the same to you."

"Of course. Bit of advice, professor? Go back to your hotel. Your wife has called three times. I'll let you know if anything changes. Promise."

Eyelids heavy. So heavy. The sounds fade, and darkness overtakes him once again.

***

The third time he awoke he felt more alert, although the first hints of discomfort were starting to creep into his bones. He wasn't in pain, but he wasn't high anymore, either. Despite this, the happiness lingered.

The TV set was on again, but this time it was showing a music video. In it, a young man with long, unkempt blonde hair was walking through a darkened forest, singing at the top of his lungs while ghostly creatures clad in white robes tried to grab him from the trees. The song was familiar, too; someone used to dedicate it to him. Then it ended, and a VJ popped into frame and smiled sadly at the camera.

"That was 'Time and Again,' coming in at number two on VH1's Quiet Catastrophe Countdown. You voted, we listened. A sad week for sure, but also a day to celebrate great music and a poignant reminder of why it matters so much. Stick around to see if your favorite made the top spot."

Then the program cut to a commercial for some fast-food joint called Pluckers Chicken. An overweight cartoon rooster with a white bib tucked beneath its wattle began belting out a song, and something about the lyrics were familiar:

Begin
To dig in
Until your plate is empty
Within
This skin
There's always more than plenty
Just savor me
Savor me

Hedley Grange, he thought suddenly. *The man in the video. That was his name.*

Then, on the heels of that, another revelation: *My name is Jensen Phillip Bennett. I was friends with the guy in the video. He hated that chicken commercial. I hate it, too.*

He searched his memory for more information, but nothing came.

Just then he heard the door open, followed shortly thereafter by a surprised gasp. He couldn't see who it was – his eyes couldn't search that far – but whoever it was quickly stormed out of the room again. He heard petite little slaps smacking linoleum as someone ran down the hallway, followed by the sound of a woman shouting something. But try as he might he couldn't tell what she was saying.

My name is Jensen Bennett, he thought. *I'm thirty-eight years old. I live in Chicago. My wife's name ... her name is ... Aimee.*

Everything seemed right except for that last part. The name was correct,

351

but the association wasn't. Aimee wasn't his wife. His wife's name was ... he couldn't remember. Something that sounded like it came from an old Knights of the Roundtable story.

She wore a pink skirt. Her hair was red. No, not red, but close. Strawberry blonde. Long and straight. Smelled like coconut.

Why couldn't he picture her face? And where was she? In the three times he'd regained consciousness, he hadn't seen anyone. If she *was* his wife, why wasn't she by his side?

The door swung open again, and this time a short, skinny nurse and a tall, plump doctor with paper-white skin came into view and leaned over him on either side.

"*See*, Doctor Cash? I *told* you he was awake."

The man she called Cash began shining a bright light in his eyes. "I'll be goddamned. Mr. Bennett? Blink if you understand me."

Jensen blinked a few times, and the doctor pulled the light from his eyes and leaned away. "Christ, I can't believe this. Cindy, let's get him extubated. He starts breathing on his own, I just may swing by and get a lottery ticket after work. Let's suction."

Cindy grabbed a long, rubbery tube and stuck it his mouth, letting it sit there for a bit before pulling it out again. "Ready to deflate the cuff."

Cash nodded and then did something near his neck that he couldn't see. Immediately after that he leaned in and put an ear to Jensen's mouth.

"He's breathing." Cash smiled. "Son of a bitch. Now let's get it out. Mr. Bennett, when I pull, take a big cough."

Jensen couldn't respond, but he blinked in affirmation. As he did as asked and coughed, an uncomfortable sensation followed, like throwing up something hard and tasteless. Then the obstruction was clear and he was breathing, his throat burning with each lungful as if someone had set it on fire. The nurse smiled as she placed a breathing mask on his face and asked him to cough again.

"*Unbelievable*," Cash said. After a moment to contemplate this statement, he turned to Cindy and nodded. "Check his vitals and respiratory rate." His voice was absolutely bursting with excitement. "Make sure everything is copacetic." Then, to himself, he added, "DeNova's going to *shit* himself when he hears this."

While Cindy carried out the doctor's orders, Cash leaned in close again, his face large and riddled with a series of small dents that looked like craters.

"Mr. Bennett, welcome back. You just became a very famous man."

✳✳✳

More sleep, and this time he dreams.

He's inside a small cave carved into an immense stone mountainside. There's a waterfall raging nearby, and its roar is amplified by the wet stone around him. He's looking down upon the soft green of distant treetops spreading out hundreds of feet below him in every direction, and the fragile mist rising from them.

Then he senses someone behind him, and he turns to see a girl wearing a pink miniskirt and white blouse with long, strawberry blonde hair standing at the back of the cave. Her face is distorted, like a reflection in a rippling pond. After an emotional reunion they make love on the soft earth, with only the roar of the waterfall and the echoed chatter of birds as background music.

Wait for me, he says afterward to the girl, whose face he still can't see no matter how hard he tries.

For an eternity if I have to, she says, and then Jensen wakes up.

✳✳✳

"I've been waiting a long time to talk to you, Mr. Bennett."

The voice was soft and friendly, but its source was beyond his line of sight.

353

"If you're a bill collector, you can just keep on waiting," Jensen replied, his voice little more than a croak.

The man laughed. "Doctor Cash *said* you were getting your spunk back. Glad to see he wasn't pulling my leg." Then a figure appeared near the foot of his bed. The owner of the voice was an elderly black man with thinning gray hair and a large pair of glasses hanging precariously from the tip of his nose. He smiled as Jensen looked at him. "You're probably wondering who I am."

Jensen blinked a few times. "The thought had crossed my mind, yes."

"Noah DeNova, professor of cardiology at Des Moines University. I was the one who found you after the crash."

Be not afraid, a voice said in his head, then was gone.

"You saved my life," Jensen muttered.

Noah shook his head and put a hand up. "No, not really. The doctors here who worked on you saved your life. I just made sure they had the opportunity to do it."

"Well, thanks anyway. I wouldn't be talking right now if it wasn't for you."

Noah brushed Jensen's words aside with a wave of his hand. "I didn't come here to bask in affection, although the effort is appreciated. I came because, ever since coming across you that morning on the mountainside, I've felt ... *responsible* for you. I know that sounds odd coming from someone you've never met, but it's true just the same."

Noah reached into the inside pocket of his dress jacket and pulled out a small voice recorder, the kind that required a cassette tape. He raised a questioning eyebrow at Jensen and held the recorder out so he could see it. "Mind if I document our conversation? I've been thinking I may write a paper on this. Your identity would remain private, of course."

Jensen looked at the recorder and tried to smile, but all he could manage was a grimace. "How could I say no to my guardian angel?"

Noah pushed a red button on the recorder and then pulled up a chair. "Pssh, I'm no guardian angel. Just a man who doesn't listen to his wife when she says to stay put."

This caused a memory to flutter to his mind. "My wife ... has she come to see me?"

"Aimee? She called when she saw the crash on the news but hasn't been here yet. I talked to her myself. She made it seem as if you two were separated."

"No, not Aimee. My *wife*. The girl with the strawberry blonde hair."

Noah's brow furrowed in confusion. "I'm sorry. I don't know who that is, Jensen. What's her name?"

"I can't remember."

Noah nodded and made a grunting sound. "I see. The doctor said you were still suffering from some memory loss. What *do* you remember?"

Jensen thought about it for a moment and decided he wasn't quite sure. Everything seemed vague and disjointed.

"I know my name," he said. It was harder to talk the more he did it, but he pressed on. "Jensen Bennett. I know I was friends with a rock star. Hedley Grange. I'm from Chicago and I'm thirty-eight. I own a nightclub on Division and Hoyne, but it's not open. My boss' name is Robbie something. He's bald and he swears a lot."

"Interesting. All true so far as I know. What else?"

Images swirled in his mind's eye. "There's my wife. I can't remember what she looks like, only that I love her more than anything. And she has a mild accent – somewhere north, somewhere like Green Bay. I can also remember a town, like a John Ford western, only not. I remember a saluki. It was tiny but mean as *hell*. It bit me, I think. There's also a man with a mustache. He's a cop, I think, but I'm not entirely sure. I can remember listening to old 45s and smoking stale cigarettes in my mom's attic. There's a guy who has a typewriter for a head ... no, that's not right ... but his mouth definitely chatters like one." He tried to make more images solidify in his mind but couldn't. "I really can't remember anything else, although it's there. Somewhere in my head."

Noah was silent for a minute, chewing on his lower lip and regarding

Jensen with kind eyes. Then he leaned forward and rested his arms on his knees. "It's common for folks in your condition to wake with a bit of memory loss, usually the result of a temporary communication breakdown between you and your hippocampus. My guess is you went on a trip to Arizona or Nevada and saw a ghost town shortly before your accident. That accounts for the strange town. And the man with the moustache is probably a friend or acquaintance. The wife you speak of might be an old lover. High school girlfriend, perhaps. Not sure what the typewriter man could mean. A half-remembered dream, possibly."

What Noah was saying seemed reasonable enough, but something in the back of Jensen's mind told him it wasn't right.

"What I *can* tell you is this," Noah continued. "You're an arts and repertoire representative for Wicked Records, having single-handedly discovered one of the biggest music acts of the twenty-first century. Quiet Catastrophe, although I'm partial to Marvin Gaye and the Beatles myself. You studied business, first at NIU for your BBA, and then Columbia for your MBA. You graduated with honors from both. Your biological father left before you were born, and your mother passed away eleven years ago. When you were eight, your stepfather committed suicide, but not before beating you so badly you were hospitalized for several weeks. You still bear a scar on your right temple from that experience. Does any of this seem familiar?"

Jensen licked his lips, the only thing he could do for himself aside from blink. "Yes. It does. It still seems like you're talking about someone else, but it *does* have a ring of familiarity to it."

"It *will* come back. Your memory, I mean. The doctors around here seem mystified by your recovery, but I'm not. I'll admit, it's been remarkable and much faster than I could have anticipated, but I never had a doubt you'd recover. Not after I got your heart beating again. You just seemed to me to be a person who keeps fighting, no matter how impossible the odds. The same goes for your memory. Right now there's a wall in your brain holding the memories in, but keep chipping away at it, one piece at a time. When the levee breaks, it'll all come flooding back to you."

Jensen looked at Noah's recorder, and suddenly a thought swam its way up from his subconscious. "Wait. I remember more. I was looking for something. Some kind of recording. It was really important that I find it, but I don't know why."

Noah frowned and reclined in the chair. "I'm sorry. I don't know anything about that. But I *do* know you're famous now, and not just because you survived. Apparently, everyone wants to talk to the man who was there when the biggest band on the planet met their maker."

Jensen blinked a few times at the words. "They *died*? *All* of them?"

Noah nodded sadly. "Yes. And I'm sorry for wording it that way. I keep forgetting they were your friends."

Jensen knew he should feel some kind of sadness at this news, but he didn't. For some inexplicable reason, he knew his friends were alright.

"Get some rest," Noah said and stood up, clicking off the recorder as he did. "You've talked way more than you should have. Dr. Cash would have my head on a platter if he knew. I'll be back, and we can talk more then."

Noah smiled, a warm and friendly sight that convinced Jensen the man wasn't just interested in publishing a paper, but genuinely concerned with his wellbeing. Then he was gone.

Alone again, Jensen kept thinking one thought over and over again in his mind:

The girl was real. And she was going to come visit him.

✳✳✳

Someone else eventually *did* come calling, but it wasn't the mysterious woman he'd been waiting for.

It was Robbie, the ill-tempered boss whose last name he couldn't remember. He entered the room, gray Stetson fedora clutched in his hands like a sleeping cat, and stopped at the foot of his bed. He was tall, perhaps six-five, and as he stood there, rubbing his shiny bald head with his left hand and nervously working the brim of the fedora with the other, he seemed to sag under the gravity of his own altitude.

"*Christ*, Bennett. They told me it was bad, but this ... it's a miracle you're still here. You look like a fucking horror movie come to life."

Jensen could see in the man's face that he was uncomfortable. Jensen couldn't much blame him; he'd seen the wrecked body reflected in the TV screen and knew it was terrifying to look at.

"*Please*. Frankenstein *wishes* he looked this good."

Robbie let out a nervous laugh and then took a single, tentative step toward him. "Look, all of us back in Chicago are just happy you're okay. I flew down the moment I heard you were awake."

But only after I started talking, he thought.

"Good of you to make the time," Jensen said flatly. His voice was still weak, but it was getting stronger the more he used it. "Send my thanks to the folks back in Chicago, whoever they are. What can I do for you?"

Robbie took another step forward, and now he was absolutely *looming* above Jensen's bed.

"They told me your brains got scrambled. Said you remembered only bits and pieces of your life before the crash. Didn't think that sort of thing actually happened to people. I wonder how much of it is real. Hell, sometimes I forget where I put my car keys. Doesn't mean I'm brain damaged."

Jensen averted his gaze, opting instead to study the TV set, which was blank again and casting an unflattering reflection of Robbie's backside. The more the man said, the more suspicious Jensen became of his motives.

"Look, if you're here to ask me something, then ask it," Jensen said. "You're clearly fishing, and this ain't Lake Okeechobee."

Robbie gave him a contemptuous look. "Okay, fair enough. You're right.

I came to ask about our deal. Do you remember it?"

"Buddy, I don't even remember your last name, let alone some business arrangement we made God knows how long ago. Is that why you're here, feigning concern? Money?"

Robbie snorted. "Not just money. We're talking millions. *Hundreds* of millions. Enough to pay the hospital bills of every sad sack *in* this place. Shit, enough to buy yourself a robotic butler to carry your crippled ass to the bank."

Three words came to him then: *Five million dollars.*

"Maybe more," Jensen whispered. The thought seemed like it should matter to him, but it didn't. "*House Made of Sound*," he said. "Quiet Catastrophe's secret last album. You sent me somewhere to find it, right before the plane went down. Springfield, I think."

Robbie began nodding enthusiastically even before he'd finished speaking. "Yes. You agreed to get it for me."

Jensen squinted at him suspiciously. "No. I said I'd *try* to get it for you. I never signed the contract."

"You remember more than you claim to," Robbie said. "But it doesn't matter. Contract or no contract, that album belongs to Wicked Records. And if you know where it is you need to tell me."

Jensen didn't remember ever finding the album's whereabouts. He remembered being in a wardrobe chest, and then something crashed outside. After that, he only recalled the void, deep and starless. There was more, though. Something happened in-between, something that involved the strange John Ford town and the man with the mustache. The mysterious girl he kept seeing was somewhere in it, too. There was another memory – something tall, something white that disappeared into the clouds. And a boy with no hair. He tried to retrieve more, but there was nothing.

"Jensen? Your silence isn't the least bit comforting. Did you find the master or not?"

"Let me get this straight," Jensen said slowly. "Three people are dead –"

"*Six* people," Robbie interrupted. "The pilots and that limey prick manager of theirs died, too."

"Okay. *Six* people are dead, and one is probably never going to walk again, and all you care about is some *recording*?"

If Robbie looked ashamed, it didn't show on his face.

"Yes. Do you realize how much money that album is going to rake in now that the band is smeared across a mountainside? Shit, it was set to break records *before* the crash. Now it'll easily be the number-one selling record of all time. And stop looking at me like that, Bennett. I'm a business man. I deal in profit. It's my job. It's also *your* job. Or did you conveniently forget *that*, too?"

Jensen blinked a few times to clear his mind, which was spinning with everything Robbie had just said. Had he really been like that before the plane crash? He couldn't remember.

"Maybe I was that person once," he said. "I don't know. But it doesn't matter, because I'm not him anymore."

Robbie took a long, deep breath before responding. "You *will* be him. You will. *If* you still want a job when you get out of this shithole."

Jensen rolled his eyes. "*Job*? Working for *you*? I'd rather plummet from another airplane." Then, confident it was what he really wanted, he added, "Consider this my resignation."

Robbie had been doing a fairly good job of masking his anger up until this point, but he could hold out no longer. "You *cocksucker*. You insignificant little *fuck*." He leaned in so close that Jensen could smell the stench of cigarettes on his breath. "Where's the master? Tell me right now or I'll fucking *bury* you, mother*fucker*."

Jensen smiled, and the sight caused Robbie's eyes to go wide with surprise. "With what? There's nothing you can do, no lawsuit you can file, no threat you could make that would *ever* break my spirit. You have absolutely no power over me anymore. *No one* does."

"*WHERE IS IT*?" Robbie screamed into his face.

Jensen didn't flinch. "I don't *know* where it is, but I wouldn't tell you even if I did, because it doesn't *belong* to you. It doesn't belong to *anyone*. Music is life, and life is art. Now kindly fuck off and get out of my room before I call security."

Robbie looked as if he would drop dead of an aneurism right then and there; Jensen could see his heartbeat pulsing through a large vein protruding from his bald head. But he didn't say anything else, just turned on his heel and stormed out.

When he was gone, Jensen smiled at his reflection in the dead TV screen. It didn't matter who he'd been before. All that mattered was who he was *now*.

It was a person he was growing to like more and more with each passing second.

***

The dream again, only this time, he's the one that comes to *her*.

The same cave, the same army of emerald treetops, the same waterfall crashing down like a million TV sets tuned to static. Her back is to him, bare shoulders and slender neck framing the cave entrance, and she's looking at the beauty stretched out below in all directions.

Still waiting, she whispers, not turning her head to look at him, but he can tell that mysterious, seductive half-smile is there all the same.

I can't see your face, he says. A rain-swept breeze flies in through the cave opening and sends her strawberry-blond hair flying like party streamers behind her. *Why can't I see your face?*

There are countless doors, she responds, still whispering but loud enough to be heard over the roar of the waterfall. *You've opened many, but others remain locked. I'm behind one of them.*

He puts one bare foot in front of the other, and her image grows slightly bigger. *Is there a key?*

There is. But it's not a key; it's a memory.

So I have to remember something to remember something else?

Yes. She stands slowly and spreads her arms out to her sides like wings, her face still turned away, her naked body sprinkled with tiny drops of rainwater that catch the meager light coming from above. *I love you, Jensen. In this life and the next.*

Then she takes a swan dive over the lip of the cave entrance and disappears. He runs to follow, but when he peers over the edge, he sees nothing but the mist rolling seductively around the tops of the trees.

The world is his alone once more.

∗∗∗

A scratching noise woke him up, something that sounded like a mouse with long claws scurrying over a wooden board. He darted his eyes around what he could see of the room, but nothing seemed amiss except for a long shadow stretched across the floor leading to the bathroom.

"Hello? Who's there?"

Seconds later, a friendly face popped into view, holding a steno notebook in one hand and a pencil in the other.

"My apologies, Jensen," the man said. "Didn't mean to wake you."

Jensen scrunched his eyes to dispel the last vestiges of sleep from them. "Noah? What are you doing?"

Noah waved the notebook in the air. "Leaving you a note. Which, now that you're awake, is completely unnecessary."

The discomfort was creeping back into his bones, and he made a mental note to ask the nurse to increase his morphine drip the next time she visited. There was also a horrible itch in his left arm that he couldn't scratch, and the realization was irritating.

"Sadly, I must go," Noah continued. "There's only so long a wife can wait in a hotel room, no matter how comfortable, before she starts accusing her husband of being a jailor. I was just saying goodbye."

Jensen couldn't help but feel a twang of sadness at the news. He not only owed Noah his life, but he genuinely liked the man, too.

"Hell hath no fury, right?"

Noah smiled and nodded in agreement. "Indeed. Nella's a fantastic woman, but she's also as stubborn as they come." He laughed to himself. "She's the most loving woman I know, but cross her once and you'll think twice before doing it again."

Sounds like my *wife*, Jensen almost said, but didn't. Try as he might, he still couldn't remember anything about her other than her hair color and the fact she was his entire world. It was infinitely more aggravating than the itch under his cast.

"But this isn't goodbye," Noah continued. "Not unless you've grown tired of me already."

Jensen chuckled. "*Never*, Noah."

"Good, because I'd love to invite you to Des Moines, once you're able. Show you around campus, maybe grab a bite or a beer. And, of course, continue our conversation from earlier."

"That paper isn't going to write itself," Jensen said. "I'd like that very much. Leave your contact information and we'll schedule something soon."

Noah shook his head. "Not *too* soon, though. I'm sure you've already figured out that the next several months are going to be very difficult for you. Despite what Dr. Cash says, I'm confident you'll regain the use of your legs, but it's going to be a long, arduous journey." Noah lifted his pant leg and showed Jensen the fake plastic appendage beneath. "I unfortunately know just how difficult. But you can do it. You just have to be patient and unafraid to fail once in a while."

Another memory came to him just then, a phrase, and he spoke it aloud.

"Let not your heart be troubled, neither let it be afraid."

Noah's head jerked back suddenly as if being struck. "That's the verse my mother used to recite to me. Where did you hear it?"

"I think," Jensen began, searching the recesses of his memory. "I think I heard it from *you*."

Noah dropped the notebook to the floor and stepped forward, eyes wide and unbelieving. "But that's impossible. You were *dead* when I said those words to you. Clinically, bodily, completely. You *couldn't* have heard me say that."

"But I did. Right before ..."

Right before I jumped out of Translucent Tower.

And with that, everything came back at once, flooding his mind with images and sounds and sensations and smells that were so intense he felt dizzy. The tower. The Warden. The disappearing boy, and his intrepid plummet from the window that followed. Coming across the bus, talking to Miguel the driver. Meeting the most wonderful woman in the world, the one with the strawberry blond hair and the bottomless brown eyes. No, not meeting; *reconnecting*, because she'd been there since the dawn of time, and would still be there when the stars winked out and the universe returned to the black, endless void it had once been.

"Guinevere Hatcher," Jensen whispered, tears standing in his eyes. "The love of my life."

[silence]

Resurrection Cemetery looks even more somber than usual in the overcast sky, but he's anything but sad. He's happy, inside and out, the mask he used to wear crumpled and abandoned in the cellars of his mind.

Somewhere nearby, a series of clicks ring out. Photographers. Some professional, others just curious onlookers, but either way, it doesn't bother him. People love sticking cameras in his face lately, and he lets them, if only because it makes them feel better about everything, like they're a part of something bigger than themselves.

Aimee Barton, formerly Bennett, pushes his wheelchair as close to the grave as the uneven grass allows. Behind him, Aimee's new boyfriend waits under the shade of an elm tree, uncomfortable with the attention that seems to follow the crippled man wherever he goes.

Want to be alone? she asks from behind.

What, and appear on TMZ all by myself? Not a chance.

Aimee laughs, but it's a respectful laugh. A *graveyard* laugh.

He looks at the large stone sitting in front of him and reads the inscription aloud.

A toast to love and friends, and to a life that never ends.

Aimee puts a reassuring hand on his shoulder. *I don't know that one. Which album was it on?*

He shakes his head. *It's not a Quiet Catastrophe song. It's a Guinevere Hatcher original.*

Never heard of her. She any good?

He smiles, tears standing in his eyes. Aimee mistakes them for sadness, as do the throngs of reporters and Grangers lined up near the fence. But he's not sad. In fact, he doesn't believe he'll ever be sad another day in his life.

She's the best, he says, and then the two friends stare silently at the grave of Hedley Grange as tiny droplets of water begin tapping their shoulders.

Until our next adventure, he says to the stone, and then rain begins falling like cold tears.

OPEN AND CLOSED
-Track Sixteen-

He was hunched over his computer desk, lost in the words spilling from his fingertips and the feelings they stirred, when he heard it: knocking, soft and polite but loud enough to cut through the sound of Led Zeppelin belting out "Immigrant Song" via the vintage jukebox by the front door.

His first thought was that it was another reporter. They didn't come around as much as they used to, back when the crash was still making headlines and everyone wanted to talk to the only man who survived. But they still came occasionally, steno notebook in one hand and a tape recorder in the other, looking to uncover some new bit of information that Jensen might have somehow forgotten.

But he hadn't forgotten anything. Not yet, at least. It was all there in the pages of the book he was now writing, pages that he had to finish, and finish soon, before it all fused together in a haze of pleasant but indistinguishable emotions, the way memories sometimes do.

Again the knock, this time a bit louder. Whoever it was clearly wasn't going away, so he saved the file he was working on and grabbed his crutches. He was finally off the pain pills for good, and feeling had returned to his legs, just as Noah had predicted. He was doing well, much better than anyone would have thought, but moving around was still a tedious affair and it took him a bit to hobble his way toward the front of the empty nightclub.

The knock came again when he was just a few steps away from the door, and he scowled. "Jesus, give a cripple a break, will you? I'm *coming*."

But the second he swung the door open, his frown faded, replaced by a big, goofy grin that stretched from ear to ear.

"Jensen Bennett," the visitor said.

"Daphne Dartmouth," Jensen replied. "Thought maybe that two-eyed ape had taken you back up his beanstalk."

Daphne smiled but she didn't laugh. "I don't remember there bein' an ape in *Jack and the Beanstalk*. 'Sides …"

She stepped aside, and Jensen now had a clear view of a red convertible idling at the curb in front of the nightclub. In it sat Johnny Two-Eyes, looking like a gorilla stuffed into a toy car. Two-Eyes didn't acknowledge Jensen's gaze, only continued staring at the road ahead with dead, unblinking eyes.

"*Jesus*, Daff. Really?" Daphne blushed.

"He's a great guy, once you get to know him." She held up her left ring finger and flashed a gaudy diamond in his face. "You guys're gonna have to get along. Bein' he's your brother and all."

Jensen did a double take. "Come again?"

Daphne smiled. "Can we go inside? It's hotter than the devil's housecat out here."

Jensen nodded and, slowly moving aside to clear the entryway, he let Daphne pass into the nightclub. "Water and pop in the fridge if you're thirsty," he said as he closed the door, giving Two-Eyes one final, disdainful look.

"You know," Daphne said, her voice echoing around the cavernous room, "for a nightclub, your drink menu sucks."

"Yeah, well it's not going to be mine for much longer. I've got a buyer lined up who wants to turn this place into a gym." Jensen nodded at a small kitchen off to the side. "Help yourself. If *I* do it, you'll have your AARP card by the time I get over there."

Daphne nodded and did as he suggested.

"So what's this about Two-Eyes being my brother? Please don't tell me my mom had a one-night stand with Bigfoot back in the '90s, because I think I'll hurl myself off the top of the Hancock if you do."

"You don't know him, Jensen." Daphne opened the refrigerator and, after scanning its contents for a moment, plucked a can of soda from within and shut the door. "He's just a sweet 'lil love bug once you get to know him."

"*Great*," Jensen said. "I'm related to Magilla Gorilla."

Daphne turned and regarded him with a playful smile. "No, dummy. You're not related to *John*. You're related to *me*. I'm your sister."

✳✳✳

Now that Jensen was sitting, his limbs had started to howl again, but he ignored the pain. Daphne was sitting across from him, her lean frame all but disappearing into a gigantic leather couch that had been left by the nightclub's previous owner. She'd asked if she could smoke, and he'd said yes, but only if he could have one too, and now they were staring at each other in silence, the haze hanging between them like a leaky exhaust.

"*Well?*" she finally said.

Jensen rubbed his eyes. He'd give anything for a stiff drink right about now, but all he had was an expired bottle of Vicodin in the upstairs bathroom, and he wasn't *that* desperate.

"Look, I get it," he said at last. "My dad, my *real* dad, moseyed on down to Missouri after my mom told him she was pregnant, to a little town called New Hamelin. Which also just so happens to be the town *you're* from. I got all that. But things start to fall apart when you look at our last names. He may have been a piece of shit, but my father was most *certainly* a Bennett. I know, because I ended up with his last name. In any case, you're a Dartmouth. I'm not. Case closed."

Daphne nodded, excitement crossing her face, and after crushing her cigarette on the heel of her boot, she pulled a slip of paper from her purse.

"I was a bit stuck at first, too. When you came to me in that hotel room, clearer than just about any other spirit I ever saw, I was stumped. Only blood'll do that, least in my experience. I was tryin' to figure it out, but couldn't. And then somethin' amazing happened – your mom came through to me. She told me where to look."

Jensen smiled. He'd been thinking about his mother a lot recently, especially how she'd always made him feel special, even when no one else thought he was. Including himself. It was hard to believe she was more than ten years gone, now.

"That's Margret Metliff for you. I don't think that woman had a malicious bone in her entire body. What did she say?"

"Well, that she loves you, and that she's awful proud of you. But also that what I was lookin' for was this."

She held out the paper to Jensen, and he took it. It was a birth certificate, dated August 24, 2002. The mother was listed as Emily Marie Stratsky, and the father was one Hershel Alan Bennett. Typed in neat, blocky letters at the top was the baby's name: Daphne Louise Stratsky.

"The baby's *me*," she said. "I didn't become a Dartmouth 'til my mamma married the man I thought was my daddy and he legally adopted me. The birth certificate was amended sometime after that, I guess. The one you have in your hand is the original."

Jensen read the document several times just to make sure his eyes weren't lying to him. But there was no denying the authenticity of the paper in his hands. His dad had fathered Daphne, almost twenty years after abandoning his mother. Even as he grappled with the enormity of it all, he realized he wasn't surprised. After all, Daphne had existed in nearly all of the past lives he'd seen along the Path of Reflection, so it made sense that she'd have some intimate connection to him in *this* life, as well.

"I loved my daddy," she said. "Still do. And he *was* my dad, Jensen, in every sense of the word. But he wasn't the one who gave me life." She looked to the right and began twirling a lock of her blonde hair. "Seems the guy who *did* was also your dad, too. Seems our pop had a bad habit of skippin' town before the bed was cold. Who *knows* how big our family really is. We could have kin all across the country!"

Then Daphne looked at him and leaned in close. "But none of that matters, right? Who cares. What's DNA but a buncha molecules? It sure doesn't define a family." Then she grabbed his knee and squeezed gently. "Either way, you're my brother. I sensed it at Springfield Stadium, I sensed it in that hotel room, and I sense it now. DNA or no. And I'll be *damned* if my own flesh 'n' blood won't visit just 'cause he don't like the guy I married."

Jensen thought for a moment. Then he returned the smile and put his hands over hers, leaning in to meet her as he did. The motion pained him, but his face didn't show it.

"Daff, you won't be able to *keep* me away from your place, wherever it is. Just make sure there's enough handicapped parking, because I'll incite a cripple riot if there isn't."

Then they wrapped each other in a hug so warm that even the incessant blaring of a single car horn outside couldn't ruin it.

***

"I best be gettin' on," Daphne said as they pulled away from each other. "He hates that Chrysler. Says it's too small." She stood up and offered him a helping hand when he did the same. "But I'm not far. John's from around here, and we found a nice little place in Tinley Park. It's just south of here."

Jensen grabbed her arm to stop her from walking away. "Wait. Could you spare a few minutes more? I need you to do something for me."

Daphne smiled. "You wanna talk to *her*, don't you. Guinevere."

Jensen squeezed her arm. "You have no idea how much."

Daphne thought about it for a minute then nodded slowly. "Okay. Can't make any promises, but I can try. Any message in particular you want me to deliver? Assumin' I break through?"

Jensen laughed. "Yes. First, don't say you're my sister. I told her we kissed, and the last thing I need is some bad Luke and Leia joke. Then ... tell her not a second goes by that I don't dream about the day I finally get to hold her in my arms again. That everything else leading up to that day is just filler." Jensen looked down, not wanting his sister to see the tears that were beginning to gather in his eyes. "Tell her I love her more than I could ever possibly explain."

Daphne tucked her hand under his chin and brought his head back up so they were once again looking eye to eye.

"I'm thinkin' she already knows all that," Daphne said tenderly. "But I'll tell her anyway."

✳✳✳

Daphne hadn't been sitting for long before she entered a deep trance. Jensen stood nearby, leaning up against the partition that separated the dance floor from the kitchen, eyes wide in excitement, the low ache in his arms and legs all but forgotten.

His sister began whispering, and Jensen had to lean forward to hear what she was saying.

"Don't publish?" he asked. "What does *that* mean?"

Then Daphne jerked her head up, her eyes a dark brown, and his heart leapt. But when she spoke, it was with the low, gruff timber of a man.

"I told you this would happen," Daphne said. Her accent was completely gone. "What did I say? You can't go telling everyone that life continues after you die."

Jensen's heart dropped. Daphne hadn't contacted Guinevere ... she'd contacted The Warden.

"*Jesus*, Benjamin. This isn't a party line. Where's Gwen?"

Daphne's lips turned upward a little, a barely noticeable smile. "She's at The Terminal. Singing and playing her acoustic guitar day and night. The locals love it. And when she's not doing that, she's yammering on and on about you."

Jensen smiled at the image this created in his head. "Can you get her for me? I need to talk to her."

"Buddy," Daphne's gruff voice said, "I don't think you ever listened to a single word I said. You shouldn't be talking to *anyone* on this side. Including me. But I had to come through to ask you to please, please not publish that book. I didn't bust my hump trying to haul you back in, just for you to spill the beans about this place to everyone on that side who'll listen."

Jensen could almost see The Warden on Daphne's face, now: the round forehead, the square jaw, even a hint of a tiny moustache below her nose.

"*In My Time of Dying* isn't really a book; it's more like a personal diary," Jensen said. "And you don't have to worry, because I'm just writing it for *me*. So I won't forget. I have no doubt I could sell it for a small fortune, but lucky for you I don't really care about that stuff anymore."

This seemed to placate The Warden, because as Jensen was talking, Daphne's stern features relaxed a little.

"Good to hear. Write it and then lock it away somewhere."

Jensen debated telling him he'd already spilled the beans, as they were, to Noah DeNova, who had the entire thing catalogued on his tape recorder somewhere back at Des Moines University. He was no doubt writing a paper on it at this very moment. But Jensen decided that would only prolong the argument, so he let it drop.

"Look, Warden," he said. "Tell Gwen I love her. Tell her I'll be there before she knows it, and we'll spend night and day together, walking the streets of Paradise City or taking a ride out into the countryside, until the day comes when we want to come back here. Then we'll go to Evermore again, and live the last bits of our current lives until we walk the Path. And when the time comes, we'll go. *Together* this time."

Daphne was silent for a moment as The Warden took this request into consideration.

"Okay, Jensen. You got a deal. But I'm not telling her anything she doesn't already know. You're all she talks about. She even took over that little coffee shop in The Terminal. Named it something cute. What was it?" Daphne began to lick her upper lip, stroking a moustache that wasn't there. "The two somethings. Heck, I can't remember."

Jensen's eyes lit up. "The Two Figures?"

Daphne/The Warden nodded. "Yep, that's it. She did something really neat with the sign. The words are made of the energy ribbons, and she keeps them in place by constantly playing her music. When she stops, which she only does to ramble on about you, the words just float back into the sky. Like I said, neat stuff. I'll swing by there after my shift is over and deliver your message. Maybe even get myself a bear claw."

But Jensen had stopped listening. Suddenly, everything made perfect sense. The name of the café, the energy ribbons that formed words, the constant music needed to keep them locked in place. He'd finally figured out the mystery.

He now knew where Hedley Grange had hidden the last Quiet Catastrophe album.

***

When the man with the moustache finally left, Daphne felt herself return, much more rapidly than usual. Whenever she'd have a reading – which she was doing more and more now that she knew she could do it – it always seemed that the person on the other end wanted to linger for as long as possible. But not this Warden man, who was happy to release his grip on her the second the conversation was over.

She opened her eyes and began to apologize to Jensen – she was really hoping he'd get to talk to his girlfriend again – when she realized he wasn't there anymore.

The nightclub was empty.

***

At first, he couldn't find it. He'd had an estate sale a few months back to pay for his medical bills, and for one horrifying moment he thought maybe he'd sold it.

But he breathed a sigh of relief when he saw the large, brown package hiding behind a stack of plastic tubs. He immediately threw his crutches aside and used the closet wall to support his weight, slowly making his way to the package before crouching next to it. His legs screamed in protest, but he was too excited to care.

"Jensen? What is it?" a voice said from behind him.

"The answer," he responded, and once again tore the brown paper from the package, revealing the painting Grange had sent to him shortly before the plane crash. It was as beautiful as he'd remembered it, the two-story building still slumbering beneath the cloudless summer sky as glints of sunlight winked from its many windows.

"The answer to *what*? The mystery of your missin' *marbles*? You *do* realize that was the second time you just left during a reading without sayin' goodbye, don't you?"

Jensen ignored her for now, instead pulling his reading glasses from the front pocket of his shirt and putting them on. He leaned in close, looking intently for brush strokes on the canvas. But he didn't see any, because *this* painting was a digital replica, comprised of millions of tiny ones and zeros.

"You clever bastard," Jensen said, the smile practically splitting his face into two parts. "It's binary code."

Daphne had walked into the closet with him and was now crouched by his side, looking at the painting with a confused expression on her face. "Binary code?"

Jensen looked to her and nodded. "Yes. Anything, including sound waves, can be rendered as a series of ones and zeros. The 'one' means the switch is closed, and the 'zero' means it's open. That's binary code. CDs and mp3s use them to replicate music." Then he turned his gaze back to the painting, even more in awe of its beauty now that he knew its secret. He ran a hand across the sign in front of the building, the one that Hedley had put there as an artistic license. "*Les Deux Figures*. The Two Figures. It didn't refer to me and Aimee. It referred to *binary code*."

Daphne was beginning to feel the excitement herself; he could see it in the way her eyes bounced and she licked her lips. "So, what you're sayin' is ... this painting is the lost Quiet Catastrophe album?"

"Yes," Jensen said. "Music is life, and life is art. He wanted me to see that music is more than just money and album sales. It's *art*. And he knew I'd only find the album once I realized that. Literally."

They both stared at the painting for a bit, in awe that they were looking at a numeric representation of an album that millions of people across the world would kill to hear even a *second* of. It was an emotional experience, filled with all of the things both of them had gone through to get to that very moment.

Daphne was the first one to speak. "So now what? Do you turn it over to Wicked Records?"

Jensen smiled and shook his head. "Hell no. We give it to the people, who are the *real* owners of it. I have a buddy who specializes in this sort of thing. He can convert this back to music with both hands tied behind his back."

"What then?"

He turned to her, his sister, his family. They were closer now than they'd ever been before, crouching down in a musty closet, staring at a painting that was drawn by a famous man who'd created it in a time that now seemed as distant as the stars. He realized in that moment that he truly loved Daphne. It was more than just the tingle of emotion he'd felt when she'd wished him luck with a kiss at Springfield Stadium in that other life, eons ago. This was *real* love, and he couldn't think of anyone other than Guinevere that he'd rather share this very intimate moment with.

"We send it out to the world. Radio stations, bloggers, YouTubers, TV stations. File sharing networks. Everyone is going to get a copy of this album, and some asshole who had nothing to do with its creation will never see a single cent."

He gazed into the picture again, into that imagined nightclub that never was and will never be, and everything began flooding back into his mind, every single moment of his life. He smiled at the memories, even the bad ones, because they had all taught him something important. Life hurt sometimes, but the pain never held as much sway as the friends and family and lovers that made it all worth living. And in the end, that's all that mattered.

"Come on," Jensen Bennett said to his sister. "Let's rock the world."

... Beyond the Shade ...

She hadn't expected her favorite see-saw to be open; it was, after all, the last weekend of summer, and seemingly every kid in Harrisburg was out enjoying the last vestiges of freedom before books and boring teachers ruled their world once again. But today, Lisa Ashford was lucky: The park was empty.

She walked up to the see-saw and straddled it, knowing she was too big now for such childish things but not caring in the slightest. She lifted her legs up and down, smiling at the sensation of flight that came with the motion. It was much more fun with someone else on the other end, but today it didn't matter that she was alone. It had been a good day, filled with a trip to the mall and a last-minute decision to visit the State Museum of Pennsylvania. Her dad knew she loved history, and it didn't take much convincing before he'd agreed to take her.

Then another girl, short and cute who had to be pretty close to her age, walked up from nowhere and stared at her with bottomless brown eyes that almost caused her to fall from the see-saw at the sight. The girl looked familiar, somehow, like someone from a dream she'd once had. Lisa shook away the thought as she realized she'd probably seen her at the park before.

"Are you gonna sit or just stand there like a dunderhead?"

The newcomer kept looking at her. If Lisa didn't know better, she would have thought the girl, too, was trying to recall an old memory.

"Okay, kid. Starting to creep me out a bit." Yet even as she said this, she knew it wasn't true. She liked this girl for some reason. It was like running into an old friend after a long absence.

"Did you go to Melrose?" the girl finally said.

381

Lisa shook her head. "Nope. Paxtang. I start at Susquehanna on Monday."

The girl smiled, a mysterious half-smile that only seemed to cover the left side of her face. "Hey, me too! Wonder if we'll have any classes together."

"Doubtful. I'm in all honors."

The girl staggered back in fake offense, the smile never leaving her face. "Woah, easy there. I may be cute, but I'm not dumb." Then, with more than just a hint of pride, the girl added, "Have a few honors classes myself."

Without another word, the girl straddled the see-saw and began pumping her legs. Lisa smiled and did the same, and a giggle escaped her chest as they bounced up and down, up and down, their eyes never straying from one another. A strange feeling began to spread throughout her body, something she'd never felt before. It was a pleasant feeling. A happy feeling.

It was a feeling of coming home.

Acknowledgements

Many thanks to Vicki Sanchez and Sharon Jackson, who read an early draft of *House Made of Sound* and let me know what worked and what didn't. If you enjoyed this book, the blame is partially theirs.

ABOUT THE AUTHOR

 FREEMAN JAYCE has spent the better part of his life telling stories, many of which made it to paper. In his past life he was a reporter, editor, and entertainment columnist for the Daily Southtown newspaper in Chicago, having penned hundreds of articles under his real name, Jason Michael Freeman. You can contact him via email at FreemanJayce@gmail.com or follow him on social media at Facebook.com/AuthorFreemanJayce.